I0573370

First Edition Copyright © 2021 Brian Jay Nelson

Digital Book ISBN: 978-1-64873-150-1
Paperback ISBN: 978-1-64873-150-1
Hardcover ISBN: 978-1-64873-151-8

Printed in the United States of America

Published by:
Writer's Publishing House
Prescott, Az 86301

Cover and Interior Design by Creative Artistic Excellence Marketing Project Management and Book Launch by Creative Artistic Excellence Marketing https://lizzymcnett.com

Acknowledgments

"For loved ones who have passed to another life, but still watch over us from a distance."

Branchview
–By Brian Jay Nelson

Table of Contents

Chapter One:

The Murder of Matthew

A bitter, cold wind howled outside the mansion's windows, as yet another tragic event unfolded inside the Branchview house. "Please! Someone help!" Loraine screamed. Steve Spencer had been transported back through time within a dream, to personally experience the events leading up to the death of Matthew Branch.

Daniel Sr was woken from a sound sleep by Lori's desperate cries. He quickly grabbed his robe, fastened the tie, and rushed down the hallway. "Lori! What on earth is going on?"

"It's Steven! Something's dreadfully wrong."

Daniel hurried to the bedside, where Steven was thrashing violently. He was fighting to breathe, grabbing at his throat. "Steven! What has happened?" He responded only with heavy terrified breathing.

Then suddenly, he looked at Loraine. "Those look like rope marks around his neck. Was there someone else in this room?"

"No! No! No one, or nothing that I could see."

Steven shifted his eyes toward Loraine and attempted to talk in a shrill, strained voice. "Lori! Water! Please!"

She looked horrified. "Oh yes, darling! I'll get some for you right away."

Loraine hurried from the room, past Heather and Daniel Jr who were standing in the doorway. "Father!" Heather cried out. "Is everything alright?"

"Yes! Steven has just had a terrible nightmare that's given him quite a shock."

"It's Charlotte! I know it is! She gave him that nightmare," Daniel IV announced.

"Now Daniel, that'll be enough of that talk. You and Heather go back to your rooms."

"Dad… I'm scared!"

Heather moved over to comfort him. "Come on Daniel! I'll stay with you until you get back to sleep."

They headed down the hallway hand in hand. Loraine rushed past them with a water glass. "Here Steven! This should help."

"Thank you," he started to recover, "sweetheart!" Still breathing heavily, and with a strained voice, he continued: "I need to speak with my brother for a few moments, please?"

Loraine looked perplexed. "Very well! I'll prepare an ice pack for your neck." Daniel gave a wink of assurance as she reluctantly left the room once again.

Steven shifted his attention. "Daniel, who is Matthew Branch?"

Daniel looked off in momentary deep thought. "I believe he was one of my grandfather's brothers. Not much is known about him, other than the fact that he was murdered, and his killer was never brought to justice."

Steven's eyes grew wide with the revelation. "He wasn't among the spirits present at the ceremony the other night, was he?"

"To be honest, I really wouldn't know. There are no known pictures of him or his brother Andrew in any of the family archives."

Steven propped himself up in the bed. "But… Andrew was there. I would've thought Matthew would be present as well."

Daniel grew impatient. "With all due respect Steven, could you please get to the point of what all of this is about?"

"I had a dream about Matthew, but he looked a lot like me, and I felt like I was him. He was with Amy, and they were both dressed in Victorian style attire."

Daniel chuckled. "He was with Dr. Seagraves? That's impossible! He lived over a hundred years ago."

Steven continued, "She went by the name of Amanda in the dream. They were in a fancy place called The Camden Hotel."

Daniel raised an eyebrow. "The Camden? That place burned down in the 1930s. It was where the Stop and Shop is presently located."

Steven continued, "After that, they were walking down the path near Lighthouse Point. Amanda mentioned something about a fire at the Locke Estate. Do you know anything about that?"

Daniel looked uneasy. "Neither my father nor my grandfather would ever speak of it. But I do know that the Locke family had an estate near there, and it burned to the ground. I believe that lives were lost as well. What happened next in your dream?"

"They said goodnight and kissed. I could feel her lips touching mine."

Daniel gave him a sly grin. "Now I know why you sent Lori from the room. Hopefully, it wasn't the beautiful Dr. Seagraves that tried to strangle you in a fit of passion."

Steven shook his head no and continued, "Matthew turned to walk away, and out of nowhere, someone slipped a rope around his neck."

Daniel reacted with shock, as Steven touched his neck and flinched with great pain. "You need to rest that throat. There will be ample time later for more discussion."

"Wait, Daniel! I have to say this. I believe Matthew Branch was trying to communicate with me in that dream."

"Perhaps he was. I think there's enough mystery surrounding Branchview to fill several volumes." He looked off in deep thought for a moment. "But… right now, we all need to get some rest. As well, we mustn't keep Lori waiting in the hall for much longer." Daniel patted Steven on the shoulder, and the two men exchanged a slight smile.

Steven smiled with an uncertain nod as Daniel left the room; he knew it was going to be a difficult conversation with Loraine as to why he wanted to speak with his brother alone. The idea of talking with his wife about another woman kissing him made Steven feel very uncomfortable, even if it was over a hundred years ago.

All was quiet after the incident in the north wing. Dr. Grayson slept soundly in her bed. However, everything was about to change, when the door creaked open and woke her up. Maggie stepped inside holding a candle, and once Dr. Grayson was awake, she motioned for her to follow. Dr. Grayson's actions were as though she was in a trance, her movements almost robotic in nature. Maggie floated along toward the grand staircase, her captive quietly obeying the request.

On the first landing, the candlelight caught a glimpse of the portrait of a stern-faced woman whose eyes seemed to be watching their every move. Dr. Grayson could not help but be disturbed by the intense emotion of the eyes as they passed. At the bottom of the stairs, they proceeded to the hallway leading to the study. As they entered the room, Maggie walked over and pointed to a spot on the wooden panel.

"Inside here, Dr. Grayson… It's what everyone is looking for."

"What's in there, Maggie?"

"You'll see." Dr. Grayson moved closer to the panel and tested the rigidity with both hands before pulling on it lightly. "Oh!" She jumped when the panel suddenly opened. It revealed a hidden storage space.

Dr. Grayson took the candle from Maggie, and its illumination exposed a mass of cobwebs. "I don't think anyone has opened this for years, Maggie." As she brushed away some of the cobwebs, the light caught something interesting. "Maggie…" The room went silent. Dr. Grayson turned around and Maggie was gone. *They're keys…* She looked around the room, but Maggie was nowhere in sight.

A few hours later, Dr. Grayson woke up in her bed, baffled. It took her a few moments to gather her senses, then she sat up perplexed as to what had happened. She glanced around to make sure it was her room when she noticed the large key ring lying on the nightstand. *What is going on…?*

Early the next morning, there was a knock at the door of the cottage. Lucretia rushed from her bed to answer it. The door knocker slammed against the solid wood one more time as she tried to tie the belt of her robe. "Ok! I'm coming!"

She flung the door open. "Agent Smith… what do you want?"

"It's nice to see you too. Is that any way to greet a friend?"

"I wasn't aware that we were friends. Besides, isn't it a bit early in the day for a social visit?"

Adam chuckled. "I'm an early riser. I like to take care of most of my business in the morning." Lucretia moved aside and motioned for him to come inside.

"Please have a seat, Agent Smith. I suppose you'd like a cup of coffee as well."

"Oh… since you are offering, yes! A cup of coffee would be just splendid. Black with two sugars."

Lucretia flashed a look of revulsion and went into the kitchen. "I would have thought a strong man like you would drink it black, without sugar."

Adam grinned and changed the subject. "I'm sure you're aware that we've been unable to locate Tyronde, Chaco, and Lomax."

"Perhaps you haven't been looking in the right places."

"And where might those places be, Ms. Darknight?"

Lucretia came back into the room. "Coffee… two sugars. How should I know? Maybe Mexico! I'm not in charge of the investigation. However, from the sound of things maybe I should be—" She settled into a chair opposite him. "You should know that someone can go pretty far with three million dollars."

Adam took a sip of his coffee and flashed a sly grin. "I suppose! But I'm not buying into that theory. It's not like

Tyronde to just up and disappear. He had too big of a stake in this area of the state. Even if he did, we would've found your body, as well as Lomax's and Chaco's, scattered somewhere along his trail. That's how he usually handles things."

Lucretia rolled her eyes. "Would I be correct in assuming that you're trying to make some sort of accusation against me, Agent Smith?"

"Not at all, Lucretia! I'm simply trying to shed light on a very curious and rather stagnant investigation. There seem to be more questions than answers in this case."

"I'd have to say that your poor investigative skills would be responsible for that. I've told you everything I know."

Adam set his cup down on a side table and rose from his seat. "Such a shame! With all this animosity brewing between us, do you think our relationship could ever blossom into something more?"

Lucretia turned rather snarky. "Perhaps on a day when Hell freezes over."

"You never know. That day might just happen sooner than you think." She walked ahead to open the door for him. Without further word, he moved through the doorway quickly, as Lucretia slammed it behind him.

The sun had made its way over the horizon by the time Agent Smith left. Lucretia took a deep breath and started to settle down, ready to start her day when she noticed a large shadow at the edge of the woods outside her window. Its brandishing staunch physique brought a feeling of terror that flooded throughout her body. A biting cold wind still howled outside. Old man winter had truly settled in for the long haul of the season. Lucretia shivered at the thought. She turned from the window quickly and tried to unsee the image of the shadow that was now burned into her brain.

The mantle clock in the main house chimed at 11 am. Dr. Grayson stood firmly in front of the fireplace, warming herself, and watching the orange flames dance. Loraine entered the room with urgency. "I just got your message. Is everything alright?"

"Please, close the doors, Loraine." Loraine paused and closed them. "I understand my sleep was undisturbed by some terrifying events last night?"

Loraine nodded. "Steven had a horrifying nightmare, and he's very reluctant to tell me about it."

"Perhaps he's trying to protect you from something."

She looked relieved. "That thought did cross my mind. He woke up violently choking, and he had rope marks around his neck. I believe that the witch may have been responsible for whatever took place in that dream."

Dr. Grayson raised an eyebrow. "I had a rather unusual experience myself last night. I dreamed that Maggie came to my room, and led me to the study." Loraine moved closer. "She showed me a secret hidden compartment in a panel of the wall that hadn't been opened for quite some time."

"What was in there?"

"There was a large ring filled with several old keys. Then, suddenly I woke up, and found those very keys lying on the nightstand near my bed."

Loraine's eyes grew wide as Dr. Grayson showed her the keys.

"Those have to be the keys to the East Wing."

"How do you know that?"

"Maggie was telling me about some old portraits that are stored in the East Wing. When I mentioned it to Mrs. Branch, she said that portion of the house had been locked for years, and only her late husband knew where the keys were."

"Obviously then, you're right. These must be the missing keys."

"We must tell Mrs. Branch about this right away."

"I think that's a good idea. Would you mind going to the south wing to summon her? I'm absolutely freezing this morning, and am not thrilled about leaving the comfort of this fireplace."

Loraine giggled. "Of course, stay here where it's warm."

Steven had somewhat recovered from his experience and decided to consult Amphitrite for further information about his dream. He tightly clenched the aquamarine pendant in the palm of his hand. On his way down the stairs, he passed Loraine and updated her on his quest. She waved him on his way, as she was too preoccupied with finding the matriarch of the family. As he approached the clearing at the end of the pathway near Lighthouse Point, he noticed a black cat prowling along the tree line by the ruins of the old Locke Estate. Then a few seconds later, Amy emerged through the thick, cold fog, and into the clearing. "Steven! It must be very urgent for you not to have waited for me at Branchview."

Steven nervously motioned to a park bench. "We need to talk. Let's sit down." They both settled on the bench, and Amy waited for Steven to speak first. "I had a dream last night about Amanda Green and Matthew Branch." Amy gasped. "Until that dream, I never knew about Matthew or the fact that he even resembled me."

Amy bit her upper lip and gazed downward for a moment. "He greatly resembled both you and your father." She paused with much emotion. "He knew me as Amanda Green, and we were deeply in love with each other. This coming summer will mark 112 years since I last kissed him near this very spot."

"I know… that final kiss was in the dream, and it seemed as though I was in Matthew's body. Amazingly, I could even feel the sensation of your lips touching mine." Amy's sad blue eyes fixed emotionally on Steven as he continued. "After that kiss, Matthew started back on the path. Then someone slipped a rope around his neck from behind." Amy reacted with great emotion when Steven pulled the collar of his coat down to reveal the bruises. Amy looked away momentarily in horror. "Amy! Do you know who killed Matthew?"

"No, Steven… I wish I did. Poseidon was very jealous. I've always thought he was involved, but he firmly denies it."

"Do you know of anyone else who may have wanted him dead?"

"He was a very kind and gentleman. I can think of no one who would have wished to harm him."

"I don't understand it, but somehow I feel oddly connected to all of this." Amy stared into Steven's eyes and reacted with sudden enlightenment. She gently placed her hand over his heart, then gasped emotionally, as tears welled in her eyes. "What…?" Steven exclaimed.

"It can't be! I can see and feel Matthew's spirit within you."

"Are you saying that I'm the incarnation of Matthew Branch?" Amy nodded emotionally.

"I'm sorry Steven…" She paused to regain her composure. "It's been a very long time since I've felt Matthew's presence. This is just so overwhelming." She buried her head into his shoulder and cried while Steven held her in a comforting embrace.

Chapter Two:

An Introduction to Holdsclaw

In the distance, along the tree line, a shadowed image stood with keen attention focused on the embracing couple. It was the black shrouded spirit of Charlotte Locke, watching the scene with a sly smirk.

"Well, well! This is shaping up to be very interesting… very interesting indeed." The scene held Charlotte's attention for some time, as Steven continued to comfort the Mermaid goddess.

In Washington D.C., within the elaborate confines of his government office, Holdsclaw sat behind his desk, smiling in deep thought. There was a knock on the door, and Representative Lapino sauntered in and settled into a seat across from him. "Congratulations Richard! I can't believe that bill we've been working so very hard on passed through the Senate."

Holdsclaw took a confident breath. "By a very slim margin, I must say. We were able to bribe a few members from the other side of the aisle to sway the vote."

"Brilliant! Without that effort, there's no doubt that we'd be back to square one."

Holdsclaw leaned back in his chair, very pleased with himself. "Tell me, Linda. Where do you plan to go for your New Year's recess?"

"I plan to go home in my private jet and spend time with my grandchildren. What are your plans?"

"I think I'll go back to Connecticut, and pay a visit to Branchview." He paused in sinister thought. "I think it's time for me to see what my future home looks like."

Lapino reacted with surprise. "Your future home? You promised to hand that over to Ms. Darknight."

Holdsclaw laughed. "Linda! We're politicians! You should know that we never follow through with our promises." He gazed off with a perverted smile. "Besides, I'm not saying that she can't live there. On the contrary, she'll serve me quite well in a more pleasurable role."

"And what about Mrs. Holdsclaw?" He looked away with revulsion. "Oh yes! That's just one more unpleasant situation that I'll have to eliminate."

"What do you intend to do?"

"I haven't quite decided yet."

Lapino peered at him curiously. "With all your money and power, you'll be able to have almost any young woman of your choosing. Why are you so fixated on Lucretia Darknight?"

Holdsclaw lowered his gaze. "Because, through her connection to the spirit of Charlotte Locke, she possesses immortality and eternal youth. I want those attributes as well, and she will give them to me." Lapino only responded by uncomfortably squirming in her seat. His sinister plot swept through her mind with worrisome anxiety.

Back in Lockeport, Lucretia decided the best way to spend a cold winter day was to shop for clothes at the mall. While browsing, she noticed a mannequin of a young woman in a colorful spring dress, with straight black hair styled in a feathered bob, and lively blue eyes that stared down on her.

She stopped to admire her with deep thought. *You're exactly what I've been looking for.* After looking around, she grabbed the mannequin's fiberglass hand. "With this touch of my hand, you shall live and breathe." The mannequin transformed into a living woman and looked around with clueless surprise. Lucretia stepped back and admired her creation. "Here! Let me help you, dear." She held her hand as the mannequin stepped down from her perch.

Lucretia turned to see an older, well-dressed woman observing the occurrence. Thinking fast, she quickly waved her hand in the woman's direction. "You saw nothing. Your mind will erase this experience." The woman stared straight ahead, nodded hypnotically, and slowly moved away.

"My dear, everything will be alright." The mannequin looked at Lucretia with a blank stare. "I will call you Tina."

The living mannequin glanced down at her body and examined her outstretched hands before smiling at Lucretia. "Tina?"

Lucretia laughed. "Yes, Tina. And my name is Lucretia. Now, I must buy you a winter coat, and some warm clothes. It's far too early in the season to be wearing that skimpy spring outfit."

Lucretia made her purchases and led her newly created friend outside to the car. She opened the door and helped her get into the passenger side. With a half-smile, she reached over and placed her palm over Tina's forehead. "I must program your mind so that you don't talk and act like a robot." Tina convulsed for a few minutes as the energy transferred. Then she settled into a natural, relaxed state after Lucretia removed her hand.

Lucretia put the car in drive, turned on the radio, and heavy metal guitar riffs blasted from the speaker, causing Tina to react with enthusiasm. "What is this music?"

"That is Black Sabbath."

Tina smiled with vigor and looked over to Lucretia. "I like Black Sabbath."

Lucretia grinned wickedly as she drove away. "I have a feeling that you and I are going to get along quite well, my dear."

At Branchview, Loraine, Penelope, and Dr. Grayson proceeded on their mission to the East Wing of the house. They were all carrying flashlights as they approached the locked double door entrance to the wing.

Loraine held the keys but graciously handed them over to Penelope. "I think it's only proper for the mistress of the house to do the honors."

Penelope looked perplexed. "Perhaps now isn't the best time to have that title." The woman urged her on, and she turned the key.

They all paused with apprehension before opening the door. "I must say that I'm quite nervous. We could very well be the first people in nearly a hundred years to enter this portion of the house." The heavy doors creaked as Penelope pulled, but it required the weight of all three women to finally budge them open.

Loraine recoiled from the stench that belched outward from the inner room. "I do suppose it will require some heavy-duty air fresheners to rid the place of that nasty smell."

The women slowly entered, with their flashlights barely piercing the darkness through a maze of cobwebs.

Penelope unpleasantly waved her hand in front of her to clear the path. "It might have been better to wear some old clothes. I'll look like a dust mop by the time we're through in here." Loraine giggled.

The women stood in the middle of the room, trying to get their bearings. Loraine was focused on finding a lamp or a light switch. "Oh…!" she shrieked. The other women jumped. "I think a mouse just scampered across my foot."

"Loraine…" Penelope blurted out, "you nearly scared the life out of me."

Dr. Grayson chimed in, "Girls--- let's just find some light." They nodded.

"Oh, look over there… a torch lamp. But how…?"

Penelope spoke up, "It turns like a key switch near the top."

"Oh, hang on… wait I see." The room suddenly lit up.

Loraine moved over to the south wall, eyeing the stern-faced portraits that were vintage 18th and 19th centuries. "I have no idea who any of these people are,"

Penelope stated, as Dr. Grayson gazed upon the lamp with awe. "Amazing!"

Loraine turned to see what she was talking about. "What? What's so amazing?"

"This bulb, it must be one of the first edition Edison's." The women walked over to look for themselves. "Can you believe this?" Loraine shook her head.

Dr. Grayson then noticed the blind that covered the large window to the room. She strolled over and rested one knee on the window box as she tried to pull it open. "These old spring mechanisms can be quite difficult." The spring suddenly let loose, causing the blind to clatter upward, stirring a cloud of dust, and sending daylight into the musty room.

"Ladies, do you realize that is probably the first natural light that this room has seen for at least a hundred years?" Penelope stated.

The women all marveled at the sights within the room.

"This was their sitting room. These are all one of a kind antiques. They're virtually priceless."

Penelope's eyes curiously scanned all around her. "If only this room could talk. Oh, the stories it could tell."

"Do you feel that?" Dr. Grayson asked.

"Feel what?" Penelope asked.

"That…." Loraine spun around. An apparition moved along the far wall of the room.

A sober faced Maggie stepped forward into the light, and all three sighed. "Thank heavens! It's only Maggie."

Maggie motioned for them to follow, and they entered a long dark hallway that had several doors. About halfway down the corridor, she stopped and looked back. "The pictures are in there."

Dr. Grayson led the way, and slowly opened the door to the room as Maggie vanished. Loraine turned to both of them with a concerned look as they entered. "It's so cold in here," Penelope announced.

"There's some type of presence in this room with us," Loraine stated.

"I agree. But I don't think it's a negative or aggressive energy."

The room was faintly lit from shards of light leaking through the tattered window blind. Loraine noticed another torch lamp on the desk and reached to turn it on. "It's obvious by all this flotsam and jetsam that they used this room for storage, but I do believe it was once someone's living quarters as well."

Dr. Grayson glanced around the cluttered room in deep thought. "Yes! I very much agree. I'm picking up on a male energy."

Penelope noticed a framed picture on a dresser and picked it up. "Oh, this dust." She brushed off the glass and frame with her blouse. "Oh my! The woman in this picture looks exactly like Dr. Seagraves." The statement got Dr. Grayson and Loraine's attention, and they turned to see the photo.

"It most certainly does look like her. Where do you suppose it was taken?"

"I'd almost have to guess that it was taken on the pathway leading to Lighthouse Point."

Dr. Grayson returned to her search of the room when she caught sight of a group of rectangular-shaped objects covered with a drop cloth. "I think those might be the portraits we've been looking for." She walked over, pulled off the dusty cloth, and held the first portrait to the light.

"That's definitely Andrew. I remember conversing with him in the Corridor the other night." She set the portrait aside and grabbed another one. "Look… hopefully, this one is Matthew Branch."

Penelope took the picture and held it up to the light. The three women gazed at it with shocked surprise. "Oh, dear Lord! If he didn't have sideburns and a mustache, he'd look exactly like Steven and his father."

"The resemblance is definitely uncanny," Loraine replied.

Loraine jumped. "What's wrong?" Dr. Grayson asked.

"I just got the chills. This was most definitely Matthew's room."

"Do you think we should take Matthew and Andrew's portraits back into the main portion of the house, or just let them be?"

"Of course, there's no question. We must display them in their rightful place in the Grand Corridor."

Dr. Grayson flashed her light onto a door to the right. "We need to see what's in that room. I feel very drawn to it for some reason."

"If the floor plans are consistent with the rest of the house, I'd have to say that it's a small study," said Penelope.

Loraine moved ahead of them and reached to open the door. "Be careful," Dr. Grayson blurted out.

Loraine nodded, and illuminated the room, flinching from the stench. "It's a maze of cobwebs in here." She looked further. "I see a small roll top desk in the corner with a chair facing it. Wait…" She paused. The others got nervous. "It looks like an old blonde wig lying on the top of that desk chair."

"What— a wig?" Penelope asked. "Let me see…."

"What is that? It almost looks like someone is sitting in that chair," Loraine said.

Dr. Grayson moved closer, then reached forward to slowly turn the chair. "Oh, the stubborn thing doesn't want to turn…" She struggled. The chair creaked, then spun around suddenly.

The women huddled together, startled by the grotesque sight, and screams of horror filled the East Wing. The skeleton of a woman in a Victorian dress, with much of her blonde hair still attached to the skull, sat in what was more than likely her final resting place.

Chapter Three:

Hidden Identities

The always faithful mantle clock chimed at 4 pm, while Penelope maintained a steady gaze out the sitting room window. It had been a dreadful cold, dreary day on the East Coast. However normal for January weather, the inhabitants of Branchview found themselves chilled, not from the cold, but the horrifying discovery made in the East Wing. As the women waited patiently for Steven to return home, Dr. Grayson remained close to the fireplace, holding her crucifix between her trembling fingers. She resolved many years before its power of relaxation in a time of crisis. Loraine was lost in thought, along with Sharie and Mrs. Porter, while Daniel Sr. nursed his glass of brandy, and Gerard sat silently in a nearby chair.

Penelope continued to stare out the window, but couldn't remain silent for another second. "I can't get that horrible image of the skeleton out of my mind."

"Yes, I know…" Dr. Grayson blurted out. "It's hard to imagine that poor woman's remains have been up in that room for over a hundred years."

Penelope turned to address Loraine. "Were you able to reach Steven?"

"Yes. He's been at the public library searching for some bit of information in the archives. He said he would be here in a snap."

Sharie shifted uncomfortably in the loveseat. "Why can't we just go ahead and start without him?"

"Steven is an important part of all this," Penelope said, "and he needs to know all the details."

Mrs. Porter sat up straight. "I know I haven't been here long, but I wasn't even aware that there was an East Wing in this house."

Sharie let loose with a sarcastic laugh. "There are secrets in all corners of this place. You'll learn that quick enough." Daniel Sr shook his head, and sarcastically raised his glass of brandy toward Sharie in agreement.

"Sharie! Was Mrs. Blakely able to stay on with the children for an extra hour?" Daniel asked.

"Yes. They're all upstairs in the study room."

"Good! I wouldn't want Heather or Daniel to know anything about this." Penelope agreed.

Amid their banter, the front door swung open, and Steven quickly strode in. "Good! Now that Steven is here, we can begin this meeting."

"I apologize for keeping all of you waiting." Steven and Loraine exchanged glances, and he gave her a quick wink.

Penelope spoke up. "By now, I'm sure you're all aware of the stunning discovery that Dr. Grayson, Lori, and myself made in the East Wing."

"And I must formally protest! You women should have waited for either myself or Steven to escort you," Daniel implored.

Penelope answered with a stern look. "I'd appreciate it if you would remain quiet until I finish, Daniel." He sheepishly lowered his head and nodded. "Aside from our ghastly discovery, we also recovered these lost paintings that Maggie told us about."

She lifted the tarp from both paintings, and Steven drew an anxious breath when he saw the portrait. "That's the man that was in my dream. Matthew Branch and his brother, Andrew." Everyone looked at him with much surprise. "Well! The plot thickens." All listened with heightened attention as Steven strolled over next to his mother to further address everyone. "I also believe that the remains found in that room might be those of Elizabeth Branch. She was the wife of Daniel Branch the first, and she mysteriously disappeared shortly after Matthew's murder." Everyone in the room gasped.

Daniel Sr. chimed in, "And how, may I ask, did you come about discovering this bit of information?"

Steven replied, "I've spent the entire afternoon searching the archives at Lockeport City Hall. I've discovered a lot of interesting facts from that time."

Mrs. Porter announced, "With all due respect, shouldn't we just notify the police about this?"

Penelope jumped in. "We decided not to involve the authorities since her death obviously took place so long ago, and the last thing we need is to make this public news."

"I fully agree with that decision," Daniel said. "We certainly do not want to have reporters and curiosity seekers snooping around the estate. There are already way too many rumors circulating about this house."

"What do you intend to do with her? You can't just leave her up there," Sharie protested.

"Of course not. If she is indeed Elizabeth Branch, we need to investigate how she died, and then we need to give her a proper family burial."

Gerard chimed into the conversation, "How do you intend to do that without having a professional do forensics?"

Dr. Grayson answered, "We decided among the three of us to do a seance and try to summon her spirit."

Mrs. Porter replied with much nervous anxiety, "I want no part in such a thing. I believe in letting the dead take care of the dead."

Sharie responded, "I somewhat have to agree. We're not quite sure of what sort of spirit we may be conjuring up."

"I assure you all," Dr. Grayson stepped in, "that I'm quite experienced at this sort of thing. If there were any type of negative energies associated with this woman's spirit, I would have picked up on it right away."

Daniel belted down a long swallow of his brandy and boldly added, "I think that Steven, Gerard, and I should examine the remains and the rest of the East Wing before we make any further decisions on the matter."

"Do what you must, Daniel, but the decision has already been made. Since I am head of this house, we will go ahead with the seance at 10:00 tonight. Anyone who wants to be a part of it should be here at that time."

While the house contemplated the evening's events, Tina sat in a plush chair in the cottage with her feet propped up, painting her fingernails as heavy metal rock music played on the radio. Lucretia entered from the other room and stood in the doorway watching. "I think it's time we discussed the reason I brought you here, Tina." Tina paused to look up at Lucretia while she sauntered over and turned the radio off. "Once a month," she sat down, "my life energies need to be charged so that I can continue using this body." Tina listened with heightened interest. "Since I don't have a desire for women, I choose to seek out handsome young men for that purpose."

"I prefer men as well."

Lucretia added, "I'm certainly glad about that." She smiled and continued. "Because of the respected position I hold at Branch Consolidated, and the fact that I have a certain FBI agent watching my every move, I need you to find those men for me."

Tina reacted with excitement. "Can I also have one for myself?"

Lucretia was irritated. "No, Tina! It doesn't work that way."

A pouty face overcame Tina. "Can I share a man with you?"

Lucretia placed her hand to her forehead in frustration. "No! That isn't possible either." She leaned in closer and continued. "You must bring the man to me so that I can draw his life energy, and then dispose of him. Do you understand?"

Tina reacted with disappointment and reluctantly nodded. "That's not fair. You get to have all the fun."

"Maybe I can arrange a way for you to get out once in a while and have a little fun of your own. But remember, if anyone ever asks you any questions, just tell them that you're my cousin from Ohio and that you're staying with me here at the cottage. Are we clear on that?" Tina answered with an enthusiastic nod.

The family meeting ended in the main house, and Steven, Daniel Sr, and Gerard gathered their flashlights to enter the East Wing. When they entered what was once the quarters of Matthew Branch, Steven suddenly halted, as though scared of his next step.

"Steven! Are you alright?"

"I just got this chilling feeling that I've been in this room before."

Daniel answered, "Dr. Grayson and Lori did mention that they felt this may have been Matthew's living space. Perhaps he's trying to tell you something."

Steven nodded and continued to scan the room. His flashlight caught the photograph of Amanda Green, and all three men moved to check it out. "Mother was quite right. It's amazing how much that woman resembles Dr.

Seagraves." Daniel cast an all-knowing glance at Steven, and he reacted by looking away, trembling with anxiety.

Gerard led the way toward the study. "Let's get the unpleasant part over with." Steven and Daniel exchanged a foreboding glance before following.

The men all entered to investigate the stale, dusty room when their flashlights caught the skeletal figure that seemed to stare at them sorrowfully through its empty eye sockets. Daniel recoiled at the sight. "This scene is every bit as grotesque as the women described it."

"It's tragic that this poor soul's remains have been up here for over a century, just waiting to be discovered." Gerard was saddened by the incident.

Steven shined his flashlight on the skeleton and moved in closer to inspect. "I think I know how she may have died." He then shined the light into the other room momentarily, then back onto the skeleton. "See that rope around her neck?" Daniel and Gerard moved in for a closer look. "That's an exact match to that rope holding one side of the drapes back in the adjacent room."

"So, it's quite obvious that someone strangled her. We just have to figure out who did it, and why." Steven gave Gerard a long glance to confirm his statement. "It will be interesting to see if we get an answer in the seance."

Daniel flashed his light around the room and spotted a covered picture in one of the corners. The other men waited curiously as he threw the drop cloth aside to reveal the portrait of an attractive blonde woman in a regal pose. "Well! Now we supposedly know what Elizabeth Branch looked like when she was alive."

Steven and Gerard strolled over to take a look. "She was a very pretty woman," Gerard stated.

Steven studied the painting, then gestured to Daniel. "It hardly seems real that she was our great grandmother."

Daniel answered with a thoughtful nod. "I should take her picture downstairs with us to the seance."

"I agree! Perhaps her spirit can give us a clue as to why her body and portrait were left in this room."

At the City Diner, Suzie was working behind the counter in the near-empty restaurant. Heather Branch and Andrea Hill entered, and sat down at the counter to converse with her. Across the dining room in one of the booths, hiding under his alias Luke Underwood, Hades patiently nursed a cup of coffee. His dark, evil eyes were fixated on the young women. Heather felt the intense stare and turned to glance at him momentarily. "Who is that weird guy that keeps staring at us?"

Suzie replied, "I don't know. This is the first time I've ever seen him in here."

Heather stated, "It's like his eyes are looking right through me. He's definitely creeping me out."

Suzie wiped the counter down with a wet cloth as she spoke to them. "The police usually come around closing time, and escort me to do the bank deposit. Hopefully, they'll get here early tonight." Suzie glanced up at the clock with anxiety, as Luke got up and strolled toward them. "Oh no! Here he comes."

Luke leaned against the counter, close to the girls. "Good evening, ladies!" His eyes were fixed on Andrea, and she reacted uncomfortably. "Aren't you the girls who had the confrontation with the wild dogs several months ago?"

Heather looked puzzled. "How did you know about that?"

Luke laughed. "I make it my business to know things. Besides, this is a small community, and word does get around." He then sat down on the stool closest to Andrea. "Which one of you looked directly into the dogs' eyes?" Andrea nervously looked away, and Luke cued in on it. "It was you! I should have known."

"Please! Just leave me alone. I don't want to talk about it."

He brushed his fingers against her straight blonde hair and smiled wickedly. "You're a virgin, aren't you?"

Suzie erupted with anger. "Whoever you are, you need to leave right now, or I'm calling the cops."

Luke raised his hands in surrender. "There will be no need for that. I was simply trying to be friendly."

"Inquiring about someone's virginity isn't being friendly. It's perverted!" Heather blasted back at him.

Luke laughed, as another person entered the diner. "Did that spunkiness come with your privileged upbringing, Miss Branch?"

Heather furiously fired back, "Who the hell are you?"

The outburst was overheard by the newcomer. Triton, the immortal son of Poseidon and Amphitrite, under his human guise of Tony Freeman, casually strolled over. "I do believe this man goes by the name of Luke Underwood."

Luke cowered when he saw him, and the three young women shifted their full attention to Triton. "Do you know this creep?" Heather said.

"Let's just say I know of him. Is he bothering you?"

"Yes!" Suzie replied. "As a matter of fact, I was just getting ready to call the police."

He shook his head and focused on Luke. "Up to your old tricks again, I see. I think it would be a good idea for you to leave now, Luke."

Luke responded with a look of disgust. "You'll regret this, Triton."

Tony turned and watched as Luke left the diner. After he was safely out of the building, he directed his attention back to the girls. "With that irritating matter out of the way, I was wondering if any of you ladies might know a woman named Amy Seagraves."

Heather perked up. "Dr. Seagraves! Yes! I know her well."

"Great! Have you by chance seen her tonight? I was sent into town to look for her."

"Sorry, but I haven't seen her for a few days. Is everything alright?"

"I'm sure she's just fine. She has a nasty little habit of leaving home without telling her husband where she's going." All three women exchanged a glance. "If she happens to turn up, tell her that Tony was looking for her."

Andrea replied, "I thought that guy just called you Triton?"

"That's just a nickname that some people like to call me. For some strange reason, they think I resemble a Greek god."

Suzie replied with dreamy eyes, "Imagine that!"

Tony looked at Andrea with an eye of interest. "I really should be going. I promise to make sure Luke never bothers you again."

Andrea noticeably sighed. "I do hope we'll see you again…" she trailed off.

Tony gave her a wink and a smile. "Oh! I'm sure you will." The girls adoringly watched him walk out the door.

Heather blurted out, "That was one handsome hunk of a man." Andrea agreed.

"No wonder people think he's a Greek god," Suzie stated.

Then Heather suddenly looked perplexed. "That's funny! I never knew that Dr. Seagraves was married."

"Oh really?" Suzie questioned. "Heather! Everyone has their little nasty secrets. Do you believe that her husband sent a guy like that to look for his wife? I'd rather think that he and the good doctor are scheduling after-hours house calls." All three girls giggled.

A short while later, Steven and Amy strolled along the path toward Branchview. Tony swiftly approached them from the opposite direction. "Mother!" he shouted. "Where have you been? Did you forget about the meeting with my father and me at the cave room?"

Amy placed her hand to her forehead. "Oh, dear! It slipped my mind."

Steven interrupted, "Wait a minute! Did I hear correctly? Is this your son?"

"Oh! I apologize, Steven. Yes, this is my son, Triton."

Tony looked Steven up and down in a wary manner. "Actually, my land name is Tony. I noticed my mother called you Steven, but you look exactly like..."

"...Matthew Branch!" Amy answered. "But of course, he isn't. Matthew was his great uncle." Tony and Steven continued to exchange calculating stares, and Amy nervously turned toward Steven. "I know you're wondering how I can have a son so close to my age. You must remember that he's an immortal. I've forgotten his exact age, but I can say for certain that he is over a thousand years old."

Tony burst out laughing, while Steven reacted with wide-eyed surprise. "I'd have to say that like you, he is very well preserved."

Tony turned his attention back to his mother. "He knows about us?"

"Yes! He's one of the few that does." Tony continued to eye Steven with a smirk. "Tell Poseidon that I apologize for my absence and that I'll speak with him later tonight."

Steven checked his watch. "If we're going to be at Branchview by 10:00, we better hurry."

"Just one more thing, Mother. I saw Hades at the City Diner tonight."

Amy reacted with surprise, but her thoughts were interrupted by the howling in the distance. "That's the first time I've heard those dogs in quite some time."

Tony replied, "Yes. Something definitely is in the air tonight, and it certainly doesn't feel right."

Tony looked around into the darkness surrounding them. "Something has stirred those hounds, and I wouldn't be surprised if Hades was responsible."

"He very rarely shows his presence above ground. What do you suppose is his purpose for being here?" Amy questioned.

"Nothing good, Mother. I'm sure of that. He was harassing a group of young girls in the diner, and I chased him off."

"I'll definitely need to discuss that issue with Poseidon later tonight. But we really must go now."

"Very well! Goodnight, Mother!" Amy and Steven hurried along, and Tony watched them with contemplative thought.

By the time Steven and Amy arrived, it was about five minutes to ten, and the family was already gathered in the sitting room. During the afternoon, they had moved the furniture out of the way and had a large table moved to the center of the room. As they prepared to get started, Steven and Amy took their place at the table just as the clock chimed at 10 pm. In the center of the table was a candle that dimly lit the room.

Daniel started to grow restless as Dr. Grayson began the evening's activities. "It's getting to be a rather common occurrence for my brother to be fashionably late to important family meetings." Steven glanced over at Daniel, while the hounds continued their howling outside.

"I'm sorry for being late. Amy and I had a slight delay on our way here." Steven gave Loraine a quick wink, and she responded with a weak smile.

"If you're all prepared, I'd like to begin." Dr. Grayson glanced at each person in attendance, and they all nodded. She immediately began the seance. "I want each of you to take a deep breath and completely relax. Let go of whatever stress, or stray thoughts you may have brought to this room." She glanced around the table once more, as everyone relaxed. "I want everyone to lay their hands on the table with fingers outstretched and connecting to the person next to you. At no time during the ceremony should this connection be broken."

All paused in the silence for a long, anticipating moment. "Spirit of Elizabeth Branch, I call upon you from your peaceful slumber to appear to us now. Help us find the answers to your murder and others that took place in your time. I beckon you. Come to us now…" The room was silent.

Then suddenly, a gentle breeze filtered through the room, disturbing the candle. A bright light flashed outside the window, illuminating the whole room. The portrait of Elizabeth lit up. The double doors of the sitting room flew open, then promptly slammed shut, startling everyone at the table. Dr. Grayson reminded them to stay calm and continue holding hands. An apparition then appeared, floating near the ceiling before it settled in a spot near the table.

A beautiful young blonde woman in her twenties appeared, wearing the same blue Victorian dress she wore when she died. She addressed the room in a stern tone, "Why have you disturbed my death quarters in the East Wing? What answers could I give that would even matter in your time?"

"We apologize for disturbing you. We were unaware of what had happened and hoped to find answers to some of the strange occurrences within Branchview. We also need to identify the person who killed you, Matthew, and possibly even Andrew Branch, and Beth DuPont."

Elizabeth looked perplexed and pointed her finger toward Steven. "How can it be…?" She moved closer. "Matthew Branch sits at this very table with his lover Amanda Green. He died before me, and surely she would have been dead long ago as well."

"We are not those people, Elizabeth," Steven spoke up. "Matthew was my great uncle."

"That's impossible! You are both the same. I can sense your energies."

Loraine glared at Steven with hurtful eyes, while Steven and Amy exchanged tense glances. One of the double doors to the room opened slightly, and no one noticed as Daniel Jr peeked in with wide curious eyes from the foyer. Elizabeth then pointed a finger at Daniel Sr. "And how is it that you are here? Everything was your fault. Your greed and hate caused all of the grief within this household."

Daniel Sr emotionally pleaded with her. "I am not your husband Daniel the first. He was my grandfather, and he died in 1959."

Elizabeth curiously glanced around the room with anxiety. "He's still nearby. I can still feel his evil presence lurking in every corner."

"Elizabeth! Did your husband kill you?" Dr. Grayson inquired.

She shook her head no. "All I could see were the hands of the person who strangled me from behind. I believe it was Aaron Locke that killed me, and most likely all the others you mentioned. He had sworn vengeance on our family after that terrible fire."

"Was your husband responsible for that fire?"

She shook her head no once again. "He was accused by many, but I know for a fact that it was not him. We were together during that entire evening."

Dr. Grayson continued, quite perplexed. "Why did your husband leave your body in that room, and close off the East Wing?"

"I do not know. Perhaps he was afraid the authorities would find him responsible for my murder."

"Why were you even there? That was Matthew's personal quarters."

Elizabeth sighed with great sorrow. "I had hoped to find clues among the papers in his desk as to who may have killed him. All I found were the beautiful love letters that Amanda Green wrote to him. I remember my last thoughts were of wishing that their kind of love could have existed between me and my husband." Amy noticeably choked up with emotion. "I wish I could tell you more, but this is all that I know. Please refrain from calling on my spirit again, for all I want is peace and eternal rest."

"I promise that you'll have that…" Dr. Grayson looked around the table for acknowledgment from the others. Elizabeth slowly faded away, and a gust of wind wafted through the room, blowing out the candle. Dr. Grayson looked upward. "Goodbye, Elizabeth! And thank you!"

Everyone looked at each other with silent astonishment, but Loraine's eyes were only fixed on Amy, displaying an equal measure of hurt and sympathy.

Out in the foyer, Daniel Jr remained unnoticed by anyone but was understandably confused by what he had just witnessed. As he turned to tiptoe away, the front door suddenly flew open from a strong gust of wind that nearly blew him over. The spirit of Daniel Branch the first materialized right before his eyes. He was dressed in nineteenth-century clothing, with a heavy wool overcoat. He peered down at the young Daniel, and the terrified boy screamed and ran upstairs. Daniel's wicked laugh echoed throughout the house.

The disruption was heard by all at the table. They quickly moved toward the closed door to inspect the situation. "Dear Lord! That sounded like young Daniel screaming," Penelope announced.

Steven was in the lead, heading to the door when it flew open, almost catching him in the face. A large black shadow breezed by and entered the room. The group gradually moved backward, away from the spirit. The now relit candle revealed a glimpse of the figure's evil grin. "Well, hello dear family and friends. I understand that you're looking for answers." He paused with a sinister chuckle. "I too, am looking for answers." The horrified group remained perplexed by the aggressiveness of the apparition.

Chapter Four:

What the Séance Foretells

The peaceful outline of the giant mansion could be seen against the darkened winter sky. A dim light in the sitting room window gave little clue as to the drama that was playing out within that section of the house. In calling on the spirit of Elizabeth Branch, the participants of a seance had unknowingly roused the restless spirit of her husband, Daniel Branch the first. It seemed that hidden within the East Wing was yet another unforeseen secret that still waited to be uncovered.

As Daniel the first materialized in the large sitting room, he sauntered through it, scanning each person with an intimidating glare. However, his attempt to scare the inhabitants was interrupted when the mantel clock chimed at 11:00 p.m. He was immediately drawn to the massive fireplace to look at it. "I always loved the sound of that clock. The finest quality piece of its time. It was custom-made in Germany by the world's premier master clockmaker. And I see it still rings true to his mastery."

Daniel spun around with a narcissistic stature, as everyone returned to their place at the table. "Now, I demand to know why my wife was summoned here tonight!"

"You have no right to barge in here and demand anything. You are no longer the master of this house," Daniel III said.

Daniel the first laughed arrogantly. "It's very daring of you to speak to me in that tone. Even if you do hold a striking resemblance to me, I was here long before you were. This will always be my house and don't ever forget that. Do you understand?"

Penelope interrupted, "Mr. Branch! I am the matriarch of this household, and I command that you keep your arrogant remarks in check."

He moved closer and peered at her. "I remember you! You're Penelope, and your twin sister was the witch. It's a disgrace that a Locke would ever become the matriarch of Branchview."

Penelope boiled with anger, but Dr. Grayson calmed her with a stern glance, as Daniel shifted his attention to Steven and Amy. He looked at them with great wonder. "My brother and his mysterious lover? It can't be possible!"

Loraine cast another venomous glance at Steven and Amy. "No, it isn't! I simply have a strong resemblance to my late great uncle."

"Indeed. But the rumors of immortality were obviously true about you... Amanda Green."

Amy gripped her glass of water and fired back a reply. "My name is Amy Seagraves! Dr. Amy Seagraves!"

"I seriously doubt that."

The conversation began to bore Daniel and he turned his eyes to Loraine. "And who might this lovely creature be?" He flashed a fake smile.

Steven interrupted, "She is my wife— Loraine."

Loraine flashed a hostile glance toward Steven. "I'm quite capable of speaking for myself, Steven."

Steven responded with a perplexed expression, as Daniel the first offered up a dismissive grunt, and then cast a disdainful look toward Gerard and Sharie. "Why are these Negro servants here in my sitting room?"

Gerard erupted with anger, "I beg your pardon, sir...!"

Daniel III intervened. "I will not tolerate such racist remarks in my house. Gerard and Sharie are honored members of our family, and I demand you treat them with the utmost respect."

Daniel the first cowered sheepishly. "I see quite a few things have changed over the years."

Sharie jumped in, "And for the better, I might add."

Dr. Grayson impatiently took charge of the conversation. "Mr. Branch! I'm Dr. Sheila Grayson, and I'm in charge of this seance. We've answered your questions and put up with your ego-fueled insults. Now it's time for you to answer some of our questions."

Daniel spun around once again, intrigued by her demanding behavior. "What do you wish to know?"

"For starters, sir… if you didn't kill your wife, then who did?"

Daniel the first looked upward in thought. "Elizabeth was my first wife, and she was very special to me."

Sharie burst out in laughter. "She couldn't have been all that special for you to have left her in that room to rot."

Daniel barked back in frustration, "I had no other choice. All the evidence pointed to me as a suspect, and I would have surely hung for that crime."

"Could you please," Steven asked, "just answer the question, Mr. Branch?"

Daniel the first flew into a rage. "I believe it was that scoundrel Aaron Locke that killed her." His eyes suddenly filled with hate. "In fact, I think he committed the other murders as well."

"But… Daniel, can you prove that?" Dr. Grayson asked.

Daniel the first looked away, shook his head no, and continued, "I'll fully admit that I was responsible for the death of my second wife Daphne, but I swear that I didn't kill Elizabeth or any of the others."

Daniel III questioned, "You killed my grandmother? I was led to believe that she left you for another man."

Daniel the first shook his head once again. "It was a tragic accident that your father, unfortunately, witnessed firsthand. We were quarreling, and I grabbed at her as she turned to walk down the stairs. She lost her balance and tumbled to the bottom landing."

Daniel III said, "Really… and how many more bodies are we going to find in this house?"

The apparition moved in closer. "You'll find her remains in the East Wing as well. She's inside the window box of the sitting room." Dr. Grayson rolled her eyes in disbelief.

As Daniel the first tried to speak again, the angry spirit of Maggie marched in through the open doors. The room was taken back by her presence. "Did you forget that you killed me too, Daniel? You're nothing but pure evil!"

Daniel the first cowered to her. "Oh, Maggie! I never meant for that statue to fall over. I was only trying to scare you."

"You're a liar! You were happy when I died. You always bullied me!"

Daniel the first angrily bit back, "What did you expect? You were always the little darling who got all the attention in the family."

Penelope had been quiet long enough. "Mr. Branch! You're a pompous, deplorable excuse for a man. I command that you leave this house, and never return."

A frustrated Dr. Grayson slapped the table with the palm of her hand before anything else could be said. "Enough! I refuse to serve as a referee to a spiritual family feud." Maggie turned and stormed back out of the room.

"I have nothing more to say. If you want to know who killed the others, you must go to the ruins of the Locke Estate, and call upon the spirit of Aaron Locke. Since being here serves me no more value, I will take my leave. Good night!"

Dr. Grayson drew an exasperated sigh. "In all my days, I've never encountered a spirit that was as overbearing and difficult as that man."

The room exchanged looks with each other in agreement. Penelope jumped from her seat. "Now that he's gone, I must go check on Daniel and make sure he's alright."

As the others watched Penelope leave the room, they prepared to exit as well. Daniel III stepped back and allowed Dr. Grayson to go ahead, following her to the foyer. "Thank you, Daniel. I bid all of you a good night." The group nodded.

As Dr. Grayson began to ascend the stairs, she stumbled and fell against the banister post. Daniel III lunged forward to grab her arm. "Dr. Grayson! Are you alright?"

"Yes, Daniel! I'm just a bit drained. If you'll all please excuse me, this evening has been very demanding, and I really do need to go rest."

Gerard turned to Daniel. "Should we wait until tomorrow to check on those other remains in the East Wing?"

"Yes, Gerard! It's very late, and I doubt that any of us has the energy to withstand any more supernatural surprises."

Sharie replied, "I'll just be happy to never have to deal with another pompous, bigoted spirit like Daniel Branch the first-ever again."

Daniel III replied, "I can assure you both that no one presently living in this household shares the views of that despicable man."

Gerard gave a friendly pat to his shoulder as they prepared to leave. "I'll see you tomorrow, Daniel."

In the back corner of the foyer, Loraine sulked with her arms tightly folded in front of her. "Before you go, Dr. Seagraves, I would wish to have a word with you in private."

Loraine glared at Steven, trembling with anger, then back to Amy. Daniel noticed, casting a quick uncomfortable glance as he waited for a reply from Dr. Seagraves. "Of course, Lori! We can talk in the study."

Daniel III said, "I think this is the point where I should say goodnight as well."

He exited up the stairwell, fleeing the uncomfortable moment, and leaving Steven alone in the awkward situation. Amy led the way into the study, while Loraine swiftly closed the door behind them. She stopped just inside, leaning against it, peering at Amy with intense eyes. "Are you and my husband having an affair?"

"Lori! That's the most ridiculous thing I've ever heard."

"Is it really? I heard how those spirits spoke of you and Steven, and how your energies were connected. I also know that the two of you have been seeing quite a bit of each other."

Amy sighed in bewilderment. "You're so wrong about all of this, Loraine! How can I ever explain this to you? It's hard for even me to understand."

Loraine strolled away from the door. "It's already quite clear to me, and I could care less that you're an immortal goddess. If you think you can waltz into our lives and steal my husband without me giving up a fight, you're greatly mistaken."

"Oh, Lori! It's not like that. Let me try to explain." Amy sunk into a chair, and took a deep breath, as Loraine remained standing firm and listening. "After Matthew died, I couldn't bring myself to walk on land for many years. I also left the beaches at Lighthouse Point, and occupied my time elsewhere in the world." Loraine relaxed a bit and sat down to listen. "Matthew often came to me in dreams and promised that somehow he would return to me. One day, out of curiosity, I returned to Lighthouse Point and saw Jack Branch. I immediately knew that it was Matthew, and was broken-hearted to find that he was in love with Penelope."

"But Penelope was already married to Daniel Branch II. You could've tried to win his heart."

"I had hoped to do just that, but Jack died before I had that chance. I know now that Matthew's energy transferred to Jack's unborn son."

Loraine gasped. "That was Steven."

Amy nodded. "When Penelope gave him up for adoption, I lost him again. By the time Steven came back to Branchview, he was already in love with you."

"Amy! I plead with you. I know you possess the powers and the beauty to win his heart. But please don't take him away from me."

Amy forced a smile. "I have no intention whatsoever to do that. But I have found out another way that Matthew and I can finally be together." Loraine listened curiously. "When I laid my hand on Steven's heart, I felt two separate energies. One was Steven's, and the other was Matthew's. Those energies are supposed to be merged as one when a spirit is reincarnated." Loraine was totally perplexed. "I found that if I were to draw Matthew's energy from Steven's body, then we could finally be together."

"How could you accomplish that? It doesn't seem rational."

"It can be done with my powers. By simply kissing Steven passionately, Matthew's energy would leave his body, and become a separate independent spirit."

Loraine took hold of Amy's hands. "I hope you understand that having a beautiful woman such as yourself kissing my husband bothers me greatly. But if that's all it would take for you and Matthew to finally be together, then, by all means, I will allow you to do just that."

Amy looked away in despair. "I wish that was all there was to it. If I were to do this, I would only be able to join Matthew in spirit."

"Are you saying that you would die?" Amy responded with a sorrowful nod. "Oh, Amy! We'll get through this somehow, and we shall do it together." In a moment of sorrow, the two women embraced the truth behind Amy's motives. Loraine realized that she had been hard on Steven without provocation. She had violated their trust by assuming the worst and jumping to conclusions.

Meanwhile, just off the shore of Lighthouse Point, a small speed boat was anchored just out of the sights of the lighthouse beacon. Two drug smugglers dressed in black wet suits hauled a large storage bin onto the beach. The men each grabbed a handle and hurried up the beach before anyone noticed their presence. Along the edge of the beach, under the large cliffside, were ancient caves. Once they were inside the cave, they could finally speak without having to raise their voice above the sounds of the ocean. "I think they packed a few extra bricks into this bin," one smuggler stated.

"It's definitely heavier than normal."

The first smuggler stubbed his toe while trying to carry the bin over the large boulders inside the wet cave and yelled out, "Dammit!"

The other man quipped back, "Why don't you just announce to the world that we're in here?"

"Okay, smartass! I didn't stumble on purpose." He regained his balance and pushed aside an old fishing net, revealing an archaic-looking wood mechanism.

"What do you see over there?"

"Some type of an old lever. I think it's been here for quite some time."

"Pull on it, and see what happens."

He turned to glance at his associate, but curiosity took over, and he pulled on the lever. He put all of his weight into it, but it refused to budge.

"Hey, dude… I could use a little help here."

"Don't 'dude' me. Why are you such a pansy?" They both pulled hard, and the rotten lever broke off, sending them both reeling onto the cave floor.

In the wake of their attempt, the entire cave echoed with a loud rumble. A large boulder slowly rolled to one side, revealing a hidden room. "Hey, look at that."

"Yea, come on. Let's check it out." They walked over hesitantly to the darkroom and shined their flashlights into it. "There's nothing in here. I wonder what the purpose was for this place—" One of the men shined his light to every corner. "Hey! Over there! Something's covered up with a large tarp."

They both walked over and pulled the heavy tarp aside, and found a beautifully ornate, and colorful carved wood box. "Oh, dude! Check out all that fancy old carving. I can't believe it's so well preserved for being down in this damp cave for so long."

"This room is extremely dry. I guess that's why they stashed it here."

His buddy looked at him with pent-up excitement. "Let's open it and see what's inside. It might be some old pirate's buried treasure."

"No! Come on. We don't have time. Let's just take it with us," he replied.

"Fine, let's go…" They picked up the box with the side handles, and a loud, ominous chant echoed through the cave.

"What in the hell was that?" He looked at his friend.

"I don't know, but it sure sounded creepy. Let's get out of here!" the other exclaimed. The walls in the room began to shake and crumble. As they rushed past the boulder, that part of the cave collapsed in a cloud of choking dust.

They both recovered, stumbling and coughing, but did not drop the box. As they exited the cave, Agent Adam Smith was waiting outside with a host of other armed agents. "FBI! Put the box down and raise your hands over your heads." The chant echoed louder. "What was that? Is there someone else in there with you?"

One of the smugglers replied, "No... I don't know what the hell that noise is, but we don't want anything to do with it. The drugs are in that bin over there."

"Fine, but what's in this box?" Adam inquired.

"We have no idea. We found it in that portion of the cave that collapsed."

The other smuggler spoke up, "Just get us the hell out of here before that chanting starts again." Adam turned to direct his agents, as two others handcuffed the smugglers.

"Let's get this stuff out of here now. I don't know how secure this place is." As the agents went to pick the box up, the chanting could be heard again. The agents noticed and looked toward the interior of the cave with fearful eyes.

A few moments later, Adam Smith exited the cave and approached the Lightkeeper, Bill Crawford. The other agents were not far behind him. "Thank you for the tip on that suspicious boat, Mr. Crawford. We've been trying to crack this drug ring for quite some time."

"I figured they'd be back again tonight. They've been out here for two straight nights before this."

"Will you be available for further questioning as a witness?"

"Absolutely, I'll make sure that I am." Adam smiled and patted him on the shoulder.

Chapter Five:

The Precise Time

B ack at Branchview, the large clock in the foyer chimed precisely at 2:00 a.m. Steven emerged from the sitting room with a book in his hand. As he approached the staircase, he reached over to turn out the lamp mounted on the base of the banister rail. But something caught his attention, and he looked up at the wall on the first landing. He paused to stare at the pastel painting of the stern-faced woman whose eyes seemed to eerily follow his every move. As he continued to climb the stairs, an apparition appeared at the top landing. It was a beautiful dark-haired woman. She looked to be in her early 30s and wore fashionable clothing from possibly the 1940s. She stepped back to allow Steven passage, but he stayed put on the first landing. He took careful notice as she raised her hand, pointing toward the stairs. "He lied! He pushed me down those stairs."

Steven eyed her with much curiosity. "Are you, my grandmother? Are you Daphne Branch?"

She slowly nodded yes. "You recalled my husband's spirit, but he should never be allowed to dwell in this household. He has been the cause of too much grief here at Branchview, and he will surely cause more."

"Why did he kill you, Daphne?"

"I discovered that he had arranged a pact with the witch."

"Charlotte Locke?" Steven exclaimed.

She shook her head. "Her name was Liddy McPherson. She was the grand witch of the Secret Society. Before he and I had ever met, he had promised her that she could assume the body of his second wife, and become the mistress of Branchview in exchange for 20 extra years of his youth."

"I don't know of this Liddy McPherson, but obviously, that transaction never took place."

"She held up her end of the bargain, but he killed her on the very night I died."

"How did that happen?"

"He shot her in the back while she waited for him in the garden, and then he burned her body."

Steven rolled his eyes in disbelief. "Sounds like my grandfather was a real sweetheart of a guy." The door creaked open from the north wing, startling Steven, and causing Daphne's spirit to quickly fade away.

Loraine stepped onto the landing dressed in her nightgown. "Steven! I was just coming to look for you. Were you just talking to someone?"

Steven answered with joking sarcasm, "Only to one of the many spirits that inhabit this place."

"You must hurry to bed. We need to talk immediately."

Steven said under his breath, "I guess that means no sleep tonight."

"I'm sorry dear! Did you just say something to me?"

"No! Go on ahead, sweetheart. I'll be there shortly." She smiled, and exited back to the north wing, as Steven climbed the last set of stairs, and wearily said to himself, "I think I need to start drinking." As he reached for the door to the north wing, he hoped the conversation with his wife would be short-lived.

As the night pushed onward at Branchview, Philip and Amy strolled the beach. "Now, since Loraine knows what's going on, why can't you just arrange a time that you can share a romantic kiss with Steven? You most definitely have my blessings on that as well."

"I can't go away with Matthew until my work is finished here. I'm sure that his spirit understands that."

"You've waited long enough, my dear. I'll uphold my promise to help the Branch family and defeat the Secret Society. I can do it without your help."

"Absolutely not! I'm committed to solving the very problem that took Matthew away from me in the first place, and now that I know Hades is walking above ground again, I am even more determined to stay the course." Philip shook his head in amazement.

"I always admired your persistence."

Philip halted and stared toward the cliffs. "Philip! What is it?"

"There's someone over there near the entrance to one of our caves. I must check this out."

"I'm going with you." They marched up the beach with determination.

Officer Hawley of the Lockeport police department, a pudgy man in his mid-forties, was standing watch over the entrance, which was cordoned off with yellow police tape. "Stop right there! This is an official crime scene."

"Crime scene? What took place here tonight?"

"They caught a couple of drug runners, and part of the cave collapsed. I have to make sure that no one goes in there until it can be inspected in the morning." Philip and Amy exchanged worried glances, and Hawley curiously inquired, "What are you two doing out here in the middle of the night?"

"We couldn't sleep, so we decided to take a stroll on the beach."

"This is private property. The beach is fenced in, and the only open access is either from Branchview or the water. Do you two have identification?"

Amy intervened, "We're Philip and Amy Seagraves. We're guests at Branchview, and I'm afraid we left our IDs back at the house."

Philip took note of the policeman's name tag. "My wife is right, Officer Hawley. Being that this is Branch property, I'm sure that the family would like to know the details of tonight's event. Is there something more you can tell us?"

Officer Hawley thought for a moment. "Well! The Branch's may be interested to know this. When they arrested the two guys, they were carrying an old wooden box. They claimed they retrieved it from the portion of the cave that collapsed."

Philip and Amy exchanged a quick foreboding glance. "Yes! I'm sure that they would be very interested. Can you tell me who has the custody of this box?"

"I'm not sure where they took it, but the FBI agents hauled it away. Just for the record, you didn't hear that from me."

"Of course! I would never put your position in jeopardy, Officer Hawley." The officer gave them a nod of gratitude, then shivered as he glanced out into the dark. The wind howled eerily through the interior of the cave.

"You two should really get back to Branchview. This place can get rather spooky at night."

"We'll do just that. Thank you for your information and concern, officer."

Philip and Amy turned and strolled away. They began conversing when they were a good distance from the cave. "That box has been hidden away for centuries. I can't believe that someone found it," Amy stated.

"This is terrible! We must get that box back. I shudder to think what would happen if someone were able to open it. It does have a seal that can only be opened by the gods, but human curiosity can only lead to negative results, as you and I know all too well."

"I agree. But what can we do?"

They came to a halt and faced each other. "You must get back to the water and re-hydrate yourself. I'll contact Zeus immediately to inform him about that box, and to also have him confront Hades on his intrusive business above ground."

"I'll meet you at dawn, near the end of the path by Lighthouse Point."

"Yes! I should know more by that time. Until then, rest well my dear." Philip and Amy parted ways, while the rest of the innocent world still slept.

Inside the Grand Corridor of the main house, it was still and silent as the living inhabitants of the house slumbered in the wake of a very tedious day. In the darkened recesses of the room, the spirit of Daniel Branch the first appeared. He eyed the splendor of the room as he conversed with himself. "I always loved this room. Now since my spirit has been called back, I refuse to ever leave again."

Maggie appeared before him, holding a sword at her side. "No Daniel! You will leave this house, and you will never come back."

Daniel gave a sinister laugh. "And do you plan to dispel me from this house on your own accord, you little runt?"

As Maggie stood brave, Daphne stepped in from the shadows, as did Andrew Branch, a tall brown-haired man in his 20s, along with Beth Dupont, a pretty blonde, also in her 20s. They were all carrying swords at their sides, as they took their stance next to Maggie.

Daphne spoke up, "We all intend to dispel you from this house, and send your soul back to the depths of hell, where you belong."

Daniel cowered in front of them. "I never intended to harm you, Daphne. You weren't supposed to find out my plan."

"And that is supposed to make everything alright?"

"I realized after you died that the witch could not assume a dead body. I knew she would be furious and curse me."

"So, you shot her in the back before she had the chance to harm you. What a self-absorbed, pitiful man you are, Daniel Branch."

Andrew stepped forward and pointed his sword at Daniel. "And now, brother, after all the suffering you caused, you want to return and dominate the very place that was also once our home?"

"I deserve to be here. I told you that I had no part in any of the murders or mishaps during your time."

Beth spoke up angrily, "Our murders, and everyone that took place here at Branchview was caused by your actions, Daniel Branch. There was someone who committed those crimes, and they were obviously responding to some selfish, destructive act that you inflicted upon them."

Daniel quickly replied, "I swear that you have the wrong person. Aaron Locke and that dreaded Secret Society were responsible for everything."

The spirit of Jack Branch stepped from the shadows, also wielding a sword and shaking his head. "Yes, grandfather! Perhaps they were. But your insistence on revenge-fueled the fires of retaliation that affected generations of this family, and several other lives as well."

Daphne concluded, "So, in your selfish quest of pride, wealth, and power, you robbed us all of the right to live a long and happy life."

"The ending of all that grief begins tonight," Andrew firmly stated.

Daniel's spirit grew increasingly anxious. "Just what do you spirits intend to do?"

Maggie took up the conversation she started, "All of us will bring change to Branchview."

The room lit up in a blinding light of all the spirits of past Branchview inhabitants, and Daniel cowered in fear. "No! Not the light! I can't tolerate the light!" Maggie led his accusers toward him, all wielding their swords. The illuminated spirits behind them converged as well. Daniel recoiled, and his terrifying screams echoed throughout the large room, and across the high ceilings of the Grand Corridor.

Chapter Six:

True Love Blossoms

A horrifying night of events had left the Branchview inhabitants taking refuge in sleep. However, it seemed as though no matter the day or time, unseen terror always lay in wait to claim yet another victim. In another part of the estate, a more terrifying, sinister event was about to take place.

In a silent dimly lit room of the cottage, Lucretia Darknight waited patiently for her evil plot to play out. The door of the cottage swung open, and Tina swept into the room giggling, while in the embrace of a handsome young man in his early 20s, known only as Trevor.

They passionately kissed as Lucretia sauntered in from the adjacent room, wearing only a sexy red lace teddy. Trevor's interest quickly shifted toward her seductive approach. "Well! When Tina told me she had a roommate, I never imagined she'd be so gorgeous." Lucretia moved closer, without saying anything, and ran her long red fingernail the length of Trevor's throat to his chin.

"Tina… you have brought me a delicious specimen. I am proud of you on your first attempt." Trevor reacted awkwardly to her comment, as she gently squeezes his bicep. Her wicked desire entranced him immediately. "What is your name, handsome?"

"It's Trevor. But you can call me Trev." Lucretia turned to look at Tina, who stood silently with her jealousy openly displayed.

"Tina dear! Would you be willing to share Trev with me?"

Tina stared at her sullenly and answered with a nod. Trevor laughed, uncertain as to his fate. "Whoa! Really… is this for real?" Lucretia smiled at him, and they passionately kissed. As Lucretia moved in for the kill, she took his hand and led him to the bedroom. Tina remained in the other room, pacing with pent-up anger over the circumstances. After it was certain they had begun their engagement, she decided to escape the cottage. Tina went to grab her coat but nervously held back and sat down for a moment. Then she jumped up and reached for the doorknob. She tilted her head, and listened for a moment as Trevor exclaimed, "Hey! What the...? No! No!" The cottage fell silent a few seconds later.

In the deep recesses of the cliffside, within the hidden cave, Poseidon sat on a large throne carved from crystal, on the altar of the gods. Within seconds, Zeus, known also as Ezekiel Sphere when functioning in the real world, materialized in front of him. Like his brother, he was in his early 30s, with a thick musculature, and long curly brown hair. They greeted each other with a nod of respect. "Poseidon! It's good to see you, my brother." Poseidon stepped down from his throne, and greeted him with a smile, while Zeus looked around. "Where is Hades?"

Poseidon laughed. "He's late, as usual." As they assumed some pleasantries, Hades stepped out from the shadows. "Talking about me already?"

Poseidon sneered, "I was getting ready to mention how much I loathe seeing you again."

"That feeling is quite mutual for me as well."

Zeus intervened, "That's enough! Put your petty differences aside, and let's get to the real issues that prompted this meeting."

Poseidon paced in front of them. "It appears that Hades has broken his oath by appearing above ground under his alias, Luke Underwood."

Zeus looked to Hades, who flinched slightly at the charge. "Is this true?"

"Yes! I'm seeking out a young woman that my hounds have chosen as my next mistress. As you well know, anyone who stares into the eyes of a hell hound belongs to me."

"You will stop immediately. I absolutely forbid you from doing this. You must not seek a mistress among the innocents in the world above ground. I'm certain that there are many to choose from in your world."

"None that are virgins. I must have this woman…" His voice trailed off.

Zeus erupted with anger. "The same way you had to possess my daughter?" They were inches apart. "Persephonia? We all know how that ended. If you dare defy me this time, I will bring down the wrath of the Heavens. Do you understand?"

Hades held back his response, as Zeus stepped away. Poseidon couldn't help but grin. "Now, with that issue resolved, let's move on to the next."

Poseidon got very serious. "Someone has found and confiscated Pandora's Box." The other two gasped in astonishment. "How could this happen? It was well hidden for several centuries."

"I don't know the details, but the authorities have possession of it. If they try to destroy the box to get to its contents, we all know very well what the consequences would be."

Hades replied, "The last time that box was opened, over half of the world perished from disease and pestilence."

"And might I remind you that it was your naive and curious mistress, Pandora that used the powers you bestowed upon her to open it," Poseidon stated while pointing an accusing finger.

Hades balked right back. "And I'll remind you that she did so without me knowing, and rightfully, she paid the price for it."

Zeus paced nervously and erupted with frustration. "You two must quit squabbling over the past. This is one instance where we all need to work in harmony." They both exchanged a glance. "We must get that box back and hide it away from the world forever."

"Zeus is right, Hades."

Zeus eyed both Poseidon and Hades. "Whatever strategy we choose, it's most important for us to be as tactful as possible in our human form."

"I most certainly agree. We must not let our real identities be exposed to the world," Hades replied.

Poseidon looked at his watch. "It's almost dawn, so I'll spend the day gathering information, and work on a plan with Amphitrite."

Zeus turned to Hades. "Leave the fact-finding to Poseidon. You're not to appear above ground unless I grant you the privilege." Hades turned with a half sneer of defiance and faded into the shadows, while Zeus turned his full attention back to Poseidon. "Beware of Hades. We can't fully put our trust in him." Poseidon gave an assured nod as Zeus faded from the room.

In the bedroom of Senator Holdsclaw, a cell phone rang on the nightstand by the bed. "Who is that in the middle of the night?" Holdsclaw reached over to silence his wife.

He looked at the caller ID, and answered in a loud whisper, "Why are you calling me at this hour?" He listened for a moment, then quickly sat up at the edge of the bed. "How much do they know?" He got up and paced away from the bed as he listened some more. "Don't worry! I'll take care of this on my end. You just need to make sure none of this can be traced back to me. Am I clear?" He ended the call and looked off into the dark of the room with a very concerned expression.

Poseidon took his meeting with Zeus and Hades very seriously. Under the guise of Phillip Seagraves, he paced along the clearing above the cliffs, waiting for Amy in the pre-dawn hours. He turned when he heard footsteps approaching, and saw Tina walking toward him, appearing to be quite upset.

Philip curiously strolled toward her. "Well! Hello there!"

Tina quickly changed her demeanor and eyed him with obvious admiration. "Well! Hello to you, too."

Philip was taken by her beauty. "What's a fine-looking young lady like yourself doing out here alone at this hour?"

"I thought it might be a good morning to watch the sunrise on the beach. What about you? Are you waiting for someone special?"

Philip answered with a clever smirk. "Perhaps I am! My name is Philip."

"Hi, Philip… my name is Tina." She stepped closer and flirtatiously brushed back his long locks of hair with her hand. "You look just like a rock star."

"I've never had anyone describe me quite in that manner." He shook his head with amusement. "Are you a guest at Branchview?"

"Yes! I'm staying here at the estate with my cousin." Philip stared into her eyes with curious wonderment, and she took notice. "Is there something wrong?"

He recovered quickly. "No! Nothing at all! I was just noticing what beautiful eyes you have." She reacted in a giddy manner as he continued, "Do you suppose it would be possible for me to visit you at Branchview sometime?"

Tina childishly grinned as she thought about Phillip's statement. "Perhaps it would be better if you met me someplace else. Like, maybe right here?"

"Tonight… at seven?"

"I can do that." She looked off toward the ocean as the sun began to peek above the horizon, and she saw Amy approaching. "I think that special someone that you're waiting for has arrived." Philip turned to look as well, as Tina left him with parting words: "I'll see you tonight. Don't keep me waiting."

She and Amy exchanged cordial nods as they passed, and Amy greeted Philip with an all-knowing grin. "She's very pretty."

"Yes! I'm very much intrigued, but also quite baffled by her as well."

"What do you mean?"

Philip gave his reply very careful thought. "Although she seems like any other living being when I looked in her eyes, I saw no light from her soul."

Amy reacted with confusion, "Perhaps she's one of the many spirits that wander the property."

He pondered the suggestion for a quick moment. "I suppose I'll find out tonight when I meet with her again."

Amy shook her head. "You never cease to amaze me, Poseidon."

He smiled in amusement. "On a more serious note, you and I need to find the whereabouts of that box immediately."

Amy sighed. "I think we have a very long and busy day ahead of us."

In the state crime lab, Agent Smith looked over evidence reports near a table holding the cocaine bricks confiscated from the cave. Senator Holdsclaw entered with his enormous bodyguard Seth following. "Agent Smith! I wanted to stop by and congratulate you and your team for the big bust."

"I wouldn't call it all that big, Senator. We have just one load of cocaine, and two hired runners in custody. The source of all these drugs is still out there."

Holdsclaw picked up one of the bricks and examined it. "At least we created a temporary disturbance in their operation." Holdsclaw then noticed the ornate box and strolled over to examine it as well. "What a beautiful box. Where did this come from?"

Adam sauntered over to join him. "The smugglers were carrying that out of the cave when we caught them."

Holdsclaw replied, "Does it have any connection to the crime?"

Adam sighed. "I have no idea. It has a vacuum seal on the lid that we haven't been able to break. There's a good chance we may have to destroy it in order to find out what's on the inside."

"You can't destroy it. It's a work of art." Holdsclaw examined it even closer. "I want this box, Agent Smith."

"I'm afraid that's not possible, Senator. For the time being, it's criminal evidence. If it turns out that it contains no drugs, then we must turn the box and its contents over to the Branch family. After all, it was confiscated from their property."

Holdsclaw paced away in thought. "I see!" He turned with an arrogant smirk and confronted Adam. "Agent Smith! Do you like your job?"

"As a matter of fact, I do sir… why?"

Holdsclaw chuckled and exchanged a smug grin with Seth. "You do understand that I can eliminate that job with one simple phone call." Adam gave a defeated nod, while Holdsclaw countered with an intimidating stare. "Since you understand how that process works, I fully expect this box to be delivered to my office by the end of the workday."

Adam answered with much anxiety, "I'll have it there by this afternoon."

Holdsclaw tapped Seth on the arm and prepared to depart before turning with a condescending smirk. "No one else needs to know about our little transaction, Agent Smith. The box simply disappeared from the evidence room. I'm confident that you can create a valid excuse for that." Holdsclaw sauntered out of the room, satisfied with his acquisition.

Outside the lab, Holdsclaw turned to Seth with a whisper. "Oh… I need to make those two smugglers disappear before this day is done. Can you make that a reality?"

Seth gave a confident nod. "Consider it done."

As the family gained some sense of understanding of the recent events, Steven, Daniel III, and Gerard walked toward the entrance doors to the East Wing, dressed in casual work clothes. All the men were clear as to their tasks. Daniel was in the lead and opened the door first. It creaked due to the age of the hinges, but a sudden rush of fear overtook Daniel, and he paused before entering. "Daniel! Is something wrong?"

"I must apologize. You two will have to go on without me. After hearing of Steven's experience with our grandmother last night, I can't bear to see what we'll inevitably find in that window box."

"I understand, Daniel. Gerard and I can handle this."

"Thank you, I'll wait right here. If you need anything, just shout."

Steven and Gerard walked into the dimly lit room and set their eyes on the large window box that beckoned their attention. Steven handed Gerard a face mask, as he slipped one on himself. "We need to wear these. The odor and dust in that sealed box will be rather pungent after all this time."

Gerard nodded reluctantly, knowing the task they were facing. "Do you want to open the box, or should I?" Steven asked Gerard.

"Give me the crowbar, I'll do it." A large cloud of dust belched into the room as the lid was removed, momentarily driving the two men backward. Steven glanced at Gerard, and they both turned to look toward the door. They could see Daniel pacing impatiently. "Oh, here we go…" Steven bent forward and looked into the box. The remains were in the box, just as Daniel the first had told them.

"Good Lord! She's wearing the same dress she had on when I was talking with her spirit last night."

Distressed, Steven sat down in a nearby chair. Gerard's eyes grew large with shock as he loudly whispered, "Steven! You need to see this!"

Steven glanced up at Gerard, as he pointed to Daphne's spirit standing before them. She slowly glanced toward Gerard, then back toward Steven with a rather concerning look. "It's okay, Grandmother! Gerard is a friend. What do you wish to tell us?"

"He's gone from Branchview. He cannot harm anyone else."

Steven looked puzzled. "Who's gone? What's happened, Daphne?"

"Myself and the others have driven Daniel Branch the first from this house. His spirit will never dwell here again."

Steven and Gerard exchanged a look of surprise. "Daphne, I want you to know that we plan to remove your body from here and give it the proper burial you deserve."

"I'd like that, Steven. But I would also ask you to allow my spirit to remain here so that I can help you and the others in the inevitable battle that lies ahead."

Steven considered her words carefully before answering. "You're certainly welcome here for as long as you want to stay. I'd love to learn more about you. I mean, it's not often you get to know your dead grandmother." They both chuckled.

Gerard replied, "Daphne! Is there any further information you can offer that might help us in any way?"

She slowly nodded yes. "You will find many answers within the Secret Society, and in the tunnels below Branchview. In the hidden room below the cottage, the gardener overheard Daniel and Liddy McPherson plot out their plan against me."

"Can you explain this plan a bit further?" Steven asked.

"On the night I died, I was supposed to accompany Daniel for a stroll in the garden. It was there that the witch was to assume my body."

Both Steven and Gerard listened with heightened interest. "Why did Daniel kill you before that? Surely, he knew that the witch couldn't assume the body of a dead woman," said Steven.

"The gardener had tipped me off beforehand. When I refused to go to the garden with Daniel that night, I was forced to confront him with what I knew. I tried to run away, but he grabbed me, and threw me down the stairs."

"And young Daniel Branch II witnessed all of this?" Steven asked.

"Regretfully! The poor child was only 4 years old, but he was already heavily under the influence of his father."

Steven stood up, and both he and Gerard shook their heads in disbelief. "I have to know this. Aside from money, why did you ever marry Daniel? He was obviously an evil man, and by my calculations, he would have been more than thirty years older than you."

"It was never about money or love. I could never possibly love that horrible man." She looked away momentarily with grief, then continued. "He threatened my parents with financial ruin unless they permitted me to marry him. Because of the deal, he struck with the witch, everyone including myself believed that he was a man in his late 40s."

Steven paced in thought. "That describes some of the inconsistencies that I found in the family journals." He paused. "I'm so sorry that you had to endure all that."

Daphne strolled closer, and lightly placed her hand on the side of Steven's face. "You're definitely your father's son. He was only a year old when I died, but he was such a sweet baby." Steven reacted with a warm smile. "I must say goodbye for now, Steven."

Daphne faded away, while Steven and Gerard looked at each other with subtle astonishment. In the doorway, Daniel Branch III emotionally reacted to what he had just secretly witnessed.

Agent Smith was still contemplating his next move after his visit from Holdsclaw. He desperately wanted to be a good agent and follow the law but was being forced by Holdsclaw to lie. Just then, an unexpected visitor entered the FBI field office. Amy sauntered into the disheveled office, dressed impressively, and Adam took immediate notice. "Hello! How can I help you?"

She extended her hand to him, and he stood, awkwardly fumbling the papers in front of him as he accepted her handshake. "I'm Dr. Amy Seagraves. The Branch family sent me here to identify a box that was taken from their property during the drug bust last night. Can you help me with that?"

"I'm Agent Smith. I would love to help you, but I don't know of such a box."

Amy stared at him in an intimidating fashion. "Could I sit down?"

Adam replied nervously as he hurried around the desk. "Of course! Let me move the papers in that chair. I apologize for the mess. I've been working on two different cases, and I'm trying to categorize everything."

Amy sat down after he cleared the chair, and Adam moved around the desk to settle across from her. His nervousness was obvious. "We were hoping that the box may have been the same one that was stolen several years ago from the main house. It was a very valuable family heirloom."

Adam looked at her with a gawky, clueless expression. "If there was a box, I have no idea where the agents may have taken it, Dr. Seagraves."

Amy challenged him with a confident glare. "Agent Smith… Do you find me to be an attractive woman?"

Adam reacted in a somewhat nervous tone. "As a matter of fact, I find you to be very captivating."

Amy stared straight into his eyes. "I want you to look directly into my eyes and tell me what you see."

Adam stared dreamily at her and answered as though in a trance, "They're so blue. They're like a tranquil ocean on a summer day."

Amy leaned over and came within inches of his face. "I know that you're lying to me about the box, Adam. You cannot lie to me while you're in this trance. Now, where is the box?"

Adam immediately responded, "Senator Holdsclaw has it. He threatened to eliminate my job if I didn't give it to him."

"Do you know where he's keeping it?"

Adam nodded slowly. "It's being delivered to his office as we speak."

Amy gave a slight sigh. "Very good, Adam. When I snap my fingers, you will not remember anything you just said." Amy sat back down and snapped her fingers.

Adam responded in confusion, "What just happened?"

"I think you zoned out for a few moments, Agent Smith. Are you alright?"

He shook his head with a perplexed expression. "I think I'm fine. I've just been working too many hours, I guess. Perhaps I should lie down and take a nap this afternoon."

"Yes! Perhaps you should." She smiled pleasantly, then checked her watch as she stood up to leave. "I really should be getting back to Branchview. The family will be very disappointed that I couldn't recover their heirloom."

Adam got up and walked her to the door. "I promise that I'll notify the Branch's personally if the box happens to turn up."

Amy turned as she reached the door, and smiled while giving him a long seductive look. "Thank you so much, Agent Smith. You've been very kind." Adam nodded as Amy exited his office. *Oh man, that was weird.*

The men returned from the East Wing, highly informed about the circumstances. Daniel Jr. was seated in the sitting room looking very depressed. "Hello there, Daniel! No classes today?"

"Mrs. Blakely gave me the rest of the day off."

Steven moved closer. "I know it's been a tough couple of days for you. It hasn't been all that pleasant for the rest of us either."

"I can't get that evil spirit's face out of my mind. He looked so much like my father."

Steven gave an understanding nod. "You'll never see him around here again. I can guarantee that." Steven quickly glanced out the window. "You know what, Daniel? It's a beautiful day out there today. How would you like to take a ride in Uncle Jack's Corvette?"

Daniel jumped out of his seat with renewed excitement. "Can we go now?"

"Sure! Come on, let's go!" Steven and Daniel Jr exited the room.

Daniel hurried ahead and opened the front door. "Hold on there, young man. It's still very cold out there. You need to go grab your coat."

Steven walked past, and out the door ahead of him. "Okay, Uncle Steven."

"Good, I'll bring the car around."

Daniel ran out of the room and left the front door wide open. A black cat scurried into the house, and quickly ran through the open doors to the South Wing, just as Daniel re-entered the room, now wearing his coat. The cat quickly moved out of sight as young Daniel rushed past. Steven was waiting out front, revving the engine, as the boy climbed into the passenger seat. "How about some music, Daniel? Let's see what my dad used to listen to back in the day."

Daniel watched with a perplexed expression, as Steven opened the carrying case. "They had pretty weird ways of listening to music back then."

Steven smiled and continued looking at the cassette titles. "Okay! We have Genesis, Yes, Jethro Tull. It seems like he was really into Progressive Rock. Ah! Alan Parsons! Let's try this one."

He selected a cassette and inserted the tape. Daniel looked up at him quizzically. "What's Progressive Rock?"

"Well Daniel, back in those days there was a group of musicians who actually knew how to play their instruments, and they put together long musical arrangements that took your mind on a journey of imagination. They called it Progressive and Art Rock."

Daniel laughed. "You have a funny way of describing things, Uncle Steve."

Steven smiled, and lightly tapped on the boy's shoulder. "Are you ready to go?" Daniel replied with an eager nod as he turned up the stereo, and they sped away.

Chapter Seven:

The Mysterious Black Cat

The black cat sauntered in as Penelope sat meditating on the bench in front of Jack's portrait. She suddenly sensed a presence in the room, and she called out without turning around. "Who's there? Jack, Maggie, is that you?" She took on a curious expression when there was only silence. After a few long moments, footsteps could be heard echoing across the tile floor, and she turned around quickly with a stern demeanor. "I don't think it's very funny to sneak up..." She stopped mid-sentence and took on an expression of horror when she saw the spirit of her sister. "Charlotte... what are you doing here?"

"Hello, sister! Long time no see...." Penelope could only respond with trembling fear, and Charlotte found that amusing. "What's the matter, Penelope? Cat got your tongue?" A wicked laugh echoed through the room.

On a bright sunny day, which was rather rare for the time of year, a classic Corvette Stingray drove through the enormous gates of the Branchview Estate, and onto the main road. As Steven accelerated beyond the estate, music blasted out from the speakers and mingled with the humming of the finely tuned engine. The joyride temporarily eased the tension of both the man behind the wheel and the child who was his passenger.

Some events of the distant past had returned to haunt the living in Branchview, along with those who live outside the property's borders. The immortals were scurrying to retrieve Pandora's Box before it could have disastrous effects on the mortal race. A powerful elite in the Senate had obtained the box, not knowing its lethal contents. Meanwhile, others began to break emotionally and wondered what the dismal hand of fate would deliver next. While Steven and Daniel Jr. were enjoying their ride, an unexpected event was unfolding in the Grand Corridor that would drastically alter the lives of all that live on the estate.

Inside the Grand Corridor, Charlotte strolled menacingly closer to her sister. "Why are you here, Charlotte? Why can't you just let us live in peace?"

"Dear sister! I've come back to finish what I started so very long ago, and what your dear late husband so rudely interrupted." Then, out from the shadows, Jack's spirit emerged into the light, carrying a sword at his side.

"I'd like to know what your evil plans are as well, Charlotte…"

Charlotte sighed at his question. "Well! If it isn't handsome Jack himself. You're looking so much healthier than the last time I saw you."

"My spirit has healed quite well."

She strolled closer to him and gestured toward the sword. "I see you have a new toy."

"I'm sure you're quite aware of what it is."

Charlotte rolled her eyes. "Oh yes!" She paused to scan both of her targets. "I have several spirits pursuing me with that same dreaded sword."

Jack pointed to the sword. "It's the tips of those swords that will thrust you back into the bowels of hell where you belong."

She threw her head back. "Oh, Jack! You're so naively dramatic. No wonder you and Penelope made such a cute couple." She arrogantly grunted, "What you both don't realize is that I've mastered the art of existing as a spirit, while also occupying the body of a living woman at the same time."

Jack rolled his eyes. "As if we didn't know... Lucretia Darknight!"

Penelope was surprised. "I knew there was something about that woman I didn't trust."

"Oh, bravo sister! You always were a bit slow at figuring things out." She spun around, clapping. "Now, I'm sure you'll understand that to get rid of me altogether, you would also have to destroy an innocent woman as well," she snickered. "I'm also sure that in all your goodhearted nature, you wouldn't harm poor, innocent Lucretia. Or should I call her by her real name, Kristin Wiler?"

Jack glared. "You redefine the word evil."

"Ahhh...." She shrugged. "Before I leave today, I want to enlighten you both with some answers you've been seeking for a very long time." Penelope and Jack watched her intently. "You both know how jealous your late brother was of you Jack, and how he lusted after my precious sister." They both answered with hardened stares. "Once upon a time, he struck a deal with my father, and I got Penelope to marry him instead of you, Jack."

"That's when you tricked me into thinking you were Penelope, and we eloped to Niagara Falls."

"Yep. I cherished the look on your face when you realized you married the wrong sister." She turned to look at Penelope. "And you! You were so emotionally distraught from it all, that you literally ran into Daniel's open arms without giving your precious Jack the benefit of the doubt."

Penelope looked at Jack with regret. "I should've known at the time that you would never knowingly betray me."

Charlotte made her move to seductively connect with Jack. "If only you hadn't had our marriage annulled, and that blasted mermaid Amphitrite hadn't tried to win your heart. Imagine the possibilities of what I might've accomplished."

"I wasn't aware of that other woman being involved," Penelope stated.

"And I'm sure you weren't aware that Jack also possessed the soul of the mermaid's long-lost love,

Matthew Branch. That's why I needed to kill him. I knew he would never be mine."

"But you killed all those other innocent people on the plane as well."

Charlotte moved closer and shrugged arrogantly. "Every battle has casualties, my dear." She paced away. "When the first plan failed, Daniel and I struck another deal. I would kill Jack, and then he would allow me to assume your body and become the mistress of Branchview." She looked away with deceit, while Penelope's heart shattered. "When he found out that you were carrying Jack's baby, however, he postponed the plans. Somehow through it all, he developed a conscience, and decided to kill me before we could complete our deal."

Penelope and Jack exchanged saddened looks. "Don't look so sad, Penelope. Your long reign here at Branchview is almost over, and soon you'll join your beloved Jack. And after you're gone, I shall destroy the remaining members of the Branch family, and assume control of everything."

"I'll never allow that to happen."

Jack tightly gripped his sword and sneered, "Neither will I, Charlotte. You have laid your cards on the table, and we now know your plan."

"We'll just have to see about that. Won't we?" Charlotte faded away, but her laughter echoed throughout the room. Penelope was suddenly stricken with great pain and grabbed at her heart.

"No… Penny! No! Oh my God, no!" He caught her as she collapsed, gently lowering her body to the floor as she desperately stared into his eyes.

"I never stopped loving you, Jack—" Her voice faded. Jack held her gently, sobbing quietly.

Dr. Grayson was in the sitting room getting ready to go meet Penelope when Loraine entered the room. "Doctor Grayson, I was just coming to find you."

"I was just on my way to the Grand Corridor to meet Penelope for meditation, and tea afterward. Would you care to join us?"

"Yes, thank you! I believe I will." The women exited into the Grand Corridor as the black cat ran out and scurried up the stairs. "How in the world did that cat get into the house?"

Dr. Grayson paused with a peculiar expression. "I don't know. Something isn't right..." Loraine looked at her with great concern.

As they entered the room, the sight of the apparition of Jack on his knees next to Penelope's body left them trembling in horror. They both paused to watch as a stream of sunlight flowed through the window, peacefully casting its light upon the couple. In the next few seconds, they watched Penelope's spirit leave her body, transforming into a younger version of herself. Jack stood astonished by her beauty. He grabbed his beloved by the waist and lifted her in the air. She then placed her hands on both sides of his face, and passionately kissed him.

Loraine whispered, "She's so young and beautiful." Jack took her by the hand, and they walked away together, disappearing into the shadows, and leaving only the shell of Penelope's body behind. The women moved closer to the body, which seemed to be asleep in peaceful rest. They noticed the joyful smile that seemed to grace her lips.

Dr. Grayson drew an emotional breath as she knelt on one knee over the body. "She's gone, Lori. She's gone." Loraine emotionally turned away, as the tears streamed down her cheeks.

Chapter Eight:

The Deception Begins

In the local office of Senator Holdsclaw, the tensions continued to heighten between the Senator and Lucretia, as they waited for a third party to arrive. Holdsclaw stared across the desk with lustful eyes that would've made the boldest of women shudder with disgust.

"Where is this Reverend Hightower? There are more pressing matters I must attend to, other than sitting here waiting on a hypocritical televangelist."

Holdsclaw never broke his stare. "He'll be here."

Just then, the door opened and a brash, well-dressed man in his early 40s entered. Reverend James Hightower confidently strolled into the room. "I'm sorry for being late, Richard. I was delayed at another appointment." He eyed Lucretia keenly. "Ms. Darknight, I assume. Richard never told me that you were such a lovely woman." Lucretia reacted with little enthusiasm and offered a limp handshake. "I understand you're in a management position at Branch Consolidated?"

"Yes. And I understand that you're a self-proclaimed minister who defrauds poor, ignorant people of their hard-earned money, with a grand promise of heavenly redemption."

"Oh, my dear lady! If I didn't do it, someone else would."

Lucretia looked toward Holdsclaw with disbelief. "And you think that *I'm* evil?"

Holdsclaw straightened in his seat. "The good reverend has agreed to help us in our situation with Audrey Branch. That will open the door for us to carry out our plan much easier."

Hightower looked at him with curiosity. "What exactly is that plan, Richard? You never did tell me."

Holdsclaw said, "You are being paid quite well for your services. I suggest that you don't ask questions, James."

Hightower glanced around the room and saw the box. "What a beautiful, ornate box. What's in it?"

"I have no idea. The lid has some sort of seal on it that no one can seem to break."

Lucretia listened with interest, while Hightower strolled over to check it out. "These carved creatures on the lid almost look like demons." He turned to Lucretia with an amused expression. "That is if they do in fact exist."

Lucretia replied with a sly grin. "Oh yes, Reverend! I can assure you that they do in fact exist, and they're probably closer to you than you would ever guess."

"I'm very curious about this box, Richard." Hightower paced for a moment in thought. "I'd like to be present when you open it."

Holdsclaw shrugged. "I see no problem with that, but first we have to find someone who knows how to break that seal." He looked to Lucretia. "Perhaps you could snoop around, and see if there's anyone at Branchview that knows anything about it?"

"Wait a minute! Are you saying that this box was taken from Branchview?"

"No. It was confiscated in a drug bust in the caves at Lighthouse Point. I made sure, however, that that fact was omitted from the crime report."

Lucretia was quite intrigued. "How interesting! Very interesting indeed." She rose from her seat, seemingly with her mind elsewhere. "I really should be going. I just remembered that I have another appointment this afternoon."

Holdsclaw settled back in his seat with a smirk. "Then perhaps I could visit you at your cottage later this afternoon, and we could discuss our strategy further. I promise that I'll be a complete gentleman."

Lucretia glared at him with a straight, sober face. "I'll be there at 4:30 sharp. And yes, I would advise you to act appropriately, or I'll be forced to turn you into a horny toad." Holdsclaw reacted indignantly, and Rev. Hightower tried to conceal his amusement.

As Lucretia sashayed from the room, Seth entered to hold the door. He immediately marched over to Holdsclaw's side and inaudibly whispered something in his ear, and he reacted with a sarcastic smile. "Well done,

Seth! I trust you've taken care of the issue with Mrs. Holdsclaw as well?"

Seth gave an assuring nod. "As we speak, Senator."

In the FBI field office, Agent Smith was at his desk, filling out paperwork on his newly arrested drug smugglers when the phone rang. "Good afternoon. Agent Smith, how can I help you?" The other voice responded with alarming news, and Agent Smith immediately reacted to it. "I demand to know how two suspects being held under your jurisdiction somehow, mysteriously, ended up being poisoned and killed." He listened to the reply with much impatience. "Look! I'm sick of excuses. I want a full report on my desk by tomorrow morning. Is that clear?" He slammed the receiver and stared straight ahead in a rage-filled huff. *Holdsclaw! He must have something to do with this.*

While Adam was stewing over the news, Lucretia sauntered into his office, and his attention immediately shifted to his seductive guest. "Surprise, surprise! I certainly hope you're bringing me good news."

She moved in and sat on the edge of his desk. "Actually, I'd like to talk about a certain box that was taken from the grounds at Branchview."

Adam reacted nervously. "I don't know what you're talking about."

"Oh! Come now, Adam! Don't play with me! I just came from Holdsclaw's office and saw it with my own two eyes. He told me where it came from."

Adam sighed. "Did the Branch family send you here as well?"

Lucretia reacted with surprise. "Oh! There was someone else inquiring about that box?"

"Yes! Another extremely gorgeous woman like yourself. Her name was…" He thought for a moment. "Amy, Dr. Amy Seagraves."

Lucretia stood up and paced in front of the desk. "Is that so? Did this woman by any chance have red hair?"

"Yeah, and beautiful eyes. Do you happen to know her?"

"You could say that. We're somewhat acquainted." Lucretia paused with a sigh, "Did you tell her who has the box?"

She paused and turned toward Adam, who shook his head in a definite no. "She has no idea, and I'd appreciate it if you kept this revelation private as well. Holdsclaw has a way of wielding his power in a very damaging way."

"Yes! I know that all too well, and can assure you that anything mentioned between us will remain confidential."

Lucretia paused with emphasis. "Thank you, Agent Smith. Your bit of information has been quite helpful." She offered a cordial nod, leaving Adam with much nervous anxiety.

Recent events had left the Branch family in utter devastation once again. Daniel Sr was suffering the most from the recent loss and was blindsided by the news. Steven, Loraine, and Dr. Grayson sat solemnly in the sitting room and reflected on the events that had taken place.

Daniel III broke the silence first. "I can't believe that our mother is actually gone. I curse this house for all the sorrow it has produced. First, Audrey is rendered catatonic, and now my dear mother is gone. What tragedy will happen next?"

Steven got up to comfort his brother. "We'll get through this, brother. If it's any consolation, we both know that she's with Jack now, and she'll no doubt be offering her spiritual strength beyond the grave. That is one comfort most people never get to experience."

Daniel turned and forced a sad smile. "I really should go inform young Daniel about his grandmother. This will not be easy." The group watched him leave the sitting room.

Dr. Grayson got up and moved closer to Steven and Loraine. "Steven! There's something we urgently need to tell you." Steven gave them his full attention. "A black cat ran from the Grand Corridor just as we entered."

Steven grunted, "That cat seems to have some sort of connection with Charlotte Locke. How did it get in the house?"

"We don't know, but it ran upstairs and is still hiding somewhere."

Steven was frustrated. "We have to find that cat, and get it out of this house. If Charlotte Locke's spirit takes up residency here, she could systematically eliminate all of us." There was a loud knock on the door, and all three glanced at each other. "I'll answer the door. I need the two of you to meet with the staff in the dining room, and notify them of my mother's death."

As Steven finished his statement, another loud knock echoed throughout the house. Steven hurried to the door and opened it to find Senator Holdsclaw. "Hello! Can I help you?"

"Are you Steven Spencer?"

"Yes, who are you? This is not the best time for me to entertain visitors."

Holdsclaw's ego was bruised. "You mean to say that you don't know who I am?"

Steven gave a less than enthusiastic answer, "Oh, yes… now I remember. You're the senator that I often see on the news."

"Could I come in?" Steven stepped aside and reluctantly ushered him into the foyer. Holdsclaw eyed his surroundings with a keen eye. "What a marvelous house. I always wondered what it looked like on the inside."

Steven said impatiently, "I hate to be abrupt with you Senator, but we've had a very unfortunate circumstance befall us today."

"May I ask what that was?"

Steven sighed. "We haven't gone public with the news, but my mother, Penelope Branch, passed away late this morning."

Holdsclaw reacted with false sympathy. "I'm so very sorry, Mr. Spencer. I've heard that your mother was a fine woman."

Steven nodded in agreement. "Who exactly did you need to speak with?"

"I was hoping someone here at the main house could direct me to Lucretia Darknight's residence?"

"Fine… fine, I can help with that." Steven directed with his hands. "If you continue down the driveway past the carriage house, her cottage is just to the right, in the first grove of trees."

"Thank you, Mr. Spencer." He paused before walking out the door. "I understand that you and your wife had a devastating fire at your Florida estate."

Steven answered rather cautiously, "Yes, that's correct."

"I'm curious. Do you plan to rebuild and return there, or remain here at Branchview? I'm sure your now departed mother must've left you a generous portion of this place in her will."

"I don't know how you know all these things. But with all due respect, it's none of your business."

Holdsclaw arrogantly snapped, "Being in my position, I make it my business to know things about people, Mr. Spencer. Trust me, it's far more beneficial to have me as an ally, rather than an enemy."

Steven countered sarcastically, "No doubt! But perhaps if you weren't so concerned about other people's personal business, you might be able to better serve the fine people of Connecticut." Holdsclaw conceded with a defensive smirk, as he indignantly stepped outside. "Good day, Senator!" Steven slammed the door and shook his head in disbelief.

As Steven settled from his altercation with Senator Holdsclaw, Loraine and Dr. Grayson performed a sorrowful task. The staff at Branchview loved Penelope dearly. She treated all of them with respect and love. The two ladies gathered the entire staff to tell them all at the same time.

Loraine remained sitting, while most of the staff solemnly filed out of the room afterward. "Dr. Grayson… you know, Penelope was one of a kind. I know she is happy now, and with the man she loved, but I will miss her terribly. I must admit, that wasn't the easiest news to deliver. The staff sincerely loved her, as did I. "

"Yes, I know. I became very fond of her as well. She'll truly be missed." A few minutes later, Sharie and Mrs. Porter approached Loraine with sadness covering their faces. "I'm in total shock. I simply don't know what to say," Mrs. Porter stated.

Sharie gave her a consoling pat. "We can't expect the men to step into Mrs. Branch's role as head of the house. We'll all have to pull together to fill the void."

"I fully agree. Dr. Grayson and I will do whatever we can to help during this very difficult time."

Sharie turned to Mrs. Porter. "I'll need you to step up and help me manage the household and staff, Mrs. Porter."

"I appreciate your confidence in me, Ms. Sharie. Mrs. Spencer here can attest that I'm quite capable of the task." Sharie glanced at Loraine with an assured wink. Sharie and Mrs. Porter put their arms around each other. "We can do this."

In the foyer later that evening, Daniel Sr slowly made his way down the stairs, grabbed his coat, and prepared to leave as Steven entered from the sitting room. "I didn't see you, or Daniel Jr at supper. I was quite concerned."

Daniel turned with a slight smile. "He chose to eat in his room, and I thought it wise to join him."

"I can imagine he took the news very hard."

Daniel responded with an expression of remorse. "He was very close to his grandmother. But I'm sure he'll get over it in time, as we all will."

Steven responded with a thoughtful nod. "Are you going for a walk? Perhaps I could go along with you."

"I appreciate the offer Steven, but I think I'll go spend the evening in my office. It's the only place I can truly be alone with my thoughts."

Steven rested an assuring hand on his back. "I fully understand." As Daniel III walked out the door, Steven stood and watched him leave. He was concerned about his safety with everything that had happened.

A little later, Mrs. Porter entered the upstairs hall from one of the rooms, with Bumpers wandering behind her. She immediately spotted the black cat preparing to enter the partially open door of Daniel Jr's bedroom. "You little scoundrel! You get away from that door."

The cat arched its back, and hissed, while Bumpers began barking. A chase ensued down the hall, and the evil tyrant scurried down the stairs with Bumpers in pursuit. Just as Loraine was entering the front door, the cat reached the foyer, and slid across the marble tile, with Bumpers hot on its tail. The cat scurried out the open door, and Loraine slammed it behind the fleeing feline. She leaned against the wall, taking deep breaths, while Bumpers continued to bark at the closed door.

Mrs. Porter ambled down the stairway, while Dr. Grayson quickly entered from the sitting room. "What in the world is going on out here?"

Mrs. Porter replied, with heavy breathing and a shaky voice, "That cat! He was trying to get into Daniels Jr's room."

"Bumpers chased it right out the door just as I was coming in. Our little man is the unlikely hero of the day," Loraine proclaimed.

Dr. Grayson replied with an overwhelmed expression and raised an eyebrow as Bumpers stopped barking, and looked up at the women, while still shaking with excitement.

"I think he deserves an extra snack for his efforts." Loraine and Mrs. Porter smiled down at the dog, while Dr. Grayson remained serious and sober-faced.

"Now that the cat is out of this house, we have to be certain that it doesn't get back in. We must notify the groundskeeper and have him construct and post wooden crosses at every entrance. Oh, and also the first-floor windows, as soon as possible."

Mrs. Porter replied as she nervously hurried away, "Good idea Dr. Grayson. I'll do that right now."

Loraine and Dr. Grayson leaned over to pet Bumpers. "Thankfully for Bumpers, that cat is one less issue we'll have to worry about for the time being."

Meanwhile, Daniel finally found some peace in his darkened office. He was able to cradle a glass of brandy and wrestle with the idea of losing his mother. However, his solitude was interrupted by a light knock. "Who's there?"

The door slowly opened. "It's just me, Lucia."

She sauntered in and turned on a table lamp. "If you came here to discuss business, I'm hardly in the mood," Daniel said.

"I tried to call you at Branchview to offer my condolences, and Steven said I might find you here."

"Surely, he mentioned that I wanted to be alone."

She strolled closer. "He did. But I was concerned about you."

Daniel smiled slightly. "Would you care to join me for a drink?"

"Yes! I'll get it myself." She strolled over to the liquor cart to pour a brandy and glanced up at the bookcase where a small camera strategically peeked out at the room from between two books. She then reached into her pocket and glanced down to look at the remote device in her hand. Her plan was going smoothly. "I know it's a hard time for you, but sometimes it helps to speak to a friend outside the family."

Daniel flashed a grateful smile. "I appreciate that, Lucia."

She held up her glass toward him. "Cheers!"

Their glasses clinked. "Indeed! To my dear mother, Penelope Locke Branch."

Daniel became very emotional but tried hard to conceal it. Lucretia set her drink down and placed her hand in her coat pocket. She then walked around behind Daniel's chair and began to massage his shoulders. "It's okay! Just go ahead and let it out."

She took off her coat and tossed it aside. "I'm sorry! It's just so tough. First, I lose Audrey, then Marcus, and now my mother. I worry about what tragedy might happen next."

"These are just things that we all have to deal with in life at one time or another," Lucretia replied.

"I know. But recently, I also found out how corrupt, cruel, and evil my grandfather and father were. I feel ashamed to even admit my relation to such men. Before now, I've always been proud to be a Branch."

Lucretia listened attentively with rising anger, aggressively digging her fingers tighter into Daniels's shoulders and causing him to react. "Can you let up a bit? You're being rather rough there, Lucia."

"I apologize. Sometimes I do get a bit carried away." She turned his chair around to face her, and slowly straddled his lap while he reacted with nervous surprise.

"Lucia! This shouldn't be happening. I'm your boss, a married man, and a father. It just isn't right."

Lucretia stared dreamily at him with a wicked smile. "Just look deep into my eyes, and forget about all that for now. Just live for the moment." Daniel instantly went into a trance, and before he could say another word, she bent forward and engaged him with a passionate kiss.

Chapter Nine:

The Kiss of Death

A theater marquee displayed the latest Transformers film "Bumblebee" above a quiet, late-night street view. It was early April in the town of Lockeport. Spring had finally arrived, and love was blooming in many quarters. Those who were lucky enough to discover newfound love on this cold night were blind to the spoilers that hid in the shadows of their lives, waiting for their chance to crush that precious discovery before it had the chance to flourish. As patrons of the theater emerged into the darkness, Andrea Hill and Triton, under his human guise of Tony Freeman, followed along behind the first moviegoers to enter onto the sidewalk.

Andrea paused to securely entwine her arm with Tony's. "I thought that was a pretty good movie. What did you think?"

Tony responded with enthusiasm, "I thought it was amazing! I can't believe how that large robot could transform itself into a car."

Andrea reacted like a young girl filled with infatuation, "I'd guess that you haven't seen any of the other Transformer movies?"

"You mean there are more of these movies?"

"At least six or seven."

Tony shook his head enthusiastically over the possibility. "I have to admit that I haven't seen an actual movie in quite a while. I keep a very busy schedule, and hardly have time for that sort of thing."

"Well, I'm certainly glad you took the time to share this one with me."

"I can only hope that it's the beginning of many more shared moments between us."

"I hope so too."

They paused to face each other, then slowly embraced and kissed. In the shadows, Hades lurked under the guise of Luke Underwood, fuming over the engagement between the two lovers.

At the Branchview Estate, Poseidon walked along the pathway with a bounce in his step, as he made his way toward Lighthouse Point. He was anxious to meet up with Amy, who was patiently waiting for him in the clearing. She sensed something different about him. "You seem to be in a rather chipper mood tonight."

"I just spent the evening with the most remarkable and charming young woman."

Amy smiled at seeing him so happy. "Would this by chance be the young woman with no soul? Obviously, she isn't a spirit as we initially thought."

Philip took on a more serious and thoughtful demeanor. "Her name is Tina Lane. I can assure you that whatever she lacks in an inner light, she more than makes up for it with an exuberant outward glow."

She smiled in amusement. "It appears that you're quite smitten with her."

He sat down next to Amy on the bench and glanced up at the sky. "Yes, my dear, you are so right. I do believe I'm in love with her."

Amy burst out laughing. "If I only had a gold piece for every time, I've heard that line over the years."

"I should've known that you'd make fun of me. It's quite consistent with your nature."

"Oh, Poseidon! If you truly love this woman, I'm quite happy for you. Now, let's just move on, and discuss the issue at hand."

Philip nodded and turned to face her. "What were you able to find out today?"

"Actually, quite a bit. The box is in the possession of Senator Holdsclaw. He has it in his local office, but he's due back in Washington by Monday."

"That doesn't leave us much time. We can only hope that he doesn't take it back with him."

Amy replied with much stress, "I agree! That might take the situation totally out of our hands."

As Amy and Philip conversed about their issue, Tina sat comfortably in an oversized easy chair at the cottage, daydreaming about her evening with Philip. She was startled when Lucretia burst through the front door. "What are you doing up so late?"

"I just got in. I had a date with the most marvelous man and had the time of my life."

Lucretia marched over and proceeded to scold her. "I did not permit you to go out. Who was this man?"

"Well, if you must know, his name is Philip Seagraves. I met him on the pathway this morning." Tina sighed. "He's so handsome, and such a gentleman."

"Seagraves? Did he by chance mention a relative by the name of Amy Seagraves?"

Tina cluelessly shook her head. "No! But he is a friend of Steven Spencer."

Lucretia took on an enlightened expression. "Really? How interesting!"

Tina jumped out of her seat with excitement. "Oh, Lucia! I think I'm in love."

Lucretia laughed out loud and sneered sarcastically. "You're nothing but a stupid, brainless, department store mannequin that I brought to life. You're incapable of loving anyone."

Tina became enraged and barked back, "That's not true! I do have feelings, and I'm much more capable of loving someone than you are."

"Don't you dare talk to me that way?"

Tina grabbed her coat and began to cry as she hurried toward the door. She turned to confront Lucretia once again. "You're an emotionless, evil monster, Lucretia Darknight!" She ran out, slamming the door behind her, leaving Lucretia shaking her head in frustration.

The large foyer clock struck at 12:30 a.m., and Daniel Sr was returning home from his office. After reaching to hang his coat, he turned toward the sitting room. He stumbled to the entrance, noticeably drunk. As he paused to regain his balance, he noticed Steven in the room, reading a book by the fireplace.

"Daniel! I was beginning to get concerned about you." Daniel continued on to a side table, where he poured another glass of brandy. He was hoping the alcohol would alleviate the extreme guilt he was now feeling.

"I would've thought you'd be in bed by now."

Steven stood up and strolled over toward him, still holding the book. "I was looking over this old family journal to see if I could get some answers. There certainly are a lot of inconsistencies and gray areas."

Daniel sarcastically blurted out, "That's an understatement if I ever heard one."

Steven moved closer. "Are you okay? You seem rather distraught."

"That is another understatement. I guess you could say that I'm somewhat drunk and disgusted with myself and my family lineage."

"I hope this isn't a bad time to ask, but I was wondering if it might be possible for Lori and I to refurbish the East Wing, and move into it?"

Daniel answered with little enthusiasm, and a bit of surprise. "My dear brother, it's yours to do as you wish. If you want to live among the tragic memories in that part of the house, then so be it."

"I just thought with the baby on the way, we could use more room, and a bit more privacy."

Daniel answered by saluting him with his drink glass, before downing a large swallow. There was a knock at the front door, and both men glanced at each other with puzzled expressions. "Who in the world can that be at this hour of the night?"

Both men moved toward the foyer with curiosity. Daniel Sr. strode ahead and swung the door open to find Tina standing there, crying and very emotional. "I need to see Philip Seagraves. Do you know if he's still awake?"

Daniel reacted with a perplexed expression. "I'm Daniel Branch, and I'm sorry, but I don't know anyone by that name."

Steven quickly intervened. "I'm Steven Spencer, and I do know Philip. Please, come in out of the cold Miss...?"

Tina shuffled in. "Tina! Tina Lane! I'm staying with my cousin, Lucretia Darknight. We had words, and I stormed out of the cottage."

Steven and Daniel exchanged a fleeting glance. "How do you know Philip?"

"He just walked me home from a date no more than an hour ago, and he told me that he was your guest here at Branchview."

Steven thought quickly for a moment, while Daniel observed, still quite perplexed. "We've recently had a death in the family, so Philip thought it might be best to make accommodations elsewhere for a few days."

Tina wiped her tears and settled down a bit. "I wish he would have told me. I'm so sorry I disturbed you."

"That's certainly alright Miss Lane. Let me get my coat, and I'll escort you back to the cottage."

Tina got emotional once again. "No! Please... I don't want to go back there tonight."

Daniel quickly intervened, "Then I insist on you staying here. We have a spare bedroom in the servants' quarters."

"Thank you, Mr. Branch. That's quite kind of you."

"The staff has retired for the night. But I can escort you to the room, and supply you with clean linens and a blanket."

Steven gave Daniel a curious look as he passed. "While you do that, I'll notify Lucia and tell her she's here." Steven dreaded having to call Lucretia at this time of the night, but even his curiosity was getting the best of him. Since the knowledge of her true identity had been made a reality, he kept on high alert when it came to any dealings with her. There was no telling how this newcomer to Branchview might fit into the devious plans of Charlotte Locke.

Chapter Ten:

Charlotte's Wrath Continues

D own on the beach, just before dawn, the skies over the Atlantic remained stormy and dark. This was Amphitrite's favorite time to stroll the beach naked. She savored those rare times she could walk on land without the restrictions of clothing. She turned, sensing that someone was watching. Lucretia had risen early that morning, and walked to Lighthouse Point. She watched the waterline with calculating eyes, as she worked her way towards the beach, hoping to converse with Amphitrite. A smile graced her face when the revolving beacon of the lighthouse caught her presence. She moved with eagerness to where the goddess stood near the water's edge. "I must say that I'm quite envious. You've managed to maintain an awesome figure for a woman of your advanced age."

Amphitrite fluttered her hands in front of her, and fashionable clothes appeared on her body. She then sternly addressed Lucretia. "I was summoned to Branchview by

Steven Spencer. I was simply waiting for the sun to come up. What business do you have seeking me out in my domain?"

"Actually, I spoke with Steven several hours ago, and told him that I urgently needed to talk to you."

"What would you so desperately have to say that would be of any interest to me?"

They began to stroll along the beach. "Plenty! But for starters, were you aware that your husband was seeing a woman here on the Branchview grounds?"

Amy rolled her eyes. "My husband and I have been mutually estranged for centuries. He's free to see anyone he wishes."

Lucretia laughed. "You might be surprised to know that this woman is in fact, a department store mannequin that I brought to life in order to be my servant."

Amy came to a complete halt and eyed her with disbelief. "If this is as true as it is demented, I must tell Poseidon as soon as possible."

"I can assure you that it is quite true, but there is another issue of more importance that we need to discuss."

Amy listened with renewed interest. "It concerns a box that I know you've been looking for. What can you tell me about it?"

"I know that Senator Holdsclaw has possession of it, and the gods need desperately to get it back."

Lucretia took on an enlightened expression. "If the gods are that concerned, it must surely contain something very valuable. What's in it?"

Amy thought hard for a moment. "Have you ever read about Pandora's Box in Greek mythology?"

Lucretia took on a look of foreboding disbelief. "Are you saying that...?"

Amy gave a definite nod. "The contents of that box could be just as devastating as a nuclear bomb."

Lucretia looked away in horror. "This could be very troublesome. Holdsclaw is a self-absorbed, arrogant ass. He'll never surrender that box."

Amy continued, "Then I suppose we only have one option." Lucretia answered with a clueless expression. "Even though we're sworn enemies, we need to put our differences aside long enough to resolve this issue before it turns disastrous."

Lucretia gave a concerned and agreeing nod. "We really should discuss this further at my cottage." The two women walked off into the now dim light of the pre-dawn.

At Branchview, the house's inhabitants were waking to start their day. Dr. Grayson was standing in her normal position by the fireplace in the sitting room, sipping on her morning tea, while Steven paced, dreading the day ahead. Loraine entered and handed him a fresh cup of coffee before settling onto the loveseat. They were all dressed in black, awaiting the early morning funeral service for Penelope.

Loraine broke the silence, "You know… I do wonder if Lucia will show up to pay her respects."

"Surely, she couldn't pass up the opportunity to gloat over her handiwork," Dr. Grayson replied.

Steven jumped in, "My intuition tells me that she'll make a late appearance at the gravesite, and act as an innocent, grieving friend. I'm sure that cat will be there as well, lurking somewhere in the underbrush."

Loraine trembled with anger. "I so despise that woman. If Charlotte ever decides to show herself beyond Lucia's image, I swear I'll do everything within my power to destroy her spirit."

Steven appeared oblivious and lost in his thoughts. "You look rather troubled, Steven… is everything alright?" Dr. Grayson asked.

"I'm just curious about why Lucia was so desperate to meet with Dr. Seagraves. Obviously, it must have something to do with Philip's involvement with her cousin."

"Her cousin? I highly question that fact. My intuition tells me there is something very suspicious about this Tina Lane."

"I agree, and am sure Dr. Seagraves will keep us well informed."

Daniel III entered the room unnoticed. "Did I hear you-" he began. The women jumped, startled by his presence. "Oh, I am sorry to frighten you both. Did I hear you mention Dr. Seagraves's name? I certainly hope she'll be at the funeral. My mother was quite fond of her."

He strolled over and poured himself a brandy. "I see you're starting rather early, Daniel… perhaps a little hair of the dog?" said Steven.

Daniel turned to confront him. "I don't need to be lectured about such things on the day of our beloved mother's funeral."

Dr. Grayson intervened. "Please! Let's not let our emotions get the best of us. We all just need to stay calm and get through this difficult day."

Daniel began to pace and changed the subject. "Is our lovely young house guest still with us this morning?"

"No. Heather gave her a ride into town."

Daniel continued to pace in deep thought. "How odd that Lucia never mentioned her to us." Steven, Loraine, and Dr. Grayson exchanged fleeting glances.

At the City Diner, Suzy Mc Vea was busy working the counter, where Jeff Manus sat drinking coffee, and reading a textbook. Tina had entered earlier and sat just a few seats away at the counter.

Suzy stopped by to refill his cup. "You must be reading something quite interesting."

Jeff looked up for a moment. "I'm studying for an exam. I'm taking classes over at the community college."

Suzy paused in her routine, as Tina observed their exchange with interest. "I'm quite impressed by the way you've put your life back together since Kim's death. I know it hasn't been easy for you."

Jeff set the book aside and smiled. "I'm working through it the best way I can. Are you still seeing the same guy I saw you with a few months ago?"

Suzy rolled her eyes. "I'm glad to say that I'm not, and I'll leave it at that."

Jeff chuckled and nervously continued, "If there's no one else in your life right now, perhaps we could get together sometime?"

Suzy reacted with slight embarrassment. His request for a date took her quite off guard. Tina swooned over the conversation, though she tried to conceal her eavesdropping.

"That would be quite nice. I think I'd really like that." Suzy replied.

She tore a page from her order pad and quickly jotted something down. "Here's my number, call me!"

Tina spoke up. "Excuse me! I'm ready to pay my bill." She went into her small designer purse, and began to count out one-dollar bills and change, then paused with embarrassment. "It looks like I'm a few dollars short. Can I leave you what I have, and bring the rest by later?"

Suzie replied, "That's usually not our policy here."

"I'm staying at Branchview with my cousin, Lucretia Darknight. Perhaps you might know her?"

Jeff's eyes widened with fear when he heard Lucretia's name. He quickly intervened before Suzy could answer. "Don't worry, miss! I'll cover the remainder of the tab, and leave a generous tip as well."

Both Tina and Suzy were impressed by his offer. "Thank you so much." She turned to Suzy, who scooped the money from the counter as Jeff added a five-dollar bill and two ones. "He's a very nice guy. Don't let him get away," Tina whispered. Suzy reacted with a fleeting, but cordial smile as she walked away. Jeff tried to hide his anxiety with a quick smile, and a nod toward Tina as she departed.

In the shadows of the wooded area surrounding the mausoleum, a black cat slinked unnoticed by most, hiding between the headstones, and watching the Branch family hover around Penelope's casket. Steven was wise to its presence and kept a keen eye on it. As the untimely event had shocked the town, close friends emerged on a cold spring day to pay their respects. Attendees stood respectfully as the minister delivered the eulogy.

A few seconds after the cat arrived, Lucretia appeared, lingering near the cat. Both stayed hidden in the back of the congregation, cautious to avoid eye contact with any type of religious symbolism. Steven glanced at Loraine and Dr. Grayson with a told-you-so expression. After the minister concluded, Lucretia approached Steven and Daniel. She maneuvered her way to stay clear of the women. "I want you both to know that I'm so very sorry for your loss."

Daniel acted rather sheepishly, simply nodding to her and walking away, while the rest of the immediate family shunned her. Steven didn't want to be rude, so he replied, "Thank you for paying your respects, Lucia."

Lucretia sighed. "I don't know what's colder, my reception by the family, or the breeze from the ocean."

Amy and Philip strolled over to offer a gesture of condolence to Steven, but a steady glance of irritation remained directed at Lucretia.

Phillip addressed Steven in a whispered tone. "Could you possibly meet me at the diner for coffee in the morning?"

"Sure, I'll be there at 7:30 sharp." Philip nodded, and Steven turned to Lucretia. "If you'll excuse me, I need to have a final moment before they place her coffin in the crypt."

"Of course, Steven. I understand." Lucretia hurried to catch Dr. Grayson who was walking alone toward the main path. "Dr. Grayson! Would you mind if I walked along with you?"

Dr. Grayson answered with indifference, "Feel free to do whatever you want."

The two women strolled along with Dr. Grayson refusing to be amicable.

"You don't like me much, do you?" Lucretia quipped.

"How can I like the person who was indirectly involved with the death of my dear friend?"

"That's absurd! We both know that Penelope died from a heart attack."

Dr. Grayson came to a halt and faced her with a stern, sober expression. "Let's be straight with each other, Lucretia. I know you're really Charlotte Locke, hiding behind the pretty face of Kristin Wiler, and I know of your intentions to destroy this family."

Lucretia matched her with an equally smug expression. "Is that so? If that's true, what do you intend to do about it?"

"Everything that I possibly can to stop you."

"Then I must simply wish you luck with that. You'll definitely need it."

Dr. Grayson chuckled sarcastically. "A wise witch would know that a grand practitioner of white magic is many times stronger in spirit than they are in living form. Consider that, before you make any plans to harm me." Lucretia answered only with a harsh expression of contempt. "With that said, I would much prefer to walk the rest of the way by myself. Good day, Lucretia."

Steven meditated for a few moments over his mother's casket, then gently laid his hand on it as a final gesture. He solemnly strolled over to where Loraine stood watching and sighed. "You know honey, Mother is the third Branch woman that we've laid to rest this week."

Loraine nodded sadly. "I stopped by and left flowers at Elizabeth's and Daphne's graves earlier today."

Steven affectionately kissed her forehead. "We need to do that seance at the ruins of the Locke Estate tonight. Out time is running out, and we must have answers."

"I'll notify Dr. Grayson of our plans as soon as we get back to Branchview."

"I'll join you shortly, I'm going to linger here just a bit longer."

Loraine answered with an understanding nod, and a gentle squeeze to his hand, before hurrying to follow some of the family members back to the house.

Having been spurned by the family, and put in her place by Dr. Grayson, Lucretia stormed back to the cottage in a huff. Tina was sitting in her easy chair, brooding over a romantic scene on a TV show when she entered. "I see you finally found your way back home."

Tina ignored her, so Lucretia grabbed the remote, and shut the TV off. "Tina…!" she barked. "You need to listen to me!"

Tina shouted back, "I was watching that!"

She turned, "I don't know how you can sit, and watch that emotional garbage. You'll learn just as Kristin did that love is fictional, and lust is reality."

"That's not true! You're a liar!"

Lucretia snickered and stood in front of her. "Really? I bet you weren't aware that you were carrying on with a married man."

Tina got emotional. "You're just saying that because you're jealous. You don't have anyone special in your life."

Lucretia slowly boiled with anger. "I'm sure that Philip Seagraves probably failed to inform you of his true identity as well."

Tina jumped up from her seat. "What do you mean?"

"Your dear Philip is in fact Poseidon, the Greek god of the sea, and his lovely wife is the mermaid goddess Amphitrite. They are both immortals."

"No! That can't be true! He's human, just as we are."

"Oh, Tina! It is very true. But what gave you the idea that you're human? You're just a stupid mannequin from Nordstrom. Someone like you is hardly worthy of an immortal god."

Tina trembled with anger. "I hate you, Lucretia Darknight!" She ran out of the room in tears. Lucretia reveled in sinister amusement. But her toying with Tina's emotions would be short-lived. There were other more pressing matters to attend to.

Steven tarried at the gravesite for almost an hour before the groundskeepers respectfully carried the coffin to its final resting place in the mausoleum. He had only just found his beloved mother, and now she was gone. The only consolation he could find was being able to see her in spirit. Hopefully, in the very near future.

Chapter Eleven:

The Locke Family Secrets

Once evening had settled in, and darkness consumed the world surrounding Branchview, the trio of Steven, Loraine, and Dr. Grayson made their way to the ruins of the old Locke Estate. Steven took the lead, with a large lantern in one hand and Loraine's hand in the other. Dr. Grayson followed close behind. "Steven…" He turned to look at her. "This looks like it might be the center of the old house. Set the lantern down right there, and we'll join hands in a circle around it." The group took their places, holding hands. "Please everyone, concentrate on the lantern's flame." She paused and looked straight at it with a steady gaze. "Eternal flame of life, we ask you to help us call upon the spirit of Aaron Locke. If you can locate him, please summon him into our presence tonight."

A sudden gust of wind blew across the area, whistling through the trees, and creating a low, mournful howl. "I can feel a presence getting closer." She raised her voice. "Aaron Locke! Please reveal yourself! Give us a sign that you're here."

Loraine shivered. "Oh, do you feel that?" she whispered. The others nodded.

The lantern flame jumped around as the bushes rustled. A figure stepped from the darkness and moved toward them. "Do not break the chain of hands."

Arron Locke, a man with a sad, weathered face, stepped into the faint light. "Why have you summoned me from my grave?" his gravelly voice echoed.

"We need to find answers to many unsolved mysteries."

"What do you wish to know?"

"We need to know if you murdered the Branch's as everyone believes you did."

Aaron emphatically shook his head no. "I had nothing to do with any of those murders. I admit that I was indeed a warlock and a member of the Secret Society, just as Daniel Branch was."

Steven interjected with great surprise, "Daniel Branch was a member of the Secret Society?"

Aaron slowly nodded. "He was the Grand Master of the Secret Society, but he wasn't a member of the Locke coven or any others that I knew about."

Loraine spoke up, "But, was he responsible for the fire that took the lives of your family?"

Aaron looked sadly at the ruins. "For many years I believed he was. But the witch confessed that she was responsible, just before she killed me several years later. She also admitted to all the other murders as well. Unfortunately, that information was never told to my only surviving son. And that streak of vengeance was passed on to his daughter, Charlotte Locke."

Dr. Grayson said, "Why did the witch kill you, Aaron?"

"She was my second wife. I dare not speak her name. She had struck a deal with Daniel to assume the youthful body of Daphne Branch, and become the mistress of Branchview. I became expendable when I no longer figured into her evil plans."

Steven blurted out, "Your wife was Liddy McPherson?"

Aaron shuddered in fear. "Shhh… you-" He was interrupted.

The ground began to rumble beneath their feet, and a huge gust of wind blew through the trees, extinguishing the flame in the lantern, and nearly knocking the trio over as they struggled to hold the circle together. Just as quickly as the turbulence all began, everything calmed and became normal once again. Aaron continued with fear in his voice, "You should have never mentioned her name here among these ruins. I fear now that you've unlocked the portal and released her spirit upon the earth once again." They were shocked by his words. Aaron began to look all around with nervous anxiety. "I should have never come here. She's very angry with me." His eyes darted with terror at the empty, dark sky above. "No! It's too late! She's here!"

Aaron began to moan in agony as his spirit quickly dissipated into the darkness, leaving only the echoes of his terrifying screams in its wake. The group glanced around with extreme anxiety, and Steven spoke up with urgency in his voice. "We need to get the hell out of here. Right now!"

The next morning at the City Diner, Philip Seagraves arrived just before 7:30. Suzy noticed right away that his mind happened to be unusually preoccupied, as he waited patiently for Steven to arrive. The topic of his thoughts was a common subject to mortal men, but not so normal for an immortal god. Philip had fell victim to a force that had toppled many a powerful man. Despite his immortal qualities, he was falling hard and deep into the hopeless throes of love. Steven arrived right on time, and also sensed the difference in his demeanor. "Good morning… everything alright?"

Philip tilted his head and waved at Suzy with his coffee cup. "I appreciate you meeting with me, Steven." He turned as Suzy approached. "Another for me please, and one for Steven here."

Suzy poured the coffee, and departed with a smile, as Steven inquired, "What urgent issue did you need to speak with me about?"

Philip sighed. "There was a meeting between Amy and Lucretia Darknight yesterday."

"Yes. I was aware that Lucia was eager to talk to her. What was that all about?"

Philip emotionally shook his head. "It appears that the woman I'm in love with is in fact a sculpted mannequin that was brought to life, and is under the supervision of Ms. Darknight."

Steven looked at Philip, dumbfounded. "I assume we're talking about Tina Lane?"

Philip nodded yes. "What do you make of it?"

"If I was thinking logically, I'd say that it was totally ridiculous. But since I already know how the witch is working through Lucia, I'd have to believe it was true."

Philip reacted with much disappointment. "What would you do in such a situation?"

"I would back away and reevaluate the situation. I don't need to tell you how dangerous things can be when a witch is involved. Even for an immortal such as yourself."

Philip's frustration poured out. "But I care deeply for Tina. Even if she is a mere, fabricated concoction with no soul."

"Then the only thing I can say is follow your heart. But I certainly wouldn't put any trust in Lucia for anything."

"I'm afraid Amy and I have no choice. She's agreed to help us in another matter of greater importance."

Steven rolled his eyes and took a deep breath. "I knew that couldn't be the only thing she wanted to talk to her about. What's this other matter?"

Philip paused before responding to make sure no one nearby was listening. "I know you're rather familiar with Greek mythology. Do you remember the story…" he leaned forward and whispered, "of Pandora's Box?"

"What?" He leaned back. "I thought it was just a fable. Are you telling me that it really does exist?"

Philip looked across the table with a stony, sober expression. "It was stolen from its hiding place, and is now in the possession of Senator Richard Holdsclaw." He paused while Suzy dropped off two menus, and promptly darted away. "You must promise me you won't tell anyone about this."

"Like any sane person would believe me. But yes… absolutely!" Steven took a sip of his coffee, before continuing onto a different subject. "Tell me this. What do you know about a woman named Liddy McPherson?"

Philip froze at the mention of her name. "I know that she's a very powerful witch that plagued this area for centuries. Hades vowed that he would never let her spirit roam the earth again. Why do you ask?"

"I found out through a seance last night that she killed Matthew Branch, set the fire at the Locke Estate, and committed all the other unsolved murders."

Philip took a deep breath. "Should I inform Amy of this?"

Steven shook his head. "I'll tell her at the appropriate time. Besides, I think it's better if she hears it from me." Philip agreed while Steven added, "There's a lot more that she and I need to discuss as well." He paused in deep thought, then continued. "What do you know about the Secret Society?"

"They've been around nearly as long as I have. They comprise elite figures such as media moguls, politicians, big business, and celebrities. Their ultimate goal is world domination, but fortunately, they've yet to succeed."

Steven absorbed the information with great thought. "The pieces to this puzzle are starting to come together.

Hopefully, Gerard and I can find some more answers in the tunnels below Branchview. "

Philip looked across the table with a foreboding stare. "You must be very careful in those tunnels, Steven. Many evil beings dwell there."

"Be cautious in your dealings with Lucia as well. As I mentioned before, she's definitely not one to be trusted."

"If what's in that box escapes, trust will be the last of our worries."

Philip stood up, as Steven slapped a ten-dollar bill on the table. "Thank you, Philip." He held out his hand. "Good luck, my friend."

"You as well. If you need anything I won't be far away." Steven nodded.

At the Branchview cottage, an unwanted visitor entered without invitation. Senator Holdsclaw quietly strolled in, looking about the room with casual interest. Lucretia also entered from another room, dressed only in a very short, silk lounging robe. She was quite startled, and became angry when she found him standing in her living room. "How dare you come into my house uninvited. What do you want?"

Holdsclaw strolled closer. "I come bearing both good news and bad news." He flashed an arrogant grin and continued. "I assume you haven't heard about my dear wife's untimely passing."

Lucretia replied with disgust, "What did you do... poison her?"

"My dear Lucretia! You do make me out to be quite the villain."

"I am quite perceptive. What other news do you have?"

Holdsclaw got uncomfortably close. "At exactly eleven o'clock this morning, Reverend Hightower will pay a visit to Audrey Branch. Give him fifteen minutes, then do your magic." He paced away while talking. "By the time this day is over, I'll be one step closer to being the Master of Branchview."

Lucretia got livid. "Wait a minute! We had a deal. I was supposed to get Branchview."

"I changed my mind. I rather like it here. Although, I do plan to keep you around as the mistress of the great house."

Lucretia was repulsed. "You must be insane! What makes you think I'd want anything to do with an old pervert like you?"

He strolled over and ran the back of his fingers down the side of her face, and Lucretia promptly slapped him hard across the mouth.

Holdsclaw only laughed in response. "You'll change your mind once you grant me the same eternal youth as I know you have."

"What makes you think I'd do that?"

He paced away once again with an arrogant smirk. "My dear! I'm afraid you have no other choice." Lucretia waited for him to continue. "You see, I'm fortunate to be in a position that I can expose you for who you really are, and that would be very unfortunate."

Lucretia boiled with anger. "Get out of my house!"

"Very well! But do be waiting for that phone call from the good reverend. We must be sure that all goes smoothly." She answered only with a hardened stare as he casually strolled out the door.

The morning continued to gain momentum, as the minutes ticked by. Steven returned to the main house and gathered some much-needed supplies for his journey to the secret caves beneath the cliffs of Branchview. Afterward, he went to meet Gerard at the carriage house.

Loraine and Sharie accompanied their husbands as they prepared to embark through the entrance below the carriage house.

Steven leaned in and kissed an anxious Loraine. "Do you think you two have everything you need?"

Gerard replied, "I believe so. Let's see, we have a rope, a small shovel, and shredded rags to mark the way back. According to some of the old maps, these tunnels branch off for miles below the town and connect to the sewer system, as well as to the caves at Lighthouse Point. It would be very easy to lose our way."

Steven quipped, "With that in mind, we'll just have to hope it doesn't rain as well."

"Oh, Steven! If I wasn't pregnant, I'd put on a backpack and go in there with you."

Sharie shook her head. "Not me! I've heard too many tales about those tunnels, and I'm not quite brave enough to test their validity."

"We'll be fine, Sharie. If we're not back by sunset, then you need to start worrying."

Both men embraced their wives. Sharie couldn't hold back tears. "You be careful, you old poop. I'll be praying for you."

Loraine grabbed Steven's arm as he turned away. "Please do take good care of yourself. I can't bear the thought of losing you." Steven kissed Loraine once more on her forehead and gave her an assured nod.

Gerard picked up a hammer from his nearby workbench. "Are you ready to do this?" Steven answered with a definite nod, and Gerard proceeded to pull the boards away from the tunnel entrance.

Loraine and Sharie watched as their men climbed into the tunnel, and disappeared into the darkness within.

At the cottage, Lucretia waited, uncertain of the fate she was about to set in motion. The last thing she ever planned was to have a mortal man hold her secrets in check in order to get what he desired. Especially when that man was a tyrant like Holdsclaw. As those random thoughts went through her mind, the phone call she had been waiting for came right on time. "Hello…?" she answered.

Chapter Twelve:

It's a Miracle

In the dimly lit room of a convalescent center, Reverend Hightower stood at the bedside of a catatonic Audrey Branch. Audrey was sitting up, staring ahead, while rocking in place, and mumbling to herself. He paused to mockingly chuckle over the insidious vision before his eyes. After which, he glanced at his watch, then placed his hand on her shoulder. With dramatic characterization, he began. "Satan! I command you in the name of our Lord Jesus Christ! Leave this sister's body, and take your vile demons with you. Go! Now!"

A few seconds later, he shook her violently, causing Audrey to convulse and moan. Then he slammed her body hard against the headboard. In the next few minutes, her eyes widened and she began to look around in confusion. "Where am I? How did I get here?"

"My dear sister! You're in a convalescent center. You've been in a catatonic state for several months, under the possession of the Devil's demons. But by the grace of God Almighty, you are now free once again."

"What…?" she exclaimed. "Where's my husband and my family?"

"They're back at Branchview. Once you're released, I shall take you back there, and surprise them."

Audrey appeared to be very shaken by the news. "Who are you? I don't recognize you."

"I am Rev. James Hightower. Today I served as the Lord's instrument in casting those wicked demons from your body." He whirled with a smirk and threw his hands in the air. "This is a day of miracles! Oh Hallelujah! Praise God!" Audrey continued to stare at the reverend in complete confusion. She was dumbfounded by the news, as the supposed reverend paced around the room, chanting praises to God for His grace in sparing this woman's sanity.

Unbeknownst to any of the Branch family, Steven and Gerard continued to make their way into the tunnels below the Estate. Gerard paused to read the map at a spot where two tunnels intersected. "Steven… according to the map, if we go to the left, we'll end up at the north end of Lighthouse Point. But if we go right, it'll lead to other tunnels under Lockeport. If we go straight ahead, we'll be nearly beneath the cottage."

"I'm not sure, but I think the cottage is the key to what we're looking for. Let's go straight."

"I'm going to trust you, so lead on…" The two men continued forward for the next several hundred feet. "Is it my imagination, or is it getting hotter in here?"

"No! It was cold and damp where we came from, but now it feels like we're walking into a blast furnace." Both men started sweating profusely, and it became difficult to breathe. Steven placed his hand on the side of the tunnel wall to his left, and quickly pulled it away. "That wall is almost too hot to touch."

Gerard placed his hand on the wall on his right. "That's odd! This wall feels rather cold." A few seconds later, the tunnel was filled with chants. "What the hell was that?"

"Maybe…" Steven's voice cracked, "it was just the wind blowing through the tunnel."

They paused for a moment to listen. "Perhaps you're right. If we go ahead about another hundred feet, we should be directly under the cottage."

"Well, we've come this far, so we might as well see this through." Steven forged ahead until they were stopped by a heavy steel door bound with a padlock and chain.

"This door should connect with the sub-basement of the cottage."

Steven went over and pulled on the chain. "But why would someone lock it from this side?" The chanting got louder once again, and their eyes darted around them with anxiety.

Just then, without warning, they heard the sound of a pack of dogs pouncing against the other side of the steel door, growling and barking wildly.

Steven turned with urgency. "Let's get out of here!"

They quickly turned to go in the other direction but froze in shock when they saw a young black man standing in front of them, dressed in old blue jeans with a rope belt, and a white collared button-up work shirt. Gerard asked, "Who are you, and what are you doing down here?"

The man's expression was sober, and he motioned for them to follow. "I think he wants us to see something." Steven shrugged.

They followed until they reached the spot where the tunnels intersected, and the man pointed for them to follow the tunnel that went under Lockeport. "What do you suppose he wants us to see?" Gerard asked.

Steven gave another clueless shrug. "I guess there's only one way to find out." They continued to follow, figuring it was a much better option than facing the uncertainty of what was on the other side of that door.

Meanwhile, back at Branchview, Reverend Hightower arrived with Audrey, where Daniel Sr. waited in anxious anticipation. He hurried into the foyer to joyfully greet his wife.

"Audrey! I can't believe you're actually here."

"Oh, Daniel! I never thought I'd be so glad to be home."

They embraced with a loving kiss. "I missed you so much."

"It's a blessing to witness such a happy reunion," the reverend exclaimed.

"Daniel, this is Rev. Hightower. He..."

Hightower finished her statement "Performed the exorcism that drove the wicked demons from your dear wife's mind."

Daniel appeared quite baffled, while Mrs. Porter breezed into the room to announce, "Martha and I have prepared a special homecoming celebration in the dining room."

"We must make sure that Steven, Lori, and the LeRouxs are here to celebrate with us."

"The Spencer's and LeRoux's went somewhere together. We've tried to notify them without any luck." She turned to Rev. Hightower. "Will you be staying for the party as well, Reverend?"

"I'm afraid not. I have another engagement that I need to attend." Hightower turned. "Audrey! Would you mind if I had a few words with your husband in private?"

"Of course not, Reverend. I'll run along, and join the others in the dining room." She laid her hand on Hightower's arm. "And thank you again for your help."

"Thank the Lord, Mrs. Branch." Audrey departed, and Hightower turned his attention to Daniel. "You have a fine woman there, Mr. Branch."

"I very much agree, but I am quite baffled over all this. How did you come about visiting with my wife?"

Hightower smiled. "Lucretia Darknight notified me, and requested that I pay her a visit."

"I'm quite grateful that you did. We had given up hope of Audrey ever recovering from her ailment. It's quite miraculous."

"Yes indeed! All things are possible where the Lord is concerned." Hightower lowered his voice. "Mr. Branch, I must warn you that there is evil in this house that caused Audrey's ailment." Daniel listened with interest. "I understand that you have a white witch living in this household."

Daniel chuckled. "If you're referring to Lori, she's a practitioner of white magic, and she's also my brother's wife. She's a very kind person, and would never cause any of us harm."

"Any type of magic is the Devil's work. He finds his way in through the most innocent means."

"I appreciate your concern Reverend, but I'm certain it's unfounded."

"Very well. If you'll excuse me, I should be going."

"I would like to pay you for your services."

Reverend Hightower smiled pompously. "I'm sure a generous donation to my ministry would be quite sufficient."

They strolled toward the door. "I'll have a check sent out first thing in the morning."

"I'm certain that God will bless you for that. Good day, Mr. Branch!" Daniel bid his guest goodbye and hurried to rejoin his wife and the others.

Below ground, Steven and Gerard continued to move swiftly through the tunnels, trying to keep up with the stranger. "I lost sight of him. Where did he go?"

Gerard flashed his light ahead and squinted. "There he is! Over by that ladder."

The man pointed upward with much enthusiasm toward a hatch at the top. Steven went up the ladder first, and carefully opened the hatch when they got to the top. He then looked down at Gerard who was close behind and noticed the young man was no longer there. "Hey! Where did he go?"

Gerard looked both directions in the tunnel. "It's like he vanished into thin air."

Steven proceeded to hoist himself up through the hatchway, then helped Gerard as he crawled through. Once inside, they curiously scanned the area with their eyes. "It looks like we're in a back office of someone's business. Maybe we shouldn't be here" Gerard stated.

"It's okay! I don't think there's anyone here right now."

"Well, wherever we are, I just want to get out without being seen."

"Agreed. Come on…" Steven motioned to the nearest exit.

The door led them into a large circular room with rows of seats around a stage. "It looks like it's some sort of theater."

Steven was caught off guard when he noticed a painted symbol on the floor of the stage. "I wish it was that innocent, Gerard." He held his hand up to stop his progress.

"Is that what I think it is?"

Steven nodded. "It's a pentagram…"

Steven took on an expression of dread as they proceeded down a long walkway to the stage that sat directly below a high circular cupola roof. The late-day sunlight streamed through the windows of the cupola, lighting the room. "They hold Satanic ceremonies here." He pointed to the cupola. "When the moon is full, and it shines through those windows and strikes the pentagram at the right angle, it is said that the presence of Satan himself is in the room."

Gerard took on a look of terror. "There's a full moon later this week. They'll likely be having their meeting then."

Steven nodded while contemplating. "There's something about that cupola. I've seen it before… perhaps from the outside." After a few moments, he took on an expression of enlightenment. "I think we're inside the SOS Club."

"Of course! I always wondered what the inside would look like. But why was that young man so eager for us to find this place?"

"Let's go back into the office and see if we can find out."

"Are you sure? What if someone shows up?"

"We've come this far. We can't leave without answers."

"Come on, stay close…" The men moved quietly back to the office. On the far wall, Steven noticed a large bookcase. "Over there… I want to look at those books." He flashed his light on the book spines and glanced at each one of them as he moved his way along the shelving. "Hey! I think I found something." Gerard stationed himself at the door, while Steven took one of the books, and laid it open on the desk.

"What's in there?"

"It has a listing of names in it."

"What do you suppose it is?"

"It appears to be a directory of all the present club members, and the other books on the shelf are marked in twenty-five-year intervals, going back as far as the late 1600s."

"I need to see this…" Steven looked up as Gerard joined him. "There's names of important people in here. Look! There's Senator Holdsclaw's name, as well as Representative Lapino."

Steven glanced up at Gerard with amazement. "I think I know what all this is. We just uncovered the meeting place of the Secret Society." Steven snickered, "Well! Look who the Grand Warlock is…"

Gerard looked down at the open book, and read the name out loud, "Rev. James Hightower."

"Oh yes! Isn't he known for saying on TV that you can't serve two masters? How ironic is that?"

Gerard announced, "Shhhh… do you hear that?" The same chanting began to echo throughout the building from the tunnels below. "There's that chanting again. Steven, we need to get the hell out of here."

"Wait, Gerard! First, we need to grab the directories from 1900 to the present and take them with us. I think we may be able to find some answers there."

Gerard's eyes glanced around the room in desperation. "Fine! Just hurry! I wouldn't want to get caught and become the human sacrifice of the month." Steven rushed to grab the books, while Gerard placed them in his pack.

Back at Branchview, the family joyfully celebrated Audrey's homecoming. They were all gathered, conversing at the large dining room table. Dr. Grayson leaned to her left and diverted Daniel Sr's attention for the moment. "I'm beginning to worry about Steven, Lori, and the LeRoux's. I thought for sure they would've been back by now."

Daniel took a swallow of his brandy before answering. "I wouldn't worry so much, Dr. Grayson. Perhaps they were having so much fun that they just decided to make an entire day out of it."

Audrey was distracted when her cell phone buzzed. She looked at the message, then looked up again when she heard Heather's phone buzz as well. Their expressions turned to disgust, as they watched the video attachment. Audrey stayed quiet, while she and Heather watched with disbelief. Then she abruptly turned to her husband and slapped him hard across the face. His glass of brandy flew from his grip and shattered across the tile floor. "You bastard! How could you?"

Heather rushed over to condemn her father as well. "I hate you!" She then turned and ran from the room in tears.

Audrey turned sternly to Daniel Jr. "Run upstairs and pack your suitcase. We're leaving this God-forsaken house tonight."

"But… Mom, why?"

"Just do as I say!"

"Yes ma'am!"

Daniel Sr pleaded cluelessly. "Audrey! What on earth is wrong?"

"Perhaps you should let Lucretia Darknight answer that for you."

Daniel replied with frustration, "I wish I knew what you were talking about. Please...tell me!"

Audrey held her cell phone in front of Daniel. "Very well! Explain this!"

Daniel's expression immediately turned to horror. "Oh my God!"

"Hopefully, the next time I have to lay eyes on your pitiful face, we'll be in divorce court." Audrey stormed from the room, leaving a very stunned and confused Dr. Grayson alone with an equally shocked and embarrassed Daniel.

The inhabitants of the household dispersed, while everyone tried to settle down after the odd turn of events. Gerard and Sharie remained at the carriage house for the night, while Steven and Loraine finally returned home. Dr. Grayson heard them enter while she was reading in the sitting room, and hurried to greet them.

She held her hand to her head and looked quite distressed. "I am so glad you two are back. It's been one heck of a day."

"Oh, dear! What's happened now?"

"Audrey had a miraculous recovery this morning. A Rev. Hightower cast the demons from her mind, and brought her home this afternoon."

Steven reacted with disbelief. "Rev. James Hightower?"

"Yes! The television evangelist." Steven and Loraine exchanged a quick glance, and Dr. Grayson changed the subject. "Steven, you look as though you've been in a coal mine. How did you get so sweaty and dirty?"

"Gerard and I went down in the tunnels today. Where is Audrey now?"

Dr. Grayson sighed stressfully. "She's gone! She took Heather and Daniel Jr about a half-hour ago, and she said she's never coming back."

"What on earth prompted that decision?"

"I'm not exactly sure. Both she and Heather received some sort of message on their phones that upset them greatly. I do believe it had something to do with Lucretia Darknight."

Steven rolled his eyes. "Why am I not surprised?"

"What did you and Gerard find in the tunnels?" Dr. Grayson asked.

Steven took a deep breath. "Plenty! Let me take a shower, and I'll meet you two in the study in about a half-hour. We have a lot to discuss."

At the cottage, Lucretia relaxed in front of the fireplace, listening to Deep Purple on her stereo. She was enamored with her results in being able to further destroy the Branch family.

She seductively sashayed across the room in her sheer negligee and poured herself a glass of red chardonnay. As she savored the taste of her first sip, her eyes caught sight of the voodoo doll lying on a nearby table. A wicked smile appeared on her face. "Now it's time for me to put some attention toward you, Dr. Grayson." An eerie laugh echoed off the walls. *Oh no! I won't mortally harm you, I'll just give you a little prick in the arm or leg occasionally, to let you know I'm thinking about you.*

Chapter Thirteen:

The Voodoo Doll

Many new revelations were making themselves known but were grossly overshadowed by the complications of Charlotte Locke's relentless pursuit to destroy everyone that carried the Branch name, and to gain control of everything they possessed.

The large foyer clock chimed at 11:00 A.M. As Steven made his way downstairs. Gerard entered through the front door simultaneously. "Gerard! I didn't expect to see you here this early."

"I'm here to pick up Daniel. The Board of Directors called an emergency meeting."

Steven sighed. "Perhaps you'll have better luck than I had in getting him to talk."

"I can't imagine what he must be going through. The mere fact that Hightower is involved in all this makes me very suspicious."

Dr. Grayson entered from the sitting room, cradling a cup of coffee. "Good morning, Gerard!"

Suddenly, Dr. Grayson winced in pain. "Are you okay?" Gerard and Steven rushed to her aid, as she dropped her coffee cup and it shattered on the tile floor.

She responded, "I don't know what's wrong. Late last night, I had the same pain in my right leg. It was as though someone was sticking me with a needle."

"Perhaps Steven should take you to the hospital to get it checked out."

"Oh no! I'll be just fine. I need to run and get something to clean up this spilled coffee."

Dr. Grayson departed, while Steven reacted with frustration. "As if we don't have enough to worry about around here."

Gerard raised an eyebrow. "I can't quit thinking about what we saw in the tunnels yesterday. That young man, the way he was dressed, and how quickly he disappeared."

"Yes, and something came to mind. I remember you saying that those tunnels were used for the Underground

Railroad? Perhaps he was a spirit that still lingers there from that time."

"I believe that it may have been more than that. I think that young man was my great grandfather."

Steven looked at Gerard with enlightenment. "Wasn't he the one that survived when the portal opened, and the beast consumed the rest of the runaway slaves?" Gerard answered with a definite nod. "Perhaps that portal exists in the portion of the tunnel where we felt the extreme heat."

"It very well could be. It is where we first saw him."

Daniel III interrupted their conversation. "Good morning, gentlemen!" He turned his attention to Gerard. "Let's go get this unpleasant meeting over with, so we can enjoy the rest of our Sunday." Daniel stormed out ahead of Gerard.

"We'll talk more about this later," Gerard concluded.

Steven closed the door behind them, and Dr. Grayson came back with a damp towel and a whisk broom.

Steven hurried over to help. "Where's Gerard? I was looking forward to talking with him." She bent down to clean up the mess.

"Here, let me get that," Steven announced. "He and Daniel had a meeting to attend." Steven carefully swept up the broken pieces.

"Thank you…"

"I couldn't help noticing that you and Lucia walked away together after the funeral yesterday. I certainly hope you two didn't have words."

Dr. Grayson chuckled. "I'm afraid there's no way to hide my true feelings about that woman. And yes, we did have words."

"Perhaps that wasn't a good idea. We have to be very tactful when dealing with her."

"Oh, Steven! You worry far too much. Here, let me go dump that broken cup in the garbage." She took the dustpan from his hand and hurried from the room, as Steven looked away with a very concerned expression.

Near Lighthouse Point, a black-cloaked figure meandered through the ruins of a once-grand estate.

Charlotte Locke threw back the hood of her cloak and spoke out loud to herself. "Very soon, a new house shall rise from these ancient ashes, and this sacred ground of my ancestors will once again belong to a Locke." In the midst of her reminiscing, she was interrupted by another cloaked figure that emerged from the woods. She quickly pulled the hood back over her head and vanished. The second figure lurked within the shadows, watching as the black cat scurried away from the site.

Daniel and Gerard remained mostly silent on their way to Branch Consolidated. As they exited the elevator, Lucretia was waiting at the end of the hallway. Daniel gave her a stern look. Gerard took notice of the negative energy that passed between them and quickly took refuge in his office.

"Lucia! I need to speak with you in my office. Right now!" She nodded, and silently followed, as he ushered her in and slammed the door. "Pray tell me what you had hoped to accomplish from this little charade of yours?"

Lucretia acted clueless. "Daniel! I have absolutely no idea what you're talking about."

Daniel responded venomously, "No! Your little clueless act won't work this time, Lucia. You seduced me when I was emotionally vulnerable and drunk out of my mind. Then you filmed it and sent it to my wife and daughter."

Lucretia dramatically played innocent. "I did no such thing!" she sobbed. "I'm just as horrified over this as you are." She began to desperately look about the room. "Someone must be spying on you. There has to be a camera hidden somewhere." She looked over toward the bookcase and pointed. "Yes, look! There it is!"

Daniel strolled over, and forcibly tore the camera from between the two books. "If you didn't put it there, then how in the hell did you know where to look?"

"I didn't! I simply saw something peeking out from between the two books." She shook her head in frustration. "I sent Rev. Hightower to help Audrey. Why would I do such a cruel thing so soon afterward?"

There was a light knock, and Gerard peeked in. "The Board's ready to start the meeting in ten minutes."

Gerard shut the door again, and Daniel lowered his voice. "If I ever discover that you're responsible for this, I will terminate you, and make sure that you never gain employment with another company." Daniel stormed from the room, while Lucretia displayed a clever smirk.

Back at Branchview, Steven was in front of the bathroom mirror shaving when suddenly, the likeness of Matthew Branch appeared. Steven jumped back when he saw the Gilded Age version of himself staring from the other side of the mirror. "I'm sorry I startled you, Steven. I need to warn you and the others about an impending danger."

"Matthew…does that danger have anything to do with Liddy McPherson?"

Matthew nodded. "As if she hasn't caused enough grief in this family over the centuries. She's found a way to come back and inflict more."

"But how? Poseidon told me that Hades had agreed to never let her return."

"He obviously went back on his word. He and Liddy are working in concert on some sort of scheme. You need to inform Poseidon and Amphitrite of this as soon as possible."

Steven shook his head in amazement. "How does Charlotte Locke fit into all this?"

"Charlotte was deceived, just as her father was. All the while, she's unknowingly been laying the groundwork for Liddy's return."

"But…" Steven tried to probe further, but Loraine called out to him from the next room. When he turned back around, Matthew had disappeared.

"Steven! Who are you conversing with in there?"

Loraine opened the door and entered. "Believe it or not, I'm just talking to myself, sweetheart."

He kissed her on the forehead. "I swear! All this turmoil is beginning to affect us all." She turned and promptly walked out, while Steven looked back in the mirror, and smiled at himself.

Across town, Daniel, Gerard, and Lucretia had settled down in the board room to begin the impromptu meeting. Marshall Hempfield, a tall man in his mid-sixties, entered the room shortly after everyone else and called the meeting into session. "Hello, I'm glad all of you could make it here this morning. We have some very urgent business to discuss."

Daniel interrupted in an indignant tone, "I should hope that it is indeed urgent, for you to have called us in on our day off, Hempfield."

Hempfield answered with a confident nod. "Ladies and gentlemen of the Board, as you all know, due to false rumors that have circulated concerning the company's future strategy, our stock experienced an unexpected selloff on Friday."

Daniel interrupted, "And a mighty quick recovery by the end of the day, I might add."

Hempfield responded with an annoyed look before continuing. "It's come to the Board's attention that a yet-to-be-named investor quickly purchased large amounts of our stock at its lowest point."

Daniel interrupted again, "That should be good news for all of us."

Hempfield carried on, "I would say yes in most cases. However, now this individual owns the full majority of stock in the company."

Daniel leapt from his chair and slammed his fist on the table. "Why wasn't I made aware of this by our corporate broker? The circumstances obviously wreak of insider trading, and a hostile takeover."

"It's obviously something you should have been on top of, but somehow neglected."

Gerard jumped in, "Wait! I have to agree with Daniel. Our broker should have caught this. The FTC should be notified about this whole situation."

Hempfield sighed. "As I'm sure they will. Nevertheless, the Board has agreed, and voted unanimously, to replace Daniel Branch as President and CEO of this company."

Daniel flew into a rage. "That's preposterous! My family has been in control of this company for over three centuries."

"I understand Daniel, but I'm afraid the Board has spoken. A very generous severance package will be prepared and offered to you before week's end."

Daniel stood up. "You haven't heard the last from me, Hempfield."

"I'm afraid I have for now. I must ask you to leave the room so that we can move onto other business."

Daniel boiled with rage as he turned to Lucretia. "I know you had something to do with this too. You're nothing but a conniving, backstabbing witch." The room went completely silent, for no one had words for what had just happened. Lucretia couldn't help but conjure an innocent smirk, while Hempfield remained calm. "You need to leave now, Mr. Branch."

In the sitting room at Branchview, Steven received a call on his cell phone from his contractor in Florida. He paced as he listened, and displayed a slow, simmering anger. "I'll get my attorney on this right away. Something rotten is definitely going on behind the scenes." After hanging up the phone, he stomped about the room, venting his anger.

He failed to even notice that Loraine had entered the room, as he continued his rant, talking to himself out loud. "I can't believe this is happening."

Loraine was startled by his behavior. "Steven! What's wrong now?"

"Our contractor in Florida just called me. He went over to the estate to look things over, and found a cease-and-desist order that had been posted."

Loraine was flabbergasted. "Whatever for?"

"They claim that the proper permits weren't applied for and approved. When I know for a fact they were."

"Then what do you suppose happened?"

He paused for a moment in thought. "My keen intuition tells me that Sen. Holdsclaw has something to do with it. That man isn't happy unless he's wielding his almighty power and screwing somebody over simultaneously."

"Honey! Just settle yourself." she took his arm, and Steven turned to delicately embrace his pregnant wife. "He'll get his due, and we will get through this. I know we will."

In Holdsclaw's local office, the evil tyrants were holding a late-night meeting. Holdsclaw, Lapino, and Rev Hightower sat comfortably and conversed while waiting for their guests to arrive. "I would've given anything to see the look on Steven Spencer's face when he got that call from his contractor," Holdsclaw smirked.

"It seems like everything is coming together nicely. Will you and Representative Lapino be attending the meeting on Monday night?" Hightower questioned.

"Yes! Most certainly! We've delayed our return to Washington until early Wednesday."

Holdsclaw leaned back in his chair as Hightower continued to speak. "Our membership continues to grow larger each month. In this month alone, we have ten new converts to swear in."

"Lucretia Darknight has all but destroyed Daniel Branch III. All we have to do is get rid of Gerard LeRoux and Steven Spencer, and Branch Consolidated will practically be ours."

Rep. Lapino bubbled over with enthusiasm, "Oh! This is all so exciting!" Holdsclaw and Hightower exchanged an amused grin as the door opened, and Seth stepped in.

"Ms. Darknight has arrived with her guest, sir." Lucretia and Hades, under the guise of Luke Underwood, strolled into the room behind Seth.

Holdsclaw stood up to greet them. "Lucretia! I understand you had a rather productive day, my dear?"

"Very productive indeed! This is Mr. Underwood. He's the official caretaker of the box."

Luke dove right into the conversation. "That's right! My family has carried down the combination for several centuries."

"And what sort of combination might that be? I can't help but notice that there is no lock," Holdsclaw inquired.

"The seal is released by a series of spoken words. Only I know what those words are."

Lapino eagerly interrupted, "Tell us what's in the box. Is it gold?"

Luke was amused by her ignorance. "I honestly have no idea. But I'm quite confident that it contains enough good fortune to satisfy everyone in this room."

Holdsclaw gave a slight nod to Seth. "You will open that box for us, Mr. Underwood."

Seth planted the barrel of his gun into Luke's back. "There's no need for that. I do intend on opening the box for all of you." Holdsclaw nodded again, and Seth holstered his gun. Luke strolled forward. "I understand that we all have something in common. I'm very fascinated by the Secret Society and their mission." Everyone in the room exchanged a quick, cautious glance as Luke turned to Rev. Hightower. "Reverend! I understand that you're the Grand Warlock of the SOS Club?"

"How did you know that?

"I stay well informed about things that interest me. As I mentioned, I fully support the mission of what you're trying to accomplish." He continued to talk in the same cadence. "So much, in fact, that I'm willing to donate whatever is in that box toward your cause, without even knowing what it is."

Holdsclaw and Lapino looked at each other with surprise as Hightower chuckled. "And I'm sure it will be a generous donation, indeed."

Luke smiled. "With that said, I bid you all farewell and good fortune with the box."

Holdsclaw jumped in. "Wait a minute! I thought you were going to open the box. Why are you leaving?"

Luke chuckled again. "The contents of that box have always been a mystery to my family, Sen. Holdsclaw. I have no absolutely no desire to know what's in it."

Lapino spoke up, "But you will open it?"

"As soon as I walk out your front door, I shall speak the magic words, the seal of the box will open, and you can all share in the wealth it contains."

Lucretia spoke up with much contempt, "I'll go with you, Luke. I have no desire to watch these buzzards hover over that box." Luke held out his arm as the two confidently walked out of the room. In the dark, Luke and his accomplice strolled outside, quite pleased with their performance. Waiting in the parking lot were Zeus, Poseidon, and Amphitrite. "Let's get this thing over with," Hades announced.

Zeus spoke up, "I can't thank you enough for your help in this matter, Hades."

"I'm only doing this because it benefits me as well. Consider it the last time I ever cooperate with any of you."

Poseidon took charge of the conversation. "Okay! Let's all take our places."

Lucretia spoke up, "Are you all absolutely certain that the contents will lose energy against your positive force field, and return to the box?"

Amphitrite answered haughtily, "It's inevitable! They're neutralized by positive energy, and feed off the negative. With that in mind, perhaps you should keep your distance." Lucretia answered with a hard stare and walked back to her car.

Hades continued, "When it's safe, I'll speak the words again, and the box will close. That's just as it was done the first time."

"Let's hope that it works this time as well," Poseidon added.

The anticipation inside Holdsclaw's office grew by the second as the group awaited the opening of the box.

"What's taking him so long?" Lapino snapped.

Hightower then spoke up, "I think we've been duped. I don't think he ever had any intention of opening that box."

Holdsclaw shouted impatiently, "Seth! Go see if he's left yet." Seth moved toward the door but halted when a bellowing chant echoed through the room.

"What in the devil's name was that?" Seth asked.

Everyone looked around with anxiety, as the seal suddenly popped, and the lid began to slowly open. Lapino shouted, "Look! Something's happening!"

The group moved in close to get a look inside. No one wanted to miss the grand revelation. Suddenly, from within the box, large bat creatures emerged, screeching hideously, and forcing everyone to shield their ears from the piercing noise. Large swarms of black particles resembling bees mingled amongst the large black creatures flying about the room. Amidst all the chaos, the room's inhabitants screamed in terror and pain, while trying to swat away the creatures that had now proceeded to gnaw and bite at their flesh with a vengeance. Outside the building, the gods proceeded with their plan, holding their hands upward to maintain the positive force field, as the terrible noises inside the office began to slowly dissipate.

In the distance, Lucretia watched from the comfort of her BMW sedan. She flashed an evil grin in the rearview mirror, *Goodbye, Senator Holdsclaw!* With a satisfying grunt, she put the car in drive and sped off into the night.

When it was finally safe to enter the building, the ghastly carnage horrified even the gods.

Amphitrite recoiled. "The stench in here is horrid."

Zeus looked down at the four skeletal remains scattered about the floor. "Good God! The vermin consumed them right down to their bones."

Poseidon looked back toward the door. "Where's Hades?"

Amphitrite replied, "He's gone! But my intuition tells me we'll be seeing him again very soon."

Zeus turned to Poseidon. "I need you and Amphitrite to take that box as far out to sea as possible. Bury it deep beneath the ocean floor, where no humans will ever find it."

"I couldn't agree more," Poseidon replied.

At the ruins of the Locke Estate, Hades strolled along as if searching for something in the night. A hooded figure stepped from the shadows, approaching him within inches. "Everything is coming along just as planned. Tomorrow night, during the full moon, the Secret Society will meet their new leader. Then, my dear, a new era shall begin for both of us."

A bright smile emerged from the hooded figure, as the news struck a chord. Liddy McPherson tossed her hood back, revealing her strawberry blonde hair and brilliant green eyes. She appeared to be a rather attractive but weathered woman in her mid-thirties. "I've waited so long for this, and now through the valiant efforts of Charlotte Locke, it's all within my grasp."

Hades chuckled. "What are your exact plans for Miss Charlotte?"

"I really haven't thought that far ahead. I'm having way too much fun watching her and Lucretia Darknight do all my dirty work." They both laughed.

In the sitting room, Dr. Grayson sat close to the fire deep in thought, clutching at her crucifix. She knew something wasn't quite right. Steven wandered into the room, looking quite weary, and his appearance caught her attention. Simultaneously, dogs began to howl somewhere outside. "Well! It sounds as if the Hell Hounds have returned just in time for tomorrow night's full moon."

Dr. Grayson stood up and strolled toward him with much anxiety. "I know! Steven… something's happening. I—"

He interrupted, "I know. All hell is about to break loose."

She reacted with great concern. "The spirit of Matthew Branch did warn you about Liddy McPherson. If she and Charlotte Locke are working together on something, what you're saying could very well happen."

Dr. Grayson tried to shake off the anxiety. "Did you have a chance to speak with Daniel?"

Steven replied, "I told him everything about how Charlotte was working through Lucia to destroy our family."

"How did that go over?"

"Not too well! He stormed out of the study, and I'm not sure where he went."

"Let's just hope he doesn't do anything foolish."

Steven knew that he and Dr. Grayson were correct in their assessment that all hell was about to break loose. He just hoped that his brother wouldn't be caught in the midst of it.

Lucretia victoriously returned to the cottage, quite pleased with the outcome of the evening. She kicked off her shoes and poured herself a glass of wine before selecting a book from her collection. She had just set about getting comfortable in an easy chair when suddenly, there was a knock on the door. *Who dares to disturb me at this hour of the night?*

She opened the door hesitantly and was quite surprised at who was on the other side. "Daniel! What do you want?"

Daniel stood rigid and hostile. "I want you out of this cottage, and off my property by sundown tomorrow. Or, I'll have the sheriff escort you if necessary."

"Daniel just hold on. I told you that I had nothing to do with what happened."

Daniel shook his finger. "You can't lie to me anymore Lucia. Steven told me who you really are, and why you're here."

She turned away from him defiantly. "Is that so? Just what do you intend to do about that?"

"I intend to do everything within my power to prevent you from succeeding, Charlotte."

Lucretia laughed. "Oh! So now it's Charlotte?"

Daniel answered with raging anger. "I'm warning you! If you're not gone by tomorrow, you'll be very, very sorry."

"Get out of here. Now!" she demanded.

"Just for tonight, Lucretia. I shall return tomorrow, and have you forcibly removed." Daniel turned away in a huff, and Lucretia slammed the door behind him. *You should know that it's never wise to threaten a witch, Daniel Branch.*

Lucretia returned to her seat, trying to calm her anger, as she focused on the flames in the fireplace. *Spirit of darkness, spirit of fire, I command you to carry my words on the wind and let them become embedded in the mind of Daniel Branch III. When I speak those words, he will do exactly as I tell him.*

Daniel's anger raged as he walked back to Branchview, but suddenly he paused amid confusion. A blank expression slowly covered his face, as though he were falling into a trance. His pace slowed, and became more methodical, but with a purpose.

Steven completed his conversation with Dr. Grayson and bid her good night, before heading upstairs to retire for the evening. He entered the bedroom where Loraine sat in bed, reading a book. "Hi, sweetheart! I just spoke with Dr. Grayson. We're both very concerned about Daniel. He hasn't returned to the house yet."

Loraine set the book down and shifted her full attention to Steven. "Where do you suppose he went?"

"Well, they were showing the hockey game on the big screen at The Mermaid Inn tonight. I was thinking maybe he went there."

"Don't you think he would've been back by now?"

Steven stressed over the question as he settled in the bed next to her. "I don't know! I just hope he didn't get drunk and have an accident. Or worse yet, I hope he didn't go against my advice and confront Lucia."

"Oh, dear! Steven… you don't suppose he would've actually done that?"

"He'd already had a few too many drinks, and he was very upset with her."

In the midst of their conversation, Maggie unexpectedly appeared near the foot of their bed, exhibiting great anxiety. Bumpers growled for a moment, then calmed when he realized it was a friendly spirit.

"Daniel's in trouble! You have to hurry!"

"Oh, dear! Maggie, what's happened?"

Steven leapt from the bed, while Maggie impatiently persisted. "We have to hurry…"

Maggie ran ahead, as Steven followed with Loraine and Bumpers in tow. Maggie hurried down the hallway and swung open a door leading to a dusty stairwell. "Maggie… where does this lead?"

"The attic! Steven, we must hurry!" Steven raced ahead, and up the stairs.

He reached the top to find a horrifying sight. Daniel was hanging from the rafters, swinging from the end of a rope. Maggie began crying. "Oh no! We're too late!"

She disappeared, but her sorrowful cries echoed throughout the high ceilings of the attic. Steven hurried to set the toppled chair upright and desperately tried loosening the knot around his brother's neck. Loraine arrived in the attic and watched with stunned horror. After Steven hoisted his brother down, he laid him gently on the floor. "Come on… Daniel." He desperately performed CPR. He tried again, then again. He checked for any sign of a pulse, then looked up at Loraine with an agonizing expression. "He's gone!"

Loraine replied bitterly, "This is the final straw. Charlotte Locke must suffer for this."

Chapter Fourteen:

The Nightmare is Real

Morning had mercifully arrived at Branchview. The unexpected death of Daniel Branch III only added to what seemed like a horrible nightmare that would not end. In a short period of time, Charlotte Locke had almost destroyed the entire Branch family. Their lineage had been narrowed to just two male descendants, Daniel Branch IV and Steven Spencer.

As Steven sat with his wife and Dr. Grayson on that sad day, he realized that they were part of the dwindling number of living beings in that great house. He also knew it was time to take drastic measures to stop Charlotte and Liddy McPherson before they annihilated the whole family.

In the sitting room, Steven sat in between Loraine and Dr. Grayson on the love seat. The two felt safer being close to him in their time of sorrow. After some time, Dr. Grayson broke the silence, "I just can't bring myself to believe that Daniel's really gone."

The anger had boiled beyond Steven's ability to contain himself as well. "We just have to do something to stop Charlotte. Even if it means destroying Lucia Darknight."

Dr. Grayson leaned forward and cast a long, caring look toward Steven. She could sense his pain but was at a loss of what to say. Before she could speak, Loraine voiced her concern. "Oh, come now, Steven! You know that our oath as practitioners of white magic forbids us to kill innocent people. Besides, Kristin Wiler has a family and a life elsewhere. It's our responsibility that she's returned to them safely."

"Lori's right! We also must keep in mind that Liddy McPherson is lurking about, waiting for her chance to strike as well."

Steven pondered an alternative thought. "Okay! This is what we'll do…" He leaned forward in his seat. "I need to go consult with Poseidon and Amphitrite about this, and Lori has a crucial doctor's appointment. So, Dr. Grayson, that leaves you with the chore of greeting Audrey and Heather when they arrive."

"I know they'll have a lot of questions. What do you want me to tell them?"

"Everything! We can't withhold the truth any longer. The sooner they understand what's going on around here, the better they'll know how crucial it is for us to keep them and Daniel Jr safe."

Dr. Grayson sighed. "I know they'll be furious when they find out what Lucia has done."

"I understand, but you must persuade them against any type of confrontation with her. We certainly don't need any more dead Branch's on the property."

In the busy City Diner, Suzie breezed by, waiting on tables during the breakfast hour. Jeff Manus entered as she passed. He took a seat at the counter and waited for her to get a few spare minutes. He watched admirably while his special girl hustled around, serving patrons. "Hey, you!" she said as she passed.

He nodded. "How about some coffee?"

"I think the magic word is please, their mister." He chuckled and obliged.

She poured his coffee and paused to sneak a quick kiss that failed to escape the curious eyes of an older woman sitting nearby. She winked and smiled warmly at the couple before turning her attention back to her tasty Belgian waffle.

"Are you free tonight?" he asked in a mellow tone.

"I have a class at 6:00, but I can be at the Mermaid Inn afterward?"

"Fair enough! I'll meet you there…."

"You better! I need you to protect me from all the weirdos. It's a full moon tonight."

The cook rang the order bell and yelled from the kitchen window. "Order up! Come on Suzie…"

"I gotta go!" She flashed him a smile before hurrying away.

Jeff looked serene, however. He remembered all too well the past issues that came about during a full moon. He sipped on his coffee and mumbled to himself. *Oh… I hate full moons…*

Inside the secret cave room, Amphitrite escorted Steven, while Poseidon and Zeus waited on their crystal thrones. Poseidon stood immediately when they entered, and held out his hand to give Steven a firm handshake. "Amphitrite sensed a great urgency when you summoned her."

Steven emotionally looked around the room, reluctant to talk about his sorrow. "My brother Daniel Branch III is dead, and Lucretia Darknight killed him."

Poseidon and Amphitrite were staggered by the news, and Zeus stepped down from the throne to join them. "Please accept my deepest sympathies."

"Steven, I know this may be hard for you to believe, but this is my brother Zeus. He goes by the land name of Ezekiel Sphere."

Steven shook hands with great admiration. "I've read quite a few stories about you."

"And I assure you, they're all true."

Steven took a deep breath. "I desperately need your help. We must end this killing spree before the witch destroys what remains of my family, and everyone else that lives at Branchview."

The two gods and Amphitrite all exchanged concerned glances. "We have to help them. I'm sure she'll try to kill Steven next, and if she succeeds, she'll also kill my Matthew in the process." Amphitrite struggled to speak as the tears rolled down her cheeks, and Poseidon reacted with an expression of empathy. "Poseidon and I were just discussing a related subject. We have reason to believe that Hades allowed Liddy McPherson to return in order to achieve some objective, and I'm sure Charlotte Locke is also involved."

"I think that objective has something to do with the Secret Society, and a takeover of Branch Consolidated." The two gods exchanged an enlightening glance. "Without your intervention, I have no doubt they'll succeed."

Poseidon interrupted, "You must know that we do intend to help, but it will be difficult to offer you constant protection."

Zeus paced in deep thought. "This is a very serious issue indeed. We must find a way to prevent any further mishaps."

Amphitrite eagerly spoke up, "I think I may have a solution." She turned to Steven. "If you could grant us a few moments in private, I'd like to discuss this idea with Zeus and Poseidon." Steven obliged, and strolled to the far end of the throne room, while the three immortals huddled in serious discussion.

After several seconds, they broke the huddle, walked to the edge of the marble altar surrounding the throne chairs, and each chose a gold sword from the weapons rack. "We have made a decision. Would you please join us on the altar, Steven?" Steven slowly approached, quite baffled by their actions. "We've all agreed that in order to properly protect Branchview and its inhabitants, it would be best to grant you the powers of a god until this ordeal is finished."

Steven stepped back in disbelief. "I don't quite understand. I'm just a mere mortal."

"Yes, true, Steven," Poseidon stated, "but by the power granted through us, you shall acquire the strength of fifty men, the fighting skills of a great warrior, and powerful psychic abilities."

"You shall also possess the immortal ability to defy death. Only another god can harm you. Thus, I must warn you to avoid Hades in every way possible. He is your greatest enemy."

"I've never even seen Hades. How will I know who he is?"

Poseidon answered, "He walks on land under the name of Luke Underwood. We will send you a vision of his likeness so that you'll be aware."

Amphitrite smiled benevolently. "You shall also have the abilities to call on all of us in any moment of need. For with these powers, you will become one of us." Steven was astonished as the three gods stepped forward, and raised their swords in the air.

"Steven Spencer! Will you accept this power, and use it only for good?" Steven answered with a slow, sure nod. Poseidon backed away.

Amphitrite spoke next, "Will you promise to never reveal your powers to any mortal outside your trusted family, or say anything about what took place here today?"

Steven nodded again. "You have my word." Amphitrite and Poseidon rested their swords upon each of his shoulders, while Zeus placed his cutlas blade on the crown of Steven's head.

Zeus then began the ceremony. "Almighty God of all gods, I petition you today to grant immortal powers to our brother Steven Spencer, who we have deemed to be pure in heart. I summon you through the power of the golden swords to infuse your mighty energy into this man's body, so that he may readily be able to protect the ones he loves."

A bolt of light shot through the cave room with the sound of a powerful jet engine, striking the three swords, and sending surges of energy into Steven's body. The impact drove him to his knees, sending spasms through his body. After a few moments, the light quickly left in the same manner that it came, and Steven was left dazed and struggled to stand up. Zeus and Poseidon helped him to his feet, and Amphitrite stepped forward and kissed him on the cheek. "Welcome to our family, Steven." He nodded.

Loraine left for her appointment shortly after Steven had departed the house, while Dr. Grayson waited for Audrey and Heather to arrive. She paced the floor for what seemed like hours trying to gain some insight into how to put her thoughts into words. It was one of the hardest things she ever had to do. When she finally came to a conclusion, it was time for some tea. It would hopefully settle her anxiety. About three sips into her cup, the front door opened, and the spirit bell rang. She hurried out into the foyer to greet the visitors "Audrey! Heather! Please come join me in the sitting room." The two women followed her to the sitting room, and they all sat comfortably close.

"I can't believe Daniel actually committed suicide. I can't help but feel guilty that I may have been partly responsible," Audrey lamented, while Heather stared downward in solemn silence.

Dr. Grayson sighed. "Actually, there's more to the story than you could possibly ever imagine. This may take a while but bear with me. I'll explain it the best I can." Audrey and Heather exchanged a quick, perplexed glance, before turning their full attention to Dr. Grayson.

An hour of intense conversation went by quickly, and the foyer clock announced to all that it was 11:00 a.m. Audrey and Heather were shell-shocked by Dr. Grayson's revelations.

"Everything you've told us sounds so impossible," Audrey stated.

"I assure you, it's all true."

Audrey fumed, "If Lucia were here right now, I'd rip that bitch's face off."

"Remember what I said, Audrey. Lucia is very dangerous, and we need to keep you alive and safe for the sake of Heather and Daniel Jr."

Heather spoke up, struggling to fight back her emotions. "She's right, Mother. We must listen to her." She paused with great emphasis. "And to think Lucia actually saved Deanna and I that night in the warehouse."

Dr. Grayson looked at her with a puzzled expression. "Wait a minute! What warehouse? I thought they made the exchange in a parking lot near the harbor."

Heather looked sheepish. "We promised not to tell anyone, but it took place at an old warehouse that was owned by Branch Consolidated. They've since torn it down."

Dr. Grayson got up and paced with new, enlightened thoughts. "And I would bet anything that those three missing kidnappers are buried beneath the rubble. We must let Steven know about this."

The front door opened, and Loraine wandered into the room, looking rather lost in her thoughts. She brightened up when she saw Audrey and Heather. They both rose to greet her. "Audrey! Heather! It is so good to see you both."

The three women exchanged hugs. "Was everything alright with your doctor's visit? You looked rather troubled when you first walked in."

"Oh yes! Everything is coming along quite well."

"Is it going to be a boy or a girl?" Heather inquired

Loraine sighed. "Actually, it's going to be both. The doctor confirmed that I'm having twins."

All the women expressed surprise and happiness. "Amazing! Little Maggie was right all along. Steven will be so happy," Dr. Grayson announced.

Audrey appeared rather confused. "Who's this Maggie? Heather and Daniel tried to get me caught up on all I've missed, but I'm still quite lost."

Loraine sighed. "Oh, Audrey! So much has happened while you were in convalescence. Perhaps we could get caught up over a cup of hot tea?"

"That would be marvelous."

Loraine turned to Heather and Dr. Grayson. "Would you two ladies like to join us?"

"Sorry! I need to go into town and run a few errands. I'll talk to you later," Heather replied.

Dr. Grayson stated, "I'll have to pass as well. I need to research these books that Steven and Gerard brought up from the tunnels. I'll be sure to catch up with you all later."

Loraine, Audrey, and Heather exited the room, while Dr. Grayson settled behind a small desk, and began paging through one of the books. She suddenly grabbed her arm, winced with pain, then looked upward with simmering anger. "I know it's you that's causing this pain, Lucretia. It will not hinder me."

Inside the cottage, Lucretia stood in deep thought staring out the window. A few minutes later, Tina casually walked in. "Where have you been?"

Tina answered defiantly, "It's a nice day, so I decided to take a walk. Do I have to report to you every time I leave the house?"

Lucretia strolled closer, as she mildly vented her frustration. "We need to get you some new clothes. You must go out tonight, and find me another man."

"I'm not going to do it. I won't have any part of your sick plans."

Lucretia tried to contain her anger. "You will do as I say, or I'll send you back to the display floor at Nordstrom."

"I dare you to go ahead and do it. That will give Poseidon a reason to destroy you."

Lucretia laughed. "He'll never know what happened to you. I'll simply tell him you ran away."

Tina fumed with frustration. "I hate you!" She turned to walk away when she noticed the voodoo doll on the nearby coffee table. She reached over, quickly grabbing the doll, and held the pin inches from the heart. Lucretia froze in panic. "I wish this doll were you. I'd jab this pin right into your heart like this."

"No, Tina! No!" Lucretia lunged for the doll, as Tina planted the pin deep into its heart.

In the sitting room, Dr. Grayson dropped the book she was reading and desperately clutched at her heart in great pain. She managed to stand and stumble a few feet before she collapsed to the floor, holding the crucifix around her neck tightly in the palm of her hand. After a few moments, the music box on the fireplace mantle started to play as the spirits of Maggie and Penelope appeared in the room. They both knelt next to Dr. Grayson's lifeless body.

Maggie lightly shook her arm. "Dr. Grayson! It's time for you to come with us."

Dr. Grayson's spirit left her body, and they all stood together. Penelope smiled benevolently as she took hold of Dr. Grayson's hand. "It's almost time for our afternoon tea, Sheila." Little Maggie took hold of her other hand, as they all walked away and vanished from the room with a loud whoosh.

Lucretia was now in possession of the doll and quickly pulled the pin from its heart. "You stupid little fool! Do you realize what you just did?"

Tina was confused. "What are you talking about?"

She paced toward Tina, shaking the doll at her. "You just killed a Grand White Witch! You killed Dr. Grayson!"

Tina became emotional. "I didn't mean to! I didn't know!"

Lucretia went into a panic. "Maybe she's still alive. Maybe there's something I can still do for her."

Lucretia swiftly headed for the door, but it flew open before she got to it, and the caped figure of Liddy McPherson strolled in, slamming the door behind her. "Going somewhere, Lucretia?"

"Who the hell are you?"

Liddy laughed. "Someone you should know very well. You've been working in my best interests for a very long time." Liddy swiftly pointed her finger toward Tina, and the young woman instantly crumbled to the floor as a dismembered mannequin. "That takes care of that problem. And by the way, it's too late for Dr. Grayson as well. Unfortunately for you, she's dead."

Lucretia looked at the crumpled remains of Tina, then back at Liddy. "Why did you do that? And for the last time, who the hell are you?"

"My dear! I'm Liddy McPherson." Lucretia looked at her with shock, as simultaneously there was another loud knock at the door. Both women glanced that way, then back at each other. "I must go. But we will talk later." Liddy vanished in a cloud of purple smoke. Lucretia opened the door to find Poseidon there, in the guise of Philip Seagraves.

He immediately forged ahead into the room and looked around. "Where's Tina? I must talk to her."

Before she could answer him, Philip saw her dismembered remains and rushed to them. He cradled her fiberglass head and looked into her deep blue marble eyes that stared blankly back at him. "Lucretia! What have you done?"

She answered with frustration, "It wasn't me! It was Liddy McPherson!"

"You're a liar!"

"No Philip! She was just here. She disappeared when you knocked on the door." She shook her head with despair and continued. "Believe me! I'm just as sad as you are. Tina was my creation."

Philip looked to her with renewed energy. "Then you have the power to restore her to what she was."

"No! It was Liddy's power that destroyed her, and there is no way that I can reverse it." Philip looked around the room for a moment, then pulled a tablecloth from the nearby dining table, sending placements flying and crashing to the floor. "What are you doing?"

"I'm taking her with me." He grabbed the pieces and rolled them in the cloth.

"Oh, Poseidon! I'm so sorry this happened."

Philip answered with a hardened stare as he departed, "I assure you, Liddy will pay for this, and so will you." Lucretia reacted with much anxiety.

The buzz of conversation filled the crowded hall of the SOS Club as the meeting proceeded on this first night of the full moon. Hades, under the guise of Luke Underwood, confidently walked to center stage. He motioned with his hands for the assembly to be quiet before he spoke. "My brothers and sisters of the Secret Society, I welcome you to our monthly meeting. My name is Lucas Underwood, and I have been sent by special order of our Master." He paused with overbearing emphasis. "It's with a heavy heart that I tell you what many already know. Your leader, the Rev. James Hightower, has tragically, and unexpectedly passed away." The crowd erupted into further loud whispers before he continued. "On a brighter note, from this night on you will have a new leader and that leader…" He smiled. "Shall be me."

A roar of dissent erupted in the audience. One of the elder gentlemen of the assembly stood up and pointed to him. "You can't appoint yourself leader without the assembly's vote. We don't even know who you are." Without a reply, Luke pointed two fingers in his direction, and the man immediately fell to the floor.

The assembly grew quiet as another man in the crowd hurried to his aid. A few seconds later he looked up soberly. "He's dead!"

Luke glanced around the room. "Are there any other members of the assembly that object?"

The room went dead silent, as a flash of elation spread across Luke's face. In the corner of the room sat a concealed figure adjacent to Luke. Liddy glanced around with a sober expression, almost giddy, and begging someone else to object. Then her expression turned to a belligerent smirk as she sauntered from the room.

Suzy swiftly made her way into the Mermaid Inn to meet Jeff. He was waiting patiently inside the door for her to arrive. The two affectionately embraced each other. "I'm sorry I'm a little late," Suzy stated with slight embarrassment.

Jeff smiled and nodded in reply. "You were definitely worth the wait."

She took his hand as the hostess escorted them to a table.

Their love truly blossomed during the course of the meal, and now they sat gazing into each other's eyes. "I can't begin to tell you how much I enjoy being with you," Jeff stated.

"Oh, Jeff! I feel the same way." She looked out the window at the darkening skies over the Atlantic. "The sun's already down, but perhaps we could take a moonlight stroll along the waterfront." Jeff nervously looked out the window, and Suzie noticed. "Is everything alright?"

"Yes! I just tend to get a little anxious when there's a full moon. I don't really know what causes it."

Suzie smiled. "If you're ready for that walk, let's do it." Jeff nodded. A few seconds later as he began to stand, an extreme pain shot through his abdomen, causing him to buckle over in pain. "Jeff! What's wrong?"

Jeff began breathing heavily, and his body began to spasm. "Whatever happens to me, just know that Lucretia Darknight was responsible."

Suzie blurted out, "Lucretia Darknight?" Jeff immediately ran from the table and into the men's room without a further word. Two men sitting nearby followed to help but found the door was locked. After a few seconds, the door blasted open, and off its hinges. The transformed werewolf ran to the center of the dining room, growling ferociously, while patrons ran in all directions. A horrified Suzie screamed and ran as well.

The owner, Bob Hartley, entered the chaotic scene with a shotgun. As the werewolf turned and charged, Bob shot at it. The bullet grazed its shoulder, sending it into a whimpering retreat. The werewolf then leaped through the large plate glass window and disappeared into the darkness outside.

Back at Branchview, the family was reeling over another tragic death. It had come to the point where no one knew who might be next. Steven, Loraine, Audrey, Heather, and Mrs. Porter sat horrified as they attempted to comfort each other.

"Did Dr. Grayson say anything significant before she passed?"

Mrs. Porter emotionally shook her head. "She was already dead when I found her."

Steven sighed. "I should've been here. I had a terrible premonition that something else was going to happen."

"Oh, Steven! Don't be so hard on yourself. You had so many things to do today. You couldn't be in two places at one time."

Heather spoke up, "She's right, Uncle Steven. The coroner said that Dr. Grayson died of a heart attack. There wasn't anything that any of us could do."

Audrey spoke with pent-up anger. "I don't believe that for a minute, Heather. I think that bitch Lucia Darknight is responsible."

Steven spoke up again, "I'm afraid I'd have to agree with you on that, Audrey."

"Have any of Dr. Grayson's relatives been notified?" Audrey replied.

Loraine replied, "She never married, and from what I understand, she had no surviving family at all."

Steven shook his head defiantly. "She was one of us. We were her family. And for that reason, she'll get a proper burial in the Branch family cemetery."

Audrey replied, "I most certainly support you on that, Steven."

Steven stood up and took a deep breath before speaking. "Now, on to other issues." He looked at each of the women. "Audrey, Heather! After the two funerals, I'll make arrangements for both of you, and Daniel Jr to stay with a friend of mine in Canada. I can't take the chance of anything happening to you." He turned around. "Mrs. Porter! You've taken care of me since I was a child. You'll be going with them." He looked to Loraine next. "Lori! I love you and our unborn children more than anything. Regretfully, I must send you away as well."

Loraine jumped up from her seat emotionally. "I absolutely object. I love you as well Steven, and I will never leave your side. We're in this marriage for better or for worse."

Steven couldn't help but be amused, and Heather visibly swooned at the romantic drama of it all. "I thought you might say that. So, I notified your mother, and asked her to come to the States to care for you during your pregnancy."

"Steven! Not my mother! I won't have any part in that!"

"I'm afraid it's too late, sweetheart. Her flight from England arrives tomorrow afternoon in Boston."

Loraine plopped back down in her seat and pouted, while Mrs. Porter timidly raised her hand to talk. "I have to ask that you would let me stay as well, Steven. I can't bear the thought of leaving you and Lori here to fend for yourselves."

Steven smiled warmly. "Very well, Mrs. Porter. You can stay if you wish." He paused, "Whatever staff hasn't quit already, I'll relieve them of their duties. We can't afford to involve innocent lives in all this."

Loraine sighed emotionally. "I know it sounds dismal, but we shall get through this. The Branch family will survive." Lori's words left everyone feeling rejuvenated after their terrible ordeals.

The next day, as the happenings of the previous night, spread throughout the small community, the morning sun streamed into the living room of the cottage. Loud, demanding knocks on the front door interrupted the silence. "Lucretia, I know you're in there…" Jeff forcibly entered, looking battle-worn, with his clothes all tattered and bloodied. "Lucretia! If you're here, I'm going to tear you apart with my bare hands."

He waited for an answer, but all was silent. He winced and grabbed his shoulder where the shotgun had blasted him. As he glanced around the room, Jeff noticed the hidden door behind the bookcase was partially open. He pulled it open and stumbled down the stairs to the basement. When he reached the bottom, he called out again. "Is anybody down here?" There was still no answer.

He set his eyes on the two large steel doors that lead to another part of the basement. *Oh, what the hell...* Jeff grabbed at the doors and was startled when a droning chant echoed across the room. He flung the doors open anyway.

The room was littered with several candles and Satanic artifacts. But the biggest surprise came when he noticed the large pentagram in the center of the floor. He wiped the sweat from his brow and commented to himself, *God, it's hot down here...* In the distance, he heard the same chants once again. At one end of the room, a solid steel door seemed to beckon his curiosity. As Jeff moved closer, the silence was broken by the sudden sound of dogs barking wildly on the other side. He quickly backed away. "So much for that idea." He then turned, noticing a dry rotted, wooden door on the adjacent side of the room. He curiously walked over and pulled it open with a difficult tug. The stench nearly made him vomit. *Whew! It stinks in here. Must be some sort of a root cellar.* Then, the chanting started again. *What in the hell is that?* Jeff remembered he had a lighter in his pocket. *Oh yeah, some light-*

As he stepped further into the room, he heard a creaking sound to his right and whirled around to look. He was shocked to see a decomposing body hanging by a rope, just inches from his face. He jumped back, screaming in fear, and fell against something on the floor. He turned and flicked his lighter once again to find he was laying amongst a pile of decomposing skeletons. The sight instantly made his blood run cold, and in a panic, he attempted to flee the room. But there within the doorway, he was met face to face with a dark, hooded figure, and the growls of three vicious Hell Hounds. Jeff's final screams echoed throughout the basement but were unheard by any living soul.

It was a dark, rainy day on the grounds of Branchview, as two more Branch family members were laid to rest in the family plot. No one could fathom what fate had in store for the rest of the living members, as winter faded and the warming rays of spring lay ahead. One could only hope that along with the warmer breezes that would soon blow ashore from the Atlantic, a touch of good fortune would arrive and lift the curse that had menaced the estate for far too long.

A small gathering, beneath black umbrellas, huddled together alongside the two caskets at the Branch Family Cemetery. The minister was barely audible through the pouring rain, as he proceeded with the eulogies for

Daniel Branch III and Dr. Shelia Grayson. The scene had become all too familiar as the surviving members struggled to regain some sense of the chaos that was wreaking havoc on their lives.

As the minister concluded his sermon, the crowd dispersed, and Gerard held back along with Steven. He elevated his voice to be heard above the pounding rainstorm. "I wish the weather could've been more cooperative. I think it would've given us all a bit more optimism."

Steven glanced upward and forced a smile. "Have you and Sharie decided as to whether you're going to stay or not?"

"It was a unanimous decision. We could never leave you and Lori to fight this on your own. Besides, we can't imagine living anywhere else but Branchview."

Steven looked relieved. "I had a vision of Hades last night, and he was standing outside the house watching it. So, I got up early this morning, and placed the crosses at each entrance just as a precaution."

"Crosses or not, I don't know how we can stand a chance against him."

"Don't worry, Gerard! The gods will help us." Gerard answered with a worried nod. "Let's finish this conversation inside over a hot cup of coffee."

The members of the funeral congregation fled to the warm embrace of the main house, away from the wicked spring thunderstorm that was pounding the East Coast.

Lucretia rested comfortably in her cottage, warm and dry in front of the fireplace, and lost in deep thought. Liddy unexpectedly appeared from a darkened corner. "You look very worried, Lucretia."

She turned around, quite startled. "Don't you believe in knocking?"

Liddy confidently strolled around to confront her. "Why should I, when I have the power to appear or disappear at will?"

Liddy sat down uninvited in a seat across from Lucretia, looking very comfortable, while Lucretia grew increasingly annoyed. "Why did you have to come back anyway? I had everything under control."

Liddy laughed. "You have the swords of justice pointing at you from every direction, you've killed a Grand

White Witch, drawn the ire of the gods, and have a werewolf terrorizing the town. I'd hardly say that's having things under control."

"I lifted the spell on that werewolf months ago. I have no idea what could've brought him back."

Liddy turned away with a petty smirk. "I have no idea either. But, to answer your original question, I came back to help you, my dear."

She whirled around, while Lucretia said angrily, "So, destroying my servant is a way of helping me?"

"Oh, Lucia! She only would've complicated matters even more. Her mind was becoming far too independent. Besides, I have the power to bring life force to you without the need of killing any more men." Lucretia sat up and listened with renewed attentiveness. "When we've accomplished our goals, I can help your spirit to permanently assume the body of what will soon be the late Kristin Wiler. Then we shall rule the Branchview empire together."

"We? How do you figure into all of this?"

Liddy smiled. "The day after tomorrow, the Board of Directors at Branch Consolidated will vote on a new CEO and President."

"I know. Gerard LeRoux will probably be the obvious choice. Then I'll have to eliminate him as well."

Liddy flipped her head toward her. "No need, my dear! Trust me! Gerard will be asked to step down by the Board, and you shall be voted into that position. He won't even be a bump in the road for us."

Lucretia reacted with surprise. "What makes you so sure of that?"

Liddy stood up. "Oh! I'm very sure of that, Lucretia. Because I have devised a guaranteed plan that will enable me to be your Vice President of Operations. We will reclaim what was taken from us all those years ago." Lucretia found a sense of renewed hope with the explanation of Liddy's plans.

The family made their way back inside the main house, warming themselves with hot coffee to stave off hypothermia. Steven spoke up, "We must try to figure out what Lucia's next move will be."

Gerard replied, "We need much luck on that one. It's nearly an impossible task."

"I can't quite understand how she was able to convince the Board to fire Daniel," Loraine answered.

"What's equally puzzling is why they didn't fire me as well."

Steven stood up and paced in deep thought. "I think they still intend to do that. Just out of curiosity, what was the name of the secretary of the Board?"

"Marshall Hempfield. Why?"

Steven strode over to the desk and retrieved one of the SOS Club directories. He tapped his finger on the page and displayed an expression of enlightenment. "He's a member of the Secret Society." He strolled closer with an open book in hand. "How about the company stockbroker you were telling me about?"

"Bernstein! Charles Bernstein!" Loraine listened intently.

Steven scrolled down through the names with his finger. "He's in here too." He handed the book to Gerard.

"I want you to scan through those names, and tell me if there's anyone else from the Board that's listed—"

Gerard carefully checked out the names, and after a few seconds, looked up with astonishment. "At least half the Board members are listed---" He was interrupted by a knock on the door.

"Stay there… I'll get that." Loraine left the room.

"Now we know for sure who's behind the takeover. But how does Lucia fit into all of this? She doesn't appear to even be a member of the Society."

"Maybe someone's using her to get what they want."

Steven replied, "We have a couple of days before the Board meeting. If we can't figure this out, you know what happens?" Gerard nodded. "Let me think it over."

Loraine reentered with a very anxious Suzy McVea. "Steven! Miss McVea would like to have a word with you, if possible."

"It's very important, Mr. Spencer."

Steven motioned for her to enter. "By all means! Come on in, and have a seat."

"I'll go make a fresh pot of coffee," Loraine announced as she left the room.

As Suzy nervously settled into a seat, Steven sat down opposite her. "What's on your mind, Suzy?"

She responded with much apprehension. "First off, I'd like to express my deepest sympathies for the loss of Mr. Branch and Dr. Grayson. I know they'll be greatly missed."

"Thank you! We appreciate that." Gerard agreed.

Suzy continued, "You might not know this, but Jeff Manus and I recently started dating."

"That's great! You make a very handsome couple."

Suzy began to tremble and cry. "Oh, Mr. Spencer! You must not have heard the news. Jeff is the werewolf! I was with him last night at The Mermaid when he transformed into that terrible beast."

Steven and Gerard exchanged expressions of surprise. "I heard that Bob Hartley shot him. Do you know where Jeff might be right now?"

Suzy emotionally shook her head no. "The police have been out looking for him all night." She buried her head in her hands. "I'm afraid he might be out there somewhere, bleeding to death."

Steven took hold of her hand. "Don't worry! They'll find him."

"I have to ask you about something he said just before he ran away and transformed. It has me very confused."

Gerard replied, "What did he say?"

"He wanted me to know that Lucretia Darknight was responsible for whatever was going to happen to him. Do you have any idea what he might've meant?" Steven and Gerard shared a long glance. The answer was obvious to them.

In the backroom of the SOS Club, Luke Underwood casually strolled in, as Liddy paced nervously. Hades demanded, "Liddy! What could be so important that you'd call me on such short notice?"

"Quite a bit! We have a big problem!" Luke motioned for her to continue. "The secretary contacted me earlier today and said that when she tried to enter the new club members into the directory, it was missing, along with four other directory books from the last one hundred years."

"Perhaps someone in the Society borrowed them."

Liddy shook her head. "It's forbidden to remove those directories from the premises. If they were to fall into the wrong hands, it could spell trouble for us all."

Luke paced in thought. "Obviously, someone broke the rules. There's no possible way that anyone other than the hierarchy of the Society could gain access to this building."

Liddy paced in deep thought and then paused. "There might be one way."

She walked to the center of the room and pulled an area rug back to reveal the hidden door to the tunnels. Hades proclaimed, "How did you know that was there?"

"I'd almost forgotten. Years ago, in my other lifetime, the Society smuggled liquor through the tunnels and hid it in this back room. That hatch hasn't been used in years."

"Do you suppose someone gained access through it?"

Liddy shrugged anxiously. "As far as I know, most of the old entryways have been sealed for quite some time."

"But you and I both know that there are still access points beneath the Branch estate?"

"Yes, true! But how would someone ever find their way through the maze of tunnels and know exactly where to find the secret entrance to this place?"

Luke pondered the question for a moment. "Perhaps they had some help. I'm sure you heard the legend about the slaves who stumbled upon my portal."

"Yes! Only one escaped, and ironically enough, he was a relative of Gerard LeRoux."

Luke responded with a confident nod. "And I would not doubt that his spirit still lingers in those tunnels from time to time."

Liddy said, "All I know is that we need to find who has those directories and get them back. The question is, where do we start?"

Luke answered with a clever grin, "Perhaps we should start with Gerard LeRoux."

In the FBI New Haven office, Adam Smith was working feverishly on trying to solve his cases, when Steven strolled into his office. "Mr. Spencer! Please tell me you don't have another disaster to report."

Steven looked perplexed and sat down. "On the contrary. I have some information that might be helpful, Agent Smith."

The statement caught Adam's attention. "Mr. Spencer... I'm not sure anything you have to tell me could solve this pile of unsolved cases on my desk. I have the skeletal remains of a U.S. Senator, his bodyguard, a U.S. Congresswoman, and a televangelist in my crime lab, and my people are baffled as to what type of creature, or creatures, may have consumed their flesh." He stood up with much nervous energy. "I also have a crisis in Lockeport, with a werewolf running loose, and a backlog of unsolved crimes, mysterious deaths, and disappearances going back nearly a year." He leaned over his desk with urgency. "Now I beg you, Mr. Spencer. Please give me something that will truly be helpful."

Steven calmly replied, "What if I told you that most of those cases on your desk are related?"

Adam sat back down with renewed interest. "If I was speaking with a sane mind, I'd accuse you of being on a bad acid trip. But considering the bizarre circumstances of these cases, I'm willing to listen."

Steven leaned into the conversation. "The three kidnappers you've been trying to find are most likely buried where an old warehouse once stood, on Water Street in Lockeport."

Adam looked at him suspiciously. "How do you know that?"

"I'll answer that in a minute. But first, I want you to go to the missing person's website on your desktop." After giving Steven a long, calculating glare, Adam began the process. "Enter the name, Kristin Wiler...."

Adam shrugged defiantly but types the name anyway. After a few moments of searching, he was thunderstruck by the results. He looked at Steven, and then back to the computer. "That's Lucretia Darknight!"

Steven gave a definite nod. "They're one and the same."

Adam leaned back in his chair, totally flabbergasted. "How can that be? Why would Kristen Wiler simply walk away from a seemingly perfect life, and take on an entirely different persona?"

Steven sighed. "She wouldn't. At least not willingly. I'll explain everything to you if you promise that you won't do anything drastic. This whole scenario is much deeper and darker than you could ever imagine."

Adam replied, "I'll make that judgment after you tell me everything in detail."

Steven glanced at a nearby coffee maker, and then at the clock above it. "Okay! But you better put a pot of coffee on. This might take a while. And who knows, you might even need something stronger than coffee by the time I'm done." Adam looked suspicious but interested.

Meanwhile, a limo pulled up in front of the Branchview main house. The driver paused to put the car in park, then got out to open the door for his passenger. "Ma'am," he held out his hand.

"Thank you… bring my bags, will you Peter?"

"Yes, right away, ma'am."

Mildred Sandstorm, an attractive, impeccably dressed woman in her mid-sixties, wearing white gloves and a floppy brimmed hat to match, got out of the car and then made her way to the entrance of Branchview. Her driver followed close behind with six large suitcases on a fold-down cart, while Millie marched ahead with her carry-on bag.

She spied the immaculately manicured lawn as she took hold of the large lion's head knocker. Loraine had witnessed the limo's arrival from the large window in the sitting room. The idea of hurrying to greet her mother was a less than enthusiastic thought. She opened the door with a rather icy welcome. "Hello, Mother…."

Millie responded with a flamboyant British accent. "Loraine! Darling! It is so wonderful to see you again." She strolled closer, and gave her daughter a rather formal peck on the cheek, then gently placed her hand over her pregnant belly. "I just have to say hello to my marvelous grandbabies as well. Tell me! Are they kicking yet?"

Loraine belligerently tolerated her mother's actions. "Most certainly! I must say that they're quite an overactive duo. They're very blatant in reminding me of that on at least three occasions each night, while I'm desperately trying to sleep."

Peter, the chauffeur interrupted. "Excuse me! Is there a room that you'd like me to take Ms. Sandstrom's luggage?"

"Yes! If you go to the top of the stairs and take the door to your right, her room shall be the first one on the left."

He nodded and began his task, but Millie spoke up. "One more thing, Peter."

She dug deep in her purse to pull out his tip. "I know you've already been paid, but here's an extra hundred for making the last leg of my trip a most enjoyable experience."

The chauffeur looked down at the large bill with wide-eyed surprise. "That's very generous of you. Thank you, Ms. Sandstrom." As he lugged the bags up the stairs, Millie watched and commented, "Oh, if I were only in my 20s. I do miss the joys of flirting with handsome young men."

Loraine sighed. "I know you must very travel-weary, Mother. Please do come into the sitting room, and we can get caught up on things."

Millie glanced at the large grandfather clock that displayed 3:45 p.m. "Oh, dear! It's way past my tea time. You do still practice that tradition, don't you?"

"Of course, I do! I've already had mine, but I shall have Mrs. Porter prepare a cup for you as well."

"That would be absolutely marvelous!" She glanced upward at the high ceilings of the foyer with an expression of content pleasure.

Across the grounds, a nervous Lucretia paced the floor; and was caught off guard when someone knocked on the door. *This place is turning into Grand Central Station.* Lucretia strolled over, opened the door, and narrowed her eyes in anger when she saw her visitor's face. "What do you want?"

Steven stormed in past her. "You and I need to have a little talk, Lucia."

She said smugly, "Indeed! I imagine your love life is rather boring with a pregnant wife."

Steven responded venomously, "Don't insult my intelligence. It's been a long day, and my patience is wearing rather thin."

"Oooh! I like it when you get aggressive."

"I want you to tell me what Liddy McPherson and Hades have planned."

She turned away and defiantly answered, "I have no idea what you're talking about."

Steven sighed. "Lucia! Are you aware that Liddy killed your grandmother, her children, your grandfather, and all the Branch's that died during the same time period?"

"You lie, just like the rest of the Branch's. My father would've told me if that was true."

Steven chuckled. "Well! Hello, Charlotte! I figured I'd get you to surface sooner or later."

Lucretia grew sheepish. "So! You're aware of who I really am?"

Steven nodded. "I'm also aware that Liddy lied to your father, that lie was passed to you, and you've been laying the groundwork for her return ever since."

Lucretia sat down and pondered. "None of that's true. Daniel Branch the first killed all those people, including Liddy, and his son killed me."

"The walls are closing in, Lucia. Liddy will destroy you just as she did the others. You can't trust her." She only replied by looking away in defiance. "Why don't you just let Kristin Wiler go? She has nothing to do with all this."

"I might consider that once I'm finished with her, but certainly not any sooner."

Steven pointed at her. "I'm warning you! If anything happens to Gerard, Kristin, or any of my family, you will pay the consequences."

Lucretia jumped from her seat. "How dare you threaten me!" She raised her hand to strike at Steven, but he deflected her energy back at her, sending her reeling hard against a wall. She slumped to the floor and looked at him, rather dazed. "Who the hell are you, Steven Spencer? You're not human!"

Steven answered in a matter-of-fact tone. "Oh, I'm human alright! You just underestimated my acquired skills."

Lucretia looked beyond him with a look of dread as the shadows of justice appeared, wielding their swords. "No! Not the shadows! Make them go away!"

Steven looked behind him but was rather puzzled when he saw nothing there. "I guess I'll leave you to your demons, Lucia. Have a pleasant evening." Hunkering down in a corner, Lucretia was horrified by the fact that she had just been bested by a human. She also pondered the validity of her conversation with Steven.

In the Branchview sitting room, Millie and Loraine continued to converse over current events, while Millie sipped her tea. "How is your tea, Mother?"

She set her cup down on the table. "I'm pleased that it's black tea, but it's definitely not Tetley's." Loraine rolled her eyes and forced a fake smile as her mother continued to ramble. "Where on earth is that handsome husband of yours?"

"Steven had business up in New Haven this afternoon. He should be back quite soon."

Millie flashed a curious grin at her daughter. "Are you certain it was business?"

"Oh, Mother! Let's not start with that again. I have full trust that my husband will always be faithful."

Millie leaned back in her chair. "We shall see! Just remember, I always warned you against marrying a handsome man. You saw how things went with your father."

"My father was a philandering fool. Steven isn't like that. If I hadn't allowed you to influence me, I would've married him long before now." Millie looked away with indifference. "By the way, how is my father? I wrote to him about the wedding, but never got an answer."

Millie chuckled. "He's far too busy with his latest tramp. He managed to rob the cradle this time. She's nearly forty years his junior."

They heard someone coming in the door, and Steven strode into the sitting room a few seconds later. "Millie! I'm so glad you're here."

Millie stood up and greeted him with a kiss on both cheeks. "It's such a pleasure to see you as well, Steven."

"I certainly hope your flight was enjoyable?"

"The journey was absolutely marvelous! If you'd be kind enough to take a stroll with me in the garden, I'll tell you all about it?"

"Very well! I could use a good walk."

He exchanged a fleeting glance with Loraine as they sauntered from the room, arm in arm. Loraine rolled her eyes and commented to herself. *Good Heavens! I think I'm going to be dreadfully sick.* Loraine decided after that encounter, it was time for another spot of tea.

In the secret hidden cave, Poseidon was seated on the crystal throne, devastated by the loss of his beloved Tina. Her dismembered remains lay in a box nearby. Zeus appeared from the shadows and approached. "Have you heard any news?"

"I'm still waiting for Steven Spencer to get back to me."

Zeus glanced at the box. "What do you plan to do with her remains?"

He shrugged. "I can't bring myself to dispose of them. I pray every day that the parts will somehow come together, and she'll live again."

"You truly did love her, didn't you?" Poseidon glanced up at him and nodded sadly. Zeus placed a reassuring hand on his shoulder and smiled. "Perhaps one day your prayers will be answered."

In the center of Lockport City Park, Tony Freeman (Triton), and Andrea Hill happily strolled along, hand in hand, on a pleasant late spring evening. "I love this time of year. The air is filled with the smell of blooming flowers, and you just know that warm summer nights will be here soon," said Andrea.

"I agree. What better time would there be to say what I have to say?"

Andrea giggled. "What do you have to say to me?"

Tony pulled a small box from his pocket, went to one knee, and popped the box open to reveal a diamond ring. "I love you, Andrea Hill. Will you be my wife?"

Andrea was flabbergasted, Tony... wow this is a surprise...." She paused. "Oh, Tony! Yes! Yes, I will!"

Tony smiled, ready to respond when an imposing vision appeared from out of the darkness. "What a pity that the wedding will never happen." Andrea and Tony looked up at the intimidating figure of Hades, clad in black and holding his two-pronged staff.

"Hades! I warned you to not interfere. I will report this to Zeus, as well as my father."

Andrea listened to the exchange but was baffled. "I'm afraid you won't have the chance to do that, Triton."

In one swift move, he twirled his staff and impaled Tony. Andrea screamed and immediately rushed to his aid. "You killed him!" she yelled.

Hades laughed as he pulled his staff from Tony's body. The ring box tumbled from his partially clenched hand. "Yes, my dear Andrea. Triton, son of Poseidon and Amphitrite, has now ceased to exist."

"What are you talking about? His name is Tony. You have the wrong person." Tony's dead body suddenly illuminated and vaporized into thin air, leaving Andrea even more hysterical. "Where did he go? What have you done?"

Hades chuckled as he looked toward the night sky. "He's off on a journey to that mythical island where warriors find eternal rest. I would imagine that his spirit is just off the shores of Avalon right about now. Never to return."

"You must be out of your mind—"

"Oh, my dear! I assure you; I am quite sane. Come along! You and I have so very much to talk about."

Andrea shook her head and trembled with fear. "You must be crazy if you think I'm going anywhere with you." She turned to run away, but Hades flicked his wrist and caused her body to be immobile.

Then he waved his hand in front of her face, and she immediately fell into a hypnotic trance. "You will go with me, my sweet Andrea, and I will give you everything your heart desires." The two strolled off into the darkness.

Chapter Fifteen:

The Lines of Good and Evil

A new day began in the quaint town of Lockeport. Despite all the bizarre happenings of the past few days, all appeared normal on the surface, but in reality, change was coming hard and fast for the citizens of this close-knit community. Especially for the inhabitants of Branchview. Today would be the beginning of a long struggle, where the battle lines were drawn between good and evil, one where each side put in place a strategy that would either succeed or fail.

Inside the City Diner, Philip and Steven sat and conversed over early morning breakfast. Suzy McVea hustled about, stopping by to refill their coffee. "I was hoping you'd make it over to our table. Any word on Jeff?" Steven asked.

Suzy shook her head in distress. "It's like he disappeared off the face of the earth." She sighed and quickly scooted into the booth next to Steven. "Something…" she whispered. "Something else has happened that's just as strange. My friend Andrea never made it home from a date last night."

Steven jumped in, "Maybe she's still with her boyfriend. Who is he?"

"Oh! His name is Tony Freeman. They've been seeing each other for nearly a month." Philip's eyes grew wide with interest as he listened. "It's highly unlike Andrea to go anywhere without telling someone. I'm very worried about her."

"I'll be meeting with Agent Smith from the state FBI office today. I'll mention this to him."

Suzy gratefully placed her hand over Steven's hand, and nervously looked toward a customer who was trying to get her attention. "Thank you, Mr. Spencer! I have to run!"

As she left, Philip quickly leaned closer. "Steven! This Tony Freeman she speaks of is my son Triton." Steven was astounded by the revelation. "I knew he was seeing a woman on land, but I believe this Andrea might be the same girl that Hades is interested in."

Steven rolled his eyes. "This does not sound good at all."

Philip stood up with urgency. "I must go speak with Zeus and Amphitrite about this."

"Go ahead! I'll see what I can find out on my end as well." Philip departed with an assured nod.

Gerard arrived early at Branch Consolidated, trying to keep a routine amidst all the chaos. Just after he sat down and began working on some documents someone knocked on his office door. "Come on in! The doors open!"

Marshall Hempfield sheepishly slunk into the room. "Do you have a few minutes?"

"Sure! Have a seat." Hempfield sat down and drew a deep breath. "What's on your mind?"

"Well, sir... I'll get straight to the point. I know you were expecting to fill the vacancy left by Mr. Branch, but the Board has decided to take the leadership in a different direction."

Gerard nodded. "I see!"

Hempfield continued nervously. "We've put together a very generous buy-out package that would enable you to either retire or possibly offer you the opportunity to seek a similar position elsewhere. Either way, you'll be a very wealthy man."

"I suppose I don't have much of a choice in the matter. You will at least give me the option to look over the package ahead of time?"

"Of course, Gerard. I can have it on your desk before lunch, but we'll need you to sign off on it before the end of the day."

"No problem!" Gerard replied.

Hempfield stood up and leaned over the desk to shake his hand, and Gerard was slow to accept it. "It was a pleasure working with you, and I wish you the best in your future endeavors," Gerard answered with a nod of thanks, then sunk back comfortably into his plush chair as Hempfield left the room.

Poseidon moved swiftly to call on Zeus and Amphitrite. They both must have sensed the urgency, and by the time he reached the cave, they were waiting on him. Amphitrite sat poised, eager to hear the updates. "Were you able to contact Triton?" Poseidon asked.

"I tried, but I got no answer. That's highly unusual."

Poseidon sat down on a step near Amphitrite. "I just learned that Andrea Hill is missing and that she and Triton have been seeing each other. My senses tell me that Hades could very well be involved in all of this."

"Yes! Ms. Hill was an object of interest for him as well," Zeus added.

Poseidon then turned to Zeus. "If Hades has harmed Triton, I will break him in two with my bare hands."

Zeus gave him a friendly pat on the shoulder. "You need to keep a cool head, Poseidon. You two are equally matched, and you know as well as I do that it would be a fight to the death."

"He's right! You'll have your day with Hades, but now isn't the right time," Amphitrite said.

Zeus continued to pace in deep thought, then turned. "Amphitrite! Perhaps you could use your psychic powers to locate Andrea Hill."

Poseidon looked toward her with renewed hope. "That's an excellent idea. If you can locate her, perhaps we can find Triton as well."

"I've only seen Andrea one time at a distance, and I'm not quite sure I can connect to her energy, but I'll certainly try." Amphitrite closed her eyes and began weaving in a trance. "I call upon the life energy of Andrea Hill. If you can hear my voice, please contact me, and show me where you are." She was silent for a moment, as Zeus and Poseidon waited with anticipation. "I see a house on a shaded street. A beautiful Victorian-style house with a wraparound porch, and a round turret on each side."

Zeus inquired, "Is this house in Lockeport?"

Amphitrite answered with a nod and continued. "I'm entering the house. Now I'm walking up the stairs, and I'm being drawn to a room. It's one of the turret rooms."

"Is Andrea there?" Zeus asked.

Amphitrite nodded again. "Her energy is very strong. I can feel great fear in her being."

"Is Triton there with her?" Poseidon asked.

She emotionally shook her head no. "I'm not picking up on his energy at all."

Zeus asked, "Can you enter the room?"

"The door is locked, but my energy can walk through it." She concentrated hard for a moment. "She's sitting at the edge of a bed, and is very scared." The room got silent. "Wait…. Someone's coming! I must go quickly."

Amphitrite nearly fainted, and the two gods helped to catch her fall. "Who else was in that house? Was it Hades?" Zeus inquired.

"All that I know is that it was someone powerful enough to sense my presence."

Poseidon said angrily, "Only Hades would have the power to know she was there."

"We have to find this house and rescue that girl. I shudder to think what evil plans he might have for her," Zeus proclaimed with great concern.

Amphitrite said, "I know for sure that it's an upscale area near downtown. Perhaps if I walked around, I might be able to find it."

Zeus spoke out with authority, "Not without one of us. Hades wouldn't think twice about killing you."

Poseidon took hold of her hand and squeezed it gently. "I shall go with you. I know we've been apart for quite some time, but I could never bear the thought of losing you." Amphitrite smiled. She knew that down deep within, he still harbored a strong love for her.

Steven headed back to Branchview from the City Diner, very distraught over the newest revelation. He swiftly entered the house, looking for Loraine, but she was already entering the foyer to greet him. After a quick kiss, she informed him, "Agent Smith just arrived a short time ago. He's waiting for you in the sitting room."

"Great! Are Audrey, Heather, and Daniel in there as well?"

"No. They're still upstairs getting ready. I'll go check on them." Loraine went up the stairs, while Steven headed for the sitting room where he greeted Agent Smith. "Were you able to get everything lined up?"

"Yes, everything's all set. They have new identities, passports, and they'll be traveling with two agents that I know quite well and can trust."

They both sat down. "Are you sure that nobody will be able to trace them down?"

Adam leaned forward in his chair. "The only people outside of us that know about this is your friend Mr. Sinclair, and the two agents."

Steven replied with a worried expression, "We just have to make sure it stays that way."

Adam motioned toward the directories on the desk. "Your wife showed me those directories. I recognized quite a few names in there."

Steven said with a matter-of-fact expression, "It's frightening to know that this is only a regional chapter of a much bigger network. I can't even imagine how deep this all goes."

Adam replied, "I know. I'd like to get a snapshot of those pages with my phone before I leave. We need to study who our enemies are."

Loraine reentered the room with Audrey, Heather, and Daniel Jr, and the two men stood to greet them. Steven turned to Adam. "I know you're familiar with Heather. This is her mother Audrey, and her brother Daniel."

"It's a pleasure to meet you both."

He motioned to the pre-arranged chairs. "If you'd all have a seat, I'll go over everything with you." Everyone took a seat, while Adam retrieved three small booklets, and handed them to the two women and Daniel. "These are your passports, and new identities. Audrey, you'll now be known as Bonnie Lewis, Heather, and Daniel, you'll now be known as LeAnn and David Lewis. From this moment on you should never address each other by your real names. Am I clear on that?" All three nodded seriously, as Adam continued, "My agents will deliver you to a man they only know as Mr. Q, who will be waiting in Niagara on the Lake, just over the Canadian border. In reality, Mr. Q will be Alton Sinclair, but you are to never mention that name to either agent."

Steven picked up the conversation. "From there, Mr. Sinclair will take you to his estate in Guelph, Ontario. He'll provide you with anything you need."

Daniel jumped out of his seat and emotionally hugged Steven. "I'm scared, Uncle Steven. Will we ever be able to come home again?"

Steven held the boy firmly at arm's length. "I promise you, Daniel. I'll do everything in my power to make that happen."

Adam offered an extra nod of assurance to the boy. "Okay! Gather your belongings, say your goodbyes, and my agents will be here to get you at 2:00 sharp."

Audrey jumped in, "Thank you so much, Agent Smith."

Heather chimed in, "Yes! We are so grateful for your help."

Everyone stood; Audrey and Heather both gave Steven and Loraine emotional hugs.

Audrey explained, "We're so happy to have both of you in our lives. I pray that we'll see you again." Loraine slipped her arm around Steven and pulled him close, as the trio left the room.

Adam smiled at Steven and Loraine. "I'll snap those pictures and get going so you can have a bit of family time before my agents show up." Adam pulled out his iPhone and quickly took shots of each page, as Steven strolled over to watch.

Steven asked, "Before you leave, I wanted to mention a young woman named Andrea Hill. She's been missing since last night."

Adam spoke as he flipped the pages of the directory. "What can you tell me about her situation? Do you know any details?"

Steven replied, "Nothing! I just know that there's a lot of people that are worried about her."

Adam shot the final page and looked up. "I'll see what I can find out, and talk to you before the end of the day." Steven and Loraine gave him a grateful nod. "You two carry on. I can let myself out."

As he exited the room, Steven and Loraine turned to each other. "Oh, Steven! Once the Branch's are gone, we'll be all alone here in this place."

He chuckled. "Not quite! We have spirits everywhere we turn."

"Very true! But they have all been rather quiet lately."

Steven thought for a long moment. "You're right! When you have time, I need you to go to the Grand Corridor and see if you can contact the spirits. They might have some information that can help us."

Loraine said snidely, "Hopefully my mother won't come back and disrupt things."

Steven looked at her curiously. "I forgot about Millie. Where is she?"

"She left the house early this morning to dabble about town. I have no idea where she's at."

"We can't have her doing that. From now on, everyone that's left in this house needs to check-in and checkout. No questions asked."

Loraine broke her embrace and began to walk away in a tizzy. "Very well! But you'll have to lecture her on that subject. That woman won't listen to a single word that comes from my mouth." Loraine marched from the room, while Steven sighed. *Oh boy.*

In his former office, Gerard was packing his personal belongings into boxes when someone slowly tapped on the partially open door. "It's open! Come in!"

Luke Underwood casually strolled into the room, and Gerard faked a smile. "How can I help you?"

"I'm guessing by the nameplate outside that you must be Gerard LeRoux?"

"Yes, I am! But I'm afraid that nameplate has seen its last day here at Branch Consolidated."

Luke took a deep breath. "Yes, I know. I'm Lucas Underwood, the new President, and CEO." He extended a handshake, but Gerard was shell-shocked and slow to accept it. "You seem rather surprised, Mr. LeRoux…."

Gerard quickly recovered and shook his hand. "I'm sorry! I guess I'm a bit surprised to be getting a visit from the man who was chosen over me."

Luke responded with a bold smile. "I just wanted to get familiar with my new surroundings, and thought I'd stop by to wish you well in your new endeavors."

"I appreciate that—"

"Well, if there's ever anything I can do to make your transition easier, just let me know."

Luke started pacing the office, as Gerard continued packing. "I've only been here a short time, but Lockeport seems like a very nice little town."

Gerard paused for a moment and looked up. "I've been here for nearly thirty years. It's a great little town."

Luke moved closer. "I noticed that interesting-looking building downtown called the SOS Club. Have you ever been inside?"

Gerard looked up with a raised eyebrow. "No, I haven't. I can't say I know of anyone who has, either."

Luke paused and sat in the chair next to the desk. "I've heard that there's a network of tunnels that run beneath the city. Have you ever explored them?"

Gerard nervously paused; he knew something was fishy about the impending questions. "No. I haven't… but those tunnels have been sealed off for years. Most people around here believe that they're haunted. Myself included."

Luke responded with a smile. "Yes! I've heard about the legends of the underground railroad, and how your great grandfather escaped a mysterious explosion down there. Perhaps his spirit still lingers." Gerard looked up to reply just as Lucretia strolled in the office, and noticeably froze with surprise. "I'm sorry, Gerard! I didn't realize you had company.

Luke intervened while staring intently at her. "That's quite alright, Ms. Darknight. Please do come in and join us."

Lucretia reacted with an uneasy chill. "I had some papers I needed to retrieve from Mr. LeRoux. I'll just come back later." She turned and swiftly walked out, while Luke watched.

"She's very pretty! I understand that she was Daniel Branch the third's mistress."

Gerard replied rather stiffly, "Hardly! But I will say that she's quite a little temptress." Gerard quickly moved to end the conversation. "I don't mean to sound rude, Mr. Underwood, but I do need to get packed up, and out of here by day's end."

"Of course, I understand! Perhaps I'll be seeing you around town. At least for a while, anyway." He departed with an overbearing grin, leaving Gerard quite troubled over the bluntness of his comment.

Lucretia lingered near Gerard's door and quickly approached Luke as he left. "What are you doing here?" she whispered. "I'm simply helping to lay the groundwork for your new leadership position. I was quite instrumental in persuading the Board to choose you." They continued walking as they conversed. "You need to keep a low profile."

"I assure you, Ms. Darknight. After tomorrow, I will seldom be seen, but often heard. Have a very pleasant day!" He continued to stroll away, leaving Lucretia to ponder his words.

Along a residential street in Lockeport, Phillip and Amy posed as a couple pushing a baby carriage, out for a pleasant stroll. "It's been a long time since we played the role of parents," Poseidon stated.

Amy smiled as she daydreamed for a moment. "I always wondered what it would be like to be a mortal, and enjoy simple times like this."

"I never gave it much thought until recently. Perhaps with my old age, I'm becoming sentimental and a bit more mellow."

Amy affectionately took hold of Philips's hand. "I know you miss her very much. I felt the same way about Matthew."

Philip replied with a warm smile, and gently squeezed her hand. Amy suddenly came to a stop and looked up at the street sign on the corner. "Magnolia Street! This is it!" She looked over to her right. "Over there!

That's the house!" While they watched, a black Mercedes pulled into the driveway, and two people got out.

Philip blurted out, "That's Hades! Hurry! Turn around before they see us." They quickly turned the carriage around and began walking away, while Philip continued, "Were you able to see who the woman was?"

Amy said firmly, with underlying anger, "Most certainly! I could never forget that woman's face. She was definitely Liddy McPherson."

Branchview was filled with a silence not felt in years. Steven and Loraine sat in the dining room, picking at the food on their plates. "It all seems so bizarre! Months ago, when we first came here, this table was full. Now it's only you and I."

Mrs. Porter ambled out from the kitchen, interrupting the silence. "Can I get you two anything else?"

Steven stated, "I'd like you to grab a plate, and come out and join us."

"Yes! Please do!" Loraine added.

"Very well!" Mrs. Porter stated. "I need to feed Bumpers, and then I'll sit down for a cup of tea. I don't feel much like eating tonight."

Mrs. Porter returned to the kitchen, while Steven set his fork down and stared off for a moment. "Hasn't your mother gotten back yet?"

"Oh yes! A couple of hours ago. We had a bit of a tiff over her being gone all day."

Steven jumped in, "I'll have to sit down, and talk with her later on." He sighed. "I keep getting this premonition that something's wrong. I hope everything is alright with Audrey and the kids."

Loraine replied, "That's rather odd. I'm feeling the same way."

At that moment, Gerard slowly sauntered into the room and sat down at the table. "The front door was open, so I went ahead and let myself in."

Steven stated, "Can I get you something to eat or drink?"

He shook his head no. "I have to get home. Sharie's waiting for me."

"You seem quite troubled about something. What is it?" Loraine asked.

Gerard took a deep breath, "The Board offered me a buyout, and I accepted. I'm no longer an employee of Branch Consolidated." Steven and Loraine exchanged expressions of shock, while Gerard leaned forward, and rested his hands on the table. "You'll never guess who they chose to be the next CEO and President."

Steven answered, "My most logical guess would be Lucretia Darknight."

Gerard chuckled. "Believe it or not, they chose Lucas Underwood."

Steven and Loraine were flabbergasted. "How did you acquire such information? The Board meeting doesn't take place until tomorrow."

Gerard stated, "Mr. Underwood paid me an unscheduled visit to my office today, and informed me himself. He also asked some very pointed questions about the tunnels, the SOS Club, and my great grandfather."

Steven said with frustration, "He knows we have those directories. We must think of a safe place where we can hide them." Gerard nodded, while the three exchanged expressions of worry and concern.

The following day was slightly overcast in Lockeport. The Board of Directors gathered in the conference hall of Branch Consolidated to announce their choice for President/CEO, and Vice President. Lucretia sat near the head of the table with Liddy to her right, as Marshall Hempfield strolled to the front of the room to speak. "I promise we'll make this announcement short, and quick so that we'll have time to socialize afterward." He motioned toward Liddy, "First, we'll announce our new Vice President. She's a woman with a highly qualified background that was recommended to us by our own Ms. Darknight. I present to you, Ms. Lydia McPherson." The attendees all stood with applause, then promptly sat back down. As Lucretia took on a confident grin, she glanced confidently at Liddy in anticipation of the next announcement. "Now, for the announcement you've all been waiting for. Ladies and gentlemen of the Board, I present to you the new President and CEO of Branch Consolidated." Hempfield unexpectedly walked to the door and opened it. "Please welcome Mr. Lucas Underwood."

Lucretia watched as Luke walked into the room, and immediately cast an arrogant glare at her. The group applauded once again, while Lucretia appeared quite puzzled. She cast a venomous glance toward Liddy, before getting up and swiftly leaving the room. Both Luke and Liddy watched as she left, then exchanged a glance of mild amusement.

Lucretia breezed into her office, slamming the door. She strode over to the window and looked out with arms folded, fuming with anger. After a few moments, Liddy strolled in, closing the door behind her. Lucretia turned abruptly, boiling with contempt. "You miserable bitch! I can't believe I trusted you."

Liddy arrogantly replied, "You're a fool, just like all the other Locke's. Perhaps that's why there's none of you left to carry on the family name."

"How dare you say such a thing!"

Liddy moved closer. "Oh, Lucretia! It's all true. I deceived you, just like I did your father and all the others. I burned down the Locke Estate, killed all the Branch's, and made sure all the blame fell on Daniel Branch the first."

"But Daniel Branch did steal my family's fortune..."

Liddy replied, "Daniel was a self-absorbed scoundrel, but he could've never achieved that feat without help from myself and the Secret Society." She boldly leaned against Lucretia's desk. "Now I'll complete the task that I started all those years ago. I will destroy what's left of the Branch family, absorb their fortune for the glorious mission of the Secret Society, and finally earn retribution for my mother's murder."

Lucretia counter challenged with much fury, "I will use every ounce of my power to destroy you. I promise that!"

Liddy shrugged. "Good luck with that. I think you'll soon learn that you have other more difficult tasks to overcome." There was a loud knock on the door, and Liddy looked at Lucretia with a grin. The door flew open, and FBI agents Grant Posterle, a square-jawed, muscular man with a military haircut, and Adam Smith barged in with guns drawn.

Grant blurted out, "Lucretia Darknight! You're under arrest for suspicion of murder, and conspiracy." As the agents moved to apprehend her, Lucretia suddenly doubled over in pain, while the spirit of Charlotte Locke fled her body, pausing only to glare harshly at Liddy.

Adam reacted with concern. "Lucretia! Are you okay?"

A dazed, confused Kristin Wilder turned to Adam; her eyes filled with terror. "I'm not Lucretia! I'm Kristin Wiler! Please tell me where I am, and what this is all about." Charlotte stood nearby for a moment, unnoticed by mortal eyes. Then she promptly waved her hand and vanished. A black cat leaped from behind a startled Adam and ran swiftly from the room, while Liddy looked on with amusement.

"Where the hell did that cat come from?"

Grant simply shrugged and proceeded to place the handcuffs on Kristin. "Okay! Ms. Darknight, Wiler, or whoever else you claim to be, it's time to go." Liddy continued to observe with wicked pleasure as Posterle recited Miranda Rights to a terrified Kristin Wiler. "You have the right to remain silent…"

Chapter Sixteen:

Luke's Revenge

A long with the change of seasons, there was also a shift in the drama surrounding Branchview. In the wake of Branch Consolidated falling into the hands of the Secret Society, Charlotte Locke, a once vowed enemy of the Branch family, now sought to become an ally to fight against the witch who betrayed her and the Locke family. She also had to fight to save the young girl who was soon to be convicted of crimes unknowingly committed while under her possession. A new secret was on the verge of being discovered in the basement of the old cottage that could make that task nearly impossible.

The sun streamed through the window, illuminating the wall of the quaint cottage in the early morning of a crisp spring day. A few minutes after eight am, the door flew open, as police and FBI, led by agents Posterle and Smith, swarmed into the cottage with guns drawn. Grant hollered out, "Ms. McPherson said there was a secret entrance to the sub-basement through the bookcase."

Grant and Adam walked over to the bookcase, while the others filed through the rest of the house. Adam began pulling out books. "There has to be a latch here someplace."

He pulled on a stationary book on the middle shelf, and it began to creak open. "I'll be damned! She was right." The two men cautiously entered the staircase with their guns drawn and flashlights in hand.

In another part of town, Philip and Amy pulled up a short distance down the block from the Victorian house in Steven's white Corvette and waited for Luke to leave. They watched as he exited the house, got in his car, and drove away in the opposite direction. "That was good timing. I'll wait here, and keep an eye on the street," Philip stated.

Amy replied, "We'll have to hurry. I know he won't leave her alone there for too long."

"I'll honk three times if there's danger." Amy nodded as she got out of the car, and swiftly walked toward the house. She entered and quickly made her way up the stairs. She then quietly and cautiously made her way to the turret room. She concentrated on the door lock until it clicked, and then the door slowly opened. The wide-eyed

Andrea was seated on a large Queen Ann chair when she entered. Amy motioned for her to be quiet, but Andrea responded in an urgent loud whisper. "Dr. Seagraves! What are you doing here?"

"I'm getting you out."

Andrea hyperventilated with anxiety. "Hurry! If he catches us, he'll kill you." Amy responded by grabbing hold of Andrea's hand, and the two women exited the room.

Meanwhile, in the cottage basement, agents Smith and Posterle cautiously entered the ceremony room, and their eyes wandered to all corners. Grant wiped the sweat from his forehead. "I can't believe it's so freaking hot down here."

Adam looked toward the large, padlocked steel door. "What do you think is in there?"

"I don't know. We may have to cut the lock off to find out."

They walked closer but were halted by the sound of a ritual chant that echoed through the room. "What in the blazes was that?"

Adam responded with a clueless and fearful shrug, as they progressed a few more paces. Their presence was felt from behind the solid steel door, and the dogs pounced against it. Their barks echoed throughout the room in an almost deafening manner. "We're not going in there." Adam then turned and saw the wooden door on the other side of the room. "Let's check out what's behind that door." The men moved cautiously toward it, and the muscular Agent Posterle tugged it open with a groan. The smell nearly floored both men as they shone their flashlights inside for a first look.

"Jesus, Mother Mary! It's a freaking death room!" Grant exclaimed. Both men swallowed to hold back their vomit.

While Grant and Adam simultaneously made their grisly discovery in the basement of the cottage, Philip sat in the Corvette, watching Luke's house in his rearview mirror. He jumped to attention when a black Mercedes SUV approached and pulled into the driveway. Philip honked the horn three times as Liddy got out of the car. The noise caught her attention, and she immediately looked in his direction. *Showtime!* Phillip murmured to himself as he jumped from the car and aimed his outstretched fingers toward Liddy. He hit her with a blast of energy that knocked her backward against the side of her SUV and held her there in suspension. Amy and Andrea ran from the house, hand in hand. "Hurry! I'm not sure how much longer I can hold her there."

The two women jumped into the passenger seat, while Philip blinked, causing all four tires on Liddy's Mercedes to flatten. He then ran back toward the Corvette, as Liddy freed herself from his energy lock. She pounded the roof of her car in frustration as the Corvette sped away.

"Amanda Green? How can that be?" Liddy blurted out.

Inside the Branchview house, Loraine and Bumpers decided to take a stroll through the Grand Corridor. Loraine paused to glance at all the pictures along the wall. She halted at one particular painting and noticed something mysteriously out of place. Not believing her eyes, she moved in for a closer look. *What… no way… how can that be?* It seemed that Penelope Branch's image was missing from her portrait.

As she moved in to investigate further, Maggie appeared behind her. "I moved her to where she belongs." Bumpers barked with joy, wagging his tail.

Loraine was momentarily startled as she turned around to address the child. "Maggie! Where did you move her to?"

Maggie stopped petting the dog long enough to point to where the picture of Jack Branch was hung. Loraine was astonished to now see Penelope and Jack posed happily together in the photo with Scooter. In a distant corner of the room, Jack Branch's voice could be heard. "It's just as it should've been."

Jack and the younger version of Penelope strolled into the light from the shadows, and Loraine reacted with an emotional smile. "Where have you all been? We thought you went away and left us alone."

Maggie stated, "We've been here all along."

"Yes! We've been making adjustments and creating a strategy with the rest of the spirits. Our time for action is drawing very near," Penelope replied.

"I know that all things might appear to be bleak. But I assure you, we will prevail." Jack smiled.

Penelope glanced down at Loraine's very pregnant belly. "How are our grandchildren coming along?"

Loraine chuckled. "They're most definitely alive and kicking, and eager to come out."

Loraine stared at Penelope through tear-filled eyes. Penelope responded with a sympathetic smile. "Is everything alright, my dear?"

"I just miss you so much as you were." Penelope and Jack exchanged a glance, then Penelope waved her hand in front of herself and transformed into the older image that Loraine knew so well. "Is this better?"

Loraine nodded as tears flowed down her cheeks. "Is Dr. Grayson with you as well?"

"She most certainly is," Penelope replied.

Jack added to the conversation with assurance, "Her powers will be of much benefit to us all."

"She will visit you soon. I promise."

"I can hardly wait to see her again, Penelope."

Maggie stepped forward, hugged Loraine, and rested her head against her baby bump. "We all love you, Lori."

At the lighthouse, Bill Crawford sat at his dining room table alone, sipping a hot cup of coffee. Even after several years, he was still feeling heartsick over the loss of his wife, Alice. Seconds later, she appeared from a dark corner of the kitchen. The full-body apparition of a blonde woman in her mid-fifties quietly sat down opposite him, and Bill smiled. "Hello, darling!" Alice stated.

"I was so hoping you'd come to visit me today. I've been missing you very much these past few days." She leaned across the table and affectionately touched his face.

"I miss you every day, Bill. But this will be the last time you'll see me for a while."

Bill said emotionally, "Why? I so look forward to our visits!"

"I know, but it's time for you to move on. I've been gone for sixteen years now. We had so many wonderful moments in life, but you have so much more ahead of you."

"If you're saying that I should find someone else, the answer is no. I could never love another woman as much as I loved you."

She leaned in further and kissed him. "I know, but I can't continue to linger between two worlds."

Bill was distraught. "But when will I see you again?"

"Someday! And I promise I'll be waiting for you." There was a knock on the door, and Alice smiled warmly, gesturing in that direction. "Goodbye, for now, darling...." Alice disappeared while Bill struggled to fight back tears.

He opened the door in a rather annoyed manner but changed his demeanor when he saw Millie standing there. "Hello! How can I help you?"

Millie immediately offered a dainty handshake with her gloved hand. "Hello there, Mr. Crawford! I'm Loraine Spencer's mother, Mildred Sandstrom."

"Oh yes! Ms. Loraine visits me quite often. Now I know where she got her beautiful looks."

Millie was quite flattered. "I just arrived here from England a few short days ago, and I've been so bored at

Branchview. Lori told me that there's a marvelous view from the lighthouse tower."

"There most certainly is! Could I show it to you now?"

"Oh yes! If it wouldn't be a bother?" Millie smiled.

"None at all! It would be my pleasure, Ms. Sandstrom."

"Thank you so much, Mr. Crawford. And please do call me Millie!"

Bill gently guided her along with his hand. "Very well, Millie! And if you would, please call me Bill."

Inside Branch Consolidated, Luke had quickly settled into his new, self-appointed position. Now it was time to lean back and soak in his accomplishment. However, his reveling was interrupted when Liddy entered, looking very distressed. "I thought I sent you home to keep an eye on Andrea."

Liddy sighed. "Andrea's gone. Two people were helping her to escape just as I arrived."

In seconds, Luke's calm demeanor turned to sheer anger. "And you let this happen?"

"The one-man must've been a warlock. His powers were much stronger than mine. He flattened all the tires on the Mercedes and paralyzed my body until they escaped."

"What did this man look like?"

Liddy nervously explained. "Mid-thirties, muscular, and long, flowing black hair."

Luke thought hard for a moment, then walked around the desk. "What about the other person?"

"I know her. Her name is Amanda Green."

Luke moved closer with ever-growing interest. "Who is this Amanda Green? Another witch?"

Liddy shrugged and answered with much frustration. "This is what I don't understand. She was a woman who lived over a hundred years ago in my previous life. She was in love with Matthew Branch. They were together on the night that I killed him. I planned to have her blamed for his murder, but she disappeared and was never seen again."

Luke leaned back with intense interest. "Until now!"

Liddy desperately searched for an answer. "She must be a witch. But she was never part of a local coven back then."

Luke paced, deep in thought. "What did this Amanda Green look like?"

"She was gorgeous. She had beautiful red hair."

Luke's eyes widened, and he slammed his fist on the desktop. "Amphitrite and Poseidon. I should've known."

Liddy reacted with a puzzled look. "They actually exist?"

Luke answered in an annoyed tone, "My dear woman! If I exist, why shouldn't they?" Liddy looked away with frustration and intense thought as Luke probed further. "What sort of vehicle did they escape in?"

"Some sort of white sports car.

Luke turned away in thought. "Steven Spencer has a white Corvette." The room went silent while he contemplated. "The gods will retaliate when they find that Triton is dead. The time has come for us to make some very aggressive moves."

Liddy gave an evil chuckle. "Let the games begin." The pair smiled as they devised a strategy.

Zeus paced on the altar as a dejected Poseidon and Amphitrite slowly entered with a blindfolded Andrea. "I was beginning to worry about you two. Where's Triton?"

Amphitrite sadly replied as she removed Andrea's blindfold, "He's dead. Hades killed him."

Poseidon slowly walked onto the altar and slammed his fist on the marble stone in anger, causing the entire cave to rumble.

Andrea ducked for cover, unfamiliar with her surroundings. She trembled with fear as Poseidon roared, "I want to know exactly how it happened."

Andrea cried as she emotionally recalled the event. "It all happened so fast. Before Tony could even react, that terrible creature of a man impaled him with his staff." The details of Andrea's story caused Amphitrite to look away with much hurt.

Poseidon replied, "What did he do with his body?"

Andrea looked down and shook her head. "I don't know. His body just disappeared before my eyes."

Zeus entered the conversation. "Surely Hades must've transported his body somewhere. But where?"

Andrea thought for a moment. "He did say something about a place called Avalon. It didn't make any sense to me." Poseidon and Zeus exchanged an enlightening glance. "Honestly! I don't know anything else…." The intensity of the situation caused Andrea to collapse with emotion. Amphitrite's quick reaction caught her before she hit the hard marble floor of the altar.

Zeus commanded, "We must take Andrea to a safe place where Hades and his hounds cannot find her."

Poseidon and Amphitrite nodded in agreement, as Andrea turned and boldly faced the two gods. "Where is this place called Avalon?"

Poseidon replied, "It's an island where the spirits of great warriors go when they die."

Andrea was very perplexed. "Who are you people, and where do you intend to take me?"

Zeus jumped in quickly, "We're your friends. I promise all we want to do is keep you alive."

Amphitrite chimed in, "There is a secret city named Alfheim in the far north country, where the Light Elves dwell. Poseidon and I will take you there."

Andrea was more confused than ever. "But… what about—" she sobbed, "my family?"

Zeus took hold of her hand and looked into her eyes. "I promise you will see them again. Trust me on that." She forced a smile.

Poseidon approached Amphitrite. "You and Andrea will have to travel without me. Pegasus will transport you there safely."

A worried Amphitrite asked, "Where are you going?"

Poseidon sighed. "To visit our son's spirit in Avalon."

Andrea shouted, "I want to go too. I must see Tony one more time so that I can tell him I love him."

Amphitrite cast a pleading glance at Poseidon. "It is on the way to Alfheim. I'd like to visit Triton as well."

Amphitrite and Poseidon then looked to Zeus, who endorsed their request with a slight nod. "I'll go to Branchview and inform Steven Spencer of the recent events. Have a safe journey."

Poseidon gave an assuring wink at Zeus, then turned to the two women. "If we leave now, we should be there before sunset."

Inside a jewelry store in downtown Lockeport, a homeless man in dirty tattered clothing was seeking answers from the clerk, as Suzy McVea entered. The clerk was examining a diamond ring for the man and spoke up when he saw her. "I have that necklace ready for you, Ms. McVea. I'll be with you in just a minute."

Suzie caught a glance at the ring, and immediately addressed the man. "Where did you get that ring?"

The homeless man got nervous, and the clerk took notice. "I found it in the park. I swear I didn't steal it."

"That's my friend's engagement ring. I helped her boyfriend pick it out in this very store."

The clerk interceded, "I thought I recognized it. I remember showing it to the two of you."

Suzy replied, "You can check your books. He came back and bought it the next day."

The homeless man felt ashamed. "I'm so sorry! You can have it. I had planned to turn it into the police, but they didn't believe the story I told them."

Suzy stepped forward with vigor and immense interest. "What story?"

"I saw a man and a woman in the park. They were confronted by this guy that was dressed in a long black duster, and he carried a large two-pronged staff."

The clerk laughed and shook his head. Suzie sternly glared at him, then turned her attention back to the homeless man. "And what happened next?"

"The man in the duster impaled the other man with the staff. He was lying there dead. But all of a sudden, his body just disappeared."

The clerk began laughing uncontrollably. "I can understand why the police didn't believe you. That's the most ridiculous story I've ever heard."

Suzy ignored him and stayed focused on the homeless man. "I believe you. What happened to the woman?"

"She walked away with the man in black. It was like he had put her in some sort of a trance."

Suzie's eyes remained fixed on him. "Who did you talk to at the police department?"

"Some fella named Detective James Fuller."

Suzie nodded as she thought, then dug into her purse and pulled out a twenty-dollar bill. "I know this Detective Fuller all too well. I think I'll march right over to the police department and have a little chat with him." She handed the twenty dollars to the homeless man. "You take that money over to the diner, and get yourself a good meal."

The man emotionally eyed the bill. "Bless you, ma'am! Thank you so much!"

He hurried out the door as the clerk shook his head and looked at Suzie. "I guarantee, he'll head straight to the liquor store."

Suzy said, "If that's what makes him happy, then so be it."

The clerk said sheepishly, "I'll get that necklace for you."

"Don't bother! I'll pick it up later." She turned to leave, but turned back and grabbed the ring from the counter. "I'll be taking that! As I said, it's already been paid for."

The police department was bustling from the events surrounding the Branchview cottage. Kristin Wiler sat across the table from agents Smith and Posterle within the interrogation room, while detective Fuller, an arrogant man in his early 40s, stood nearby, listening to the ongoing conversation.

Posterle glared at Kristin with intimidation. "Lucretia, if you want to keep denying that you had anything to do with these murders, I'll keep sitting here until I get a confession. All the evidence points to you, and you alone."

Kristin reacted with frustration. "Will you quit calling me Lucretia? My name is Kristin Wiler. I told you everything that happened."

Grant slammed his fist on the table, and pointed at Kristin, while Adam squirmed uneasily in his chair. "I'm finished listening to all of this hocus pocus. I'm not buying into this ridiculous story that a woman that's been dead for 39 years somehow came back to inhabit your body, and now she's left you to pay the ultimate price for her crimes."

Kristin looked down and said quietly, "It's all true."

Detective Fuller's phone buzzed, and he glanced down at the message. "You'll have to excuse me, gentlemen. It appears I have a visitor."

Adam looked to Grant, while Fuller exited. "Why don't you take a break? I'll try to talk to her."

Grant got up and left, then Adam leaned into the table and stared straight at Kristin with urgency. "Listen to me! I know that everything you're saying is true." Kristin was surprised. "I'll do everything I can to get you out of this. It may take some time, but you'll have to trust me."

"What should I do in the meantime?"

Adam said seriously, "I don't want you to say another word until your appointed attorney gets here. Do you understand?" Kristin responded with a serious nod.

Detective Fuller was conversing sarcastically with a very emotional Suzy McVea, while Agent Posterle lingered nearby, sipping on a cup of coffee. "You expect me to believe the story that crazy drunk told me, and that the man I'm looking for, that was supposedly dressed in a black duster, is none other than Lucas Underwood, who by the way, is the new President and CEO of Branch Consolidated?"

Grant perked up when he heard Luke's name mentioned and moved closer. Suzy held the ring in front of him. "He had this ring. It's the one that Tony Freeman was going to give to Andrea. He dropped it when Luke killed him."

Fuller replied in an annoyed fashion, "Ms. McVea! We have no proof to show that this Tony Freeman, or whoever he is, even exists. You can't stand there and tell me that his body just disappeared."

Grant interrupted, "You also have to have more evidence than the word of a town drunk before you can cast suspicion on one of Lockeport's more upstanding citizens."

Suzy narrowed her eyes and said, "He's been harassing Andrea ever since he got into town."

Fuller shouted back, "Andrea Hill is a very attractive young woman. I would imagine quite a few men are trying to win her attention."

Suzie rolled her eyes and reacted with frustration. "You have to be the worst detective there is. I bet you haven't even tried to find Jeff Manus."

Grant interrupted again. "Oh! I'm very sorry Ms. McVea. Obviously, you haven't heard. Jeff Manus was one of the men they found dead in the cottage basement at Branchview."

Suzy crumpled with emotional pain. What…?" she exclaimed. "When did this happen?"

Grant replied, "Earlier today." He pointed toward the interrogation room. "We have the killer in custody. It's Lucretia Darknight."

Suzy was distraught and staggered, as Fuller spoke sober-faced, and with little concern for her feelings. "I should've said something sooner. It just slipped my mind."

She responded with much contempt. "Go to hell!" She stormed from the room in tears.

Grant strolled up to Fuller. "She might be a problem for us."

On the beach at Lighthouse Point, a black cat wandered along the shoreline on a calm night. As the spirit of Charlotte Locke appeared at the waterline, the cool Atlantic waves gently tumbled to the shore. She desperately looked out over the dark waters and called out in a shrill, haunting voice. "Amphitrite! Amphitrite! Please, come now! I need you!"

She paused and listened as a high-pitched sound responded, with dolphin-like clicks that echoed back from the waters. Charlotte waited patiently, listening to the sounds. After a few moments, two young Nereid Nymphs, the blonde Damaris and brunette Hermia, both armed with bows and golden arrows, emerged from the water.

They boldly strolled within inches of Charlotte and surrounded her with their bows armed and poised to strike. Damaris stated, "What business do you have calling on our queen, spirit witch?"

"I assure you that I've come here in peace, bearing important information for Amphitrite."

Hermia responded, "You should know very well that these gold arrows can pierce your spirit and instantly destroy you?"

Charlotte humbly nodded. "I have no other hidden agenda for being here. I'm desperate to speak with her."

The two Nymphs lowered their bows, and Damaris explained, "Amphitrite was called away on important business. You may speak your purpose to us."

Charlotte took a deep breath. "As you might know, Hades and Liddy McPherson have joined forces with the Secret Society."

Damaris answered, "Yes! We're also aware that they accomplished that with your help."

Charlotte sighed. "Unfortunately, that's true. But they betrayed me! Even after I was warned by Steven Spencer. I can't simply walk away now, knowing of all the unnecessary destruction and sorrow that I've caused."

The Nereids eyed her with much contempt, and Hermia replied, "We do not need to hear your penance. The Shadows of Justice will surely deal with you."

Charlotte nodded sadly. "Yes, I know. But perhaps I could earn some sort of redemption through offering my services to the struggle."

The Nymphs glared at her with calculating eyes, and Damaris inquired, "What have you done with Kristen Wiler?"

"She's in grave danger. She was arrested for the crimes that I committed while in the guise of Lucretia Darknight. Something must be done to save her."

They both looked at her hard and soberly for a moment. Then Hermia replied, "I fully sense that you are telling the truth, Charlotte. But I must warn you, if you betray us, death and destruction will be swift to find you."

"I assure you that I'm determined to shed my wicked ways for the good."

Damaris concluded, "We shall speak to Amphitrite on your behalf when she returns. She will summon you telepathically when a decision is made."

"How long must I wait?"

Damaris said, "It may be a very late hour."

"I will wait here all night if necessary. I have nowhere else to go." Charlotte gave them a grateful bow before the two Nymphs turned and walked back into the ocean. She watched them disappear below the water, then saw their finned tails flip above the gentle waves as they swam away to the depths of the Atlantic.

Chapter Seventeen:

He Can Be Trusted

A cool breeze blew across the Atlantic on this early summer night. Despite the calm and pleasant conditions, boiling turbulence surrounded Branchview, as the forces of good and evil began a real-life game of chess that would lead to an inevitable showdown. On this very night, Andrea Hill would begin her journey to places hidden from human sight and would meet people only known to exist in mythology. It was within the mystical land of Alfheim that she would remain in safekeeping until the coming battle had played out.

In the shadows of the glistening moonlight, somewhere over the Atlantic Ocean, Poseidon and Andrea glided just above the water on the back of the winged horse Pegasus, while Amphitrite swam with lightning speed in the waters below them. Pegasus slowed as they reached the dark landmass, and the horse gracefully landed on the stony beach with the riders intact. Poseidon dismounted, then lifted Andrea safely to the ground as Amphitrite approached from the water through the thick sea fog.

The night sounds echoed an eerie beckoning from the deep woods. "I had hoped to reach here before dark. It can be a rather scary and foreboding place at night. "

The three slowly walked toward the tree line, leaving a patient and calm Pegasus behind. As they got nearer, a host of figures emerged from the mist, bearing torches.

Andrea fearfully clutched at Poseidon's arm. "It's alright, Andrea," Amphitrite stated. "The spirits will not harm you."

The figures surrounded the three of them, and Magnus, a very large, and weathered-looking warrior, stepped forward. He went to one knee and bowed. "Poseidon! We've been expecting you."

Poseidon stepped forward and helped him to his feet. "It's good to see you again, Magnus."

Triton stepped from among the figures and planted his torch upright in the ground. When Andrea saw him, she immediately ran to him with much emotion. "Tony! I missed you so much."

Magnus turned to Poseidon with a clueless smirk. "Tony?"

Poseidon replied, "It's a long story—"

Amphitrite moved toward her son as well, and Poseidon followed suit. Triton then turned his attention back to Andrea. "I'm so glad my parents were able to save you from Hades."

"I'm so sorry we couldn't have saved you as well, my dear son," Amphitrite sadly stated.

Triton smiled at his mother. "None of us could've known that Hades would do this. I suppose it was simply my fate."

"He will surely pay for what he has done. I promise you that, son."

Triton embraced Andrea, then pulled away and looked at her strangely. "There is another life force living within you."

"Are you saying she's with child, Triton?" Amphitrite asked.

Before Triton could answer, Andrea spoke in her defense. "If this is true, the child is surely yours. You're the first and only man that I've ever been with."

He looked at her with much joy. "I'm going to be a father…."

The joy quickly faded between all, as the reality of the situation sunk in. "I don't want to leave you. I want to stay here with you."

Triton shook his head. "This is no place for the living, and you have so much life to live. Not just for yourself, but our child."

"I assure you, Andrea, you and the child will be cared for properly. You're one of us now," Poseidon stated.

A few seconds later, loud dolphin-like clicks could be heard echoing across the beach. Amphitrite answered in a piercing, high-pitched clicking chant of her native language, which caused the others to cringe. She then walked over to address Triton and Andrea. "I must go. I am being summoned by Damaris and Hermia. I will visit again very soon." She embraced her son, then turned to Andrea. "Poseidon and Pegasus will take you the rest of the way to Alfheim. You'll be greeted there by the god Freyr, his wife Geror, and his twin sister Freya."

Andrea emotionally embraced her. "Thank you so much for everything."

Amphitrite answered with a warm smile. "Have a safe journey, my dear."

Magnus turned to Poseidon as Amphitrite departed. "If you should need us in this battle with Hades, our warrior spirits will all proudly fight beside you."

Poseidon answered with a gracious nod. "I would be honored to call on you, my friend."

In the meantime, Zeus assumed his alias of Ezekiel Sphere and arrived at Branchview to meet with Steven. Rather than discuss the issues at hand in the sitting room, they both agreed it would be wise to move to the privacy of the study.

"We should be able to talk in here without being interrupted," Steven said.

Ezekiel settled into a plush chair, while Steven sat behind the desk. "Pardon my ignorance, but where exactly is this place that they took Andrea? I doubt it even exists on any map."

Ezekiel chuckled. "I'm certain that you've heard of parallel worlds."

"I have. But I always thought they existed somewhere in another galaxy."

Ezekiel leaned forward to explain. "There are many hidden vortexes that exist in our oceans and waterways. Occasionally, they open, and anything that happens to be passing by at that time is pulled in."

"You mean like the Bermuda Triangle?"

"Precisely! However, the immortals have control of these vortexes, and we can enter and return at any time we please." Ezekiel paused with a smile as Steven listened with great interest. "It is when we pass through these vortexes that we enter the parallel world and the hidden lands of which I speak."

"Amazing!" There was a light knock on the door, and Steven chuckled. "So much for not being interrupted."

The door opened and Millie walked in. "Please pardon the intrusion, Steven. There's an Agent Smith that's here to see you."

"That's okay, Millie. You can send him in." Millie left to usher Adam into the room, and Steven quickly commented to Ezekiel, "Don't worry! He can be trusted." Millie returned with Adam, then stood for a moment admiring the men with her hands cupped in front of her.

"I swear! I've yet to see an ugly man since I've been here at Branchview." Steven responded with a raised eyebrow, and Millie snubbed her nose indignantly. "Very well! I'll leave you, handsome gentlemen, to talk." She sashayed out, and the men all looked on with amusement.

Adam said, "Your mother-in-law is quite a card."

Steven chuckled. "You don't know the half of it."

Adam sat down. "What's with all the drop cloths and dust out in the foyer?"

"The workers started renovating the east wing today. We hope to have it done before the babies arrive." Steven motioned toward Ezekiel. "This is a good friend of mine, Ezekiel Sphere. He's a trusted ally as well."

The two men shook hands. "It's a pleasure to meet you, Agent Smith."

Steven leaned forward and shook his head. "It's been quite a day. I'm certain the whole town of Lockeport is all abuzz over the discovery at the cottage."

"And the problems keep getting worse…." Adam said emphatically. "Charlotte Locke's spirit has left Kristin Wiler's body, and that leaves Kristin to take the fall for all of the murders."

Steven said, "We can't let that happen. There must be something we can do."

"We better figure out something quick. She gets transferred to state prison tomorrow evening."

Ezekiel sighed. "I'll speak to my associates. Perhaps we can come up with a plan."

"Whatever that plan is, I want to be a part of it."

Ezekiel cast a concerned glance at Steven, who gave him an assured nod. "Very well! Everyone involved will meet on the beach near Lighthouse Point just before dawn, and there we will plan out our strategy."

Adam wearily put his hand to his forehead in careful thought. "You know, I'm very concerned about where Charlotte Locke might be. She could very easily throw a wrench into our plans."

Steven said intently, "I'm certain she's still lurking somewhere in the shadows. We'll just have to be careful."

Adam nervously ran his hand through his hair. "Were you able to hide those directories?"

Steven and Ezekiel exchanged a glance. "They're in a safe place. Why?"

"I started looking over the photos I took and found that my immediate supervisor, Grant Posterle, and Detective Fuller were among the members' names." Steven and Ezekiel looked at each other with wide-eyed surprise. "That got me thinking about just how big their network is. If we were able to tap into the nationwide directory, we could bring down some pretty heavy hitters."

Steven asked, "How do you propose we do that? None of us here are computer geeks."

"There's someone that the bureau arrested about a year ago that was hacking into the mainframes of several large corporations. She is considered one of the best in the game. She's been cooperating with the FBI in helping to bring down other large hacking rings. Perhaps I can convince her to help us."

Steven questioned further, "How do you intend to do that without Posterle finding out?"

Adam looked away for a moment in thought. "I'll think of something. I'll set the wheels in motion on all this tonight, and we'll talk more about it in the morning." Adam stood, planning to leave, as Steven and Ezekiel moved to accompany him to the door. Adam then turned to the two men and held out his hand, palm down, in a gesture of unity, and the others promptly placed their hands over his. "Let's defeat these bastards."

Below the cliffs at Lighthouse Point, Charlotte sat on the rocks, gazing out into the vast darkness of the Atlantic. She suddenly sat up straight and listened attentively. "Yes, Amphitrite! I'm here!" She jumped to her feet and strolled to the waterline.

After a few long moments, Amphitrite emerged from the dark waters, strutting toward her with a stern demeanor. "You have a lot of nerve showing your face after all the negative history we've shared."

"I trust that Damaris and Hermia spoke with you on my behalf?"

"They did. I just haven't decided whether it's wise to trust you."

Charlotte looked up at the dark sky. "You and I can do many things with our powers, but unfortunately, we can't turn back the hands of time."

"Yes, I agree. That is a very cruel reality."

"I can't begin to tell you how much I regret the things I've done. But I'm sure we can both agree that Liddy McPherson was the catalyst for all those sorrows and tragedies."

Amphitrite responded with vigor. "My life won't be complete until I see that woman locked in the deepest regions of hell."

"It appears that you and I now share the same sentiments."

Amphitrite stared at her with calculating thought. "Tell me what she and Hades have planned."

Charlotte said seriously, "It's absolutely maniacal. The Secret Society is plotting to overthrow the country, and kill the President of the United States."

"Do they have the capability to do such a thing?"

Charlotte responded with a nervous nod. "Oh yes! They are quite organized. I can say that with great certainty."

Amphitrite began to walk past her. "I must notify the gods and Steven Spencer of this immediately."

"Amphitrite! Wait!" She turned to listen. "The way I see it, you have several options here. You could easily destroy my spirit here and now, leave my fate to the shadows of justice, or trust and accept me as an ally. I have a feeling you'll be needing all the help you can get, and possibly more."

Amphitrite studied her for a moment, then gave her a stern nod. "I'm sensing that it might be the right thing to do. But I'm warning you. Don't ever do anything to make me regret this decision."

Chapter Eighteen:

Destroy the Enemy

A s the Branch family braced for the onslaught of their impending battle to save Branchview, Luke Underwood sat comfortably with his companion in crime. They were leaned back, seated across from each other at a small round table, sipping a glass of wine by candlelight in the Underwood parlor. Liddy proclaimed, "You seem rather calm and content this evening."

Luke smiled. "I must admit that I am a bit pleased knowing that those missing directories will be back in my possession by this time tomorrow."

"How can you be so sure of that?"

Luke confidently leaned back in his chair. "I now have a bargaining chip. Earlier today, my men apprehended Deanna LeRoux outside of her apartment in Boston. Late this evening, they did the same to Sharie LeRoux in the parking lot of the Stop n' Shop. I'm sure that when Gerard hears about this, he'll do whatever he has to do to get his precious wife and daughter back safely."

"Even if we do get those directories, many of the names have surely been compromised," Liddy said.

Luke chuckled arrogantly. "My dear Liddy! You should know that I have a failsafe method in place to make sure those names never become public knowledge. Our network is so large that our enemies have no idea of the adversity they face."

"I don't understand the point of all this then."

Luke leaned forward and webbed his fingers in a sinister way. "It's called undermining the very foundation of your enemy to destroy them." He paused to smile across the table. "It's also a way for me to find out where they are hiding the Branch family, and where they took my beloved Andrea."

Liddy erupted in frustration. "Andrea! Why should you even care about her? She doesn't love you, and she never will." Luke was very perturbed by her statement, and Liddy leaned into the table with the intent to persuade. "Beside the point, you and I could make a much stronger union."

Luke reacted with much contempt. "What makes you think that I'd be interested in an ancient old hag like yourself, whose body has been defiled by more men than I can ever imagine?"

Liddy fired back with prideful vigor, "You think no different than any other typical man. You seem to forget that you've been around much longer than I have, and have done far more despicable things."

Luke chugged down the last swallow of his wine, then fired back equally, "And you seem to forget that I am a god, and I can reduce you to a pile of dust with a wave of my hand." Liddy cowered at his remark, and timidly took a sip of her wine. Luke then stood up, tossed his chair to one side, and pointed at her with boiling anger. "This conversation is over! You're to never speak of this nonsense again. And that, my dear, is a warning that should be wisely heeded."

The day was winding down in the Branch household, but Steven found himself concerned over not hearing from Gerard. It was unusual, and after recent events, he thought it was necessary to check on him. At the carriage house, Steven found Gerard pacing nervously. "Gerard…What's happened? You look very distraught."

Gerard spoke in a voice wavering with emotion. "Luke Underwood kidnaped Sharie and Deanna. He wants the directories back in his possession by tomorrow afternoon, or he'll kill them both."

Steven reacted with much anxiety. "It's okay! We can have the gods return them. We've already been able to gather more than enough names from the pages."

A troubled Gerard placed his hands squarely on Steven's shoulders. "We have to make sure that nothing happens to Sharie and Deanna. They're all I have left in life."

Steven gave a sympathetic nod. "We'll get them back, but there's not much we can do tonight. Come stay at the main house, and we'll meet with the gods before the sun comes up."

Across town at the McVea household, someone was paying a late-night visit. A loud knock echoed throughout the dark house. A light came on, and while Suzy hurried to the door, fastening her robe, there was another loud, more aggressive knock. "Okay! Okay! I'm coming!" she shouted. She stopped short of opening the door. "Who is it?"

"It's Detective Fuller."

Suzy rolled her eyes and opened the door. "What do you want? Isn't it a bit late to be knocking on someone's door?"

Fuller arrogantly strolled in, uninvited. "I thought it best for you and me to have a little chat." He moved further into the house and looked around, as she nervously held the top portion of her robe closed with one hand. "Your uncle has a nice little place here." He turned to address her face to face. "I understand that he's all you have left since your parents passed away."

Suzie reacted with concern. "Just what are you getting at?"

Fuller chuckled. "It would be a great loss to the community if something were to ever happen to you, him, or the diner he owns…" His voice trailed off. He shrugged with a clueless expression before continuing. "I mean, there's always a chance of a fire and the possibility that you two would never make it out in time."

"Is that a threat, Agent Fuller?"

He stood within inches of her face. "No! It's a warning to keep your mouth shut about what happened to your friend. It'd be a shame if you met the same fate as poor old homeless Eric."

"What did you do to him?" she exclaimed.

Fuller responded in a matter of a fact way. "I like to think that we put the poor soul out of his misery. Kind of like the same fate that your werewolf boyfriend encountered."

Suzy pulled the door open and responded with a smoldering anger. "You're despicable! I should call the police department and file harassment charges."

Fuller laughed. "Now you listen to me, little Suzy! I'm the law in this town, and you're just a lowly citizen that's required to do as I tell you."

"Get out!"

Fuller arrogantly strode by her on his way out the door. "You have a pleasant evening, Ms. McVea." He strolled out, and Suzy slammed the door behind him.

A faint band of red emerged on the horizon over the Atlantic. The warming summer season was arriving, leaving a crisp breeze gently floating along the beach. Steven, Gerard, and Adam approached to meet with Ezekiel, Philip, Amy, and surprisingly, Charlotte Locke. As they all came face to face, Steven and Gerard were quite perplexed. "Charlotte?"

Adam looked at Steven with surprise. "That's Charlotte Locke?"

Gerard smirked. "None other! The witch we all knew as Lucretia Darknight."

Charlotte stepped forward. "I'm finally able to stand face to face with my nephew."

Steven cautiously halted her approach with his hand. "I don't understand all of this."

Amy stepped up. "Charlotte has approached us, and offered her help."

Steven began to speak in frustration, but Ezekiel cut in. "She's assured us that she regrets her evil past, and now wants to use her powers to help destroy Luke, Liddy, and the Secret Society. It is a battle that will not be easy to overcome, and we need all the help possible. Plus, she has intimate knowledge of their inner workings."

Charlotte humbly nodded. "It's true, Steven. I realize now that I should have listened when you spoke the truth to Lucretia."

Philip spoke up with great impatience. "There'll be time for explanations later. We have much more important things to discuss."

Amy stated, "I agree! Charlotte has informed us of a much larger scheme by the Secret Society that involves a government takeover."

Adam replied, "I just might have a way to counter it. I plan to call in a request to the warden at state prison to get our hacker out on assignment release. She should be able to help us thwart that coup before it ever takes place."

Steven spoke up, "Well in the midst of this, another problem has arisen."

He motioned to Gerard, who emotionally spoke. "Hades kidnapped my wife and daughter. He wants the directories back."

Adam interrupted, "Who the hell is Hades?"

Everyone cautiously glanced at each other, as Gerard quickly recovered and back-peddled. "My apologies. I'm so distraught that I meant to say Luke Underwood, and the guardian of hell is the first thing that popped into my mind."

Amy replied, "There's certainly not much difference between the two of them."

Phillip spoke up as well, "Ezekiel and I will promptly tend to that issue this morning."

Adam looked toward Ezekiel and spoke with vigor. "What about Kristin Wiler? You told me last night that you'd have a plan."

Ezekiel motioned toward Amy. "Dr. Seagraves is a psychiatrist. She'll request to see her..."

Charlotte interrupted, "Wait! I have a better plan to get her out."

Adam burst out, "Absolutely not! She'll be terrified when she sees you. Besides, I'm not quite sure if I can trust you."

Charlotte held up her hand to calm him. "I know you're in love with her. If you want her to escape all of this safely, you must trust me."

Adam reluctantly nodded in agreement, then shook his head in disbelief. "Who are you people anyway? This is all like some crazy episode of The Twilight Zone."

Steven laughed. "If I told you the whole truth, you probably wouldn't believe me anyway."

Adam slapped him on the back of the shoulder. "Maybe someday you can tell me over a good cup of coffee."

Steven replied, "Preferably when this is all over."

The group went quiet as the sun peeked over the horizon. Ezekiel then stated, "Okay! You all have your tasks…. let's get this done."

Philip motioned to Steven and smirked. "Ezekiel and I will meet you this afternoon at the cave entrance. We'll need you to bring Gerard." Steven countered with a puzzled expression but then nodded in agreement.

The foyer clock promptly chimed at 7:00 a.m. Millie hustled energetically into the room, wearing a jogging suit, as Loraine slowly waddled along down the stairs. "Mother! Mrs. Porter will have breakfast ready shortly. Where on earth are you going?"

"I shan't be long! I'm simply going for a short zip around the property."

They were interrupted by a loud knock on the door. "That's rather odd. The workers don't usually start until 9:00."

Millie shrugged cluelessly and opened the door to see a very tall, dark-skinned construction worker standing there with two others behind him. "You gentlemen are a tad early, aren't you?"

The worker strode forward, pulled out a gun, and pointed it at Millie. "We like to get an early start on things." From out of the shadows, Liddy sauntered in through the doorway behind them and quickly spotted Loraine, who was halfway down the stairway. "If it isn't Mrs. Steven Spencer herself. You're the one we want, sweetheart." Liddy brandished a small, curved saber knife, motioned for two of the men to follow, and they started toward her, while the other held the gun on Millie.

Loraine waved her hand and created a wall of fire between herself and Liddy and the two men. Millie used the distraction to attack the man with the gun. She employed a quick roundhouse kick, knocking the gun across the floor, and followed with a series of quick martial arts moves that snapped the man's leg at the knee. Liddy ambitiously waved her hand to one side, easily dismissing the wall of flames, and took off after Loraine, who was trying to waddle back up the stairs. The two men turned to fight off a now pursuing Millie.

Liddy caught up with Loraine and pulled her down near the top of the landing. Loraine struggled, while Liddy raised the saber knife and prepared to strike. "I'm going to enjoy this. First, I'll kill you, then I'll carve those despicable offspring from your womb."

"Not in this lifetime, bitch!" Loraine blew a mist that froze Liddy's eyes, sending her tumbling backward. In a swift move, Millie snapped the neck of one of the men, dove for the gun that was near her on the floor, and shot the other man who was charging toward her. Loraine got to her feet but quickly fell back to her knees in pain. Liddy recovered and continued her pursuit. A split second later, Steven barged through the half-open front door with the ferocious roar of a lion, and his eyes glowing like red hot coals. He pointed his finger at Liddy, and the saber knife flew from her hand, impaling the portrait of the woman hanging on the landing wall. She tried to hurl energy at him, but he easily deflected it, leaving her quite surprised. As the monstrous Steven leaped up the stairs toward her, she wisely snapped her fingers and vanished in a cloud of purple smoke.

Steven recovered to his normal form and rushed to Loraine, who was visibly stunned. "Oh, sweetheart! Are you okay?"

Loraine answered in a breathless tone, "Steven! Where on earth did you acquire such powers?"

"I'll tell you all about it later." He looked down toward the foyer. "Are you okay, Millie?"

Appearing quite dazed and winded, she replied, "I'm a bit bruised and battered, but far better off than these two stiffs, and this other bloke who has a badly broken leg."

In response, Steven shook his head in disbelief and amazement, while Loraine began hyperventilating and went into a panic. "Honey! What's wrong?"

She looked at him with desperate eyes. "The babies! Oh, dear! I do believe my water just broke."

Chapter Nineteen:

The Grand Mansion

The grand mansion of Branchview was surrounded once again by the endless struggles of fighting evil forces. Yet behind closed doors, the family revels in the joy of birth. On an early morning in June, the house would see a shining light during all the chaos. It was as though all the ugliness had faded for just a moment. The flowers were blooming, while the sun shone brightly over the inhabitants. Nonetheless, their respite was fading quickly. While Luke was lost in contemptuous thought, his secretary paged him on the intercom. "Mr. Underwood! There are two gentlemen from Oceanus Industries here to see you."

Luke took on a perplexed yet curious expression. "Very well! Send them in." The door opened, and Philip and Ezekiel strolled into the office wearing business suits, with their long hair tied back in ponytails and stuffed beneath their shirt collars. Luke barely flinched, then smirked sarcastically. "What a clever way to get past my gatekeepers. I must say, both of you do clean up quite well." He stood and motioned. "Please sit down! Can I offer you two gentlemen a drink?"

Philip sneered in response. "No thanks! This is a far cry from being a social call."

Ezekiel opened his briefcase, removed the directories, and tossed them on his desk. "I do believe you've been looking for these?"

Luke grinned. "I should've known that you two had possession of them."

Ezekiel exclaimed, "We demand that you release Sharie and Deanna LeRoux immediately."

Luke settled back into his seat. "Not so quick! First, I demand to know where you're keeping the Branch family and Andrea Hill."

Philip interjected, "They're both hidden in places where you'll never find them."

Luke became serious. "You greatly underestimate me. I will find out sooner or later, and I will kill the rest of the Branch's and take Andrea as my wife."

"Even if she's carrying Triton's child?"

Luke flew into a rage, slamming his fist on the desk. "You lie!"

Ezekiel seriously shook his head no. "I'm afraid he's telling the truth."

The secretary buzzed in on the intercom once again. "What is it?" he demanded.

The secretary replied in a meek voice, "I'm sorry to interrupt, but I believe this is the phone call you've been waiting for."

Luke settled a bit, glanced up at the clock on his wall, and smiled. "Give me a few moments, then I'll have you connect me." He glanced up toward the two men and grinned. "That's one of my men calling to inform me that Steven and Loraine Spencer and their two unborn children are dead."

Philip and Ezekiel looked at each other in shock, as Luke pushed the button and spoke to his secretary again. "You can put that call through to me now."

Millie was on the other end. "Hello! Mr. Underwood?" Luke's smile turned to a perplexed expression when he heard Millie's distinct British accent.

"Who is this?" Luke demanded.

"This is Mildred Sandstrom. I'm calling on one of your henchmen's cell phones. You'll find your men inside their van, on the second level of the company parking garage." Philip and Ezekiel began to smile as they listened. "One of the poor chaps has a very badly broken leg, and will require an ambulance, while the other two weren't quite as fortunate." Luke's expression turned to shocked anger. "Despite all of this calamity, I do hope you have a very good day."

Millie ended the call, and Ezekiel said confidently, "Well, Hades! It appears things didn't turn out quite as you had planned...."

Luke answered with an angry scowl. "Never address me by that name. The LeRoux's will never see the light of day until I'm in full control of Branchview and the Branch's fortune."

Ezekiel stated, "How foolish of me to believe that you'd simply be satisfied with having control of the United States."

Luke leaned forward with urgency. "You know of our plans?"

Ezekiel nodded. "Thanks to Charlotte Locke, who is now an ally of ours."

Philip pulled out a very old, long, twisted blade dagger from his suit jacket, and aggressively plunged it into the wooden desk in front of Luke. "I believe you know what this means."

Luke sneered, "A declaration of war that I gladly accept."

Ezekiel stood with great prowess. "As do we. You shall meet us on the beach at Lighthouse Point on Friday, June 21st at exactly noon. It will be a battle to the death."

Philip added a further threat: "If any harm comes to any of the Branch's or the LeRouxs, we will move on you sooner, and without warning."

Luke pulled the knife from the desk, laughing. "The battle will take place on the Summer Solstice. How appropriate! I shall celebrate my victory by drinking your blood."

Philip yanked the knife from his hand and tucked it back under his jacket. "We'll just have to see about that. Things haven't exactly gone in your favor so far."

Ezekiel announced, "If the LeRouxs are not released by this evening, we will take actions to expose you and Liddy McPherson for who you really are."

"Please don't disappoint us. I savor the chance to face you in battle, and avenge my son's murder," Phillip replied.

Luke peered at them with a scowl as they turned to leave. "Have a pleasant day, Mr.... Underwood," Ezekiel stated.

The foyer clock chimed at 10:00 a.m. Mrs. Porter busily cleaned up broken glass and debris from the earlier conflict, as the loud noises of construction could be heard from the east wing. Suddenly the house became silent. A few moments later, the construction foreman, a stocky man in his early 30s, called from the top of the stair landing. "Excuse me, ma'am. We have a bit of a problem up here. Is there anyone in authority that I can speak to?"

Mrs. Porter looked up at him. "I'm afraid not. Everyone has gone to the hospital. Mrs. Spencer is about to give birth." The foreman let out a sigh of anxious frustration. "Is there something I can help you with?"

The foreman strolled down to the middle landing, as Mrs. Porter moved to the bottom of the stairs. "My workers were taking up the floor in the sitting room, and they...well, they found what appears to be human remains. They look like they've been there for quite some time."

Mrs. Porter reacted with much nervous anxiety. "Oh no! What should I do?"

The foreman walked the rest of the way down the stairs and tried to calm her. "I'll call the sheriff. I'm sure it's nothing for anyone to be concerned about. Those bones have probably been up there longer than anyone in this house has been alive." Mrs. Porter nodded in agreement.

Meanwhile, back at Branch Consolidated, Luke swiftly entered Liddy's office, slamming the door behind him. He marched over to her desk, poised for a confrontation. "I demand to know how you managed to bungle your assignment at Branchview."

Liddy struggled to talk. "Steven Spencer arrived just before I was ready to kill his wife. There was something different about him. He barged in like a wildly possessed beast, and his powers were much greater than mine. I was lucky to escape unscathed."

"Did he take out my entire crew as well?"

Liddy shook her head no. "It was Loraine Spencer's mother."

Luke rolled his eyes. "You mean to tell me that an old woman took out three of my best men? Did she have superhuman powers as well?"

"I've never seen a woman of her age in such great shape. She's very skilled in martial arts."

Luke paced back and forth. "Steven Spencer must have received some sort of special powers from the gods. But now, I'm very intrigued by Mildred Sandstrom as well. It appears there's more to her than meets the eye." Liddy looked ready to pass out, and Luke took notice. "What's wrong with you?"

Liddy answered with great frustration, "I don't know. Suddenly, I'm so weak, and I have this dreadful feeling that something is wrong."

Luke moved closer with concern. "Perhaps if you used your psychic powers, you might get a vision."

"I'm not sure I have enough strength."

Luke sat down and placed his hands across her desk. "Take hold of my hands. I'll help you." She grabbed his hands, and they both closed their eyes.

Liddy began to weave back and forth. "I see Branchview. I'm in the east wing. There are construction workers. They've found something."

"What is it, Liddy? What have they found?" Luke demanded.

Liddy continued with a pained expression. "Remains! Human remains!"

Liddy groaned in agony and opened her eyes. Luke immediately helped her over to a couch and forced her to lie down. "Whose remains are they, Liddy?"

She managed to answer with wide-open eyes. "I think they might be mine. If so, we must take and bury them as soon as possible in a place where no one will find them."

Luke was perplexed. "Why would we have to do that?"

Liddy replied urgently, "Because if those remains are exposed to this world, my present body will continue to erode. I will eventually die."

Luke tried to comfort her. "You just lie here and rest. I'll take care of this issue immediately."

Agent Smith had made his way to the state prison processing room. He was waiting for the staff to complete the release papers when the steel door opened and a very tall, muscular guard entered. He was escorting Joey Arcovio, a tiny mousy looking woman in her early twenties. Adam got up to greet them, as the guard planted the orders on the table in front of him. "Hello, Joey! It's been a long time." The girl only responded by shyly looking over the top of her large, round, wire-framed glasses.

"Just sign that release, and she'll be in your custody."

Adam looked at him with great seriousness. "I'm signing her out for a top-secret assignment. When you sign your portion of the copy, remember that I'm holding you accountable to keep this confidential."

The guard smirked. "You sure you can handle this wild one all by yourself?"

Adam replied sarcastically, "What's that supposed to mean?"

The guard replied in a matter-of-fact way, "She bit another woman's ear off who tried to steal her fruit salad last night at supper. Then she kicked the guard that was trying to separate them in the groin." The guard glanced at her. "That guy will be speaking in a higher octave from now on." Adam looked at her with much surprise, but she avoided eye contact. "She's a quiet one, but she has a proven mean streak."

Adam tore off his copy of the release and handed the other to the guard. "I think I'm quite capable of keeping her under control."

Back at Branchview, a rattled but stable Gerard entered through the front door, and was quickly greeted by a frantic Mrs. Porter who was shadowed closely by Bumpers. "Oh, Mr. LeRoux! I'm so glad you're here."

"I got here as soon as I could, Mrs. Porter. Have the police already taken the remains?"

She answered in a shaky voice, "Yes! They've been gone for at least twenty minutes now. A Detective Fuller told me that they'd be processing them at the police crime lab."

Gerard sighed and looked upward. "We never seem to get a break from all the chaos, and drama, do we?"

"I know! It's terrible! Have you heard anything about Sharie and Deanna?" Gerard emotionally shook his head no. "What about the hospital? Have you heard any word on Mrs. Spencer?"

"The last I heard, she's still in labor."

Mrs. Porter responded with much anxiety. "The poor dear! I do hope everything will be alright."

"I'm heading over there right now. Just settle yourself down, and I'll notify you when something happens."

"I'll do just that, Mr. LeRoux. I'm not a drinking woman, but after this morning's events, I think I'll go to the sitting room with Bumpers and pour myself a large glass of brandy."

Gerard chuckled. "Maybe have an extra one for me as well." She nodded with amusement.

Chapter Twenty:

It's Time…… Babies Coming

In the hospital waiting room, Steven's mind was flooded with all the turmoil happening, not only at Branchview but also in the world surrounding it. While deeply lost in his thoughts, the spirit of Daphne Branch appeared in the chair next to him, and Steven reacted with surprise. "Grandmother! What are you doing here?"

Daphne gazed around the room. "This is the first time I've left Branchview since my death. The world has become quite modern since then."

She turned her full attention to Steven. "I came to warn you about the remains that were found at the house this morning."

Steven sat forward and said in a low voice, "What remains? I thought we accounted for all the people that Daniel the first killed."

"They belong to Liddy McPherson."

Steven reacted with great concern. "I thought he buried her remains on the grounds after he burned the body."

"I thought so too. But obviously, he must've put them under the floorboards shortly before he permanently closed off the wing." Daphne looked at Steven very seriously. "You must get those remains, and make sure they never get buried again."

"Wait... I don't understand."

"If they remain exposed, Liddy will die. If they are buried once again, she will remain living." Steven pondered and tried to wrap his mind around the idea, while Daphne spoke again with urgency. "I must go now, but I will peek in later to see my grandbabies."

Daphne disappeared, just as Millie entered the room and Steven shifted his attention. "Millie! Did everything go smoothly?"

"Just perfect! I did have much difficulty, however, trying to hail a cab. I thought surely I was going to have to flash my breasts to get someone to stop."

Steven managed to contain his amusement, as Millie sat down next to him. "Tell me! Where did you attain the fighting skills you displayed this morning?"

Millie sighed. "I suppose my secret would've revealed itself sooner or later. For years, I was an MI6 agent with the British Intelligence Service. I retired just a few short years ago."

Steven leaned back in his seat and looked at her with complete surprise. "You were a secret agent? Does Lori know?"

"Oh! Good grief, no! She always believed that I was a foreign relations envoy for the Parliament. I couldn't dare to tell her the truth. It would've put us both in grave danger."

Steven nodded and smiled. "Don't you think it's about time she knew the truth?"

Millie looked down thoughtfully. "I do suppose you're right. I shall have a serious conversation with her when this is all over, and she feels up to it."

They both looked at each other, and Millie began to inquire, "And what about those powers you displayed?"

Steven was spared an explanation when Dr. Scotnicki, a woman in her early 40s, walked into the waiting area, looking quite exhausted. Both Steven and Millie stood up in anticipation. "Mr. Spencer! I'm pleased to say that you are now the proud father of two very healthy babies."

Steven and Millie reacted joyfully. "Is Lori alright?"

"Yes, yes! She's exhausted, but resting in recovery as we speak."

"Can I—we—see her?"

"Only for a few moments. She's been through quite an ordeal." Steven grabbed Millie's hand, and they followed the doctor to Loraine's room.

After Adam left the prison with Joey, he decided the best place to keep her safe was at his home. When they entered the house, Adam invited her to sit and get comfortable. Joey shyly took a seat on the couch. "Can I get you a drink? Water or a soda?" Joey shook her head no, and Adam sat down opposite her. "You haven't said a word since we left the prison. Am I going to be able to trust you?" Joey nodded. "Okay! Here's the deal. We have some really bad people called the Secret Society who want to take control of the United States. We have to somehow get into their database to find out what major players are involved."

"Where's the host computer?"

Adam shook his head with frustration. "I don't know. But it can be accessed through a computer in the back office of the S.O.S. Club."

"Can you get me in there?"

Adam looked upward in thought. "I suppose with some careful planning, we can."

"You get me in there, and trust me, I'll crack it in no time at all."

Just then, Grant Posterle casually sauntered in from an adjacent room with his gun drawn. "It's too bad neither of you will get the chance to carry that plan out."

He motioned to Adam with his free hand. "Toss your gun over to me."

Adam rolled his eyes, slowly took the gun from his holster, and tossed it to him. Grant then took the gun, holstered his own, and aimed Adam's gun at both of them. "A good agent would've checked his back door. You're getting careless, Adam."

Adam replied, "How did you know?"

Grant said, "The warden at the state prison called to see what plans we had for Ms. Arcovio."

Adam shook his head. "What do you intend to do now?"

"Kill you with your gun, of course." Grant paced closer. "I'll make it look like there was a struggle, she got your gun and shot you. Then I'll take her somewhere in your car, shoot her, and say she was trying to get away."

The cuckoo clock on a nearby wall chimed and distracted Grant just long enough for Adam to quickly charge at him. The gun went off into the ceiling as they struggled. Adam was able to knock the gun from his hand and kicked it across the room. They continued to fight, but Grant was stronger and began to overpower Adam. A few seconds later, while Grant had him in a chokehold, a gunshot echoed through the house. Adam looked up at the shocked expression on Grant's face as he released his grip and slowly collapsed onto the floor. Adam was dazed, as he turned to see Joey, trembling and aiming the gun at him. Adam got to his feet cautiously, as Joey quickly tossed the gun aside. "Joey, it's okay… he's dead. You shot the bastard right between the eyes." She looked at Grant's dead body with terror in her eyes.

"I didn't mean to kill him."

"I know, but he would have killed both of us." Adam sighed. "Now we another problem to solve."

Steven slowly entered Loraine's room to find her peacefully resting. As he strolled closer to the bed, she opened her eyes slightly and managed a weak smile. "Hello there!" he stated.

He grabbed a chair and pulled it close to the bed, while Loraine reached for his hand. "Did you see our babies?"

"Only for a moment. They're beautiful. Just like their mommy."

"I'm certain it helped for them to have such a handsome father as well."

Steven smiled. "I came close to losing you this morning. I dread to think what may have happened if I hadn't arrived when I did."

Loraine looked at him with a perplexed expression. "What did I witness in you this morning? It was superhuman!"

Steven looked down. "The gods granted me the powers so that I could protect you and the rest of my family."

Loraine was flabbergasted. "It most definitely worked. I'm baffled by my mother's performance as well."

Steven giggled. "You'll have to have her explain that to you. I'm sure she will when the time is right." Steven gently brushed her hair back with his hand. "I should leave now, so you can get some rest. I'll be back soon." He kissed her forehead. "I love you!" She smiled, and silently mouthed the same words back to him.

He quietly closed the door to her room and made his way back to the waiting room. Once there, he found it filled with unexpected guests. "Hail! Hail! The gang's all here." Phillip, Ezekiel, Amy, Gerard, and Millie all stood, eagerly waiting for an update.

Amy anxiously asked, "Is everything okay?"

"Yes, she and the babies are doing just fine. They should be able to come home in a few days." He looked at Philip and Ezekiel who were still dressed in their suits. "If I should say so myself, you two gentlemen are looking quite dapper."

Ezekiel responded, "I do think I could grow quite accustomed to this look."

Steven turned serious. "Something strange happened earlier. The spirit of Daphne Branch appeared to me..."

Gerard interrupted, "...And told you about Liddy McPherson's remains?"

Philip picked up the conversation from there. "Gerard just finished telling us all about it. We have to get those remains back before Detective Fuller buries them."

"If he hasn't done so already. We know his name is in that book."

Ezekiel turned to Amy. "Perhaps you, Charlotte, and Agent Smith can find something out when you go to get Kristin Wiler."

Amy answered, "Perhaps Officer Hawley could be of assistance. We already know he can be trusted." Millie stayed quiet but listened to the conversation attentively.

Phillip responded, "If all goes well, Ezekiel, Steven, Gerard, and I will meet you back at Branchview at around eight o'clock."

Ezekiel looked at his watch, then glanced at everyone. "It's 3:15 right now. Let's go get this done."

As all turned to depart, Millie took hold of Steven's arm and spoke in a loud whisper. "Steven! You must tell me what's going on—"

Steven reacted impatiently. "There's no time for me to do that. I promise that we'll talk later. Right now, I need you to be here for Lori and the babies."

Millie nodded and looked at him very seriously. "Please be safe!"

In the Branchview foyer, someone knocked on the large mahogany doors, and Mrs. Porter ambled as quickly as she could from the sitting room, with Bumpers tagging closely behind. "Oh, Bumpers! I swear this place is as busy as an airport terminal." She opened the door to find a very nervous Agent Smith and Joey. "Agent Smith! Was Steven expecting you?"

"No! Actually, I need your help… desperately!" Mrs. Porter reacted nervously and ushered them into the foyer. "I have to be somewhere, and I'm running rather late." He motioned to Joey, who had gone down to one knee to pet Bumpers. "This is Joey. She's in my protective custody. Can I trust you to watch her for a few hours?"

Mrs. Porter looked her up and down. "Well of course! The poor child looks like she's emaciated. I'll fix a nice meal for her."

Adam said anxiously, "Thank you, Mrs. Porter! Hopefully, I'll be back by early evening." He turned to Joey. "I need you to stay right here with Mrs. Porter. If you try to escape, your life could be in great danger. Can I trust you to do as I say?" Joey looked up at him, rapidly nodded yes, while Adam turned back to Mrs. Porter with urgency. "I have to get going, but there's one other thing I need."

"What might that be?" she replied.

"Since you're the housekeeper, you know this place better than anyone. Where can I hide a dead body?" Mrs.

Porter was rendered stunned and speechless by Adam's request.

At Branch Consolidated, Luke sat comfortably in his office as Liddy wearily entered and sat down in a nearby chair. "How are you feeling?"

"Weak, but much better! That was a very close call."

Luke's cell phone rang. "Speak to me." Luke listened, then broke into a slight smile. "You found them! Good job! Now, I fully trust that you'll make sure I have three fewer problems before the end of the night?" He ended the call, completely pleased with his dealings. *Oh... finally.* He leaned back in his chair, smiling.

Chapter Twenty-One:

Can We Trust Her Really?

T he drama escalated as the day progressed in this crucial struggle to save innocent victims caught within the ambitious path of Luke Underwood, Liddy McPherson, and the Secret Society. In the case of Kristin Wiler, Charlotte felt especially obligated to help her escape prosecution for the crimes she regretfully committed. As the team worked hard to solve not only this issue, but many others in the world surrounding Branchview and Lockeport, another issue arose that would very quickly demand their attention as well.

Amy was seated outside on a park bench in front of the police station, patiently waiting as a black cat strolled up next to her. Amy stared straight ahead and sternly said, "I'm so glad you could make it, Charlotte. I was beginning to think you stood me up." The cat jumped up on the bench next to her, and Charlotte appeared. "I must say you do create quite a dramatic entrance."

"Where is Agent Smith?"

"He's late, and I have an anxious feeling that something isn't quite right."

Charlotte seemed unusually concerned. "It's nearly seven. She's due to be transported at seven-thirty."

"I know! We may have to do this without him. It's our only chance."

Charlotte thought for a moment. "Perhaps I could sneak in, put a sleeping spell on everyone inside, and simply walk out with her."

Amy spun around and sternly faced her. "Absolutely not! Kristin will be terrified when she sees you."

"What type of plan would you suggest?" Charlotte replied.

"Just follow my lead, and don't appear until I've had a chance to talk with her. Then you can do your little cat thing and create a distraction." She smiled.

Charlotte nodded, and Amy strolled inside by herself. A young female officer was standing behind the admittance desk. "How can I help you?"

"I'm Dr. Amy Seagraves. Kristin Wiler's appointed attorney requested that I give her a brief psychological evaluation before she gets transported."

The officer quickly checked out the release file as Officer Hawley entered the work area. "There doesn't seem to be any paperwork indicating that request, ma'am."

Hawley interrupted, "I happen to personally know Dr. Seagraves, and I'm sure that request is valid if she says it is."

"Thank you, Officer Hawley. I realize that I am pushing it a bit late, but I absolutely must see her before she gets transferred out."

"No problem, doctor. I can walk you back to the holding room."

Kristin Wiler sat waiting, wearing an orange prison jumpsuit, as Amy was ushered in by Officer Hawley. "This shouldn't take too long. By the way, I was wondering if you knew where they're keeping the remains that were found at the Branch estate this morning?"

"They're downstairs in the crime lab. Why do you ask?"

Amy smiled. "Steven Spencer was interested in knowing. I'm sure he'll be checking on it later."

"Just have him ask for me when he calls." She nodded.

Hawley left the room, and Amy quickly sat down on the bench next to Kristin. "We only have a few minutes, so I have to make this quick." She took hold of Kristin's hand. "I'm going to get you out of here, but you might be startled by the spirit who is going to help me." Kristin gave her a puzzled expression. However, deep inside, she had a rough idea of who it might be.

In the deep caverns below the cliffs of Lighthouse Point, Poseidon ushered a blindfolded Steven and Gerard into the Secret Cave. Zeus rose from one of the two throne seats to greet them. Poseidon reached up and pulled the blinders back on each man, and Gerard was in awe as his eyes searched the impressive perimeters of the large Cave Room. "I'm glad to be rid of that thing. I'm afraid I could never function very well as a blind man."

Poseidon gave an understanding nod. "As I mentioned before, it's traditional protocol. No mortal can know the secret entrance."

Zeus stepped down from the altar to greet the arriving party, as Gerard continued to scan the room with amazement. "What is this place?"

Zeus stated, "For now, we'll just refer to it as the secret Cave Room. We'll explain further when we have more time."

Zeus nodded to Steven. "Gerard! Now that Hades has Sharie and Deanna, you're more involved in this than ever. The two of us, as well as Amphitrite, have agreed that it's time to grant you the powers necessary to transform you from a bystander to an ally."

Gerard stepped back in fearful anticipation. "I don't understand what you mean. I'm far from being superhuman material."

Poseidon approached him with a chuckle and laid an assuring hand on his shoulder. "We're willing to grant you the powers needed to help us fight Hades, and Liddy McPherson. Will you accept our offer?"

Gerard looked to Steven for further assurance and was answered with a nod of certainty. "By all means then. How could I possibly say no to the gods and my friends?"

As Gerard was being weaponized physically, Charlotte was pacing outside the police station, watching the time on her wristwatch. *Oh, she should've had enough time by now.* With a wave of her hands, she abruptly disappeared. Moments later, inside the police station, a black cat wandered into the squad room, and everyone turned their attention toward it. The female officer from the front desk reentered the room. "How did that cat get in here?"

A handsome male officer was on one knee, scratching the purring cat under the chin, while others in the room gathered around. "I have no idea! But isn't she a cutie?"

Charlotte suddenly appeared on the floor next to him. "Meow… You're kind of cute, too." Everyone was taken aback, as Charlotte then waved her hand in the air, and all attendants in the room slumped to the floor, and into a deep sleep. As the thrill of victory rushed over Charlotte, she strolled toward the holding room. *Sweet dreams, everyone!*

Charlotte opened the door and was surprised to find Amy and Kristin leaning against each other, fast asleep. *Oh… that spell was a bit more potent than I thought.* She flicked her fingers toward the two. "Time to wake up, ladies." The two snapped out of their slumber, and Charlotte motioned toward them with urgency. "Come on! We must get going!" The women hurried toward the door just as Agent Smith entered. He paused to look at all the slumbering bodies, then looked to the three women with a clueless expression. Amy replied, "Don't even ask! We must move, now!" All four swiftly exited.

As the four made their way to Adam's car, Detective Fuller was getting out of his. Fuller quickly drew his weapon. "Agent Smith! Stop right there!"

Adam slowly turned around, while the others momentarily froze in place. "She's in my custody now. In case you've forgotten, I'm a Federal Agent."

Fuller replied, "Ask me if I care. I see someone helping a murderer escape." Without warning, he fired a shot that hit Adam in the arm. Before he could shoot again, Charlotte pointed two fingers toward Fuller, and flames engulfed his hand, causing him to quickly drop the gun, and scream out in agony.

Amy looked relieved, and Charlotte quickly commanded, "Hurry! I'll hold this bastard off, while the rest of you get away." Kristin helped Adam into the back of the car, while Amy got into the driver's seat.

Fuller swatted out the flames on his long sleeve shirt, then struggled to get back to his car. Amy sped away, while Charlotte had a bit of fun with Fuller. She aimed her outstretched fingers toward his car, causing the engine to stall out. Then, amidst a blinding light, she vanished.

At Lighthouse Point, Steven, Gerard, Zeus, and Poseidon were heading back along the beach. Steven asked, "How do you feel, Gerard?"

"More energetic than I have in years."

Poseidon chuckled. "Just try to keep that energy in check until it's needed."

Steven's cell phone rang, and he gave it a long look. "It's Agent Smith." He took the call and turned on the speaker. "Agent Smith! Did everything go as planned?"

Adam said with desperation, "Not exactly. We need your help. I got shot, and we need to ditch my car."

"Where are you?" Steven replied.

"The shopping center, just outside of town on Old Saybrook Road."

"Okay! Hang tight! We'll get there as soon as we can." Steven ended the call, and all four men acted quickly.

Zeus spoke up, "Poseidon! You go with Steven. Gerard and I will go to rescue Sharie and Deanna. Then hopefully, we'll all meet safely back at Branchview."

Poseidon asked, "What about Hades? He won't let you just march in there and take them without a fight."

"If he gets in our way, then either he or I will have to die. It's as simple as that."

Gerard responded with a look of great concern, while Steven impatiently tapped Poseidon on the arm. "Come on! We haven't much time!" The men all nodded and went about their plan.

At the Underwood residence, Liddy descended the stairs, while Luke waited for her at the bottom. "Did you get the women fed?"

Liddy replied, "All taken care of. I think you're treating them far too well."

"I have no animosity toward them. They're simply a means to an end." They were distracted by a knock at the door. "I wasn't expecting anyone. Do you know who that might be?"

Liddy cluelessly shrugged, and Luke moved to answer the door. He pulled it open to find an anxious Detective Fuller. "I got a problem. I need your help." Without a word, Luke ushered him in. "Agent Smith helped Kristin Wiler escape a short time ago. I shot and wounded him, but they still got away."

Luke noticed his loosely bandaged hand. "What happened there?"

Fuller replied with agony in his voice, "Some dark-haired bitch burned my hand with some sort of magic."

Liddy, who had been listening, strolled the rest of the way down the stairs. "Charlotte Locke!"

"Who the hell is this Charlotte Locke?"

Luke looked down. "She's the spirit witch that possessed Kristin Wiler and is responsible for all the murders."

Fuller shook his head in frustration. "I don't know what the hell you're talking about."

"I'll explain it to you some other time. You mentioned others were helping him. Do you know who they were?"

"There was just one other. Some hot looking redhead that looked a heck of a lot like the mural painting over at The Mermaid Inn."

Liddy rolled her eyes and stepped forward. "That would be Dr. Amy Seagraves." Liddy and Luke exchanged a glance.

"You seem to know a lot about these people," Fuller responded.

"Let's just say that our paths have crossed more than a few times."

Luke replied, "I don't know what you expect me to do. This is obviously a police matter."

Fuller chuckled arrogantly. "There's something more. I talked to Agent Posterle earlier, and he mentioned that he had reason to believe Smith was onto us. He said that he'd get back to me, but never did."

Luke nonchalantly stated, "He's probably busy working on a case."

Fuller shook his head. "He usually gets back to me right away. Even if it's just a text. I have a feeling something's gone wrong."

Luke thought for a moment. "I see where you're going with this. If Agent Smith has any knowledge of the Secret Society, that could be trouble for us all."

Liddy chimed in, "Perhaps I could use my psychic abilities to locate all of them."

"Good idea! But we'll deal with Posterle's disappearance later. Right now, we must find Agent Smith before he has the chance to share what he knows." Luke glanced back at Fuller seriously.

On the outskirts of town, Amy parked Agent Smith's car at the far end of the mall parking lot, along the bordering tree line. Kristin took the opportunity to attend to Adam's wound, while Amy stayed behind the wheel, watching for Steven and Poseidon.

Kristin explained, "The tourniquet helped to stop the bleeding. We just have to get him somewhere so that I can get that bullet out."

"How do you know so much about treating wounds?"

"I was a nurse in my previous life."

Adam looked up at her, and said weakly, "Lucky for me…."

Amy's attention shifted to an oncoming car. "There he is! It's Steven!" They all took a deep sigh.

Across town, Ezekiel and Gerard parked down the street, but within sight of Luke's house. "As soon as it gets dark, we'll have to move, regardless of whether he's there or not," Ezekiel stated. Suddenly, Luke and Fuller exited the house and got into Fuller's squad car. "I think we just got lucky. They're leaving."

"Liddy's still in there, but it should not be a problem in her somewhat weakened state."

"Duck down! They're driving this way."

Fuller's car drove by, and they sat back up. "Let's do this!"

Inside the house, Liddy paced slowly, but nervously. In the cover of the swiftly increasing darkness, Ezekiel and Gerard snuck up onto the porch. A black cat followed close behind; Gerard tried to shoo it away, but Charlotte appeared, startling both men.

"I thought you could use some help," she whispered. Both gave her a silent nod.

Liddy paused her nervous fidgeting long enough to peek out the side window. She then turned on the porch light and walked away from the foyer. All three tried to conceal their presence in the shadows of the porch. Ezekiel blinked toward the porch light, and it went dark. He then turned and signaled 'go' to Gerard and Charlotte. The front door popped open, and the trio barged in. Liddy hurried from the parlor, and Ezekiel hit her with a bolt of energy that sent her flying hard into a wall.

Charlotte yelled out, "They're probably in the turret room upstairs." The men nodded and headed in that direction.

Liddy struggled to regain her senses. She sat upright and pulled a chain from her blouse. At the end of it was a dog whistle that she abruptly blew into.

The door to the turret room flew open and Gerard entered, followed by Ezekiel and Charlotte. Sharie shouted, "Gerard!"

Deana hollered, "Daddy!" They both ran to embrace him.

"Come on! We have to hurry!" The thunderous sound of barking dogs erupted within the house.

Ezekiel shouted, "The hounds! I'll take care of them. Just don't look into their eyes." The three dogs tore up the stairs, forcing them all back into the turret room before Ezekiel could act. They slammed the door just in time, as the dogs wildly pounced against it.

Charlotte said, "I have an idea. I'll distract the dogs, while all of you escape." Before anyone could respond, Charlotte disappeared. In the hallway outside the room, a small black cat appeared at the top of the stairs. Liddy, still dazed, began to make her way upstairs. The cat meowed, and the dogs turned to give chase down the stairs. The cat scampered out the open front door with the dogs in hot pursuit. The dogs whisked past a still unstable Liddy, causing her to tumble back down the stairs, while the others escaped the room. Outside, the cat scurried up a tree, and the dogs attacked the trunk, trying desperately to reach it.

Charlotte then appeared behind the dogs, taking them by surprise. "Here doggies! This is my version of mace." She blew dust from her cupped hands into the dogs' eyes, and they immediately began howling and whimpering like helpless puppies.

As the four exited the house, Liddy stumbled out behind them. Ezekiel and Deanna raced ahead toward the waiting car, but Sharie tripped on the front step, taking Gerard down onto the ground with her. Liddy shot webbing from her fingers, and it tangled their feet. Gerard transformed as he turned toward Liddy, roaring, with eyes glowing red. He easily broke the webbing on his feet and shot bolts of energy from his tiger paw hand that pined Liddy halfway up a porch pillar. He held her against the pillar with his massive paw throttling her throat.

Sharie watched in horror. "Gerard! No! You're killing her!"

Ezekiel ran back. "Come on, Gerard! We'll deal with her later." Gerard snapped to his senses and released Liddy. She slid down the pillar to the porch deck, striking the hardwood surface as she landed. He picked up Sharie in his massive, muscular arms, and all three hurried toward the car.

As Liddy slowly struggled to her feet and looked angrily toward the now retreating car, Charlotte boldly approached. "Don't even think about it, Liddy." She held up her hands, creating a blinding wall of light energy that sent Liddy reeling once again.

Chapter Twenty-Two:

Nothing Can Stop Our Success

By the time Detective Fuller and Luke found Agent Smith's car, all the occupants were long gone. Fuller jumped from his car to question Officer Hawley and the other patrolman who had arrived first. "What have you got?"

"They were already gone when we got here."

Fuller pitched a fit, as Luke calmly walked over and peeked in the car. "Somebody must've been helping them."

Office Hawley stated, "They couldn't have gotten too far. There's a lot of blood in that back seat."

Luke strolled up to the two men. "My educated guess would be that you'll find them at Branchview."

Hawley turned to Fuller. "Speaking of Branchview, what happened to the remains that were in the crime lab?"

Fuller aggressively answered, "That's a top-secret issue that doesn't concern you, Hawley. If you like your job, you'd be wise, not to ask about it again." Hawley simply nodded, and walked away from the conversation, as Luke and Fuller exchanged a serious glance. Fuller's cell phone rang. "Fuller here!" He listened. "I see! When did this happen?" He looked to Luke with concern. "Fine, hold tight. I'll be right there." He ended the call.

Luke jumped in, "What was that all about?"

"A disturbance at your house. A neighbor claims she saw some pretty crazy things going down."

Steven and the others finally arrived back at Branchview. Mrs. Porter greeted them at the door and ushered them all in. Steven helped a very weak Adam to a chair in the foyer, as a nervous Mrs. Porter hovered over them. "What on earth happened?"

Kristin stepped forward and took control of the situation. "He's been shot! I need to work on him right away. I'll need a bottle of whiskey, plenty of hot water, clean linens, and a sterile knife and tweezers."

Mrs. Porter nervously replied, "That shouldn't be a problem in this house."

Adam spoke up, "Wait! We have to move Posterle from the east wing. Just in case Fuller shows up with a search party."

Mrs. Porter and Joey looked at each other. "We already did."

Steven asked, "Where did you put his body?"

Mrs. Porter replied with anxious vigor, "We buried it under the dirt floor in the hidden portion of the basement. No one will ever find him there." All exchanged a shocked look of disbelief.

Steven then eyed Joey. "Who are you?"

Adam answered for her. "This is Joey Arcovio. She's the hacker that's going to help us get into the database of the Secret Society." Joey looked at the floor shyly, while a black cat wandered in through the open door.

Mrs. Porter pointed anxiously. "That cat!"

Phillip exclaimed, "It's okay, Mrs. Porter! She's one of us now." Charlotte appeared before a very stunned Mrs. Porter and Joey.

Joey shouted, "Wow! Things get stranger by the minute around here."

Amy strolled up to Charlotte's side and commented with a smirk, "I must admit, I was pretty impressed by your performance tonight." She smiled.

A very impatient Kristin spoke up. "With all due respect, could I please get those things I need? We have very little time."

"Oh, yes! I'll get right on it!" Mrs. Porter exclaimed as she quickly ambled from the room.

Joey chimed in as she followed, "I'll help!"

Steven took command. "We'll move Agent Smith to the dining room table. You'll be able to work on him easily there." Steven then helped Adam from the chair and said in a low voice, "Are you sure about this Joey? She looks rather meek to me."

Adam smiled. "Looks are deceiving! She's the best at what she does, and whatever you do, don't get her mad."

Kristin tended to Adam in the dining room, waiting for Mrs. Porter and Joey to return with the supplies. She then shooed everyone away but Steven, so that she could work on Adam's wound.

The group waited patiently, watching the minutes tick away on the mantel clock in the sitting room. Kristin and Steven finally entered, and Phillip boldly stepped forward. "How is he?"

Steven smiled. "A bit drunk, but he should recover just fine."

Charlotte strolled over next to Kristin and motioned her toward the foyer. "Can I talk to you for a minute?" She nodded. Charlotte and Kristin entered the foyer and faced each other. "I never had the chance to apologize for everything I did to you."

Kristin shook her head. "You more than made up for it by helping us tonight. But it will take me some time to forgive you."

"I understand." Charlotte paused with solemn thought before continuing. "Agent Smith always did have a thing for you, and I think you like him as well."

Kristin replied with a grin, "He is kind of hot, isn't he?"

Charlotte grinned. "Take it from an old spirit witch, who regretfully never took the time to fall in love: March right back in that dining room, and tell him how you feel." Kristin looked away in anxious thought, then back at Charlotte with wonder. "Just do it!" Kristin eagerly nodded and hurried back toward the dining room as a tear trickles down Charlotte's cheek. *Way to go, girl…* Charlotte disappeared from the foyer, just as Ezekiel and Gerard entered with Sharie and Deanna.

All four marched triumphantly into the sitting room and were met with applause. Mrs. Porter greeted Sharie with a hug, "Oh Sharie! Thank heavens you and Deanna are back with us."

Amy stepped forward, "Well! It appears that we all had a somewhat successful night."

Ezekiel announced, "We could have never done it without the help we received from Charlotte. Has she shown up here yet?"

Mrs. Porter looked around the room. "She was just here a minute ago."

Steven grew impatient and motioned to Philip and Amy. "We have to move Kristin right away. She can change into one of Loraine's outfits, and I'll take her prison jumpsuit and burn it somewhere on the grounds later."

Amy responded, "What about Agent Smith? They're looking for him as well."

Steven rolled his eyes and shrugged. "He's determined to stay here and help us."

Phillip replied, "That's impossible! He's now wanted for helping two prisoners escape custody." A knock interrupted him.

Steven whispered, "Everyone be very quiet. I'll take care of this." The group huddled together.

Steven pulled the sitting room doors shut and entered the foyer. He took a deep breath as he opened the front door. "Detective Fuller! How can I help you?"

Fuller tried to look around him, and into the house, "Mr. Spencer! I have reason to believe you may be harboring criminals in your house. I'm sure you wouldn't mind if I came in and took a look around?"

Steven shook his head defiantly and blocked the door. "Not without a warrant. I know my rights."

The two men had a stare down for a long moment, and Fuller reluctantly backed off. "Okay! If that's the way it has to be, I'll come back later tonight with officers and a warrant."

"I'll be here," Steven replied boldly.

"So be it!" Fuller backed away from the door, and Steven closed and locked it. Ezekiel, Philip, and Amy opened the door from the sitting room and entered the foyer. "That was Fuller! We need to move those two out of here ASAP."

Steven, Ezekiel, Philip, and Amy all quickly moved with urgency toward the dining room, where they discovered Adam and Kristin engaged in a passionate kiss.

Amy then turned to the three men behind her and flashed a mischievous grin along with a naughty raised eyebrow. "Well! I do believe we'll need to make accommodations for another passenger." All three men looked at each other with wide-eyed amusement and unanimously nodded in agreement.

Chapter Twenty-Three:

The Magnificent Winged Horse

A mild summer breeze blew in from the Atlantic on this seemingly endless night. Once again, Amphitrite found herself in the role of a guide, leading innocents to the haven of the parallel world. Once there, two lovers could begin a new life together, far from the false persecution they faced in this unjust world. For all of those who remained in this dimension, there would be no rest in the days ahead, as they sharpened their strategy and continued their arduous behind-the-scenes battle with the evil that would lead them to the inevitable showdown on the Summer Solstice.

On the beach at Lighthouse Point, the magnificent, winged horse stood poised and ready for yet another journey across the ocean. Adam was standing close to Kristin with his arm around her waist for balance. The whole scene was incredible. Only a few short days ago, Adam Smith would never have imagined working in concert with mythical beings that were only believed to exist in fables.

Adam exclaimed before mounting Pegasus, "Are you sure I didn't die? This seems like some fairy tale dream."

Poseidon reassured him, "I assure you that it's very real. In the coming days, you'll learn a great deal about us and the hidden world."

Adam shook hands with Poseidon and Zeus, then moved to Steven. "I wish I could stay to help."

Steven replied, "This is the only logical thing to do. You and Kristin need each other."

Adam turned to glance at Kristin who walked over and slipped her arm around him. He then turned his attention back to Steven. "Please take care of Joey."

Steven gave him an assured nod. "I promise you; she'll be in safekeeping."

Adam answered with a smile, "Thank you again for everything."

Kristin approached Steven and gently kissed him on the cheek. "I'll always remember you, Steven Spencer."

Steven blushed. "You'll be hard to forget as well. On the other hand, I'd rather not remember you under the guise of Lucretia Darknight." She smiled and gave a definitive nod of agreement.

Kristin glanced around the dark beach. "I'd hoped that Charlotte would've come to see us off. Tell her I said thanks. She'll know what I mean." Steven answered with a wink.

Amphitrite stroked the mane of Pegasus and spoke with urgency, "Come! We must be going! We have a strong headwind that will make our journey a bit longer than normal."

Adam approached the horse and shook his head in amazement. "Here we go!" Zeus and Poseidon hoisted him onto the horse, then followed suit with Kristin. Once mounted, she securely wrapped her arms around Adam and comfortably rested her head against his back. Amphitrite noticed Adam's nervousness as they prepared for flight. "Just lean forward, and grip his mane. I guarantee it will be a smooth ride."

Zeus turned to Amphitrite with sober concern. "Be safe, Amphitrite."

"We'll be fine. Damaris and Hermia will join us a few miles out, and the Nerieds will be following in our wake." Amphitrite then seductively sauntered out toward the ocean. She loosely waved her hands in the air as her earthly clothes disappeared, and she continued strolling naked into the deeper waters.

Poseidon looked at Steven with a bright-eyed smile. "That's a sight that I shall never grow tired of seeing."

Steven shook his head. "I can't think of too many men that would grow tired of it."

Once Amphitrite was neck-deep in the water, she turned and waved toward Pegasus, calling, "Onward until the morning!" She submerged, as her finned tail rose in the air. Her high-pitched, dolphin-like clicks echoed loudly across the dark ocean.

Pegasus neighed, while gently striding toward the water, his wings spread wide. Amphitrite led the way in the water, as the magnificent beast took flight. The revolving lighthouse lamp intermittently offered a glimpse as they flew away into the night.

A lone figure stood watching from the cliffs above, as the winged horse gracefully glided off into the darkness, carrying Adam and Kristin to their new destiny. Charlotte sadly said to herself, *Goodbye, Kristin Wiler. I wish you a good life.*

In Canada, Alton Sinclair, a rugged-looking man with dark features, played Monopoly with Audrey, Heather, and Daniel IV in the Sinclair parlor. The family was settling in nicely to their new surroundings. Audrey finally felt like they had arrived somewhere they could relax and enjoy some freedom. Daniel jumped from his seat with excitement. "I have Park Place."

Alton and the others giggled. "At this rate, Daniel will own this house before long." A few seconds later, there was a brief, loud buzzer noise, and the lights flickered.

Audrey exclaimed, "What in the world was that?"

"It was my burglar alarm. But if someone tripped it, it should've stayed on until I shut it off."

"Maybe there was a short circuit," Heather added.

Alton stood up and walked to a computer monitor at the other end of the room. "I'll check the property cams to see if they're picking up anything." He leaned over the monitor to check things out. "That's rather odd. None of the cameras are working." There was a loud thud outside the window. Alton then grabbed a remote, entered a combination, and a wall slid open to reveal a hidden room. "Hurry! Everyone into the safe room."

Alton stood at the door ushering everyone in. "Aren't you coming in too?" Audrey inquired.

Alton shook his head. "I'll let you all out when the danger has passed."

Audrey commented, "Be careful, Alton!" He entered the combination code again, and the wall slid shut. The lights flickered, then went out altogether. Alton looked around anxiously in the dark. He went to a large cabinet in the room, opened it, and chose a high-powered crossbow from among an array of other weapons, and also grabbed some ninja stars from a nearby drawer. He then crouched down behind a chair and waited, as he heard the front door slowly creak open.

The hardwood floor gave way to the intruder's footsteps. A voice called out in the dark, "Mr. Sinclair! We know you're home! Come out quietly, and bring the Branch family with you." Alton waited and listened closely to the footsteps that revealed at least three individuals. The lead assassin stood in the doorway to the parlor. "We will find you!"

Alton took a coin from his pocket and tossed it across the floor. The assassin paused, and cautiously entered deeper into the parlor. Alton waited silently, hidden securely behind the large chair. As the intruder made his way into the line of fire, he jumped up and released the trigger. Since Alton was an expert marksman, the arrow struck the criminal square in the heart. Alton kicked off his shoes and quietly made his way across the floor. He checked to be sure the man was dead, then set out to find the next two assassins.

Audrey broke the silence inside the saferoom. "I think I heard something out there."

Heather whispered, "I can't believe they found us."

Audrey listened closely and commented with dread, "I can't hear anything now. Can you?"

An emotional Daniel stirred. "I'm scared! What if they can get in here?"

Audrey hugged the boy to comfort him. "That wall is made of thick steel, and Mr. Sinclair is the only one who knows the combination."

Heather added assurance, "They'll have to tear this house down to get to us, Daniel."

The second assassin searched the area, lifting the dining table cloth, then moved on to the kitchen pantry. Alton quietly stalked him from a distance, watching his every move. As the intruder turned after checking a back-entry way, a ninja star whizzed through the air, digging into his shoulder. He let out an agonizing groan, shooting his gun wildly in Alton's direction. A second star quickly followed, striking him in the carotid artery. The assassin fell to his knees, rapidly bleeding out as he gasped his last breath of air. Alton walked over and kicked the gun away from under his limp hand. Then before he could turn to check his six, a serrated knife struck him deep in the upper bicep.

The assailant immediately pulled it out, while Alton grimaced in pain. He then felt the cold steel of the blade against his throat, as the assailant backed him against the kitchen counter. He spoke in a loud whisper within an inch of Alton's face, "Now! Before I slit your throat, I want to know where you're keeping the Branch family."

"They're not here…" he stated.

The assassin pressed on Alton's wound, causing intense pain. "Try again—"

"Okay! Okay! They're outside in the utility shed!" He gestured toward the back door, and the assassin looked away just long enough for Alton to grab a tea kettle from the stovetop. He swung it wildly, striking the assassin in the head, and sending him reeling backward. A violent struggle ensued between the two men, and Alton painfully fell to the floor after delivering a solid punch to the jaw of his opponent. Out of his peripheral vision, Alton saw the dead assassin's gun just a few inches away. He quickly grabbed it, rolled, and shot the pursuing assailant dead. A wounded, exhausted Alton struggled to his feet, holding his bleeding arm as he stumbled out the back door. A few seconds later, a generator was heard starting up, and the lights immediately went back on. Alton reentered the room, and leaned over the third assassin, rifling through his pockets until he pulled out a wallet and opened it. The sight brought a new light to the situation as Alton mumbled with disbelief, "These guys are CIA!"

Alton then hurried back toward the safe room, opened the wall once again, and a very fearful Branch family sighed with relief. "It's all over! But we must get out of here as soon as possible."

Audrey stepped into the parlor and approached him with concern. "You're hurt! We're not going anywhere until I tend to that arm."

Alton took a deep breath as Audrey examined his wound. "I'll be fine!"

"Nonsense!" She turned to Heather. "Go get my sewing kit. We must stop this bleeding, and get him stitched up."

Alton noticed Daniel staring with horror at the dead assassin in the parlor. "Run along, and help your sister, Daniel. But don't go in the kitchen." The boy quickly fled the room, as Audrey took off her blouse, tore it at the seam, and tied a tourniquet above the wound. "I'm sorry that he had to see that," Alton stated.

"It's okay! It's better if he fully realizes that it could've been us." She pulled the tourniquet tight and dabbed the excess blood from his arm with what was left of her blouse. "How were you able to take down those men by yourself?"

"Before I made my fortune in writing and real estate, I was a member of an elite Impact Team in the Canadian Armed Forces."

Audrey glanced at him with a smirk. "You're just full of all types of surprises. Aren't you, Mr. Sinclair?" Alton smiled.

Chapter Twenty-Four:

Casual Conversations

The gods had made their way back to Branchview, thinking all was well for the moment. They were seated comfortably in the sitting room, sipping brandy, and engaging in casual conversation. Zeus stated, "You know, seeing Amphitrite au natural tonight made me think of my first wife Metis. You do remember her, don't you?"

Poseidon replied, "The Oceanid! How could I forget her? That must've been around 1300 BC."

Zeus grinned. "Yes, was it really… that long ago?"

"Longer than I'd like to admit."

"I must say that I loved that woman more than any of my seven wives."

Poseidon responded, "Even more than Hera?"

Zeus looked at him with subtle surprise. "Have you forgotten that she was our sister? That would be very frowned upon in this modern world."

Poseidon reflected, "Perhaps it's time for both of us to settle into a normal life, brother. Do you know where Metis is now?"

"The last I knew; she was staying near the coast of Rhode Island on the Aegean Sea."

"Maybe you should look her up?"

Zeus answered, "What about you, big brother? Are you still in love with Amphitrite?"

"Perhaps! But more than anything, having lost Tina, I now understand how much hurt she harbored when she lost Matthew Branch."

Zeus saluted him with his drink. "Maybe when this battle is over, we will seek a change." He downed his brandy, while Steven entered the room, and both men turned their attention to him. The mantle clock chimed 1:30 a.m.

"Steven…." Poseidon asked, "do you think Detective Fuller will be back tonight?"

"I do not doubt that he will."

"Where do you plan to hide Ms. Arcovio?"

Steven pointed toward the wall, "There's a hidden passageway behind that wall panel that leads to a room with a bed. Mrs. Porter is in there cleaning and preparing it for her."

Poseidon stood up and looked around the room. "I'd imagine there's a lot of secret rooms and passages in this old house."

Steven nodded in agreement. "Luckily, my brother Daniel showed me where they all were before he passed. At least the ones he knew about. I have the LeRoux's hidden away where they can't be found as well." There was a knock, and Steven looked to the gods with certainty. "I'm betting that's Fuller now." Steven walked over to the wall, opened the secret panel, and ushered Zeus and Poseidon in. "Just don't get lost in there." Zeus looked back at him with raised eyebrows.

The wounded and still stunned Liddy sat in the parlor of Luke's house. "I'm very disappointed in you, Liddy."

"I'm beginning to think I would've been better off staying in spirit, rather than taking on my mortal body. I wouldn't have been so vulnerable."

Luke slammed his fist on the table in anger and pointed at her. "You're lucky I don't send you back to the depths of hell."

"I'm telling you! I could've held my own if it wasn't for Charlotte."

"I should've destroyed that witch when I had the chance," Luke lamented.

Liddy leaned forward with fire in her eyes. "And that Gerard LeRoux! I swear! He's just as powerful as Steven Spencer."

"The gods must've helped him as well."

Luke's cell phone rang, and he answered it with urgency and turned on the speaker mode. "You better have good news for us."

"Mr. Underwood! I'm calling on one of your assassins' phones. I'm afraid things didn't quite go as planned," Alton replied.

Luke sat forward and sneered angrily. "Who is this?"

"This is Alton Sinclair. Perhaps you should have looked into my background before you sent your hit squad."

"Perhaps I should have come after you myself…."

"Oh well! Better luck next time! You'll find all three of your men resting well in the morgue here in Guelph. Goodnight Mr. Underwood!" Alton disconnected, and Luke threw the cell phone across the room, causing Liddy to cower.

"What should we do now? Go after them ourselves?"

Luke got up and paced in thought. "No! We shall set our sights on the battle ahead. I will crush my brothers and Steven Spencer. Then nothing will stop us."

In the cool night air outside of Guelph, Ontario, Canada, Alton, and the Branch family boarded his private jet. Daniel turned to ask, "Where are we going, Mr. Sinclair?"

Alton paused to think for a moment, then answered confidently, "I think we'll go to Sweden. I haven't been there in quite some time."

Daniel said excitedly, "Cool!"

Heather sighed and walked ahead. "Too cool! Couldn't we go someplace warmer?" Alton glanced at Audrey, and she responded with a keen smile.

The grandfather clock in the Branchview foyer chimed at 4:00 a.m. Steven was relaxing in a chair with his feet propped on an ottoman, while Mrs. Porter was snoozing in the recliner. Detective Fuller entered, looking rather defeated, and Steven sat up straight in his chair. "Did you find anything other than ghosts lurking within the hidden corners of my house, detective?"

"My men searched this place from top to bottom, but I still know you're hiding them somewhere."

Steven stood and held his ground, as Fuller strolled up to within inches of his face, in an unsuccessful attempt to intimidate him. "You've already looked all night long. Feel free to stay for breakfast if you'd like. Mrs. Porter is an excellent cook."

Fuller retreated a bit and glanced at Mrs. Porter who was now awake and sitting up in her chair. "I'll have to decline that offer, Mr. Spencer." He stepped back to a more comfortable distance. "But I will keep men on the grounds, checking the woods, the cottage, and of course, the carriage house."

"Feel free to look as you may. The cottage has been closed up since the bodies were discovered there."

Fuller stared at Steven with a curious expression. "By the way! Where are the LeRoux's? I noticed they weren't home. Isn't that rather odd for this hour of the night?"

Steven looked down. "Detective Fuller! I don't make it a general practice to keep tabs on Gerard LeRoux and his family. This is not a prison camp."

Officer Hawley entered the room. "Are we about ready to wrap things up here?"

Fuller paused in thought. "Actually, I'll have you stay here to keep an eye on things, Hawley. I think I'll stop for a cup of coffee at the City Diner and swing back here later." Fuller gave one final long glance at Steven, who countered him with a sober stare before he finally departed.

"That man's arrogance is far too much to bear."

Hawley looked into the foyer to make sure he was gone, then anxiously turned back toward Steven. "Fuller is up to something. I just know it."

"I applaud your investigative skills, Officer Hawley. But I think the rest of us are a few steps ahead of you on that."

Hawley shook his head and moved closer. "He did something with the remains that were found here yesterday morning. They're not in the lab where they're supposed to be."

Steven looked concerned. "Is that a fact?"

"Yes! And I also find it odd that he would be going to the City Diner. He isn't exactly welcomed there by Ms. McVea and her uncle."

Steven looked intrigued. "Officer Hawley! I think it might be wise for you to swing by the diner and see exactly what Fuller is up to. I'm rather concerned for Ms. McVea."

The City Diner was just opening for the day, as Fuller watched from his car. Suzy McVea opened the front door and entered. He waited until she was inside and the lights were on, then he got out of the car and strolled toward the front door.

Suzy sauntered into the restaurant area from the kitchen and was startled to see Fuller standing there. "You should always lock the door behind you, Ms. McVea. This town isn't as safe as it used to be."

She glared at him with contempt. "What do you want?"

Fuller sat down on a stool at the counter. "It should be obvious. How about coffee and breakfast for one of Lockeport's finest?"

"We don't open for another half hour. Besides, you're not among the finest."

Fuller glared back at her. "That wasn't a request, Ms. McVea. That was an order."

She stared at him for a long moment in response, then noticed his bandaged hand. "What happened to your hand?"

"Just a little mishap that's no concern of yours. Now, get me some bacon and eggs."

"Fine… But it'll take me a few minutes to get things set up."

She strolled back into the kitchen, and Fuller glanced around carefully before locking the door. "Why isn't your uncle here?"

"He should be in later. He wasn't feeling well this morning." Fuller looked relieved, and a sinister expression crossed his face.

When Suzy walked out of the kitchen with his cup of coffee, Fuller was blocking the doorway. She stepped back to a safe distance, but Fuller pursued her into the kitchen. As Suzy tried to get away, he aggressively grabbed her arm, pulling her in close. "You know you want this as much as I do, you little tramp," he exclaimed.

"Get off me, you creep!"

"There's no sense in yelling. No one can hear you." Fuller managed to wrap his good hand around the back of her head, so he could force her into kissing him. She fought to free herself, and in the struggle, she bit down hard on his bandaged hand. Fuller screamed in agony and backed away. Suzy grabbed a pot of coffee off the hot plate, and smashed it against the side of Fuller's head, sending him reeling backward and bleeding. "You'll regret that, you little bitch!" he screamed.

Suzy dashed toward the back door, but he pinned her against the wall. Seconds later, officer Hawley entered from the front. "Let her go, Fuller!"

Fuller turned in a rage but had trouble drawing his gun with his bandaged hand. Hawley drew his gun first and fired. Fuller fell limp to the floor, and Hawley cautiously moved to check on his lifeless body. Suzy hysterically trembled with fear. "Is he dead?"

Hawley looked up, nodding. "I'm afraid so. Are you okay?"

"I'm just a little shaken. What should we do now? You just shot a fellow officer."

Hawley got to his feet and evaluated the situation. "Don't worry! I'll take care of it. Just get this place straightened up, and make it as if nothing happened." Suzy nodded with much anxiety.

Back at Branchview, Mrs. Porter ambled in from the kitchen. "I have more pancakes! Who wants some?"

Ezekiel and Philip looked at each other and rolled their eyes. "I couldn't eat another bite even if I wanted to, Mrs. Porter."

While everyone else shook their heads, Joey shyly held her plate up. "I'll take more." The room filled with laughter.

Phillip said, "It appears our new friend has the appetite of a hungry warrior."

"She won't go hungry as long as she's in this house." Mrs. Porter glanced at Steven. "You look so tired, Steven. Can I get you another cup of coffee?"

"No! Thank you, Mrs. Porter. I need to get over to the hospital to see Lori and the babies. She and Millie will think I forgot about them."

"I'll need to ready Mrs. Sandstrom's bed. She'll be exhausted when she returns. Hopefully, Lori and the babies can come home as well."

Mrs. Porter motioned to Joey. "I'll get those pancakes for you, young lady."

Sharie got up from her seat. "I'll help you in the kitchen, Mrs. Porter."

Steven waited for them to leave and motioned to Gerard. "While I'm gone, I need you to call this Agent Guitierez and have him meet us here at Branchview."

"What if he alerts the other agents? After all, Agent Smith is a wanted man."

"He gave me a code word to mention. It's guacamole!"

Everyone laughed. "Guacamole?"

Steven gave a clueless shrug. "He said that's the code they use to warn each other when rogue agents are discovered."

Ezekiel stated, "In this case, we have no idea how many rogue agents there are."

"Hopefully, Agent Guitierez is as reliable as Adam thinks he is."

"I guess that's the chance we have to take," Gerard concluded. "We need help from within the agency." The group all shared a very concerned glance.

Steven hustled his way out of the house, wishing for just one full night's sleep. It felt like forever since he'd slept alone with his wife, in peace. The hospital seemed unusually quiet that morning when he arrived. But he could hear Millie and Loraine talking as he got closer to the room. As he entered the hall, the sight brought him to a complete halt. In front of him was an image of perfection that he cherished greatly. His beautiful wife, and two children.

Loraine looked up with joy when she saw him standing in the doorway. "Steven! I was just telling Mother that I can't believe she was actually an MI-6 agent, and never told me."

"How many times do I have to tell you, dear?" Millie wearily lamented. "We were sworn to secrecy."

"All those times you were away, I thought it was because you didn't love me."

"Oh, sweetheart! I loved you then, and I love you still." Millie stood up, handing one of the babies over to Steven "Here! It's time for you to get acquainted with your son."

He gently cradled the baby and kissed his forehead. "He's so precious."

Millie smiled. "I'll leave you two love bugs alone, while I attempt to go find a decent cup of tea."

Steven smiled. "I am so glad you told her the truth." Millie shrugged and patted him on the shoulder as she departed.

Steven then turned his attention back to his wife. "What are we going to name them?"

"Mother said we should name the boy London, and I think we should name the girl Olivia."

Steven pondered for a moment. "London and Olivia Spencer. I like it."

Loraine was amused, as Steven brushed his finger gently across baby London's cheek. "I swear! Sometimes you're far too agreeable, Steven."

"Would you have me any other way, Mama?" He leaned over and kissed both her and baby Olivia.

"I wouldn't trade you for anything, darling."

Chapter Twenty-Five:

The Twins Arrive

The summer sun shone brightly across the quaint little coastal town of Lockeport. On this beautiful day, Luke Underwood sat behind his desk at Branch Consolidated in a rather foul mood. Liddy entered with a notepad in hand and settled into a seat opposite him. "What marvelous events are on our agenda today, Liddy?" She glared at him from across the desk.

"We still have that lingering issue between the FDA and Minotaur Pharmaceuticals."

"I thought Hempfield took care of that." Luke scowled and swiveled in his chair to look out the window. "Imagine the nerve of that company to steal the name of a noble beast from Greek mythology. We should cut that division loose on that fact alone."

Liddy rolled her eyes. "That's beside the point. Several people have died from the side effects of their

Ezedrol drug. We need to pull it from the market as soon as possible."

Luke swiveled back around, as a look of pure evil enveloped his face. "We'll do no such thing! Surely there's enough money in the reserve to bribe the FDA into looking the other way."

"I'll have Hempfield look into it."

"Did you call Detective Fuller? He should have checked in with me over an hour ago."

"Yes, but he isn't answering his cell phone, and no one at the police department has seen or heard from him since he left the Branch Estate early this morning."

Luke sneered. "I suppose this should be expected from such a man. He's an incompetent fool."

In other quarters, the day was proving to show some signs of goodness, as Steven and Loraine brought their babies home from the hospital. Millie followed close behind with Loraine's overnight bag. Gerard and the two gods were all waiting in the sitting room when they arrived. Gerard spoke up first, "Welcome home, Loraine." He gave her a friendly kiss on the cheek and paused to admire the babies.

Philip and Ezekiel both stepped closer, eagerly extending their arms. "May we have the honor?"

Steven smiled. "Of course!" They both carefully handed the babies over to the beaming gods.

Ezekiel grinned. "What beautiful, precious babies they are."

Steven and Loraine beamed with pride. "I do believe we've found the perfect godfathers."

The room burst into laughter at the suggestion.

Millie smiled. "If you would all please excuse me, I must retire and get some rest. I have a very special evening planned tonight."

"And what plans might you have, Mother?"

She turned with an arrogant smile. "I happen to have a date with a very special gentleman."

They all glanced at each other with surprise, "So! Who's the lucky guy, Millie?" Steven asked.

"I simply can't tell you right now. That would deprive you of the surprise. You'll just have to wait and see." Everyone exchanged a look of amusement as Millie proudly strutted up the stairs.

The rest of the inhabitants entered a few seconds later, and they quickly swooped in to greet the new babies. Mrs. Porter and Sharie gently took the babies from Philip and Ezekiel, while Deanna and Joey observed. Sharie said, "Look at this precious little angel. She reminds me of you, Deanna."

Deanna looked embarrassed. "Oh, Mom! You're embarrassing me!"

Mrs. Porter motioned to Loraine "Come now, Loraine! Us ladies will make you a nice lunch. I'm sure you'll appreciate that after having to eat that horrible hospital food."

"I must admit, that would be heavenly!" All the women left the room except for Joey, who felt awkwardly out of place.

There was a knock on the door, and Gerard promptly announced, "That must be Agent Guitierez."

Steven spoke up, "Just to be safe, I want you all to wait here in this room." Steven answered the door and greeted Guitierez, a tall man in his mid-30s with dark hair and kind, mellow eyes. "Agent Guitierez, I assume. I'm Steven Spencer. Please come in."

Guitierez glanced around the impressive surroundings as he entered. "From what I gathered in my short conversation with Mr. LeRoux, Agent Smith passed some important information onto you."

"We definitely have a lot to discuss. Are you familiar with a movement called the Secret Society?"

"We've investigated a few reports on that group, but it all seems to be fictional."

Steven rapidly shook his head no. "I assure you, they are real, and much bigger than you could ever imagine."

Guitierez studied Steven for a moment. "Where is Agent Smith? You do realize he is considered a felon?"

Steven rolled his eyes and thought before responding. "Let's just say that he's in a sort of protective custody until this issue gets resolved. I'll explain everything to you in the best way I can. "

"What about Joey Arcovio? What's her role in all of this?"

Joey strolled in from the sitting room and stood in the doorway. "If you quit asking stupid questions, we'll tell you everything you need to know." A rather stunned Guitierez glanced at the young girl, then at Steven, who backed up her comments with a definite nod.

Across town, Luke decided to investigate Detective Fuller's disappearance. So, he invited Liddy to accompany him on the short walk down main street to the police station. "I'm beginning to believe that our Detective Fuller may have met some unfortunate kind of fate," Luke stated.

"I think you might be right. I tried to center on him with my psychic energies and came up with nothing. That's usually not a positive sign."

"I don't doubt that my brothers and Steven Spencer somehow had something to do with it."

"Maybe! But I did strangely keep getting a vision of the City Diner."

"Interesting! But I find it hard to believe that little waif Suzy McVea could have anything to do with his demise."

Liddy wisely thought, measuring her words. "With all due respect, it seems we've been handily outmaneuvered so far. How do you plan to counter?"

Luke grinned. "Let's just say that on that fateful day of battle, not only will they face us and the powers of the underworld, but the evil dead will also rise from their graves and converge upon the great house, showing no mercy on its inhabitants." Liddy reacted with wide-eyed surprise and a sinister smile.

Back at Branchview, Steven and the others conversed with Agent Guitierez. "Everything that you say seems to be so sensational. Perhaps you should just step aside, and let me and the FBI take it from here."

Ezekiel reacted with frustration. "You don't seem to understand. Until we get access to that nationwide directory, we don't know who we can trust."

Steven responded, "Posterle was part of the scheme. For all we know, you could be part of it as well."

Guitierez took extreme offense. "Now wait just a minute here! I'm a proud American, who happens to love this country. I assure you that I wouldn't be on a list of people who wanted to kill the President and topple the government."

Gerard stepped in, "Then you're going to have to trust us, and keep this confidential until we get that list."

Guitierez eyed Philip and Ezekiel suspiciously. "You never did mention how they fit into all this…."

Phillip answered, "Mr. Sphere and myself are personal friends and allies of this family."

Steven replied, "I assure you, everyone in this room can be trusted." The music box on the fireplace mantle started playing by itself, and a gusty breeze blew through the room, causing everyone to pause and take notice.

The apparition of Maggie Branch appeared next to Agent Guitierez, causing him to jump back in his seat. "You have to listen to them. They're telling the truth."

Guitierez reacted with anxious disbelief. "Where did this little kid come from?"

Steven laughed. "Let's just say that she's one of our resident ghosts."

"No way! There's no such thing as ghosts…."

Maggie responded, "Try to reach out and touch me."

Guitierez cautiously reached out, but his hand felt nothing. "I don't understand! I see you, but I can't touch you."

Maggie giggled, while Joey sat forward in amazement. "That is so dope!"

Gerard shook his head with amusement. "I love this old house."

Guitierez made the sign of the cross in front of him. "Oh, Mi Dios!"

Ezekiel inquired, "Have we made a believer out of you, Agent Guitierez?"

"I don't understand all this, but yes."

Philip spoke with urgency, "We have to move quickly, this afternoon."

Ezekiel answered, "Absolutely! Gerard and I will accompany Ms. Arcovio to the tunnels, while Steven and Philip meet up with Amy and Charlotte in the secret room."

"Who are Amy and Charlotte?"

Phillip laughed. "You'll find out soon enough."

As everyone stood, Guitierez glanced around cluelessly. "What am I supposed to do?"

Steven replied matter-of-factly. "I could have Mrs. Porter fix you some lunch, and I'm sure Maggie would enjoy your company." Maggie giggled, while Guitierez was speechless. "Just be sure you're here when they get back with that thumb drive." Someone else knocked on the front door, and everyone anxiously looked that way. "Everybody just sit tight. I'll take care of this," Steven said.

Steven pulled the doors to the sitting room shut. *Oh, here we go....* As he opened the front door, officer Hawley burst inside. "Mr. Spencer! We were right about Fuller." A surprised Steven listened attentively. "He went to the City Diner, and tried to get a little early morning delight with Ms. McVea."

"Is Suzy okay?"

Hawley nodded rapidly. "I got there just in time. She put up quite a fight for being such a tiny little thing."

"Good... where's Fuller now?"

Hawley paused. "He's dead! He drew his gun on me, and I had to kill him."

Steven reacted in disbelief. "What did you do with his body?"

"I'll just say that I stashed it in a place where no one can easily find it."

Steven thought for a moment. "Just do me a favor: Keep an eye on Suzie, and don't trust any of your peers. Luke Underwood may try to harm her."

"Should I keep an eye on him, and that Liddy McPherson as well?"

"Yes! But no matter what happens, don't confront either one of them. They're very dangerous people."

Hawley looked at him with a rather puzzled expression. "What's going on here, Mr. Spencer?"

"Trust me! You'll know soon enough. Just keep this between us for now."

After Hawley left, Ezekiel, Gerard, and Joey all headed to the carriage house garage and prepared to embark on their journey into the tunnels. Ezekiel and Gerard pulled away the boards covering the hidden entrance, while Joey watched, clutching tight to her oversized satchel purse. Gerard then climbed up into the tunnel entrance. "Give Ms. Arcovio a boost, and I'll pull her the rest of the way up."

Joey froze with fear. "Is everything okay?" Ezekiel asked.

Joey shook her head. "I'm claustrophobic."

"Now's a great time to tell us…."

Ezekiel sighed and placed his hand on the side of the young girl's head. "Look into my eyes; absorb what you see, and listen to my words." Joey followed his command. "When I snap my finger, you'll no longer have these fears." He snapped his finger near her ear, then stood back. "How do you feel now?"

Joey hesitated for a moment and took a deep breath. "I'm ready to do this." Gerard smiled.

Inside the secret Cave Room, a blindfolded Steven cradled a black cat in his arms as they entered the throne room, with Poseidon leading them. The cat leaped onto the floor and Charlotte appeared. "Thank you for the lift, Steven. I'll take every opportunity I can to be snuggled by the likes of you."

Steven answered in a condescending tone, "Aunt Charlotte! Behave yourself!"

"How I wish you wouldn't call me that. It makes me feel so old." Steven snickered.

Steven and Poseidon exchanged an amused expression, as Amphitrite entered from an adjacent room, yawning, "Well, look who's back! I trust everything went smoothly?" Poseidon asked.

Amphitrite sauntered closer. "It was a long journey. I only got back about an hour ago."

"By chance did you see Andrea Hill?"

"Yes, I did! She's adjusting quite well to her new life in Alfheim." Amphitrite strolled onto the altar, comfortably plopped down in one of the throne chairs, and looked inquisitively at Poseidon. "Have you told Steven about our little surprise?"

"No! I thought I'd save it for the right moment." Steven looked at him and shrugged. "We brought back an old friend from the grave, who we thought you'd be very happy to see." Steven's face lit up, and Charlotte's expression turned to horror as the smiling specter of Dr. Grayson sauntered into the room. She was brandishing a sword of justice, and dressed like a warrior, with her ever-present crucifix hanging from her neck.

"I understand you all might be needing a little extra help?"

Charlotte spoke up in a panic before Steven could react. "Dr. Grayson! I never meant to kill you. It was an accident."

Dr. Grayson rested her sword on the altar and approached her with a calm demeanor. "I know all about it, Charlotte. You did me a favor without knowing it." Charlotte looked puzzled as Dr. Grayson turned to address everyone. "As you all know, I had a very nasty smoking habit, and it would've soon been discovered that I had lung cancer. I would've been dead within six months anyway."

"Oh! Please forgive me, just the same."

Dr. Grayson answered with a smile, "I know you're making a genuine effort to compensate, and I do forgive you." She looked at Steven. "It's good to see you again, Steven."

"I can't tell you how good it is to see you."

They shared a quick embrace, and then she stepped back with a keen grin. "How do you like my new threads?"

Steven giggled, "They fit your personality quite appropriately."

Joey had overcome her anxiety of tight places, and they began the enduring trip through the damp, miserable tunnels beneath Lockeport. Rats scampered close to the bricked walls, and Joey clasped tightly to Ezekiel's arm as she watched with fear in her eyes. "I hate rats!"

Ezekiel replied, "I'm not very fond of them myself, young lady."

Gerard stopped and looked around. "I think we're close, but I can't remember exactly where it is."

Ezekiel gestured ahead at a young black man, who was motioning for them to follow him. "I think he's trying to tell us." The young man stopped near a ladder, pointing upward, and then disappeared.

"Wow! Where did he go?" Joey asked.

Gerard answered, "That's a mystery that even we don't know." Ezekiel and Joey observed as Gerard climbed the ladder to examine the hatch door. "They've sealed it since the last time I was here."

Ezekiel responded, "I'll take care of that." Within a few short seconds, they could hear the inner latch pop open.

"Cool! You'll have to teach me how to do that trick," Joey exclaimed.

Gerard and Ezekiel pushed the hatch door upward with much effort, and it finally gave way. Within moments, all three entered the room through the hatch, and Joey immediately set her sights on the computer.

Gerard stated, "We have to hurry! I'm sure they've installed a modern security system since we were last in here."

Joey plugged in the thumb drive and began to rapidly type away on the keyboard, as she concentrated on the screen. "This shouldn't take long at all." Ezekiel and Gerard anxiously waited, and after a few long minutes, Joey's face lit up. "I'm in!"

"They weren't joking! She is good."

Joey continued to type away, focusing seriously on the screen. "That's a really big file, downloading should be starting...right about now."

Inside Branch Consolidated, an alarm sounded, and Liddy left her desk to investigate. She hurried back, typed in a code, and looked at her screen. *So! We have intruders.* Liddy hurried from the room and scurried to Marshall Hempfield's office. "Have you seen Mr. Underwood?"

"He left about twenty minutes ago. I believe he went to lunch. Why?" Liddy rolled her eyes with impatience and hurried off, leaving Hempfield puzzled.

The tension built as Joey rushed to get the file downloaded. Ezekiel and Gerard continued to wait anxiously. "How are we doing?"

"Just a few more seconds. Almost there! Got it!" She reached around, and pulled out the thumb drive, but remained seated in anxious contemplation.

"Come on, Joey! What's wrong?"

"I have to go to the bathroom…"

Ezekiel exclaimed, "Good grief, woman!"

"Well, what do you want me to do? Pee my pants?"

Gerard gave an anxious sigh. "I believe there's a restroom out in the main hall to the right." Joey hurried out of the room, as the two men nervously fidgeted and paced.

Liddy rushed past pedestrians walking down the sidewalk, hurrying toward the S.O.S Club. She paused when it was in sight, and ducked into an alley. Once there, and out of sight, she quickly waved her hands and disappeared in a cloud of purple smoke. In the backroom of the SOS Club, Gerard and Ezekiel heard Joey scream, and they both ran from the room.

The men kicked the door open to find a giant serpent had Joey pinned in a corner. "Great! It would have to be a snake." A large lightning bolt saber appeared in Ezekiel's hand, and the snake lashed at him, while a terrified Joey tossed the thumb drive through the air to Gerard. The snake leaped at it, causing Gerard to fumble it, and it slid beneath an antique cabinet. Joey ran from the room, as Gerard reached to retrieve the thumb drive, and Ezekiel fought off the snake. With one swift wave of the sword, he lopped off the snake's head as it lunged at him. Gerard was able to retrieve the thumb drive and placed it in his pocket. The headless serpent fell limp to the floor but then morphed into several other smaller snakes. "Okay now! That I wasn't expecting." Gerard and Joey had made it to the hatch, waiting on Ezekiel, who paused to expel a freezing layer of ice upon the pursuing, hissing vipers. They pulled the hatch closed, and escaped down the ladder as the snakes shook off their icy casing and merged to form the likeness of Liddy. She placed her fingers on her forehead and concentrated. *May the beast from hell be released.*

As the three frantically hurried to escape through the tunnels, Joey exclaimed, "Who the hell are you people anyway? I feel like I'm caught in a game of Dungeons and Dragons."

"I do believe my life may have inspired such a game," Ezekiel quipped.

Just then, the tunnel began to shake with loud booming footsteps, and a terrorizing roar echoed from further ahead in the tunnel. "Okay! What the hell is that?" Gerard shouted.

"I do believe that's the Basilisk, and it most definitely is from hell." A large, prehistoric rhino-type creature rumbled toward them from the far end of the tunnel, shooting streams of fire from its mouth. As they all desperately looked for an escape, the young black man appeared and motioned for them to follow. He directed them down an offshoot tunnel, just as a huge fireball roared past them and continued down the main corridor. The young man motioned toward the opening at the far end of the offshoot. Ezekiel and Joey ran toward the light of day, but Gerard paused to acknowledge the man. "Thank you!" The young man replied with a quick, serious nod as the beast honed in on them.

Gerard managed to leap out of the sewer outlet with the beast in hot pursuit. Ezekiel threw a bolt of lightning at the large conduit pipe outlet, causing it to collapse just ahead of the beast. Gerard fell to one knee, totally out of breath. "It'll be a cold day in hell when anyone talks me into going back into those tunnels again."

Ezekiel leaned over next to him, trying to catch his breath as well. "Who was that young apparition that helped us?"

Gerard looked up with a proud smile "That was my great, great grandfather." Ezekiel smiled. "If you should ever see his ghostly figure again, be sure to thank him for me as well."

Gerard nodded, and a still stunned Joey added, "Ditto for me too."

A short time later, the group made their way back to the main house. They entered and promptly rang the spirit bell. Millie swiftly entered from the sitting room, dressed immaculately, and quickly winced with disgust. "Good heavens! You all smell as though you fell into a vat full of flotsam and jetsam."

Gerard responded, "That's a pretty accurate assessment, Mrs. Sandstrom."

Mrs. Porter ambled into the room, followed by Sharie and Agent Guitierez, who inquired with impatience, "Were you able to get the download?"

Gerard pulled the thumb drive from his pocket and handed it over to Guitierez. "Not without great challenge."

Mrs. Porter looked to a sober and dirty-faced Joey. "Come on! I'll help you get cleaned up, young lady."

Millie commented with an unpleasant expression, "I must leave the room as well. I can't tolerate the stench."

As they went to leave the room, an explosion was heard outside the house. "What in the world was that?" Guitierez asked.

Ezekiel peeked out the door. "It's Liddy! She just blew your car up, Agent Guitierez."

"Are you kidding me? What do we do now?"

Sharie replied, "She won't come any closer to the house. She can't tolerate the crucifix outside the door."

Gerard stated, "We have to get him safely out of this house and back to New Haven with that thumb drive. But how can we do that with her watching us like a hawk?"

Sharie paced back and forth for a moment. "I think I have an idea…." All desperately looked to her for an answer. "The secret passage off the sitting room leads to a tunnel that has a hidden entrance near the main road by Lighthouse Point. He can escape through there."

Gerard replied, "Good idea! I can sneak out the back door, get the car, drive out the back gate while Ezekiel creates a distraction, and then I'll meet up with him."

"You're not getting anywhere near my nice, clean car smelling like that, mister. I'll go and meet up with Agent Guitierez in about ten minutes." She turned to Guitierez. "If I'm not there by then, you're on your own."

Guitierez anxiously interjected, "How will I know the way? I've never been in this house, let alone that passage."

Mrs. Porter spoke up, "He's right! He could end up walking in circles for the next hour."

The ghost of Maggie appeared next to Guitierez, tugged on his trousers, and looked up at him with sober eyes. "I can show you the way."

In town, Philip and Steven strolled along the sidewalk. "My intuition is practically making my brain explode. Something isn't right."

Phillip replied, "I rather feel the same way, but I'm certain that Zeus wouldn't allow any harm to befall Gerard or Joey."

The two men continued. "You're right! We'll grab a quick bite to eat at the City Diner, and they should be back at Branchview by the time we return."

As they got closer to the diner, they noticed an ambulance in the street ahead, with its lights flashing. "I wonder what's going on there?"

Steven looked on with an expression of dread. "Oh no! That's in front of the City Diner. I hope nothing's happened to Suzy."

"I hope not either, but I think we may have discovered the source of our anxious intuition." Their conversation petered out as they hurried toward the scene.

Chapter Twenty-Six:

Digging A Hole

As each day drew one step closer to the confrontation that lay ahead, tragedy continued to blaze through the world surrounding the great house of Branchview. Regretfully, there would be more casualties by the time the sunset on that fateful day of the Summer Solstice. Steven and Phillip made their way toward the City Diner with heightened anxiety. The crowd grew as rescue workers slowly wheeled a covered body out the front door of the diner.

A tearful, shaken Suzy followed them to the ambulance. Steven hurried to her side, and she was greatly relieved to see a friendly face. "Suzy! What in the world happened here?"

She answered quite emotionally. "It's my uncle, Carl! He's dead!"

Phillip inquired, "Did Luke Underwood have anything to do with this?"

She shook her head. "He wasn't feeling well the past few days, so I opened the diner this morning, and he came in around noon." She sniffled, then continued. "I went back to the kitchen to check on him, and he was on the floor. Oh, Mr. Spencer! How much more tragedy can I endure?"

Steven gave her a comforting embrace. "I know this is a difficult time for you. If you need anything, don't hesitate to call me." Steven and Philip exchanged a serious glance as Suzy buried her head in his shoulder and continued to cry.

At the Underwood house, Liddy had settled in for the day, relaxing in the parlor with a glass of wine. However, she was anxious to hear back from Luke. After her first glass, the front door opened, and she stood firm, poised for confrontation. "Where in the hell have you been all afternoon?"

Luke took great offense to the question. "Since when do I have to answer to you concerning my whereabouts?"

Liddy stood her ground. "I could've used your help today. Zeus, Gerard, and some geeky-looking young girl broke into the meeting hall."

Luke sat down in a nearby chair. "I trust you were able to stop them from getting whatever they were after?"

"Unfortunately, no! I threw everything within my powers, including the Basilisk at them. But somehow, a young black man helped them to narrowly escape."

Luke leaned forward with concern. "Were you able to return the Basilisk to hell?"

"It returned as I so commanded…."

Luke drew a breath of relief. "At least you did one thing right." He thought for a moment. "What were they able to get away with?"

Liddy sat back down. "They downloaded something off the computer. That little geek had a thumb drive that she handed off to Gerard LeRoux."

Luke rolled his eyes. "They accessed the nationwide directory—"

Liddy balked with frustration. "They would've never gotten away if I'd had your help."

"I had a good reason for being away. I'll tell you all about it. But first, I need to know more about this young black man."

"I just caught a fleeting glance at him. He had a dirty white, long-sleeved shirt, blue jean trousers, and a rope belt."

Luke responded, "I believe that was Gerard's great, great grandfather. He was the only one of a group of slaves that escaped the flames of the Basilisk."

Liddy impatiently sat down and leaned forward in her chair. "Explain this a little further. I was around back then, but I don't recall such a story."

"As you know, the tunnels were used by both the Branch and Locke families as part of the Underground Railroad."

"I remember hearing rumors. Go on…"

"I fought on the side of the South in the Civil War. In fact, I confronted my brothers at Gettysburg. I should've taken the opportunity to dispose of at least one of them when I had the chance."

"Why didn't you?"

Luke gasped, "We had a brotherly code of honor. A code that I most recently have discarded." He vented angrily before continuing. "Anyway! When I learned that they were shuttling slaves to freedom in the tunnels, I released the Basilisk to ensure they would never escape."

"But this one man defied the odds."

"And now his spirit has returned as an ally to his grandson, and the others."

Liddy absorbed the information with great interest before moving on. "So! What was this important business that kept you away today?"

"I recruited someone who can help us greatly. Someone I'm sure you'll be happy to see."

Luke snapped his fingers in the air, and Jenny McPherson, a sandy brown-haired woman in her early 30' entered the room. She seemed very hardened in appearance, with a confident and regal stride. Liddy reacted with great surprise, "Mother!"

"Hello, sweetheart! It's nice to see you…." The two had a mutual agreeing moment, quite different from what would be expected of a mother and daughter reunion.

Inside the secret Cave Room, Dr. Grayson and Charlotte sat at a table waiting, as Amphitrite strode in. "Well! Where has our favorite Mermaid been?"

Amphitrite moved closer. "I went for a swim, and then meditated for a while on the rocks."

"Charlotte has been educating me on the deceptive history that's led us to where we are today."

Amphitrite sat down with the women. "I never heard the full story of what took place in the 1600s."

Dr. Grayson replied, "Surely, you were around back then?"

"Yes, but I didn't become permanently connected with this area until the late 1800s. It was then, while resting on the rocks at Lighthouse Point, that I first saw the one true love of my life."

Charlotte questioned, "Matthew Branch?"

Amphitrite nodded emotionally and took a deep breath. "He was strolling along the shoreline without a shirt when he caught my eye. He was the most beautiful man I've ever seen."

Dr. Grayson smiled. "How romantic!"

"I know! It's hard to even look at Steven Spencer without thinking of him." The ladies giggled, then Amphitrite changed the subject. "So! What fueled the vengeance of Liddy McPherson?"

Charlotte continued, "From what I know, Liddy's mother, Jenny McPherson, was accused and tried for witchcraft. She was found guilty and sentenced to hang. Liddy watched her mother's execution."

"That's terrible! But what did the Branch and Locke families have to do with that?"

"They were her most hostile accusers. She swore on her mother's grave that she would return, and punish every generation of both families."

Dr. Grayson lowered her head. "She lived up to her word."

"I know. I became one of the clueless victims of her lies, and it ruined my life."

Amphitrite smiled warmly. "We were all victims."

Charlotte gave an understanding nod. "At least you were able to find true love, if even for the shortest bit of time. My heart was so blackened with hate that I never experienced its thrill." Amphitrite and Dr. Grayson exchanged an emotional glance.

After a long moment of awkward silence, Amphitrite stood up and began to pace about the room. "I had a vision during my meditations. It had to do with the room in the basement of the cottage."

Charlotte emotionally clenched her eyes shut. "I know that room all too well."

Amphitrite stated, "I saw Detective Fuller digging a hole."

Charlotte jumped up with a burst of enlightenment. "That has to be where he buried Liddy's remains."

"That was my first thought as well…."

Dr. Grayson then stood up with great assertion. "If we ever want to rid ourselves of Liddy forever, we must dig up those remains and incinerate them."

"We'd have to conjure heat almost equivalent to molten lava to make that possible," Amphitrite stated anxiously.

"I believe between the three of us, we can make that happen," Charlotte replied enthusiastically. "My good sisters! Let's do what needs to be done."

In the sitting room at Branchview, Ezekiel conversed with Gerard. "I think we accomplished quite a bit today. A storm will be forming over the Atlantic later tonight, and it will be of such intensity, that nearly the entire coast of New England will have to evacuate."

Gerard replied, "I hate to see that happen, but it's the only way to get innocent people out of the way."

Ezekiel got up and strolled to the window to view the evening sky. "I petitioned the supreme God for intervention, but have not as yet received an answer. Without that consent, we're left to fend for ourselves."

Both men paused in thought. "I'm curious. How did your brother Hades turn into such an evil being?"

Ezekiel smiled and strolled back to his chair. "He wasn't always that way. Being the eldest of the brothers, he was bitter that he drew the lot of being God of the underworld."

"I can't say I blame him for that…."

"On one of the rare occasions that he ventured above ground, he spotted my daughter Persephoneia, gathering flowers. He was so taken by her beauty that he abducted her and carried her off to the underworld to be his bride."

"So, he took his niece as his wife?"

Ezekiel shrugged haplessly. "I struck an agreement that allowed him to keep her, based on one condition: She would return above ground for the spring and summer months, for the sake of seeing her mother."

"How did that work?"

"It worked well for a time. That is, until she discovered Hades was having an affair with a Nereid princess, and in her rage, she turned the women into a mint plant."

Gerard laughed. "You have to be joking?"

Ezekiel replied, "It's all true. In retaliation, he turned Persephoneia into a granite statue. Afterward, he became increasingly isolated, and his heart grew evil."

"If I didn't know who you were, I could never believe what you're telling me."

Steven and Philip entered the room. "Good evening, gentlemen!"

Ezekiel stood up and retrieved the brandy decanter from a side table. "Good evening! Can I pour you both a brandy?"

"Count me in, brother," Phillip stated.

"No thanks! I never touch the stuff. I'll have Mrs. Porter brew me a cup of coffee."

Gerard commented, "Ezekiel was just giving me a lesson in Greek mythology." Steven and Philip sat down as Ezekiel poured a brandy and handed it to Philip, while also refilling Gerard's glass.

Phillip continued, "It's surprising how our histories coexist. I was just thinking that this will be the third time we've been involved in a battle on American soil. The second time in this region."

Steven stated, "You two were here for the American Revolution? "

Both Philip and Ezekiel nodded enthusiastically. "We were reluctantly here for the Civil War as well. We fought on the side of the North, but that's an unfortunate time in history that we don't like to discuss."

Gerard chimed in, "Thankfully, you chose to fight on the right side. I shudder to think what the fate of my people may have been had the slaves not been freed." Ezekiel answered with an assured wink.

Steven responded, "What about all the other wars that America was involved in? Were you there too?"

Phillip nodded. "We were present in World War I and II. We even spent time with Commodore Perry in the War of 1812. But we chose not to be involved in Korea or Vietnam."

"What about the war in the Middle East?" Gerard asked.

Philip and Zeus looked at each other, laughing. "Talk about a fruitless cause. Those lunatics have been fighting each other since the beginning of time."

Phillip nodded. "Not even divine intervention would bring total peace to that region." He took a sip of his drink. "Speaking of divine intervention, did you receive approval from the supreme God?"

Ezekiel shook his head. "We can't give up hope. There's still time."

"I've alerted the parallel world, and they're all standing ready," Phillip stated.

Steven stepped in. "I'm still waiting to hear from Agent Guitierez as well. Hopefully, he'll be able to counter the network of the Secret Society before it's too late."

Ezekiel raised his drink to the others. "We can only have faith."

There was a knock on the door, and all looked toward the foyer. "I'll get that…." Steven went to answer the door, and he was somewhat surprised by the guest. "Mr.

Crawford! This is certainly a surprise. How can I help you?"

"Good evening, Mr. Spencer. I'm here to pick up Millie."

"So! You're the mystery man. Please, come on in." Steven ushered him into the foyer as Millie gracefully descended the stairs, dressed elegantly.

Bill watched admirably. "Millie! I must say you look marvelous…."

Steven added, "I'd have to second that remark." Millie appeared quite flattered.

She stepped forward and gave Bill a quick peck on his cheek. "You look quite handsome yourself."

Steven was quite amused. "So, where are you two lovebirds going tonight?"

"Don't worry, daddy. Just dinner, dancing, and whatever."

"I promise I'll try to have her back at a respectable hour."

"Oh, horse feathers! Don't bother waiting up, Steven."

Steven tried to contain his amusement. "Very well! You two have an enjoyable evening."

"Oh! I'm certain we will." Steven smiled and shook his head, as Millie took hold of Bill's arm and gave Steven a departing wink.

In the cottage, a foretelling conclusion is about to unfold as Amy, Charlotte, and Dr. Grayson approached the door with flashlights and shovels in hand. They paused as Amy peeled the yellow crime scene tape from the door. "I didn't think I'd ever be coming back to this place," Charlotte remarked.

"At least this time it's for a beneficial cause," Amy replied, and Charlotte nodded in agreement.

Amy took a deep breath as they entered. "Let's do this…." The three women made their way into the basement and the ceremony room. They then pointed their flashlights in the direction of the closed wooden door and proceeded. The wooden door creaked loudly as it took the effort of all three women to pull it open.

They flashed their lights to all corners of the dirt floor, while Charlotte shuddered with emotion. "I did some despicable things in this room that will haunt me through eternity."

Dr. Grayson laid a sympathetic hand on her shoulder, as Amy moved ahead. "Over here, it looks like the dirt's been disturbed recently." All the women began digging gingerly around the edges until a body bag was revealed. Amy carefully opened it and pulled out a human skull. "Hello, Liddy McPherson!"

"We mustn't hesitate. We have to destroy these remains tonight," Dr. Grayson exclaimed.

Charlotte spoke up. "I know just the place to do it, too." The women paused to listen. "I think it would be fitting to burn them at the ruins of the Locke Estate. That's where all of our grief originated."

Dr. Grayson agreed. "You're right, and I also think we should perform the ceremony at the stroke of midnight to honor all the souls that perished because of her actions."

"Ladies! I couldn't agree more," Amy stated. Eerie chants echoed through the basement, and all listened. "It's just the demons that guard the portal. They know we're here."

Amy continued, "Just as long as they don't alert Hades. None of us have the power to fight him."

Under the pergola in Branchview Gardens, Steven rested on the swing bench and listened as the foyer clock chimes echoed from the house. It chimed seven times, alerting the household that it was 7 pm. Loraine slowly approached from within the house. "What do you know? We finally have a moment alone."

She sat down next to him and scooted close. "I know. These times have been few and far between lately."

Lightning flashed in the distance and they both noticed. "Looks like there's a nasty storm brewing over the Atlantic."

"By tomorrow afternoon, it should be a strong hurricane. They're already warning everyone in the coastal areas to move inland."

"It's amazing that Zeus could make all that happen."

"It's even more amazing that he'll be able to stall it before it hits the shore." Steven embraced her tighter and kissed her on the forehead. "You'll never believe this, but Millie's mystery date was Mr. Crawford."

"The lightkeeper? I would've never imagined."

Both were momentarily amused. "We received some good news in the mail today." Loraine tilted her head to listen. "We got a copy of our renewed building permit. They'll be able to start working on our house in Florida sometime next week."

Loraine sighed. "Do you think we'll ever really be able to go home again? It seems like we've been here for an eternity."

"We will. But just when, I don't know. Since Audrey has no desire to live here anymore, I suppose ownership of Branchview will logically transfer to me."

"So that will leave us with two enormous homes to maintain."

"Well! I do have to make sure that Daniel inherits this house when he becomes of age. It must remain in the Branch family."

"So, we have some decisions to make."

Steven replied with a thoughtful nod. "We'll work things out. We always do."

Loraine kissed him, as Mrs. Porter nervously made her way into the garden area. "Mrs. Spencer, I'm sorry! Sharie and I can't seem to get the babies to quit crying."

"That's quite alright, Mrs. Porter. I'll be along in just a jiffy." Mrs. Porter ambled back toward the house, as Loraine looked up at Steven. "Oh well! That was quite nice while it lasted. Would you like to come along and help?"

"As long as I don't have to change their diapers."

"Oh, come now, Steven. Just remember that at one time, someone had to change yours as well." He nodded with amusement.

The Underwood household was filled with loving embraces from two witches that had been apart for centuries.

"You are much like I envisioned you would be as an adult," Jenny stated. "You were the last face I saw before my life ended on that fateful day."

"I've done everything I can to avenge your death, Mother. I've destroyed the entire lineage of the Locke family and practically all of the Branch's."

"I wish I could've come back sooner to help. If you recall, they incinerated my remains, rather than give me a proper burial. That ensured that I could never leave the realm between purgatory and limbo."

"So, how was Hades able to bring you back?"

Jenny stood and paced, observing the knick-knacks on the fireplace mantle. "I don't know the details. He brokered some kind of a deal with Lucifer, who guards the realms between Heaven and Hell."

Liddy accepted the answer with much thought. "Nevertheless, the day after tomorrow, we will begin our quest to finish the job, and we'll do it together."

Liddy flinched with sudden pain, putting her fingers to her temples. Jenny reacted with alarm, gently grabbing her shoulders as she sat back down next to her. "Liddy! Are you alright?"

"Just a terrible headache. You'll soon realize that one of the downfalls of being a mortal is that you experience physical pain, among other things, that you never feel in spirit form."

Liddy fell back onto the bed, still massaging her temples, while her mother stroked her hair with her fingers. "Perhaps you should just rest for a while. Hades and I have much to discuss."

"Mother! Just be sure you refer to him as Luke from now on. He demands to be called that when he's above ground." Jenny nodded.

At the ruins of the Locke Estate, the three women prepared to incinerate the bones. They stood in a circle holding hands. Dr. Grayson checked her watch. "It's almost time." She looked at Amy. "Did you bring enough water with you? We can't have you dehydrate from the intense heat."

"I brought two large bottles. They're in my satchel." Dr. Grayson emptied the remains from the body bag, and they all stood waiting for the stroke of midnight.

Charlotte said, "I almost feel guilty destroying her in this way. But I know this will atone for the tragic deaths of my ancestors." She paused to glance at Amy, then continued. "As well as your beloved Matthew and the innocent victims in his family." Amy forced a smile through pursed lips.

Dr. Grayson looked at Charlotte again. "This should gladly be the end of Liddy McPherson, forever." The alarm on her watch beeped and all stood back at a safe distance. "It's time!" They stretched their hands out toward the remains, and fire shot like a white-hot torch from their fingertips. A strong whirlwind breeze surrounded them, and it carried the mournful, deafening cries of long-dead spirits.

While Luke and Jenny relaxed, enjoying a glass of wine, Liddy rested alone in the bedroom. "I think I'll quite enjoy living in the modern world. The clothes are so much more comfortable than the ones I wore in the 1600s," said Jenny.

Luke smiled and raised his glass in a toast. "Here's to a long and beneficial partnership, my dear."

They clinked glasses, just as Liddy began screaming from her room upstairs. "It's Liddy!"

They both ran quickly upstairs. They barged into the room to find Liddy standing in the center of it, screaming in agony, fully engulfed in flames. Jenny turned to Luke in a panic. "Do something!"

Luke shrugged as he watched in horror. "It's too late! It's beyond my powers!" Liddy slumped to the floor as her screams muffled to an end, and only the crackle of the flames could be heard. Jenny and Luke watched with speechless horror.

The women continued fueling the fire, as Amy collapsed to her knees. Dr. Grayson lifted her arms and ceased. "That should be enough! It's finished!" As the fire died down, wailing moans could be heard as the tortured spirits escaped into the night air. Amy collapsed onto the ground, and Charlotte hurried to her side in a panic, while Dr. Grayson frantically dug through her satchel for the bottles of water. Charlotte held her limp body in her arms, as she used the water to soothe her cracked lips, while also stroking her brittle hair from her ashen face. "Don't you dare leave us now, Mermaid?"

Amy managed to open her eyes as the water trickled into her partly open mouth. After a few anxious moments, as Dr. Grayson looked on, Amy began to cough and come around. She grabbed hold of the water bottle with her hand, and desperately chugged the remainder of the contents, then quickly grabbed the second bottle from Charlotte and did the same. They both helped Amy to her feet, as she continued to breathe heavily, and her original appearance slowly returned.

"Thank heavens! She's coming back around. We just have to escort her back to the water as soon as possible," Dr. Grayson stated.

"You had us worried for a few anxious moments there, Mermaid."

Amy eyed her with gratitude as she struggled to regain her breath. "Thank you, Charlotte." Amy weakly glanced at Dr. Grayson. "Is it finished?"

Dr. Grayson gestured toward the scorched patch of earth, where nothing remained but ash. "She's gone." They all took a deep sigh of relief.

At the Underwood house, Jenny knelt over the incinerated ashes of her daughter. Luke looked away with a distress rarely displayed. Jenny turned toward him with stern, angry eyes. "How could you let this happen? You were supposed to protect her."

"I had nothing to do with this. Surely, someone must've discovered where her remains were buried."

Jenny looked up with rage. "And they burned her, just as they did me in 1697."

"I assure you! If I would've known, I would've done something to prevent this."

Jenny sneered, "I swear upon my daughter's ashes! I will torture and destroy whoever did this to my baby."

"And I promise you that I will do everything in my power to make that a reality."

Chapter Twenty-Seven:

The Biblical Storm Arrives

The small town of Lockeport braces for a massive hurricane, before the Summer Solstice. Most inhabitants had wisely chosen to seek higher ground. However, some had chosen to stay and ride out the storm, clinging dearly to this small slice of life that they proudly call home. A patrol car slowly cruised down a nearly vacated street with boarded-up businesses, and only a few people rushing for last-minute necessities. Officer Hawley stopped by the City Diner, noticing a large number of homeless people with disheveled clothing that inhabited the booths. Suzy was working the serving area all by herself, pouring coffee, and checking on each individual.

As she made her way back behind the counter, he flagged her down. "Can I get you a cup of coffee, Officer Hawley?"

Hawley responded with a great deal of anxiety. "What are you doing here, Miss McVea? Most everyone else has boarded up their businesses and homes, and left town."

"I'm not going anywhere. This old diner is all I have left."

"And it might be the absolute last thing you ever have. There's a category 5 hurricane heading this way, and this whole area will probably be destroyed and flooded by this time tomorrow."

Suzy reacted defiantly, motioning to the people scattered throughout the diner. "Someone has to take care of these people. They have no way of getting out of town, and even if they did, they have nowhere to go. For crying out loud, they live in our city park."

Hawley said with frustration, "You've always been a stubborn one, Suzy. You have to understand the seriousness of this situation."

"I have lived here all my life, and it's not my first storm. I understand it clearly. But I've made my decision, and that's final."

Hawley shook his head. "Very well! I'll check on you again before I evacuate myself. But after that, you're on your own."

"I'll still be here, and I'll have a hot meal waiting for you." Office Hawley sighed, then left to resume his duties.

At Branchview, Loraine was settling into her new routine as a mother of twins. Millie entered the nursery to help, and Loraine couldn't resist teasing her. "Well! Someone got in rather late last night."

"Oh really, Lori! Are you going to insist on keeping tabs on your mother?"

Loraine laughed. "I hope you had a pleasant time."

"It was marvelous! Mr. Crawford is a true gentleman."

Loraine lifted baby Olivia from her crib. "Would you mind holding baby London while I feed Olivia?"

"Not at all. My little man just loves his grandmama. Don't you?"

There was a knock at the open door, and Dr. Grayson peeped in. "Can I come in?"

Loraine looked up with surprise. "You most certainly can." Dr. Grayson strolled in, as Millie watched with wonderment. "Mother, this is Dr. Grayson."

"I'm so very pleased to meet you. Lori has told me so much about you." Dr. Grayson answered with a nod. "Excuse me for staring, but I find it remarkable that a deceased woman can once again walk among us."

"I guess when there are two Greek gods and a Mermaid goddess involved, anything is possible."

"I suppose. I thought I'd seen every sort of strange phenomenon when I served in MI6, but obviously, I was wrong."

Dr. Grayson moved in for a closer look at the babies. "Oh, Lori! They are beautiful. I wish I could have been around for their birth."

A chilling breeze blew into the room, and Maggie stepped to the forefront. "It's so good to see you again, Maggie." Dr. Grayson stated.

Maggie turned her attention to Loraine with urgency. "Are you almost done feeding the babies?"

"About halfway, why do you ask?"

"You must hurry! They're waiting for us in the Grand Corridor."

Millie asked with curiosity, "Who's waiting, Maggie?"

"The spirits. They all want to see the new members of our family."

Millie sighed. "More spirits? Why am I not surprised?" Dr. Grayson and Loraine exchanged an amused glance.

On the beach at Lighthouse Point, Zeus stood at the water's edge looking out over the ocean, and Poseidon strolled up to join him. "Any word yet?" Zeus shook his head with disappointment and sighed. "That ocean has always been a major part of our existence. Its beauty never ceases to amaze me." They continued to stare across the vast expanse for a long moment before Poseidon continued the conversation. "I spoke to Amphitrite this morning. She and the other women found Liddy McPherson's remains and destroyed them."

Zeus looked at him with surprise. "She's gone?" Poseidon nodded. "That's one less problem we have to deal with."

Poseidon looked outward, flipping his long hair from his face. "It's hard to believe there's a monster storm lurking out beyond that calm horizon."

Zeus laughed. "I guess we could say it's like the storms of life. You know they're out there, but they always hit when you least expect it."

Poseidon pondered the remark. "You ever think about all the mistakes we've made throughout the centuries?"

Zeus grunted. "Every day! It haunts me like a relentless ghost."

Poseidon nodded in agreement. "I guess if there's anything I've learned throughout the years, it would be that though we're gods, we're far from being perfect."

Zeus answered with a friendly pat to the back of his broad shoulders. "So true, brother. So true."

In the Grand Corridor, Maggie led the women, toting the babies, into the enormous room. Two comfortable seats awaited them, as a long procession of spirits from Branchview's past waited to greet the new arrivals. The first to greet them was a young Penelope and Jack Branch.

Millie whispered loudly to Loraine, "They look remarkably like Steven and Charlotte."

Loraine only answered with a smirk, as Penelope and Jack moved closer with much excitement. "Oh, Jack! Our little grandbabies. They're adorable!"

Maggie stepped forward with confidence. "I'd like to introduce you all to London and Olivia Spencer, the new members of the Branch family."

Loud applause rang out, and the women looked up with wonder to see the light of countless spirit apparitions filling the room. "Oh, dear! I do believe this is going to take a while…." Millie nodded.

Across town, in the Underwood residence, Jenny McPherson sat in a large Victorian chair within the parlor, lost in reflective thought. Her meditation was abruptly interrupted when the front door opened and Luke entered. "You're home rather early...."

Before replying, Luke immediately strolled over to the decanter, and began pouring himself a glass of wine. "You and I have many strategies to discuss before tomorrow." He turned and held up the decanter. "Could I pour you a glass?"

"No, thank you."

He strolled over to an adjacent chair and sat down. "Actually, I couldn't wait to get out of that blasted office. As soon as tomorrow is out of the way, I will resign, and place someone else in the position."

Jenny only replied with a close-lipped smile, before moving the conversation forward. "So, what should I expect from our opponents?"

Luke set his glass down and seriously leaned into the conversation. "By no means whatsoever are you to engage in battle with my brothers. They could destroy you with a flick of a finger. I've made sure that you're equipped with skills equal to Steven Spencer and Gerard LeRoux. You'll have the same shapeshifting skills that will transform you into a creature that best fits your personality."

"What about the Mermaid and the Spirit Witch?"

"They're not to be taken lightly either. But Amphitrite, like any other fish, must stay hydrated. If you're able to destroy the water supply that she'll be carrying on a belt around her waist and subject her to extreme heat, she will succumb."

Jenny went on to ask, "What are some of the vulnerabilities that I'll have?"

Luke took a sip of wine before answering. "You, my dear, are only a mortal that has been granted exceptional powers. You must be careful not to be taken down. If any of those mentioned were able to snatch out your heart, you will be destroyed."

Jenny gave an understanding nod. "I'll take whatever measures necessary to make sure that doesn't happen."

The morning had been a hectic venture for Suzy McVea. Since the untimely death of her uncle, she had assumed the task of running the diner alone. It was proving to be quite a difficult endeavor for a girl of her age. With the morning breakfast rush now passed, she finally had a chance to sit down on a stool to catch her breath. Officer Hawley's patrol car pulled up outside, towing a generator on a small trailer. Suzy stood and strolled over to the window to also see a large box truck, followed by two other police cars. She excitedly moved to the door to greet Hawley. "What's all this about?"

Office Hawley shrugged. "I got thinking about it, and decided to recruit some friends to help you out here." He motioned to the windows. "I got some plywood to board up those windows, bought a generator, and the Stop n' Shop donated a generous amount of food." Three other police officers entered. "We'll all stay here with you to help cook and serve the food."

Suzy was flabbergasted, as tears flowed from her eyes. "I don't know how I can ever thank you for all this."

"No need! We're just neighbors helping neighbors. That's the way it should be."

In the main living quarters of the lighthouse, Bill nervously busied himself at his command desk. He was studying the approaching storm and listening to the weather radio when there was a knock at the door. He turned to look that way in annoyance, before rushing to answer it. "Millie! What are you doing here?"

"I came here to check on you. Aren't you going to evacuate to Branchview as we discussed last night?"

"Not until the very last minute. I have to make sure that all the fishing vessels have cleared the storm zone."

They both walked over to the computer screen. "Where exactly is the storm located at this moment?"

Bill pointed to the screen. "I have to say, it's the strangest thing I've ever seen. It's just stalled offshore, around 250 to 300 miles out, churning like an angry beast."

"Perhaps it will change direction and go back out to sea."

"We can only hope. If it decides to charge at us head-on, it could be total devastation."

Millie clutched onto his arm. "You will promise me that you'll get out of here in time? This old lighthouse is very vulnerable."

Bill nodded. "I promise." Millie smiled. "Would you like to stay and have a cup of coffee with me?"

Millie shook her head, while Bill frowned. "I will stay for a cup of tea, however." She grinned.

That evening, while most of the inhabitants of the great house busied themselves within other quarters, Philip headed for the garden gazebo to meditate. A black cat slinked up within a few steps from where he stood, and affectionately brushed against his leg. "Good evening, Charlotte!"

She appeared and leaned against the railing next to him. "I was hoping I'd find you here."

Philip pleasantly looked up to the skies. "It's a beautiful summer evening."

"Not to steal a pun, but it's sort of like the calm before the storm."

Philip laughed. "I sense there's something on your mind?"

Charlotte pondered before continuing. "Whether I survive the battle tomorrow or not, I know I'll be summoned back to hell to account for all my evil doings."

"I suppose that's true."

She turned toward him in desperation. "I've done everything in my power to atone for as much I can. Would you and Ezekiel be willing to speak on my behalf?"

Philip contemplated for a moment. "In all these years of my existence, I've come to believe that everyone deserves a second chance, Charlotte." He turned to face her. "You've been of great service to us, and I promise I will speak to someone on your behalf and do everything I can to help."

She meekly responded, "Thank you." They both leaned against the railing and gazed out into the night. "You know, now that Liddy's gone, perhaps there's a special favor I could do for you in return."

Philip curiously glanced at her. "What might that be?"

She winked cleverly at him. "Let's just keep that a surprise, shall we? Sleep well, Philip."

Charlotte walked away, and disappeared into the night air, while Philip shook his head in amazement. *Good night, Charlotte.* A loud meow rang out somewhere in the darkness.

The main house was slowly quieting down for the night, while Mrs. Porter and Joey were busy cleaning the sink and counter area in the kitchen. "Is there anything else you need me to do?"

"No. You go run along. I can finish up here."

Joey paused before walking away. "Looks like things are getting kind of tense around here."

Mrs. Porter continued to scrub away. "We'll get through it. We always do…."

Joey lingered. "You know, I never had grandparents and my parents never had time for me." Mrs. Porter paused to listen as Joey's voice cracked with emotion. "You're the only one who ever took an interest in me, and made me feel special." She kissed Mrs. Porter on the cheek. "Thank you!" She quickly exited the room, and Mrs. Porter looked up, wiping the tears from her eyes. *It's amazing how some people never cease to surprise me.*

The LeRoux family had chosen to sleep in the main house, so everyone could protect each other. Gerard was finding it very difficult to sleep. As he was sitting up in bed, lost in his thoughts, Sharie crawled in next to him. "Are you ok, baby?"

He paused before turning toward her. "I was just thinking about what might happen if we fail tomorrow."

Sharie leaned over and kissed him on the cheek. "We're not going to fail. We have too many good people on our side."

"I just want us all to be happy again."

Sharie took hold of his hand. "I've stuck with you through 26 years of marriage. We had our share of tough times. But if I had to do it all over again, I wouldn't change a thing." She looked directly into his eyes. "I love you, Gerard Le Roux. We will get through this, and we will be happy again."

"I love you too, Sharie." He leaned close and kissed her.

Steven peeked through the doorway to see the babies sleeping peacefully in their crib, and Loraine fast asleep in the chair. The sight gave him extra inspiration, as he prepared for the impending battle. The lives of all his family and friends hung in the balance. He smiled to himself as he turned out the light.

Dr. Grayson waited in quiet contemplation in the sitting room, when she noticed the now-familiar music box on the mantle. *Oh.....* The urge hit her to wind it up, and the ballerina began twirling around to the musical notes of 'Stardust.'

Steven entered. "Mother always loved that music box."

Dr. Grayson turned and smiled. "I know...." She strolled toward Steven. "I miss the long talks we had over tea."

"Seems like it was just yesterday."

Dr. Grayson sighed. "I'll be returning to the spirit world when all this is over, and I wondered if you'd do me a favor." Steven listened attentively. "While I was staying here, I began writing a book about the history of this old house, and the spirits that dwell here. My manuscripts are in the desk drawer of my old room. I would like for you and Lori to finish it for me."

"We would be honored to do so. But you have to promise that you'll come back to visit us from time to time."

She replied with a warm smile. "You can count on it. After all, I'm a part of the history of this place now."

"Yes… you are!" He smiled.

Below the cliffs of Lighthouse Point, Amphitrite rested on the rocks, emotionally staring out over the dark ocean. Zeus approached and sat down next to her. "I hope you don't mind if I join you?"

She shook her head. "Couldn't sleep?"

He shook his head. "I figured a nice stroll on the beach might help."

She paused in deep thought. "I've decided that I want Steven Spencer to kiss me tomorrow. I'm ready to go be with my Matthew."

Zeus pondered her statement. "You do realize that once you go, you can never come back as you are?"

Amphitrite nodded confidently. "I was once willing to give up immortality to be with Matthew for a single lifetime. Now, I can be with him forever in spirit."

Zeus smiled. "I do envy you for loving someone that much, Amphitrite."

"Perhaps someday, you'll love someone in the same way."

Zeus gazed out optimistically over the dark waters. "Perhaps! Only time will tell."

The family agreed to have a celebration breakfast the next morning. Amid peace before the battle, they felt the comradery might be good for everyone. Mrs. Porter emerged from the kitchen. "Has everyone had enough to eat?"

Steven replied, "Mrs. Porter if we all ate another bite, we wouldn't be able to move from this table."

Ezekiel stood and raised his coffee cup. "I'd like everyone to raise a glass, cup, or whatever you may be drinking in a toast."

Gerard noticed the serious atmosphere and decided to lighten up the moment. "We all know you probably have brandy in that cup, Ezekiel." The room erupted in laughter.

"I'll remember that comment, Gerard." Everyone raised their drinks. "Here's to family! No matter what happens today, rest assured that we all came together for a just cause."

Everyone shouted a hearty "Here, here!"

The family gathered again in the foyer shortly afterward to send the gods off, along with the others who would go into battle. Ezekiel gave the orders. "Dr. Grayson, you'll remain here at Branchview along with the spirits and the shadows of justice, to protect the house from attack." She gave an understanding nod. "Steven, and Gerard, you'll hold the front line with Philip, Amy, and myself."

Charlotte stepped forward. "I want to stand with you as well." Ezekiel and Philip exchanged a glance, then gave an agreeing nod. Steven kissed Loraine and baby Olivia then followed suit with baby London who rested in Millie's arms.

Loraine spoke up, choking back tears. "Please be safe, Steven."

A tearful Sharie and Deanna rushed to embrace and kiss Gerard. When everyone had said their goodbyes, Steven took a deep breath and opened the door. "We will prevail, and see you all very soon." The remaining household members watched till their loved ones faded from sight, along the pathway to Lighthouse Point.

Across the Branchview Estate, in the cemetery, the ground around some of the gravestones began to heave and hands were soon seen reaching upward from the dirt. The hideous, decomposed bodies emerged from the burial sites, groaning loudly. As they looked around, they slowly began to group, limping from the cemetery grounds.

In the dark recesses of the Branchview basement, the dirt around a freshly dug grave stirred, and a fist exploded upward.

On the beach at Lighthouse Point, the gods took their stand at the forefront, while Steven, Gerard, and Charlotte took their places behind them. All assembled with their backs to the ocean, as thick clouds churned in the distance over the Atlantic.

A few seconds later, Hades and Jenny, with the three Hell Hounds on a leash, boldly marched toward them. They were followed by countless winged demons that looked similar to giant vampire bats. Within their wake was the enormous Basilisk, spitting fire and shaking the ground with its thunderous footsteps as it moved toward the beach. Steven spoke to himself in a loud whisper, "What the hell is that thing?"

Gerard heard him, and answers promptly, "That is a Basilisk."

They halted within a few short feet of each other. Hades reigned in the leash of the hounds as they heeled at his feet, and let out a wicked laugh. "It appears that you're rather outnumbered?"

Jenny added with a smirk, "I'd have to agree. All you could bring to the fight is two mortals, a Mermaid, and this one, who certainly must be the little black kitty cat?"

"Who the hell are you?" Charlotte inquired.

Jenny answered boldly, "I am Jenny McPherson."

Amphitrite replied with contempt, "Liddy's mother!"

"Exactly! And you two are the first ones I'm going to kill."

Charlotte boiled over with anger. "Think again, bitch!"

She transformed into a sleek black panther, roaring wildly.

Jenny then turned her attention to Amphitrite. "What have you got, Mermaid?"

"Oh! I can more than hold my own, just as I am."

She motioned to Steven, and looked at him with great curiosity. "You and the red-headed Mermaid, I remember you two from when I last breathed air as a human. But you were both different people back then." The gods, as well as Steven and the others, exchanged clueless glances, and Steven balked at the suggestion.

"I'm afraid you're quite mistaken, I didn't exist during the last time you lived in 1697," Jenny smirked.

"Not that you know of. Nevertheless, what do you bring to the battle, handsome?"

Steven channeled his energy, and transformed into a lion-type beast, while Gerard simultaneously transformed into a tiger beast. They roared ferociously, and the hounds recoiled and cowered in response. Amphitrite smirked confidently. "These are the two testy creatures you should be concerned with."

Hades said arrogantly, "I must say, I'm rather impressed. But Jenny has a surprise of her own." He nodded to her, and she shapeshifted into a hideous, growling beast that even repulsed Zeus and Poseidon.

"That is one ugly bitch."

All the beasts returned to their human forms, as a group of Federal Agents and National Guardsmen approached in the distance from the lighthouse side of the beach. Steven announced, "It's Guitierez, and he brought the calvary."

Zeus said angrily, "I thought he agreed to let us handle this. We can't involve innocent mortals in our battle."

Steven sighed. "Agent Guitierez can be quite stubborn at times."

Hades balked. "Foolish mortals! I assumed they'd try to interfere, so I also brought an army of mortal mercenaries from the Secret Society." He gestured toward the other side of the beach, where another platoon of armed men and women approached.

As tensions on the beach unfolded, Dr. Grayson stood sentry with all the other members of the Shadows of Justice, brandishing their swords and prepared for battle. Along with them were the worthy spirits of Branchview's past, who surrounded the enormous house acting as a spiritual barrier.

A multitude of winged demons approached, and aggressively encountered the spiritual apparitions, but were repelled by their illumination. Some took flight above to the high turret roof and shrieked in loud, high-pitched chattering noises. The demons were also halted and forced to shield their eyes from the protective crosses strategically placed around the house. They were joined by the evil corpses of the living dead, whose echoes of sneering growls could be heard even within the Branchview walls.

The illuminated spirit of Marcus LeRoux stood to the right of Dr. Grayson, while Jack Branch and a young Penelope flanked her to the left. Jack spoke up, "I do believe we'll have to expend a good amount of our spiritual energy to fend off this hoard."

Marcus answered, "The walking dead are only a distraction. We need to make sure those demons don't fly up and enter through the upper story windows."

Dr. Grayson responded, "If so, we'll need to engage them by air as well. We cannot allow harm to come upon our family."

Penelope confidently looked ahead. "We shall prevail!" Just then, a bright light pierced through the gray skies like a large bolt of lightning, as the battle notes bellowed, echoing aggressively from above. As they all looked upward in awe, the clouds parted like tearing sheets, and an army of angels thundered through and formed a menacing line in midair.

Dr. Grayson clutched at the crucifix around her neck and smiled. "I do believe a higher power has intervened on our behalf."

The group on the beach were alerted by the trumpet blast as well and looked to the skies. The radiant warrior angel directed an army in an arc pattern, hovering in the sky. Zeus gestured enthusiastically toward the warrior. "Anu! The Watcher of the Skies."

Steven asked, "I take it that's the divine intervention we were hoping for?"

Poseidon nodded and turned to Hades. "Perhaps now would be a wise time to retreat."

Hades sneered, "I will never concede defeat." Just then, another winding horn sounded and echoed inward from the ocean waters. A squad of three large, wooden barquentine vessels appeared on the horizon. They were equipped with winged sails, and all fitted with some sort of silent, futuristic jet engines. They landed in the waters just offshore, ushered in by Pegasus, with Freyr and his Gigantes wife Geror riding on his back. Zeus cheered, "It's Freyr and the Light Elves."

Magnus and Triton then emerged from the deep waters, leading a legion of spirit warriors from Avalon onto the shore. In the wake of their arrival, the sea erupted with finned tails as far as the eyes could see. As they got closer to shore, Nereid and Oceanid warriors took human form, armed with crossbows and golden arrows. Hades and Jenny watched with shocked surprise, while Poseidon turned to Steven with a confident grin. "Divine intervention indeed."

Chapter Twenty-Eight:

A Day of Reckoning

After nearly a year of turmoil, the day of reckoning had finally arrived. What began as a simple dispute between a deceived witch and members of the Branch family had now grown into a full-scale battle of good versus evil. On this fateful day, there would be an outcome that even the most intuitive soul could never have imagined. The onlookers all watched as Pegasus landed on the beach. Freyr, an average-sized warrior, and his wife Geror, a towering, muscular woman, both dismounted and took their places in the standoff.

The mercenaries of the Secret Society threw their weapons down and retreated when they saw the countless multitude of Nereid and Oceanid warriors continuing to emerge from the depths of the Atlantic, flooding onto the already crowded beach. On top of that, several more Elven fighters continued rowing to the shore from the three sailing vessels.

As everyone looked on in awe, Gerard noticed the size difference between Freyr and his wife. "That is one big woman." Steven nodded in agreement.

Hades scoffed angrily as he watched his mercenary's retreat. "Useless, mortal cowards!" He looked toward Guitierez and his regimen, who now stood near the front lines. "I suggest that you and your pitiful army fall back to the safety of the lighthouse barrier."

Captain Scott, a tough, square-jawed man in his early 40s, and commander of the Connecticut National Guard regimen, aggressively stepped forward. "Do you think you're the devil himself? You have no right to give us orders."

Guitierez moved to calm him, while both Hades and Jenny mockingly laughed. "I think we should all do as he says, Captain. He's not necessarily the devil, but he's pretty damn close."

Captain Scott looked all around him. "This is almost Biblical. It's like a small-scale Armageddon."

"Not exactly. But you're close on that as well, sir."

The Captain gave Guitierez a humble nod, then turned to his men. "All fallback!"

Guitierez then motioned to his team, "Us as well!" After a few moments, when all the mortal troops were at a safe distance, both sides silently stared at each other and waited. The scene was quiet for a few tense moments until Hades pounded his staff in the sand. "Attack!"

The groups swarmed toward each other, colliding in mid-stride. The angels swooped down from the air and picked off demons with a wave of their swords. Steven paused to notice how quickly the angels moved in for the kill without hesitation.

The same scenario was taking place outside of Branchview as the walking dead and demons were unable to penetrate the spiritual energy and swords of the Shadows of Justice. The winged demons were intercepted in midair by the angel warriors before they were able to breach the windows of the upper stories.

The Hell Hounds leaped at Steven and Gerard, who had transformed into the lion and tiger. The dogs' bit at their flesh, but the beasts easily tossed the dogs away like rag dolls. In the forefront, the Basilisk charged a group of archers and incinerated them, as he belched a giant fireball.

Anu landed on the back of the Basilisk, and drove his huge sword into its neck, causing the beast to roar in agony, and throw its head to shake him loose. As the giant beast fell on its front haunches, other angel warriors jumped on for the kill. All the while, it continued to belch fire that consumes several more fighters. Charlotte, now transformed into a panther beast, bit and clawed at charging demons, while Amphitrite tossed destructive energy from her fingertips toward anything that tried to attack. Across the outlet, Bill Crawford climbed to the top of the lighthouse observation tower, surprised by the events unfolding on the beach below.

The Barquentines were stationed just offshore, a safe range from the battle. Anxiously observing from the deck were Adam Smith, Kristin Wiler, and a now noticeably pregnant Andrea Hill.

Adam spoke up, "I wish Freyr would've allowed me to fight. This is our battle as much as it is theirs."

Kristin stepped in, "I disagree! This is a battle of the supernatural. It's not wise for mortals to be involved."

Andrea added, "I somewhat feel the same as Adam. If I wasn't pregnant, I'd want to be on that beach fighting next to Triton."

Inside the main house, Millie was protecting the babies, while Loraine used her powers to help fight the demons that had managed to breach the upper windows.

While she was distracted, the decomposing hand of Grant Posterle grabbed her shoulder and whirled her around. He growled as he tried to throttle her in a chokehold.

One window in the nursery shattered, and two demons crawled into the room. Millie turned when she heard the commotion and tried to fight them off, but they easily tossed her against the wall. One demon then taunted a barking Bumpers, while the other eyed the babies. Loraine noticed the intruders as she struggled with Grant. She kicked the zombie hard in the groin, causing him to release the grip on her throat. She quickly shot energy from her hands as he charged again, causing the corpse to explode, sending rotting chunks of flesh propelling throughout the room.

She then turned her attention to the demons, who were now hovering over the children. "Get away from my babies!" The demons turned, angrily gnashing their teeth, and growling at her. She extended the fingertips of both hands toward them. "Oomda lambda nu!" They were instantly reduced to hot ash. She then quickly turned to check on Millie. "Mother! Are you alright?"

"Yes, dear. I'll never doubt your supernatural powers ever again. You are one badass mommy…"

The enormous battle raged on as the giant Basilisk was finally brought to the ground, causing a loud tremor along the beach as it fell. It let out a final, pitiful moan before it died along the edge of the cliffs. As the mighty beast took its last breath, Jenny ran toward Amphitrite, who continued to fight off demons. "Time to die, Mermaid." She transformed into the hideous beast, and also shot energy from her fingers, causing the water bottles around Amphitrite's waist to burst.

A stunned Amphitrite had little time to react, as the beast shot a wall of fire that enveloped her. Charlotte heard her cries and tossed a demon aside. In her form as an agile panther-like creature, she leaped at Jenny who continued to maniacally fuel the flames. Catching her off guard, she pounced on her chest and tore into her flesh before Jenny could react in defense. Within seconds, one of Charlotte's large paws transformed into a human hand and snatched Jenny's still-beating heart from her chest. She changed back to her human spirit form and held the plucked heart upward in victory. In anger, Hades roared, swiftly rearing his two-pronged staff, and propelled it through the air toward Charlotte. The staff impaled Charlotte, sending her to the sand next to a severely dehydrated and dying Amphitrite. With a wailing yell of vengeance, Poseidon hurled his trident like a javelin, and it tore into Hades's torso. The impact forced Hades to muster an echoing scream that shook the entire shoreline. His dying scream caused the battle to suddenly cease. All was quiet in those moments, as warriors from both sides paused to look in his direction. Hades looked down, wide-eyed at the base of the trident that had impaled him straight through. He then looked up at an equally stunned Poseidon and Zeus. All eyes watched in silent anticipation, as Poseidon pulled the trident from his body, and the once-mighty Hades slumped to the ground in death. Jenny's body turned to ash upon the sand and was quickly scattered by the wind. Poseidon and Steven then desperately rushed to aid Charlotte and Amphitrite.

Poseidon took Charlotte's dying body into his arms, as she stared back with desperate eyes. "I will keep my promise to you, Poseidon…." He knelt in the sand, struggling to maintain his composure. Within seconds, her body turned to black ash and scattered in the wind.

As Poseidon turned with tears rolling down his cheeks, he noticed Steven holding Amphitrite. "She's almost gone as well. We have to get her to the water immediately."

Just then, the ground began to tremble and shake violently. They both shielded her with their bodies, as a large crevice opened in the earth between them and the cliffs. Inside the crevice was red hot, glowing magma. It sucked in and swallowed the dead body of Hades, his hounds, the Basilisk, and all the evil dead. With a deafening shriek, the demons retreated into the crevice just as it closed once again.

Inside the City Diner, the dishes in the kitchen started breaking, as the walls shook violently. Suzy screamed hysterically, as Officer Hawley rushed over to hold her tightly. "What's happening…?"

"Well, I believe we're having an earthquake."

"An earthquake? I thought we were preparing for a hurricane?" Officer Hawley shrugged his shoulders cluelessly.

The earth continued to rock the little seaside town of Lockeport, causing the SOS Club to crumble under the stress. It finally collapsed with a groan into a heap of dust. Below ground, the steel padlocked door that protected the portal to hell exploded open, thrusting flames into the tunnels below the town. The cottage just above it exploded into roaring flames, sending debris flying everywhere.

As everyone hunkered on the shoreline, Bill Crawford hung on tight in the pinnacle of the lighthouse, as windows shattered and the tower rocked relentlessly. Guitierez, the agents, and National Guardsmen clung desperately to the crumbling barrier wall.

The main house was also being rocked by the earthquake, so Loraine and Millie hustled to gather the babies and Bumpers downstairs to safety. Before they could get down the stairs, the shaking suddenly stopped, and a deafening silence ensued. An intense peace overcame the remaining fighters on the beach, and everyone struggled to regain their composure. Steven scooped Amphitrite into his arms, rushing toward the ocean. As he waded in and submerged her body, he looked up to see a fast-approaching wall of water on the horizon. Poseidon took Amphitrite from Steven's arms and yelled, "I do believe the water is coming to us. Run!" The remaining individuals on the beach ran and scattered, while Zeus, Poseidon, the Nereids, and Oceanids all charged toward the water.

Bill gathered his senses in the top of the lighthouse, grabbing at his forehead that was bleeding from a large gash. He looked outward to the sea and noticed the wall of water heading toward them. *Tsunami!*

The ships offshore prepared for impact. Adam, Kristin, and Andrea huddled close and watched in shocked horror as the giant wave overtook them. Adam shouted, "Both of you, hold onto me as tight as you can!" The wave quickly engulfed the ship, sweeping them all over the railing.

All watched in horror from the shore as the monster wave tossed the Barquentines like they were toy ships. Damaris turned to the others. "Ready yourselves for rescue mode!"

The warriors dove headlong into the incoming water as it crashed onto land, carrying the Barquentine vessels with it. Angels swooped down, lifting as many individuals as they could to safety. The wooden ships violently crushed and splintered against the rock cliffs. Poseidon held tight to Amphitrite as the water pulled them under. Amphitrite revived, transforming into a Mermaid, and parted ways with Poseidon who had transformed into a Merman. With precision radar, she honed in on a floundering Steven and rapidly pulled him toward the surface. All around, countless Nereid and Oceanid Warriors swam swiftly to scoop up the Elves and other mortals that were swept under by the wave. Bill rushed from the tower stairs just as the wave hit, filling the room and overwhelming him.

The wave continued its relentless path onto the land, demolishing anything within its trajectory. Suzy anxiously looked at Office Hawley, as a loud rumbling sound approached from outside. "What's that noise? It sounds like a freight train." Before anyone could react, the wave hit with great impact, penetrating the diner as they all struggled against the inrushing waters.

Loraine peeked out the front door and saw the giant wall of water approaching. An anxious Dr. Grayson turned. "Get back in the house! Now!" She slammed the door shut, as Dr. Grayson and the other spirits created a wall of energy to block the impact. As the wave approached, it crashed into the carriage house, obliterating it on its way toward the Branchview house. The spirits held solid, and the wave parted to either side, sparing the great house. A loud cheer was heard from the spirits on the outside, as the inhabitants of the house huddled closely in the middle of the foyer until the waves' fury had passed.

Loraine got up, slowly made her way to the door, and cautiously opened it. A weary Dr. Grayson now stood waiting with the other spirits. "We did it!"

Loraine turned around with excitement. "We've been spared!" All cheered in response. Loraine said nervously, "I can't wait! I have to go find Steven."

Sharie shouted, "Wait, Loraine, I'm coming along as well."

"Hold on, Mom. You're not going without me," Deanna added.

Millie smiled. "You all go on ahead. Mrs. Porter, Joey, and I will care for the babies."

As the waters calmed and subsided, the carnage was revealed along the coastline. The bodies of those that did not survive were mingled in with the exhausted mortals who were being aided by the Nereids, Oceanids, and angels. Adam and Kristin wearily clung to each other, as a Nereid Merman helped them to their feet.

Triton rushed toward them in a panic. "Have you seen Andrea?"

Adam spoke up, "I'm sorry! We lost hold of her shortly after we were swept overboard."

He gave a disappointed sigh, but seconds later he heard someone yelling, "Triton!" He turned, and instinctively they ran to embrace each other.

"I was scooped to the surface by a Nereid Merman."

"Thank God!" he exclaimed.

A sudden realization overcame them as they held onto each other. "Andrea! I'm different."

She looked at him with equal surprise. "I can feel you. You're flesh and blood once again."

Poseidon wandered up and emotionally embraced his son. "Triton! You're alive!"

Triton looked at his outstretched hands with amazement. "I don't understand. I was a spirit, and now I'm alive."

"You were unjustly killed by the two-pronged staff of Hades. When he died, you were given back the life he took from you."

Triton shook with emotion. "I gladly accept it."

"I do as well," Andrea enthusiastically added. They joyfully kissed.

Triton eagerly turned to his father once again. "Have you seen mother?"

"She was saving Steven Spencer after the wave hit. I lost track of them."

A weary Amphitrite and Steven picked themselves up on another part of the beach. "We made it."

Amphitrite forced a smile. "You did! But…. Steven." She pauses. "It's time for me to go." Steven was perplexed. "I want you to kiss me."

"Are you sure? You do understand what this means?"

"I'm more than ready! I want to be with my Matthew."

They stood toe to toe, and Steven reluctantly embraced her. "Goodbye, Amphitrite! I will never forget you."

"Nor will I forget you, Steven Spencer. I'll remember you every time I look at my Matthew." They passionately kissed, just as Loraine ran onto the scene. She stopped short to watch with visible hurt. An equally perplexed Sharie and Deanna quickly moved to comfort her. Amphitrite then slumped, lifeless, to the sand, and Steven stumbled to one knee, before collapsing as well. Loraine tried to run, but Sharie held her back. Zeus, Poseidon, Triton, and Andrea arrived on the scene seconds later.

Triton tried to run to his mother but was also halted by Poseidon. "Wait!"

They all watched as the spirit of Amphitrite emerged from her body. The apparition appeared as she was under the Victorian era guise of Amanda Green. Her spirit hovered above the sand as she patiently waited. A few seconds later, the spirit of Matthew Branch emerged from Steven's body, and they embraced. A now revived Steven watched as they turned to wave goodbye to him, and the others. They strolled hand in hand a few more steps, then vanished as a strong gust of wind blew across the beach.

As the emotions flooded through Steven's body, he picked himself up, and rapidly stumbled through the sand to meet Loraine with a passionate embrace. She held him tightly in her arms. "Oh, Steven! I thought you were dead." She abruptly paused and slapped him hard across the face.

"What was that for?"

Loraine turned her nose up. "That kiss! You certainly looked as though you were enjoying it."

Zeus and Poseidon exchanged an amused glance as they looked on. "Lori! You know I had to do it."

"I know. But you didn't have to be so passionate about it." He grabbed Loraine squarely by the shoulders and pulled her in for a very long, passionate kiss. Lori sighed as he gently released her.

"It's not every day that I get to passionately kiss a goddess, as well as the woman I truly love."

Triton fell to his knees alongside his mother's lifeless body, and he was joined by Poseidon. "I'll take her back to the ocean…."

Poseidon laid his hand on Triton's shoulder and gestured up toward Andrea. "I'll take her. Your future wife and child need you now."

Poseidon scooped up her lifeless body and sadly walked toward the ocean. Magnus caught up and walked alongside him. The other spirit warriors of Avalon, along with the Nereids and Oceanids, all marched back into the sea.

Mangus spoke as they walked into the water. "I'm sorry about Amphitrite. Would you like me to take her to Avalon?"

Poseidon gestured toward the others around them. "No. I think she should be with her people, the Nereids. But I would like you to do me another favor." Both paused in their progression and Magnus listened. "There was a spirit witch named Charlotte Locke that died here today. She fought valiantly on our behalf, and deserves to find rest at Avalon."

Magnus answered with a confident nod. "I will seek out her spirit in the afterworld, and take her there. This I promise."

"Thank you, Magnus." Poseidon and Magnus continued until they disappeared, amid the wake of the countless finned tails of the Nereids and Oceanids returning to their underwater home.

Sharie desperately addressed Steven. "Have you seen Gerard?"

Steven looked beyond her to see a disoriented and exhausted Gerard struggling to make his way toward them. "If you and Deanna turn around now, I think you'll see the guy you're looking for."

They turned and joyfully ran toward him, embracing him tightly. Loraine slipped her arm around Steven as they watched the happy reunion. "It appears that most everyone is accounted for." She looked around. "Except…. Have you seen Charlotte?"

Steven sadly looked downward and shook his head. "She didn't make it."

Loraine reacted with much remorse. "Would you like to go back to Branchview now? I can fix you a nice cup of coffee."

"That's the best suggestion I've heard all day."

Suzy and a policewoman struggled to regain their composure after the wave hit the diner. They were knee-deep in water and looking around for survivors. "We have to find Officer Hawley. He was right next to me when the water hit."

They looked about for a few moments before the policewoman pointed. "Over here! I found him!" Both women pulled debris off him, and the policewoman moved quickly to begin CPR. *Come on Hawley! Come on!*

After four long tries, she gave up. But an emotional Suzy pleaded, "Don't give up! Keep trying!"

The policewoman looked up. "He's gone, Suzy. I'm sorry...."

She gently closed his staring eyes and dejectedly stood up, while Suzy proclaimed, "We have to make sure that everyone knows he was a hero."

The policewoman answered, "They will! I promise!"

Adam and Kristin walked hand in hand toward an approaching Agent Guitierez. "I never thought I'd see you two again."

Adam announced, "Hopefully, you're not going to arrest us."

Guitierez shook his head no, and glanced back at the other agents a short distance down the beach. "Come on! Let's walk the other way."

Adam anxiously inquired, "Were you able to stop the assassination attempt on the President?"

Guitierez nodded firmly. "As we speak, there is a nationwide round-up of key members of the Secret Society."

Adam gave an approving nod. "What about Joey? Is there some way we can cut her some slack for helping us out?"

"I have a plan. I'll tell you all about it." Guitierez anxiously looked back, then motioned to both of them. "Let's keep walking until we're a safe distance from the rest."

Zeus walked alongside Freyr and Geror as they surveyed the ruins of the Barquentines, along with the other Elves. The winged god Anu joined them, and Zeus said, "I can't thank you all enough for your timely intervention."

Anu answered with a pleasant smile. "It's been a long time since we've all been together. Perhaps we should arrange a future reunion under more pleasant circumstances."

Freyr stated, "Perhaps on a sunny day in Alfheim."

The group laughed, then Anu looked around with a serious, caring expression. "My angels will carry your dead home safely."

Geror nodded. "We appreciate that, Anu."

Freyr looked to Zeus, then to Anu. "Now that the wave has turned our ships into tinder, do any of you gentlemen have a suggestion on how we can get home?"

Anu looked to Zeus for an answer. "It's not been done for quite some time, but since we can't get you all to the vortex, perhaps we can bring the vortex to you."

Anu replied, "Call your people together."

Freyr turned and blew his horn. It caught the attention of Adam and Kristin. "I believe that's meant for us."

Guitierez stated, "You do know that when you're cleared of charges, you'll probably be up for a medal of valor?"

"Well, you'll just have to accept it for me." Guitierez looked at him with great surprise. "Kristin and I got married in Alfheim. We have no plans of ever coming back."

"I'm happy for you both." The breeze suddenly picked up, and a vortex appeared over the calm waters, silently moving its way onto land. Their conversation was halted when they saw it. "I do believe that's our ride home."

"Hopefully, Guitierez... you'll never tell anyone where we are."

"Ha!" he laughed. "Even if I did, they'd never believe me. As far as I'm concerned, I never saw either one of you today."

He and Adam parted ways with a firm handshake. "Thanks for everything."

"I envy you two. Please enjoy your new life." Guitierez watched as Adam and Kristin ran hand in hand toward where the vortex had settled over the congregation of Elves. They took their place among them, anxiously looking upward, while Freyr and Geror joined them.

Zeus proclaimed as he and Anu stepped aside, "May the winds carry you all safely home."

"Thank you both." Freyr and Geror clung to each other and looked upward with the rest as the vortex opened. "Here we go!" The vortex gently drew them upward. Once the last being was safe inside its churning whirlwind, it rapidly moved back out over the Atlantic, and abruptly disappeared over the horizon.

Zeus and Anu gave an approving nod. "The angels and I should be leaving as well, Zeus. There's no one guarding the portal to the Summerland."

They shared a pleasant handshake. "Until we meet again, my friend." Anu blew his horn, and he and the army of angels, some carrying the dead, ascended into an opening in the sky. In a matter of seconds, the clouds merged, and the only sounds heard were the cries of seabirds in the skies overhead. All was returning to normal, as the tide inched its way up the beach.

Gerard, Sharie, and Deanna joined Zeus, who was still looking to the heavens. Deanna was choked up by the vision. "That was awesome!"

Zeus answered with a smile, as Gerard leaned over with exhaustion, "I can't believe it's over! We won!"

Zeus took on an expression of regret. "Does anyone ever win in war, Gerard?" He answered with a subtle shake of his head.

Sharie turned to Zeus. "We're heading back to Branchview. Would you care to join us?"

"I'll be along in a short while. I have one more issue that requires my attention." Zeus wandered over to a hysterical Captain Scott. "I don't understand all of this. When that wave hit, those angels pulled me and the others from sure death. Many others were saved by Mermaids and

Mermen. It's all like some crazy fairytale dream. How can it all be real?" The group of agents voiced their inquires with mumbles in the background. Zeus simply grinned and waved his hand in the air, causing Captain Scott and the others to freeze in animation. The lone exception was Agent Guitierez, who looked around at his frozen comrades with a confused expression. Zeus stepped back and spoke calmly to the still individuals. "When I snap my fingers, all of you will come to, and not have a memory of anything that happened here today." Once the group was released from their trance, they looked around rather befuddled.

Captain Scott looked cluelessly at Zeus, "What happened here, sir?"

Zeus looked around at the empty beach. "We had an earthquake and tsunami."

Captain Scott also surveyed the beach with a confused expression, before focusing back on Zeus. "How did we all survive?"

Zeus gazed out to sea and shrugged. "Perhaps we can call it a miracle, Captain."

He nodded thoughtfully, then turned and motioned to his platoon. "Let's head out!"

Guitierez strolled closer and flashed a grin toward Zeus. "Good job, Ezekiel." He then turned and motioned to his agents. "We're done here! Let's go!" Zeus stepped back and watched as the men left the area. It was with great relief to him that all had been set right. He and Poseidon's true identity would remain anonymous, hopefully for many years to come.

The one person that had not been accounted for was Bill Crawford. He had been badly injured during the ordeal and managed to stumble his way to the main house. In the study, the family members celebrated their victory when the doorknocker echoed throughout the house. Millie got up and rushed for the door, but it opened before she got there. "Millie! Anyone! Please, help!" Bill announced as he stumbled through the door.

"Oh, Bill! I thought surely that the wave had swept you away."

He struggled to move forward, but his legs faltered under him. The others quickly gathered to help him into a chair. "I thought I was dead as well. The water swept me under, and I looked up to see my departed wife and the spirit of Silas Burke reaching for me." Everyone in the room gathered closely to listen. "Just as I took hold of their hands, a Mermaid boosted me to the surface."

Millie coddled him. "Goodness! What happened then?"

"I woke up on dry land, lying in the middle of the pathway leading to Branchview."

Mrs. Porter replied, "You were a very lucky man, Mr. Crawford."

Millie examined the cut on his forehead. "Oh, dear! That's quite a nasty cut you have. Come along, and I'll tend to it." She ushered Bill from the room.

Joey looked to Mrs. Porter with a smile. "That was pretty dynamic."

"I'm sure we'll hear about more dynamic things in the days ahead." She rested her hand on Joey's shoulder. "Come along now, we have to get the generator fired up, and get some power back on in this old house."

"Yes ma'am!"

The LeRoux family had finally made their way back to the main house and paused to examine the carnage of what once was the carriage house. On top of the wreckage was what remained of Jack Branch's Corvette, his vintage Ford truck, and their vehicles. Sharie buried her head in Gerard's shoulder and wept. "Oh, Gerard! That was the only home that I've ever known."

Deanna looked around sadly. "The cottage, the beautiful oaks, grand maples, and the gardens. They're all gone." Gerard glanced about with a pained expression as he embraced his family. "It'll all come back in time. At least we still have the grand old house, and each other."

An exhausted Steven, now showered with a fresh set of clothes, sat with Loraine in thoughtful silence. Triton entered with Andrea. "I hope we're not interrupting anything?"

Loraine was startled, "Not at all. You two are a much-welcomed guest here."

Steven first looked to Triton, "It's good to see you among the living once again." Then he glanced at Andrea, "And it's great to see you back home again."

Triton reached over and took hold of Andrea's hand. "It's a miracle that I shall never take for granted."

"Well…." Loraine asked, "have you decided whether you'll stay, or go back to Alfheim?"

Andrea looked lovingly at Triton. "We talked about it on our way back here. We've decided to stay, and make Lockeport our home."

Steven sighed. "Well! There's not much left of it. But we do need people like you to help rebuild it."

"Luckily, I work well with my hands. I should have no problem finding a job." Both Steven and Loraine looked at him with puzzled expressions as he continued. "I've decided to give up my immortality so that I can live a normal life with the woman I love." He looked again at Andrea with a smile. "As I said before, it's rare that a man is lucky enough to earn a second chance at life."

"It's obvious that you inherited the wisdom of your father," Steven responded.

"And the loving heart of your mother…. We will miss her," Loraine added.

Triton wiped a tear from his eye. "From this moment on, I'd prefer to be addressed as Tony Freeman."

Steven smiled. "And you shall! With a special emphasis on that last name."

Tony added, "Absolutely! I'm now a free man!"

Steven glanced at Loraine, then back to Tony. "I'll be needing someone to help me get this place back into shape. How would you like to be the Head of Maintenance here?"

"You'll both be able to live right here on the grounds," Loraine stated.

Tony and Andrea reacted with excitement, as Gerard stood unnoticed in the doorway, listening. "You're offering me a job, and a place for us to live?"

Both Steven and Loraine gave an enthusiastic nod. "Hopefully, you'll accept."

"Most definitely! I'd be a fool to turn down an offer like that."

Gerard strolled the rest of the way into the room. "I might have to ask for a job myself."

Steven stood with a concerned look. "Gerard! There's no need for you to ask anything of me. You're family!"

Gerard appeared relieved. "I appreciate that."

Loraine stood as well. "You may have lost the carriage house, but you haven't lost a home. There always has, and always will be a place here for you and your family."

Gerard responded with humble emotion, as Steven moved closer. "Besides, I can think of no one else that I'd rather put in the top position at Branch Consolidated, and I'm sure that when Audrey comes out of hiding, she'll overwhelmingly agree with me."

Gerard emotionally shook hands with Steven and hugged Loraine. "Thank you! Thank you both!"

"No! Thank you, Gerard. For being part of our family, and for being a valued friend." Gerard wiped a tear from his eye and tried to regain his composure.

"After you get freshened up, and Mrs. Porter feeds us, I'd like you to ride into town with me. I need to check on Suzy McVea."

Andrea spoke up, "Can we go too? I would very much like to see Suzy."

"Sure! I'm certain she'll be quite happy to see both of you as well."

Loraine stated, "I'll stay here and check with the spirits. I'm sure they're quite prepared to return to the light." Steven started to respond but was interrupted by a knock at the door. "Never an undisturbed moment at this house."

Steven strolled over and opened the door. "Agent Guitierez!"

"Steven! I hate to bother you so soon after the ordeal, but I've come for Joey."

The others had entered from the sitting room. "I'll go find her, Agent Guitierez," Loraine replied.

Steven stepped aside and ushered him in. "We've put out warrants for the arrest of Marshall Hempfield, Charles Bernstein, and several other high-level executives of Branch Consolidated."

Gerard stepped forward. "Hopefully you have enough evidence to put them all away for a good while."

Guitierez answered confidently, "With charges like conspiracy, fraud, and insider trading, I'm confident they'll be swapping their Armani suits for prison orange." Loraine returned with Joey, and Mrs. Porter ambled along behind them. "Are you ready to go, Joey?"

Joey sadly responded, "Can't I stay here on some sort of work release, or something?"

Guitierez smirked, "If you did that, then the FBI would have to find another agent for their computer fraud division."

Joey reacted with surprise. "For real? I'm not going back to prison?" Guitierez shook his head no. "How can I ever thank you?"

"By being a good agent. I went to great measures to make this possible." Joey looked back toward Mrs. Porter. "I'll come back and visit. I promise!"

Mrs. Porter shook with emotion, "You better, young lady!" Joey ran and hugged her. "Remember everything I taught you."

Joey responded with tears in her eyes, "I'll never forget! You helped me more than you'll ever know." Joey went to leave with Agent Guitierez and turned for one final wave goodbye.

Steven took a deep breath as he closed the door. Mrs. Porter quickly tried to disguise her emotion. "I'll have dinner prepared shortly." The group smiled.

After dinner, Steven and the others headed into Lockeport to check on Suzy. When they arrived at the Diner, they found her sadly leaning against the counter, amidst all the rubble.

She was startled when the bell on the broken front door clanged. "Mr. Spencer! Mr. LeRoux! Am I ever glad to see you two."

Gerard announced, "There's someone else here I'm sure you'll be glad to see as well."

Just then, Andrea entered with Tony, and Suzy's face lit up with surprise. "I thought I'd never see either one of you again." She rushed over to hug them.

"I never lost faith," Andrea replied.

Suzy looked at Tony with amazement. "I thought you were..."

"I know! But in this case, love conquered death."

Suzy smiled. "Hold on a second." She ran back behind the counter to retrieve something from her purse. "Speaking of love. I've been saving something for both of you."

Andrea huddled close as she handed a small box over to Tony, and he opened it. Andrea gleamed with joy. "My ring! I thought it was lost forever." Tony went to one knee, and before he could say a word, Andrea answered, "Yes! Yes! A million times, yes!"

Steven and Gerard glanced around at the damage. "It's going to take a lot of work to get this old diner up and going again."

Suzy reacted in despair. "I don't know if that'll ever happen."

Steven placed his hands square on her shoulders. "We'll just have to make it happen. You and this diner are an important part of this town."

Gerard stepped up. "Steven's right! We all need to pull together to restore this town, and make it better than it ever was."

Steven stepped back, giving an assuring nod. "We'd be happy to give you a place to stay at Branchview until your house and the Diner get restored."

"Thank you so much."

"Just come over when you get your things together. Mrs. Porter will help you get settled."

"I can't wait, Suzy! Andrea exclaimed. "We have so much to talk about."

Suzy smiled through her tears. "I'll see you all later." As they all filed out, Suzy called Steven. "Mr. Spencer!" Steven turned around. "That first day you were in town, and stopped at the Diner, I knew you were someone special."

Steven responded, "And I knew you were as well." They exchanged parting smiles. "I'll see you later."

Once they arrived back at Branchview, the LeRoux family, Steven, and Loraine all headed for the Grand Corridor. They were all aware of the impending goodbyes they faced. Dr. Grayson greeted them when they entered the room. "I'm afraid it's time for all of us to say goodbye."

Loraine spoke up, "Only, for now, my dear." Dr. Grayson and Loraine watched as the LeRouxs said goodbye to Marcus, and Steven approached his parents. Out of the congregation of spirits stepped a young black man that Gerard immediately recognized and moved to greet.

Gerard smiled. "I'll never forget what you did to help us, Grandfather."

The young man gave a wide smile in response. "I'm very proud of the man you've become, Gerard. When I was alive, I could only dream that this would all be possible for my family."

"Without your sacrifices, it would have never been possible."

His grandfather gestured toward Marcus. "That's quite a young man you raised there."

"I guess now the LeRoux namesake will end with me."

"But it will never be forgotten. We'll be waiting, when it's time for you and the others to go to the light." Gerard gave an emotional nod.

Meanwhile, Steven conversed with his parents as Jack gestured to the piano. "You should concentrate a little more on playing that thing. From what I've heard, the world could use a lot more beautiful music."

Steven chuckled. "Perhaps now I'll have a little more time."

"Make the time, Steven. Life is way too short."

"Hopefully, you'll both visit from time to time?"

Jack stated, "You can count on it."

Penelope gently placed her hand against Steven's cheek. "Goodbye, for now, my son." They turned and joined the procession of others, who now made their way toward a large portal of light that had opened in one end of the room. Steven went to Loraine's side, and the LeRouxs joined them.

Dr. Grayson paused. "I'm going to miss all of you."

"You better keep your promise, and come back once in a while."

"Oh, I will Steven… I have to make sure you finish writing my book."

"Goodbye, Dr. Grayson. And thank you for everything." Loraine embraced her one more time.

Dr. Grayson turned to go, leaving only Maggie, who looked very confused. "Come on, Maggie! We'll go together."

Maggie turned and looked back toward the others, and Steven responded, "Go on, Maggie! It's okay to go to the light!"

"But will I ever be able to come back?"

Loraine answered emotionally, "You can come back any time you'd like, sweetheart. This will always be your home." She smiled and took hold of Dr. Grayson's hand. With a final wave from Dr. Grayson, they walked together into the light. As they crossed the threshold, the portal closed. The quiet was almost deafening for a few long moments. The LeRoux's tearfully embraced each other, as did Steven and Loraine. The group stood huddled for some time as they regained their composure.

Later that night, Steven entered the foyer and greeted Zeus who was just entering the house. "Ezekiel! I haven't seen you since I left the beach today."

"I've been off by myself for a good bit of the day. A little time out of mind."

"I can certainly understand that. Can I pour you a brandy for a nightcap?"

Ezekiel answered wearily as he moves to ascend the stairs. "It's been a long day. I'll have to pass on that offer, but thank you just the same."

Steven gave an understanding nod, as Ezekiel began climbing the stairway. He turned as he got halfway up. "I'll be leaving in the morning, as soon as Poseidon returns."

"So soon! We'd hoped you'd stay on for a while."

"I have many things demanding my attention." He paused. "The never-ending life story of an immortal god."

Steven replied with a smile, "Rest assured, you'll always be welcome here at Branchview."

"I appreciate that, my friend."

"We'll have a good long talk in the morning over breakfast."

Ezekiel gestured with a kind nod. "Sleep well, Steven."

The next morning, after Ezekiel bid farewell to everyone at Branchview, he assumed his identity as Zeus and went to the secret Cave Room. When he arrived, Poseidon was seated on one of the throne seats, waiting. "It appears the room escaped the wrath of Hades?"

Poseidon glanced around as well. "Everything appears to be as it was."

Zeus strolled closer. "I trust everything went well on your journey?"

Poseidon gazed upward with emotion. "Amphitrite is at rest in Nereida, and I'm certain she's happy in spirit as well."

"She'll be missed."

Poseidon stood and strolled closer to Zeus. "Where will you go from here?"

Zeus shrugged. "Perhaps I'll spend some time on the Isle of Rhodes. As I mentioned before, I heard that's where Metis now resides." He paused. "Maybe I can reignite an old flame."

Poseidon laughed. "Good luck with that."

"What about you?"

"I've grown rather fond of Branchview. Perhaps I'll linger for a while until normalcy prevails."

Zeus smiled and pondered for a moment. "They're good people. I hope to visit here again sometime."

Poseidon laughed. "Hopefully under less desperate circumstances." The two men shared a firm handshake and a brotherly hug. "Until we meet again, brother." Zeus gave an accentuated nod before turning away, and quietly vanishing into the dark recesses of the room.

Poseidon then strolled over to the box that held the mannequin remains of Tina Lane. He picked up the head, and looked deep into her marble blue eyes, as tears welled within his. Broken-hearted, he then gently placed the head back in the box, and solemnly turned to walk away. After taking a few steps, a familiar voice beckoned him.

"Poseidon! Don't walk away." He whirled around with shock and surprise.

"How...?"

Tina nodded emotionally. "I'm not sure, but I believe Charlotte might have had a part in it."

Poseidon responded with much exuberance. "She kept her promise."

They passionately embraced and kissed. Then Poseidon grabbed her shoulders firmly and stared deep into her blue eyes. "Your inner light is so radiant. I can see and feel it."

Tina answered with equal disbelief through tear-filled eyes. "I have a heart… and a soul!"

A tearful Poseidon responded, "Yes Tina! You most certainly do!"

Two days later, as things began returning to a more normal state at the Branchview house, Steven casually entered the foyer after his morning walk. He was immediately greeted by Loraine, who kissed him on the cheek. "I'm so glad you're back, darling. We have guests in the sitting room."

Steven looked puzzled, and just then, Audrey Branch entered the room, followed by Alton Sinclair, Daniel Jr, and Heather.

"Uncle Steve!" Daniel Jr. ran to him with great joy, and Steven went down to one knee to greet him.

"Audrey… Heather… I was beginning to worry about all of you."

"We heard about everything on the news, and felt it was finally safe to return."

"We were in Sweden," an excited Daniel proclaimed.

Heather rolled her eyes. "It was so cold there."

Steven looked seriously at Audrey. "You and I have a lot of issues to discuss."

"I know. We'll go over a few things, but most will have to wait until I return."

Steven reacted with a puzzled expression. "Where are you off to now?"

Alton and Audrey looked admiringly at each other. "Alton and I got married in Sweden. We're leaving tomorrow morning on our honeymoon."

Steven shook Alton's hand with much surprise. "Congratulations! I must admit, I never saw that coming."

Alton answered, "Neither did we. It just sort of happened."

Steven looked to Audrey. "I'll contact our attorney, and have him start on the preliminary paperwork."

"Good! We'll need to make a few changes. I'm putting you in charge of Branchview until Heather and Daniel come of age. And of course, I'm sure you'll agree that Gerard should be in charge of Branch Consolidated."

"Absolutely! I already put him in that position until you and I could consult on it."

Alton gave Steven a sly wink. "You also stand to inherit a generous share of the Branch family fortune."

Tony, Andrea, and Suzy entered from the confines of the sitting room. They were followed by the LeRouxs, and much to Steven's surprise, Philip and Tina strolled through the doorway as well. Mrs. Porter also entered from another adjacent room and leaned against a doorway with a wide grin.

Steven was flabbergasted. "This is like a wonderful dream. Being surrounded by my entire family once again."

He shifted his attention to Philip, who hugged Tina tightly as he stood behind her and beamed with exuberant joy. Steven approached the couple with great wonder.

"How...?"

Phillip interrupted with a chuckle. "It's a long story, Steven. I'll explain it to you over a good cup of coffee."

Steven saluted the couple with a wink and a nod. "I can't wait to hear all about it."

Tina looked up lovingly at Philip, and he gave her a quick kiss.

Steven glanced at every other smiling face and held his hands up. "Okay! I have an announcement." He turned to Loraine. "Where is your mother and Mr. Crawford?"

"They're upstairs with the babies. Why?"

"We need to bring them all down here. This family deserves a worthy celebration."

Philip held his hands up as well. "And I have a declaration to add to that." All listened attentively. "May this family long-endure in peace, love, and happiness, along with this grand old house of Branchview." The room responded with enthusiastic claps and cheers.

Later that evening, Millie and Bill returned the babies to the nursery. Bill carried a very alert Olivia, while

Millie toted London, who was almost asleep. "That was some party," he stated.

"Indeed!" She glanced down at the baby. "I do believe this one is about ready to be put down for the night."

"This little one doesn't seem to want to go to sleep. Too much excitement, I guess."

They both carefully laid the babies in their cribs. Baby London drifted off to sleep immediately, while Olivia shifted her attention to a stuffed bear on a nearby dresser.

Bumpers casually observed from his usual resting place in the corner, as an unexpected event unfolded. The baby reached her little arms in the direction of the bear, and it levitated from the dresser. It then drifted toward the crib, until it was securely within the smiling infant's grasp. Bumpers sat up, and tilted his head in wonder, while Millie and Bill stared with sober awe.

"Please tell me I didn't just see that?"

Millie sighed. "It's just an absurdity that you need to get accustomed to, dear. Nothing in this house, nor this family, ever ceases to amaze me."

The large foyer clock chimed at midnight. In the garden, Steven strolled with Loraine, and they paused under the pergola to gaze up at the full moon. Steven commented, "It's a beautiful night."

Loraine exhaled with exuberance. "It's an all-around wondrous night."

Steven smiled as he continued to look up. "When we started this journey, did you ever think it would lead us to where we are today?"

Loraine clutched his arm affectionately. "I have to admit, there were times when I thought we were surely doomed."

Steven nodded in agreement, then looked out into the darkness. "The ending of all this was more fantastic than anything we could've ever written into one of our novels."

Loraine contemplated, "For all the tragedy that this family has dealt with at the hands of Liddy McPherson, they are all truly deserving of a happy ending."

A black cat wandered out of the bushes and rubbed affectionately against Steven's leg. "Look! We have a little visitor."

He reached down to pick up the purring cat, while Loraine watched in amusement. "Oh! She certainly likes you. Just like every other woman"

"I think we should adopt her. We can call her Charlotte."

"Absolutely! It would be highly inappropriate to call her anything else." Loraine gazed outward in thought. "You know, Charlotte taught me a few new tricks in the short time she was with us."

Steven responded with a curious glance. "Like what?"

She flashed a smirky grin. "Well! She said that in times when I need to refresh my mind, I should simply spread my wings, and take flight." Steven glanced at her with a perplexed expression as she continued. "I think it's a wonderful night for just that." She then turned back toward Steven. "I'll be back in a short while, darling."

Before he could respond, she waved her hands outward in front of her, transforming into a nighthawk. She swiftly flew off into the darkness, leaving a visibly stunned Steven gazing upward. He cradled the cat closer, as he said out loud, "I do believe we're destined for a life of endless, bizarre adventure." He looked closer at the cat and affectionately scratched under its chin. "What do you think, Charlotte?"

The black cat purred and snuggled into the comfort of his chest. "Meow...."

Coming Soon…….

The Portal of Time *– By Brian Jay Nelson*

If you missed **"The Unexpected Journey"** it's the first book of the Branchview Series

Follow me:

Website: Branchview.info
Amazon Central: @brianjaynelson
Instagram: @info_branchview
Facebook: @BJNScreenwriter